EVERY WORD
YOU NEVER SAID

Also by Jordon Greene

A Mark on My Soul

Watching for Comets

EVERY WORD YOU NEVER SAID

JORDON GREENE

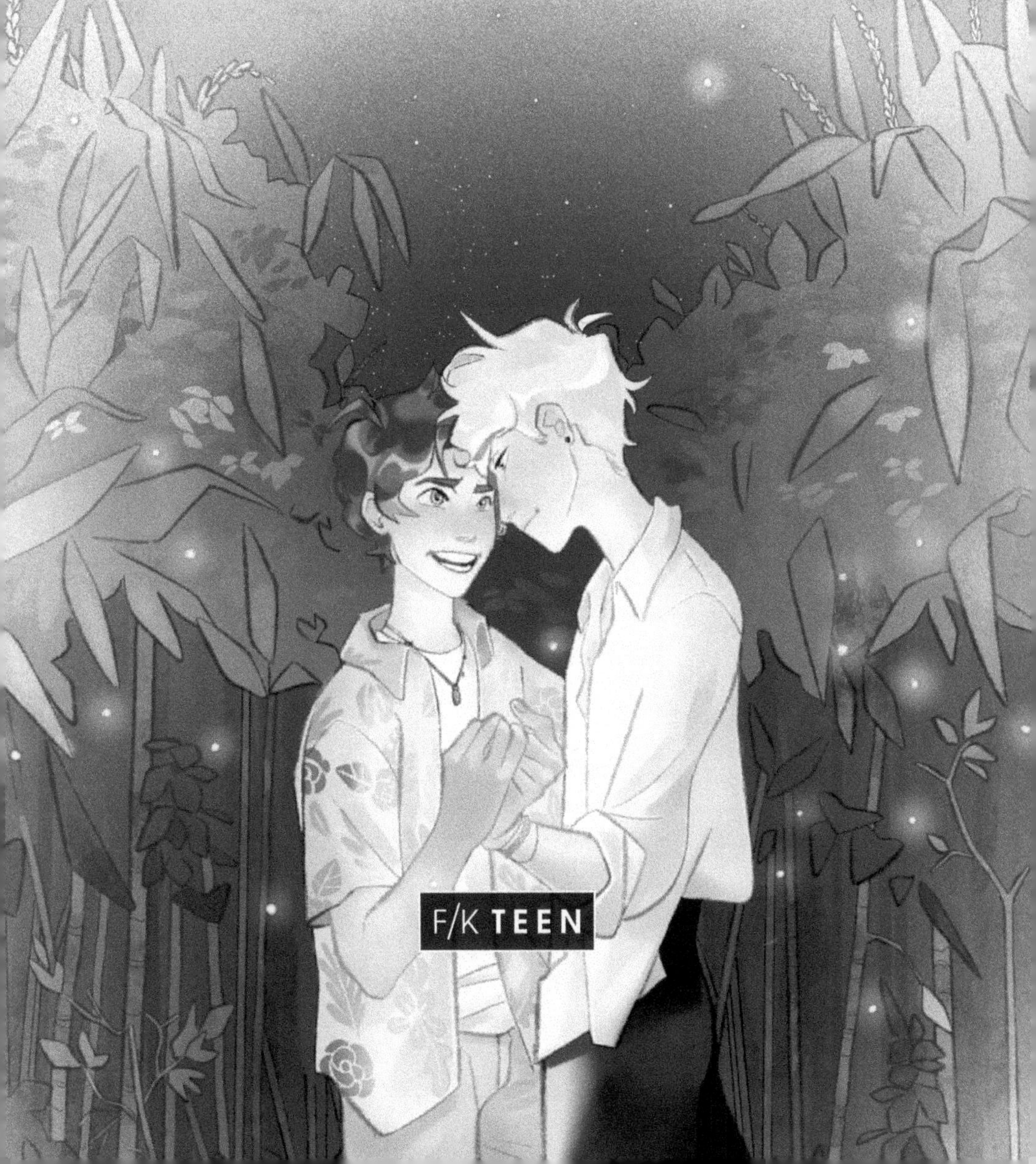

Published by F/K Teen
An imprint of Franklin/Kerr Press
Kannapolis, North Carolina 28083
www.FranklinKerr.com

Edited by Christie Stratos
Cover art and design by Lucía Limón
Interior design by Jordon Greene
Author photograph by Kim Greene

"How Beautifully Fragile" poem used by permission.
Copyright © 2020 by Sabina Laura

Printed in the United States of America

FIRST EDITION

Hardcover ISBN 978-1-7354373-6-1
Paperback ISBN 978-1-7354373-5-4

Library of Congress Control Number: 2021922816

Fiction: Young Adult Contemporary
Fiction: Coming-of-Age
Fiction: LGBT/Gay

To Amanda Jane
for being that brutally honest
judgement-free friend we all need.

how beautifully

fragile

we are

that we accept pain

when we think

we deserve it

and let it break us

silently.

- Sabina Laura, *Moonflower*

SKYLAR

WEDNESDAY, AUGUST 14

New beginnings. I'm so over them.

I swear they're overrated, and I promise you they never end up better than how the last one ended. With each change of scenery, each relocation and *chance at a new start*, comes the quick, inevitable fall back to my reality.

"I believe we have you all set, Skylar." My new guidance counselor, Mrs. Alderman, smiles warmly. It's the type of smile that's meant to be welcoming and calm but actually says *good luck on your own*. It's nothing new, changing schools has become something of a ritual, and they're all the same.

She turns her pale-green eyes and plump cheeks to Mr. and Mrs. Gray, I mean my, uh, new parents. "We'll be sure to notify his teachers of his disa—"

And there's fall number one.

She stops and coughs into a closed fist. Just say it, for God's sake. Come on! My *disability*.

"That Skylar is nonverbal," she corrects, eyeing me timidly before straightening.

I don't move, but I peek at Mrs. Gray out of the corner of my eye. She's smiling forgivingly, small hands clasped with my adoptive dad, who just let out a little huff. They were so nervous this morning, and from the looks of it, they still are.

It hasn't been a full week since I moved in and became Skylar *Gray* instead of Skylar *Rice*. That's another thing that's going to take some time to get used to. And now we're sitting in the office at the local high school, A.L. Brown, where Mr. Gray said he graduated forever ago, registering me for classes.

"I'm sorry, Skylar," Mrs. Alderman says as she nods.

I grin and start typing on my phone. When I hit play a male British version of Siri replies for me, "It's okay."

I literally can't talk. It's my "disability". Long story short, I got laryngitis when I was like five and it screwed up my vocal cords. So yeah, I can't. At all. Like nothing comes out of my mouth except incoherent noises and air. My phone *is* my voice.

Her shoulders relax and she types something out of view. The printer whirs to life and I end up with a piece of paper in my hands, my class schedule.

"Do you have any questions?" she asks.

I purse my lips and shake my head, which earns me an unruly strand of hair over my eye. I push it to the side. Even if I did have a question, I'd say no. It's annoying having to "talk" most of the time, so I avoid it when I can.

"What about your parents?" Mrs. Alderman turns to Mr. and Mrs. Gray, and I give them a small grin to let them know I'm good.

They're pretty great—so far, at least. I'm still getting to know them. But they're already *so* much better than any of my foster parents, or anyone I've dealt with in the children's homes over the past like eight years or whatever. I think I like them. But I still can't get rid of this nagging feeling that it's going to click one day they've adopted a defective son and I'll find myself back in Vermont's foster care system instead of this suburban North Carolina town. Or would they just throw me in the system here?

Like this morning, I almost put on one of my skirts instead of these black shorts, but I didn't. Mr. and Mrs. Gray say they don't mind, but I don't want to push it yet. Plus the only two I own I snuck and bought a few years ago, and they're suddenly much too short, like halfway up my thigh short.

"I think you covered our concerns," Mr. Gray — or Bob, he did tell me to call him Bob if I couldn't call him Dad yet — says.

They had a whole-ass list, from how the school would work with me in the classroom to how bullies are dealt with, and on and on. And Mrs. Alderman answered each with practiced ease.

"I think we're all done here then. We'll be sure to make Skylar at home here at Brown, I promise." Mrs. Alderman stands and extends her hand toward her office door. "I'll walk you out and have a student show Skylar around before he goes to class. Skylar, you can wait here."

"Have a good one, champ." Bob squeezes my arm just as Mrs. Gray — Kimberly — hugs me. It's still sort of weird, the whole hugging thing, but I let her. I think she's about to cry.

"If you need anything, text us," she says.

And I'm glad she stops there. I'm fifteen, going on sixteen. And sure, I might be short, but I'm not a kindergartener starting my first-ever day of school. I'm a sophomore, and I know I've dealt with more bullies and shitheads than either of them.

I nod anyway, just for her, and apparently it's enough. She lets Mrs. Alderman lead her into the main office and the door closes on its own as a bell rings. A few minutes later the door nudges open again.

"Skylar," the counselor says, waving me out. There's no point in wasting time, they're going to make me go to class eventually, so I throw my pack over my shoulder and follow. "Skylar, this is Jacob. Jacob, Skylar."

"Hey." He dips his head and his hair bounces above bright green eyes. That hair! It's pure white. Angelic, except he fell from heaven and started a punk rock band.

I nod back, fighting against every instinct to bite at my lip. He's *so* beautiful.

"Skylar just transferred. I need you to show him around the school and help him find his classes. Make him feel at home," Mrs. Alderman explains, which gets his eyes off me finally. I cough out a breath and catch his fingers fidgeting with the hem of his unbuttoned green flannel layered over a black tee. His nails are black. When Mrs. Alderman looks up from her watch and hands Jacob a slip of paper, I look away, landing on a much less interesting beige printer. "Here's your hall pass. You should have plenty of time before the end of the period. Oh, and Skylar can't speak."

"I'd be at a loss for words if I transferred here too." Jacob grins at his own joke.

"Uh..." Mrs. Alderman seems speechless. She looks between us, then grins at him in a way that says *please shut up*. "He's nonverbal, he *can't* speak. Skylar talks through his phone."

"Oh. Like dumb?" Jacob flinches, I swear it, but rebounds

quickly. "I mean… Uh… Cool, um…okay."

"No, as in he cannot *verbally* speak." Mrs. Alderman is visibly disappointed. I think she's about to say something else but looks at me instead with apology written all over her face.

"That's what I meant, like…never mind." Jacob stops talking. Instead, he nods, his cute—sort of stupid—pale lips pressed tightly together.

It's nothing I haven't heard before. And I'm sure it won't be the worst.

"All right." Mrs. Alderman forces a grin. "We're glad to have you here, Skylar. I'll let Jacob show you around now."

With that she nods to Jacob, eyes flaring, and disappears into her office. I drag my gaze up to meet his unfortunately beautiful eyes and paint an expectant grin across my face. He's just standing there looking at me. Then I guess it clicks.

"Right! Tour!" Jacob shakes it off. His voice raises multiple levels and he waves for me to follow. "Come with me."

I sigh and type furiously on my phone. "Not deaf. I can hear you."

"Oh, right." He pooches his lips, eyes darting away. "So, uh, let's go?"

This is going to be a long day.

JACOB
WEDNESDAY, AUGUST 14

Ms. Agee must hate me more than my dad does. She volunteered me to Mrs. Alderman—me *of all people*—to greet the new kid. Really?

I thought we were on good terms, I had a B in her class last semester. Sure, I like to talk, but I'm not the kid that never shuts up, that's Eric.

And I called him *dumb*. In my defense, that's what my church calls people who can't talk in the Bible. And that's what I've had shoved down my throat. Then again, it also says you can have slaves and that women should be quiet, and well, no. I wish I could just wash it all out of my head.

Just move past it. He didn't seem that fazed.

Maybe he also has memory problems. Fingers crossed, because *I'm* not bringing it back up to apologize.

"So, welcome to Brown?" I say, but it comes out like a question. I'm not going to lie and say it's the best school around. I think most people hate their school pretty universally. I mean, it *is* school.

He nods and I remind myself not to expect any more of an answer.

"Uh... Just stick with me and I'll try to make this painless."
Aka, no more painful than it's already been, for either of us.
"Don't know if you care about sports, but we're the Wonders.
Ooh!"

I raise my hands in mock awe since the halls are empty. It
earns me a half grin. I stop short of telling him I'm on the swim
team. One, I doubt he'd care, and two, I'm not going to be like
the sports jerks whose whole life is about being on the school
team.

"Can I see your schedule?" I ask.

Skylar nods and hands me a slip of paper. His finger
brushes my hand, and my eyes flick to his face for a split
second before shooting back to the paper.

He's sort of cute, in this short, brown-eyed-puppy-dog
type of way. Like even my skinny ass could pick him up
without effort. But it might ruffle his orange-striped collared
shirt that seems a tad too dressy for the black shorts he's
wearing.

He's actually *really* cute. Like, I'd tap that cute, if he was
into guys at all. Or me, for that matter. I probably shouldn't be
thinking about tapping the new kid so soon. Or ever.

Focus. Schedule. Look at his schedule.

Cool. He's in my second period. Dance. Can't say I
expected that. The rest is pretty typical for a sophomore.
Honors English 2 for first, then Civics for third, and Sociology
ending the day.

"Most of your classes are in the same wing, except Dance."
I swivel to face him, walking backward down the hall. "Did
you choose Dance?"

"Yes, something wrong with that?" Skylar's phone asks in

a British accent. Why British?

"Uh, nah." I'm a little thrown off by the voice. British?

Up until now, I figured I was the only guy taking Dance this semester. I couldn't convince Ian to, and I didn't make it to second period to confirm my suspicion since I had to pick up Can't Speak Kid. Okay, maybe I shouldn't call him that. I don't need to sound like some backwoods asshole. He'll meet enough of those.

"Me too," I give him my first genuine smile. "Same period too."

His fingers go to his phone and that's when I notice something dangling from it. It's tiny, green, and spiky. Oh my God, it's a little dinosaur. He just got cuter.

"Cool," his phone says, pulling my attention back to him.

"Yeah, cool," I say as we enter the cafeteria. "After second period you have lunch in here. It's nothing special. Just a lunchroom. You don't have to eat in here though. You can go pretty much anywhere. Oh, and I don't know about where you came from, but we have an à la carte line. The fries are amazing, like almost McDonald's amazing. But avoid the hamburgers. They're premade from hell."

That gets me a bigger smile. His head bobs and it's like he's laughing, but there's no sound. It's sort of weird.

"Let's go upstairs, and I'll show you where your other classes are," I say.

He follows me up in silence toward the Language Arts wing. I can do quiet if there's music playing or I'm at home and that's the alternative to talking to Dad, but this, I can't.

"So, you're from up north?" I break the silence. Sure he can't talk, but he can use his phone, right? I glance at him while he types.

"Yes. I'm from Vermont," Siri says, I mean Skylar, but still Siri technically. It must be weird talking through something else. Whatever, Vermont though? That's way up there.

"Vermont? Like all the way up at the tip?" I ask.

"No, sort of the middle. Rutland," comes after a few more seconds of typing. He looks at me with that same half grin from earlier.

"Was it super cold up there?" I ask. I don't know what else to ask about Vermont.

He nods ecstatically, and I swing open the doors to the Language Arts wing. Teachers' voices whisper down the hall, escaping through open classroom doors.

I ignore them and take another look at his schedule. He's got Mrs. Sangster for English. Sorry, Skylar. Her classroom is close though. We make the first right around the corner and it's two doors down.

"Your first period, English, is right here." I lower my voice to a whisper and point to my left where *Mrs. Sangster* is stamped on a cheap silver plate. Looks like he has Mrs. Moyer for Civics and Mr. Dennard for Sociology. Both of those are on the other side of this hallway. "Your Civics and Sociology classes are just down the hall. But Dance is all the way downstairs."

He nods. I guess that's that.

A few minutes later we're walking past the library and then the auditorium, where they do all the school plays. I give him quick notes on each. I've not been in the library much. For a reader, I just don't have a thing for the school library. It's all stuffy and old, and most of the books are, well, old. Skylar doesn't seem thrilled with the "classics" from the look on his face.

"You said you play sports?" his phone asks.

It throws me. Like I know it's him, but it's still so effing weird. He's like some futuristic robot from *Terminator*, but cuter, and not trying to kill me.

"Yeah." I nod. "I swim. Nothing pretentious and 'important' like football or basketball."

"Cool," Skylar says back, and after a slight pause and some furious typing, Siri comes back to life. "I'm thinking about doing track and tennis."

Speaking of sports, we're entering the auxiliary gym now. It's big and covered in green. The dance studio is on the opposite end next to the band room.

"Swimming is enough for me. Short bursts, not that constant on-the-go shit," I tell him. "Plus it's usually inside, so another bonus."

Skylar shakes his head and huffs. Ugh, why is he so cute? Why do there have to be cute boys? And I swear they're all straight. I scream internally at my doomed fate.

It's one of the many gripes about living in a small town without a car to call my own. We're like half an hour from the largest city in the state, but when you're still in high school *and* have to use your mom's car to get anywhere, that makes meeting new people impossible. Plus, how do you ask a guy out without the very real possibility that a long history of toxic masculinity connects a fucking fist to your jaw?

"And here's the dance studio. This is where your, or our, second period is." I point toward the solid wooden door with *Mrs. Lockerman* stamped next to the little slit of a window.

"Don't know if Mrs. Alderman told you, but we have to dress out for class. You can't wear that." I motion toward his clothes, including the tight black jean shorts he's wearing. I stumble over my next words. "We have to wear like tighter-fitting t-shirts and either tights, or, like…uh…leggings."

Oh my God. I'm going to get to see him in tights or leggings. I swallow a growing lump in my throat and shrug to throw him off how nervous I am. I need to get away from this. I check my watch for an excuse.

"It's almost lunchtime." I change subjects and start back in the direction we'd come, checking his schedule for his locker number. "I'll show you to your locker and then back to the lunchroom."

At his locker I let him figure out his combination before saying anything. Part of me is like, *stick around, go to lunch with him*. The other part is screaming *I'm stupid to even consider it*. Yeah, let's just nip that in the bud right now.

His lock unclicks. He looks so satisfied as he swings the door open and stows his pack in the tiny metal space.

"Be careful with your phone, they're real strict about us having them. It's draconian." I throw in a big word I never really use. I should know on the phones. I've had mine confiscated more times than I want to admit.

Skylar tilts his head and starts mouthing something, and his hands start moving. I shake my head.

"Sorry, I can't read lips." I shrug. You could say the most basic thing and I'd still not have a clue.

His shoulders slump.

"I have to have it," Siri says, and Skylar points at me. "Case in point, you."

I tilt my head, mocking him.

"Whatever." I laugh. "Lucky you."

The bell saves me from further conversation. But I can't just throw him to the wolves without a life raft.

"Let me give you my number in case you get lost or something." I don't know why I say it, but I do. At least Mrs. Alderman can't say I abandoned the new kid.

He taps his screen a few times and hands me his phone. I type in my number and name and hand it back.

"So, the lunchroom is straight down the hall." I point and start walking off backward. "See ya 'round."

SKYLAR

WEDNESDAY, AUGUST 14

Third was boring. History.

But the looks when they realized I couldn't talk spiced it up. I can never tell if they think I'm weird or they're jealous I get to keep my phone out during class. But I think it's the weird one.

I weave through the crowded hall, past the cliques, glances, and confused frowns. There hasn't been time for word to circulate about the new kid yet. But I'm already wondering if they'll call me handicapped, defective, or retarded. I've heard them all. And someone *is* going to say I'm deaf. I roll my eyes at the thought and swing into my last class of the day, Sociology.

Up front is the teacher, I think. He's leaning against the big desk up front, nodding at us like he's considering each of us carefully. And he's giving real Alexander Skarsgård vibes, from when he played in *Battleship*. I think his name is Mr. Den-something, but I'd have to check my schedule again. I nod, then pivot for the end of the room, sweeping into a seat at the back where I can watch the desks fill up.

More faces. More glares. Not because they know me, but

because they don't. And as usual, the whispers.

"Who's the new guy?" from a group of boys a few rows over, and then from two girls a few seats ahead of me who aren't even trying to hide it.

I'm right here. I can hear you. Just ask. I swear I won't chop your hand off. But they don't. They rarely do, and I'm not really sure why, it's not like they know my flaw. At least the guy in the middle is sort of cute. Light brown hair, thicker lips than he deserves, and he looks tall. I pull my eyes away so I don't stare.

People don't really care for me, even when they get to know me, and that just seems to make them care less. Not like it bothers me anymore. That's why I don't get close to people. I'm here because I have to be. It's how I'm getting to college. It's how I'm figuring out my own life. I'm not going to need any of them. So, by no means am I going out of my way to introduce myself. Starting conversations with strangers isn't me. I prefer ending them.

Finally, the class bell rings.

"Take a seat." Mr. Whatever-His-Name-Is motions for us to settle and then writes his name on the board. "I see a lot of familiar faces, but for those who don't know me, I'm Mr. Dennard. And no, it's not De-NARD, it's De-nerd. Yes, nerd, get over it."

The giggles and shuffling don't faze him. I aspire to that type of not-giving-a-shit.

"The way I see it, half of you wanted to take this class and the other half didn't have a choice. Let's try to make it through together though. Okay?"

No one answers. He gets a bunch of blank stares, minus

the huffs from the *half that didn't have a choice.*

"Instead of taking roll, we're going to go around the room and introduce ourselves," he says.

My chest tightens. No! Why? I hate this shit. Like just call the roll, don't make me do this.

Mr. Dennard points toward a petite girl with short auburn hair at the front of the room, in the same row of desks as me. "We'll start up here. Just give us your name and one interesting fact about yourself. Go."

I freeze up. It's not even my turn and my mind has left the building. Did she say her name was Hannah? It doesn't matter, she isn't going to talk to me anyway. I start typing, trying to figure out what to say about myself that's *interesting.* I'm so not interesting. So far I just have *Hey, my name's Skylar.*

Why did I choose this side of the room?

Hannah—I think that's right—sits down and there are only five people ahead of me. What do I say? They'll figure out I can't talk the moment I stand up, so that's not going to work, plus that's not interesting, it sucks. And I'm not talking about being in foster care since I was seven. That's sad. And no to finally being adopted at fifteen. That's just pathetic.

Maybe, *There isn't much interesting about me. But I'm from Verm* —

"I'm sorry, hold on a moment, Latoya." Mr. Dennard interrupts the tall girl's introduction. "Let's put away all the phones please."

He can't be talking to me, certainly he got the note that I need mine. I look up anyway, and he's looking right at me, along with everyone else in the room.

My eyelid twitches. I wish I could just say *Hey, sorry. I need it to talk, it's sort of a thing*, but I can't. I start to type it out instead, but the sound of feet stomping toward me reaches my ears as I look down.

"Phones—" His voice starts with authority and then trails off, and it's gone when he starts again. "I'm sorry. You must be Skylar."

I nod.

"You're fine then," he says and then sweeps his gaze around the class at the confused sighs. "But just Skylar."

Mr. Dennard puts his hands up to silence them. Guess he isn't going to explain. "Go on, Latoya."

She says something about adopting a beagle over the summer then sits down, and the girl in front of me gets up.

"Hiya, I'm Imani Banks," she declares in this sassy but sweet voice and brushes a few curly strands of jet-black hair from her deep-brown face. She's short, sort of like me, but there's a confidence in her sway. "And something interesting, well, I'm Wiccan."

Wiccan? Like the religion? Like witchcraft? Definitely interesting, not sure I'd tell people though.

For a moment it distracts me from the stress building in my chest. I hate these types of introductions.

"Oh... Thank you, Imani." Mr. Dennard blinks a few times and then his eyes land on me expectantly. "We already know your name, Skylar. But could you introduce yourself?"

I nod nervously. I make one small adjustment in the message I'd already typed and hit play.

"My name is Skylar Gray, and I'm nonverbal. I require my phone to speak. And something interesting is that I'm from Vermont. I just transferred," Siri explains in the British accent

I set it to years ago.

"Again, I'm sorry, Skylar. The office sent a message about your phone, but it slipped my mind at first," Mr. Dennard apologizes and sweeps his gaze over the class. "However, this is a great opportunity to see how communication is not solely verbal. There are also nonverbal components, ones made up of facial expressions, body language, touch, and gesture. And languages like sign language. These are all valid means of communication."

He looks at me when he mentions sign language. I'm not sure if he's trying to absolve himself of his mistake or validate me in front of the rest of the class, but whatever it is, it sounds pretty good.

"But on that note, while Skylar needs his phone to communicate and participate in class, that doesn't mean the rest of you can have your phones out. Only Skylar." His declaration is met with another host of groans.

There aren't many perks to not having a voice, but this is one. The only one.

"Now back to introductions," the teacher says, and some twenty uninteresting facts later the intros are out of the way. "Now that we know each other's names, I want everyone to pair up in groups of three. I'm going to write a few questions on the board. And I want you to answer them to your groupmates, who will write them down and turn them in for a participation grade at the end of class. I'll put up the first question once you're in groups."

First introductions, and now groups. This class is one hundred percent not on my favorites list.

I don't move as he starts writing on the board and the class erupts into a melee of bodies jumping from one end of the class to the next or spinning around to face the friends they're already sitting with.

My expectation to be sitting by myself until Mr. Dennard assigns me a partner quickly vanishes when the girl in front of me, the one who declared herself Wiccan just minutes ago, turns and faces me.

"Hiya, I'm Imani," she reminds me, which is good, I'd already forgotten. It's usually useless information.

I nod as a tall lanky boy with a messy brown mop atop his head straddles the chair to my left and high fives Imani.

"Hey." He puts his hand out to shake but barely meets my gaze. I look at his hand a second. Who seriously shakes hands in high school? But I take it and give him a half-baked smile. I remember him talking about reading some obscene number of sci-fi, or maybe it was fantasy, books over the summer, but I can't recall his name. At least it's obvious he's not some sports jerk.

"Sorry, what was your name?" I let Siri ask.

"I'm Seth, Seth Harrington, if that matters." He shrugs.

"It doesn't," Imani says dryly. When I look at her questioningly, she explains, "It's okay, we're BFFs. Like I literally don't remember when we weren't friends."

She's pretty. Her skin is this dark silky brown, and the pink shadow around her eyelids really makes her dark-brown eyes pop.

"We basically know everything about each other, so this should be pretty easy," she giggles. "We just have to learn about you. Skylar, right?"

I nod. She seems really nice, and so far Seth comes off more as the awkward nerd type whose complexion mirrors his obvious lack of outdoor activities.

"Mind if we call you Sky?" she asks with a shrug.

I nod.

"Sky is good," I say through my phone. Maybe it's best to talk instead of just shrugging and nodding to everything. But then again, I'm not putting too much effort into something meaningless and so inevitably finite as this is sure to be. I glance at the board and read the first question. Okay, they're not exactly questions, but whatever. "The first question says to provide further context about the interesting fact you told the class. Imani?"

I direct it to her first. I figure she got here before Seth so why not, and I don't want to answer. What I want is someone to talk and distract me from the eyes that are prodding at me from other groups, and the whispers that I just know are about me. The weird mute boy.

"Well, I'm Wiccan. But it's not like people think. It's not all that different really from, like, Christianity," she explains with her hands flying. "They have prayer, we have affirmations. They have a Bible, we have our own books."

"She's a good bitch, I mean witch." Seth smiles, earning a light punch to the gut. "I deserved that one."

"You deserve *all* of them." Imani glares, but there's a playfulness in her eyes.

These two are a handful. And I can't help but wonder if there might be more than just BFFs going on, but I suck at matchmaking.

"And you?" I look at Seth.

"Uh..." Seth ponders. I'm not sure what's hard about it.

Wasn't it just something about reading books over the summer? "I read books by Micaiah Johnson, a bunch of Marie Lu. I loved The Young Elites trilogy."

My eyes light up. He's a fan of one of my favorite authors! Everything Marie Lu writes is pure gold, like perfection. I'm about to type out a response, but he keeps going.

"Uh… And some Sarah J. Maas, and a bunch of others. Oh, and this one sci-fi—those others are all basically fantasy— called *Ark* by something Baxter. It's about Earth becoming uninhabitable and the only way to save humanity is to send a bunch of kids on a decades-long trip through space to a new world. But it—"

"We get the point." Imani stops him and looks at me like she could slap him. "He doesn't usually talk a lot, but he'll talk for hours about a single book if you let him. You can thank me later."

"Eh." Seth shrugs it off. "It was insane though."

"Sounds cool," I type out, letting Siri's voice do the talking. "Marie Lu is my favorite."

I'd prefer to stay on this train instead of telling them more about me. It's not like they really want to know. No one in this room really wants to know more about me. I'd take a bet that ninety-nine percent of them, currently buzzing on and on about who knows what nonsense, don't really care what their group partners are telling them.

"What about you?" Seth asks.

I almost forget to hold back the sigh of disappointment. My interesting fact was being from Vermont. It's broad. But it's also a small state, and I'd daresay neither of them knows much about it, and maybe it's just me, but not much was memorable.

I think about it. What's something actually worth saying about my past, about where I came from that's not depressing? I'm not telling them I was just adopted, even if that is the entire reason I'm here.

I know. I'll tell them the one thing I'm going to miss. Cocking my head and grinning slightly, I type away and hit send.

"Like I said, I'm from Vermont, and we had this soda you can't get anywhere else called maple soda," my phone explains. It was great. And it tasted just like it sounds. "It's so good."

"Sort of like our Cheerwine," Imani says, and I give her a confused look. "It's not wine. I promise. It's a soft drink made around here. Not sure why it's called that, then again I don't know what wine tastes like either."

That's something I can't say. I've had a few glasses, and I don't want a soda tasting like that.

"We'll have to get you one," Seth says.

I'm not sure I want to try it. Plus, it's awfully bold of him to assume we'll ever talk again. I've only known them a few minutes, and they seem like fun, but I know better than to think it'll last.

I shrug, and before I have to say more the teacher starts writing on the board again.

"And the next question is…" Mr. Dennard's words trail off.

Just focus on the questions and move on.

* * *

Kimberly picked me up after school. They don't want me riding the bus or walking home. Neither of them will say it, but I know why. They're afraid I'll get bullied. Which is about as certain as Disney making another Star Wars movie. Word just has to circulate first.

"Did you make any friends?" Kimberly asks, sunglasses obscuring her sky-blue eyes, as we pull into the garage.

Friends? I wouldn't say that. Acquaintances, maybe. Imani and Seth are the only people who really talked to me other than teachers. Oh, and the boy who Mrs. Alderman made show me around. Can't forget about that hottie. What was his name? James. No. Dammit. What was it?

Jacob! That's it.

"Yeah." I start typing and let my phone take over. "In my last class."

"That's great!" She places a hand on my shoulder. It still feels so foreign, but I know she's trying to be Mom. She gets out of the car and I follow. "Are they your age?"

I nod and smile for her. I don't think they're really my friends. They were nice and all, but friends?

"You'll have to tell your dad and me about them at dinner. How about your teachers?" Kimberly switches, but it's still weird hearing someone say *your dad*.

"They were fine," I type.

As Kimberly drops her purse on the kitchen counter and removes her sunglasses, my eyes catch a set of picture frames. They're on the living room wall through the archway. A happy family. My new parents and their kid, Elijah. He's not around though. Apparently he died of cancer a few years ago. I think he'd be about my age now.

"Just fine?" Mrs. Gray asks. I reel my gaze back. She's searching for something.

I've said all I plan to about my teachers. And technically I only met two of them anyway. I didn't get to school until later, and my little tour didn't end until lunch, so that's all that was left in the day. And that Jacob kid was right. The fries *were* top notch.

I give her my best grin and mouth my next sentence. *I'm going to read.*

"Okay." She sets her hands on her hips and I detect a little sigh. "Dinner will be ready around six."

Okay, I say and head toward my room.

My room. And it really is this time. It's not just a temporary holdover, another place to wonder how long I'll be there. At least that's what I'm telling myself.

My posters line the walls, creases and all, and a few new ones the Grays got me before I moved in. Everything from *Jurassic Park* to *Alien*, Taylor Swift to Ariana Grande and Troye Sivan, and of course the jumbo-sized *Maze Runner* poster with Dylan O'Brien hanging over the bed. My pictures of Myylo and Chris Pine are pinned above my little desk, crinkled from being folded and moved. And the massive *Jurassic Park* body pillow the Grays got me is sprawled on the bed.

I really hope this lasts.

JACOB
THURSDAY, AUGUST 15

"We're doing another cover soon, right?" Ian asks as we cross the street from the senior lot.

"Yeah, sure," I say, but I'm distracted, eyes scanning the path to the school entrance.

"We should do something harder this time," Ian keeps on. "A real banger. We could pull it off. Maybe some Death Punch?"

"What?" I reel myself back in. What the hell is he talking about? "Punch?"

"Yeah, Five Finger." He looks at me like I'm an idiot while His Grand Paleness leads us through the school entrance and upstairs. "You know. The band."

"Oh, yeah. Sure," I say. *Pay attention, Jacob. Stop searching the crowd for a cute boy who probably thinks you're an asshole anyway.*

"Um, okay." He surprisingly doesn't question me.

We cut through the crowd, carving a maze-like path to the math and science wing. There are so many people, too many. The hall is packed, and I hate it.

"How about 'Remember Everything'?" I throw out the

first song that comes to mind.

"I said hard, that's like their softest song," Ian complains. "Where is your head right now?"

"I'm here," I tell him, but the truth is I've been thinking about Skylar since I dipped on him at lunch yesterday.

"Then how is 'Remember Everything' hard?" Ian asks.

"I mean, it's not. I—"

"Exactly, it's not. How about 'Never Enough'?" Ian asks.

I eye him stupidly. Like, we don't suck, but that might be pushing it.

"You sure about that?" I grimace. "You think Ted can sing that? I'm just backup, so I got that, but—"

"Sure he can! And I really want to do that killer drumbeat." Ian's practically jumping down the hall.

"Whatever. Text Ted about it," I say. "But we're hitting mine nex—"

"That's what he said!" Ian blurts.

I clench my eyes shut for a brief second and purse my lips. We're in the middle of the hall. I could kill him right now. And it didn't really make sense, but it's all Ian. Ever since I came out over the summer, he takes every chance he gets, switching up *she* with *he*. He thinks it's great.

"What?" I mock punch him in the shoulder.

"Okay, yeah, that wasn't that great," he admits. Then his eyes widen like he's had a moment of realization as we glide past tac boards and a couple practically fucking behind a pillar. "But it did! You know? Like he's saying you get to bottom next time. Right? Hitting—"

"Stop. Just stop," I whisper-yell. Ian shrugs. I think he's said plenty. "And you know way too much about being gay for a *straight* boy."

"Thanks to you." He rolls his eyes.

I huff.

"*Also*, not my fault," I remind him, then do something stupid. "You seen the new kid?"

"New kid?" Ian seems befuddled.

"Yeah, short guy, can't talk," I describe as concisely as I know how. "Transferred in yesterday. Didn't I tell you they made me show him around?"

Ian looks up, which is dangerous in this crowd, and then back at me. "Maybe… Hold up, yeah. Think he's in my Civics class. And yeah, you did. He's the one you called dumb, right? I haven't seen him yet though."

That's what he would remember. I huff and nod.

"Eh," I say.

"Why?" Ian eyes me.

Why? I wasn't thinking this far ahead, and I don't think I want to talk about this. It's stupid. I can't crush on every cute guy and tell Ian every time, that's why I'm such a loser already. But Ian's looking at me with this expectation.

"Ted!" I scream as every spindly bit of my scapegoat's nearly six-foot self comes around the corner. He rolls his eyes. His name isn't Ted, it's Eric. It's an inside joke. He hates it, but it's us, so he deals with it. "Ian wants to do an FFDP song next."

Ian side-eyes me knowingly, but drops it as Eric does this clicking thing with his tongue.

"Which one?" he asks.

"'Never Enough'," Ian speaks up.

"God, you never want anything easy, do you?" Eric shakes

his head.

"What's the fun in that?" Ian shrugs.

"I'll get the music tonight," I tell them. I'm usually the one who prepares everything. Eric is the brain and the voice of the operation, and Ian basically just beats his drums. Okay, he does more than that, but I'm not giving him any more credit.

"Awesome." Eric fake punches my arm and starts off in the other direction. "Bell's about to ring, gotta go. See you in third."

I throw him a peace sign and take off with Ian toward our first class. It's only one block to get through before I know I'll see Skylar.

SKYLAR
THURSDAY, AUGUST 15

I'd almost forgotten about Jacob. Maybe forgotten is the wrong word, but I hadn't thought I would run into him again, not this soon.

I was wrong. But it still came as a surprise when I walked in on him standing in *nothing* more than a pair of cute burnt-yellow briefs, in the process of pulling his leggings up.

"You liking it here so far?" Jacob asks. It's the first thing he's said to me since I got to class, and we're back in the changing room again with maybe a minute to spare before the bell.

I put down the shirt I was just attempting to put on and pick up my phone.

"Sure. It's not bad." Siri's words slip through the cracks in the stall door into the main changing area where Jacob is. I refuse to change where he can see me. The last thing I need is to accidently look at him and for him to think I'm staring.

I pull on my shirt, making sure it hangs over my jeans. I still haven't worked up the courage to wear a skirt. I drape my dance clothes over my arm and open the stall door. Good, he's dressed. In all black again too.

"Good," he says and throws his pack over his shoulder.

It gets quiet. I smile awkwardly, checking my phone to get my locker code, and shove my clothes in my dance locker just as the bell rings.

"Well, see you later," Jacob announces behind me, and when I turn around, he's gone.

Why was that so awkward? Ugh.

I shake my head and loop my arms through my pack before taking off. A minute later I'm in the cafeteria. Voices echo off the walls and the screech of sneakers on linoleum jabs at my ears. I'm getting the usual glances now. Go me.

The word has spread. They know the new kid can't talk, or maybe they think I'm deaf. That happens a lot. I ignore it, focusing on my tray and the assortment of individually bagged burgers and chicken sandwiches and then the hot fry tray. I can feel their eyes on me. It doesn't matter how used to it I am, it still gets under my skin.

At the end of the line I pay and make for the grid of tables. I just need to find an empty one, or maybe one of the big ones with an empty seat away from the rest of its occupants.

"Skylar!" My name shrieks from somewhere among the tables.

My instinct is to change course, to move away from the voice. It's probably a group of girls who want to use me for their mocking game, or worse, the humanitarians who think they need to "take in the poor little handicapped kid." Like I'd rather you just kick me.

"Skylar!" It's the same voice, but closer. Hold up, I know that voice.

I tilt my head just enough to glance in the direction it came.

It's her. I can't remember her name, but it's her. Wiccan girl. I stop. But why? Why am I stopping?

"Come sit with us," she says once she twirls around in front of me, that curly black hair bouncing everywhere.

In my head my mind is going every which way. Screaming *no, run,* and *sure, go with her,* and *eh, I don't know,* all at the same time. I glance around the room, and eyes are glued to me. Confused, irritated, judging. I just want to get away from this, so without giving it more thought I nod.

"Sweet." She bobs her head and takes off. I follow, staring back at the dirty glares.

"Sorry about all them," her friend says when we get to the table, his mouth skewed in this way that says he gets it. I seriously doubt it. "People are stupid."

"Yeah, like what's their problem?" Wiccan girl eyes him, glaring back dangerously into the heart of the cafeteria.

I don't need their help. I want to tell them that and go my own way, but it feels super rude to pull away from the only two people in the room who aren't looking at me like I'm some freak.

"I didn't need saving," Siri says for me.

"Who said anything about saving you?" She looks at me like I'm insane.

"Of course you didn't need saving," the boy says. Even sitting down, he's tall. His head towers at least half a foot over us. "Just thought you could use some friends."

I huff and loosen my shoulders. *Okay, calm it, Skylar.* Maybe I didn't need saving, but maybe there's nothing wrong with someone trying to help a little too.

"Maybe," Siri's British voice says for me.

"Yeah, we have to stick together. There are some *real* assholes around here that thrive on making people like us miserable."

People like us? I'm not sure she understands what she's saying. They're not like me. And now I'm wondering what the hell is wrong with them.

"Outcasts, nerds, freaks." It's like she read my mind. Then again, I've been told my face is a bit expressive. "You know?"

I do, I mouth slowly.

Except most of the time, even the outcasts and freaks do better than me. What makes *them* outcasts though? Oh wait. He's a book nerd, which I can jive with, and she's Wiccan.

"You can hang with us," Seth suggests. "We're not the coolest, but we're fun! Especially if you're into nerdy stuff and have a general loathing of assholes."

Check. Check. I can roll with that. If they were ever to see my new room, they'd confirm the shit out of the nerd part. And I'd say the latter is obvious.

You two always together? I move my lips.

"Say again?" the girl asks.

I really need to ask them their names again, but it feels so rude. I move my lips slower this time. *You two always together?*

"Oh, yeah." She smiles.

"Basically," he groans, and she slaps his arm from across the table. "What the hell was that for?"

He gives her a sly grin, which makes me wonder.

"For being a bitch," she says. "He is. But he's my bitch. So annoying, but you get used to it."

"Same." He shrugs his thin shoulders. "But I'm beginning to doubt it."

She rolls her eyes and then turns to face me. "So what's your story?"

"I'm sorry, but what were your names again?" I have Siri ask as I squint in embarrassment.

"That's okay." She bounces in her seat. "I'm Imani, and this is–"

"Seth. I'm Seth," he interrupts her.

I allow a thin smile to slink across my face. These two are something else.

"So what's your story?" Imani asks again.

My story? I mouth. I know what they mean, but I don't want to get into it. They're going to have to deal with what they got in class yesterday.

"Yeah, your deal. You said you came from Vermont. Why'd you move?" Seth picks up.

I look down, fidgeting my fingers over my tray. I open my mouth and let my lips do the speaking again. *Long story. Maybe some other time.*

There's the slightest pause, but Imani doesn't let it hang for long.

"That's okay. Whenever you're ready." She smiles.

I look up and catch Jacob between the mass of faces. His white hair is impossible to miss. It's like a magnet to the eye. But then again, his face is too. There's another boy sitting at his table who's just as pale as he is. I think I saw that kid yesterday in my third period. I dig in my brain for a name, but it fails me. Why do I suck at names so bad?

"You know anything about Jacob?" I type, and let Siri ask before fully letting my mind process the stupidity of the question. They're going to want to know why I want to know.

But then again, maybe not.

"Jacob *who?*" Imani asks.

It didn't cross my mind there could be more than one. I start typing and Siri starts up, "Don't know his last name. White hair. Sort of pale."

"Jacob Walters." Imani eyes Seth and then me with a grin. I'm not so sure what that's about.

"He's a senior. *I* think he's nerdier than he lets on. Even if he's all grunge-scene boy. He and his friends, Ian," Imani turns to find their table and points to the pale boy sitting with him, "and Eric have this, like, rock cover band thing going on. Can't remember what they're called. They're decent though."

"Nah, they're pretty good," Seth counters. "They do other stuff."

I shrug. Rock isn't my favorite. But he has a band? I'm not sure whether to think it's cool or cringe.

"Depends," Imani says. She glances at Jacob and sighs. "He broke a lot of hearts over the summer, though, and put a big target on his back. Poor guy."

I tilt my head. What the hell did he do? Key one of the rich guys' cars? Steal their girlfriend? I could totally see him stealing their hearts. Or did he call someone something stupid? The way his mouth said stupid shit on our tour, that's not too unbelievable.

"He came out like right after school ended last semester." Imani sighs and Seth rolls his eyes and falls against his chair. "He's gorgeous. A lot of girls had their eyes on him. Now they're total bitches to him for no reason."

He's gay!? I mouth, unable to hide the surprise in my eyes. There's no way. He's too hot. Like usually the guys I can't stop looking at are straight.

"Yep." Seth pushes his chair dangerously onto two feet and drops it back to the floor with a clack.

I bite at my lip and smile. *Stop it, that doesn't mean he's an option. Remember what he said when you first saw him. "Oh, like dumb?"* But my mind is buzzing with possibility. I mean, he's so good-looking, but that aside, he's not going for the defective, short-as-hell guy. So just stop.

"He's single." Imani eyes me proudly.

So? I mouth as quickly as I can.

"Like, he's available." She's grinning so big, leaning in closer.

The thought sends a tingle up my spine, and I swallow down an imaginary lump in my throat. Is it that obvious I'm gay?

"Want me to introduce you?" The excitement in her voice practically rings.

Hold up!

"Oh boy." Seth shakes his head, his eyes conveying pity.

No! I mouth. *I met him.* I slow down so she can follow my lips. I'm a bit too excited right now, or maybe worried. *They had him show me around when I got here yesterday.*

"Oh really?" Imani sticks out her tongue.

I ignore it, shaking my head, but I'm grinning uncontrollably.

"Was he gay or bi?" Seth questions.

"Gay, definitely gay," Imani says, which shouldn't but does make my heart jump, even if bi would have been just as amazing. Then she breaks the ice. "In case you haven't noticed, it's okay if you're not straight here. I'm pan. Seth's a straighty, but I forgave him for that a few years ago. I don't want to assume your sexuality, though, or your gender."

She eyes me. She's trying not to ask, but she's still waiting for me to fill in the gap. Usually I'd feel like I was being pulled into a trap, being baited into some cruel game, but somehow this doesn't feel like one, which is unnerving in its own way.

I'm gay, I tell them. Definitely not into girls. No offense meant, but I'm just not. Wish I could be. Guys are trash. And she's pan? That's cool.

"Pronouns?" she digs, but I like it.

He/him, I say.

"Cool! I'm she/her, Seth's a bitch," Imani says casually without breaking eye contact.

"I'm right here," Seth sighs. It doesn't even register on her face.

"So, we got the G and the plus, still no B, L, T," Imani laughs. "I would be the L but some of the guys and theys are just too yummy."

The look on my face makes it obvious I'm a little confused.

"The alphabet mafia. LGBTQ+." She explains, "You're the G, you know, gay. I'm the plus, pan, since it doesn't have a P in there."

She seems pleased with herself.

"I'm not invited to the club, apparently," Seth jokes. "But I'm for y'all."

"He's good," Imani laughs. "My favorite straighty."

The bell rings and I'm about to get up. It's instinct when you usually sit by yourself. But I pause.

"What do you have next?" Seth asks as he gets up.

Civics, I mouth, but I get blank stares, so I type it out and let Siri say it. "Civics. Mrs. Moyer."

"Exciting," Seth mocks. "Better than math."

Good luck, I tell him, and I'm about to head back to my locker when Imani speaks up.

"You want to ride with us in the morning?" she blurts. Seth gives her a questioning glance and then shrugs.

Kimberly brings me, I mouth before I realize how lame it sounds.

"You could still ride with us, it'd be fun," she says. "Seth can pick us both up!"

I don't want to just say no. Shit like this isn't normal for me. People don't *want* to be around me, and when they do, they usually have other motives. But these two, they don't seem like most people.

I'll think about it, I tell them and nod before waving goodbye.

JACOB

"I'm clocking out, Zara," I yell, slipping past the candy counter. The theater wasn't that busy tonight, and somehow the bathrooms weren't too disgusting this time.

I step around the corner and make for the lot by the research institute. I've lived here my whole life, before it was even here, and I still don't have a clue what they *research*. All I know is that it's this sprawling campus of massive ornate brick buildings that take up half of downtown Kannapolis.

We're not in the country exactly, but after eleven this isn't the most happening place. Like it's not the sticks, but I wouldn't call it the suburbs either.

It's quiet tonight. And the sky is clear. Even with the streetlamps illuminating the path to Mom's golden Camry I can make out most of the stars beyond a full moon, and then there's the real spectacle. A comet. It's been up there a week or so, and it's especially brilliant tonight. Ty says it's almost at its closest. And damn, is it cool.

I unlock the car and fall behind the wheel. It sucks having to drive Mom's car. Besides the knowing looks in the school parking lot, it's frustrating not knowing if it'll be available when I need it. And that nagging sense that I'm stuck.

I get my phone out and check my messages before taking off.

IAN: Play Red Dead tonight?

I send a quick shrug emoji back. Then there's a Snap from Tyler. He's my long-distance Instagram friend, turned online gayming buddy last year.

I open it. A picture of his smiling face, complete with big green eyes and messy black hair, fills the screen. And there's a caption at the bottom. *I did it! Me and Aidan are back together!*

I hold up my phone, snap a picture of myself smiling, and type out a little burn, *You sure this time? JK! Congrats!*

I start my playlist and drop my phone in the cupholder. A deep beat takes my mind off everything as I put the car in drive and move across town. Home is only a few minutes from work, so it doesn't take long to hit my street, but I drive past my house and let another song start up. I'm not ready to go in yet. The kitchen lights were on, so Dad's probably still up. I know Mom is, she's a night owl, has been since I was a kid, but if Dad's up he's probably working on some campaign junk and I *don't* want to hear it.

It didn't use to be like this. I didn't use to dread going home. I mean, maybe it's not dread. I just... I don't know. I always want to delay it. I feel different around them now, Dad *and* Mom, but mostly Dad. My eyes roll into the back of my head when the thought hits me. Nothing should have changed, nothing. But I knew it would. Which is why I was so scared when I told them, when I admitted my truth to them.

I even called it that, *my truth*. And no, that went over no better than when I plainly told them I was gay. I got a lecture for it. Dad threw out, "That isn't your truth, Jacob. The truth doesn't depend on your feelings or how confused you are. Truth is never changing."

He didn't understand the words, and no amount of explaining would have changed his mind, just as it won't now. But I can't begin to say how much I wanted him to see, how I needed him to see. But he couldn't, he can't, understand that I'm finally being me, the real me, not the act I'd been putting on the last few years. That was the lie. This, who I am now, as fucked up as I feel at times, this is the true me.

The music goes silent and I snap back to the here and now. I've driven down a few side streets I hadn't meant to, so I make a U-turn and head back while the music picks up again. Leave it to me to listen to depressing shit when I feel, well, depressed.

A minute later I pull in the driveaway. I sit, staring at the door. The kitchen is on the other side, and Dad. I puff out a big breath and get out.

When I swing open the door, Dad's at the kitchen table. He's rummaging through stacks of paper, glancing through readers at his laptop, which I taught him how to use last year, like the smartphone I had to explain a few months ago, and the new TV remote. More campaign stuff. Not to be that relative, but we don't need him as our next congressman.

I put on a smile and cast a quick "Hey" behind me as I try making it to the living room without getting stopped. Mom will be in there watching some HGTV reruns, I'm positive. She's probably planning the next remodel.

The sound of a buzz saw or something grinding greets my ears, and at this hour it's definitely from the TV. I shake my head and a real smile crosses my lips. So predictable. But before I can cross the threshold, my dad calls.

"Jacob." His voice is gruff as usual. It has that sound it always does when he has a tech question, distant and confused. He's probably been waiting all night just to ask. I roll my eyes. I swear it's my only use.

"Yeah?" I stop.

"How do I get this, uh..." He points at the screen, searching for the word I assume describes whatever it is he's doing. "What's it called?"

I hold back the urge to sigh and walk around the old wooden table. It's been in the family for a few generations, and it's big enough to sit eight comfortably, even though we only really need room for six. He's got a Word document up on the screen.

"Word? A document?" I ask, giving him a few options.

"Is it just a document? Or is it *a Word*?" he asks, totally butchering its real name.

"Both, but no one really cares," I say. He can be real detail-oriented sometimes, and with getting his exploratory committee ready over the past month, he's been on overdrive.

"Okay, so how do I send this to Pastor Spencer?" His bald head shines under the kitchen light, accentuating the gray hair just over his ears and along the back of his head.

It's moments like this that are both empowering and annoying as hell. Like, I could totally screw this up for him and lead him into chaos, but he'd figure that out eventually and I'd be grounded. But on the other hand, it's just annoying that he constantly needs help with *every little thing*. I don't want to be involved in this campaign. At all. Not even tech support.

"Just go to your e-mail," I point to the icon I set up for him way back when, "and send it to him."

He clicks the icon and lets out a light bulb of a sigh before starting a new e-mail. He seems to have this part down. He even hits the attachment button like he knows what he's doing, but that's when the confusion hits again. "But where is it? I need to send these position statements for Pastor to check before I send them to Toby."

He doesn't know where he saved it? That again. I shake my head and point at the screen, tapping where I need him to click. "Go here and here. Okay, then—"

I think we're almost there when he stops me.

"Why are your nails black?" he gasps.

I sigh. It's not even horror anymore, it's aggravation. I knew this was coming. It was just a matter of time before he'd notice. I painted them Sunday night after church, before bed. I know he doesn't like it. Okay, doesn't like it is a massive understatement, but *I* like it.

"Because *I wanted* to?" I drag the words out as a question in my you-really-have-to-ask voice, which in hindsight isn't the best option.

"Jacob," he sits up straight and his voice becomes stern, "we've talked about this."

"I know." And I do. It's not the first time I've painted my nails, which is *only for girls*. "But there's nothing wrong with it."

I'm not standing down this time. I do that too much. And it's such a stupid little thing. It's *my* fucking nails. I don't think God cares if I put a little color on them.

"Yes, there is. It's not right for a man to paint his nails. There are things women do that men aren't supposed to, just like there are things men do that women aren't supposed to," he explains.

"Not buying it," I say before I really think about it. God, I should have kept my mouth shut.

"It's biblical, Jacob. Men are to be masculine, bold, not feminine." He points at my hands in disgust, repeating the sexist drivel. "Make sure that's off before you go to bed. End of discussion."

"Yes, sir," I drone, though I want to blurt *whatever*. I did that *once* when I was eleven. That was the worst spanking I ever got. One for each year of life, Dad said.

I fight the urge to huff—I don't need him commenting on my *heavy breathing* too and dragging this out even longer. Instead, I escape into the living room. Mom grins at me knowingly. There are times I'm not sure if she's totally on board with everything he says and other days when I'm positive she is. It's confusing. Like now. I'm not sure if it's just pity since I'm a fag and they're convinced I'm going to hell, or because she knows I'm irritated and Dad's way too dogmatic. But I never ask to find out.

"Hey, Mom." I nod and keep moving.

"Hey." Her voice is calm and smooth. "How was work?"

"It was…work?" I shrug.

She grins and shakes her head, and her long, flowing brown curls bounce over her shoulders. A bit of the tension lifts from my chest. I love her, even if she doesn't get me. I think she just doesn't know how to disagree with Dad and live with him.

"You work at a theater, it can't be that bad," she croons.

"It's just boring sometimes." I don't bother mentioning Connor's stupid ass. I can call myself a fag all day, but having someone else do it, knowing how they're saying it—and in public, while I'm stuck on the job and unable to say anything—is infuriating. I still can't talk to her about that type of thing, because it means she'd have to sympathize with my *sin*.

"That's work." She smiles, and I smile back.

"I'm tired. Night. Love ya," I tell her and walk off to my bedroom a bit better than I was a minute ago.

I swing my door open and sling it shut before falling on my bed. A pile of clean clothes sits on the floor by my closet which Mom told me to fold yesterday. My tiny excuse of a desk sits at the foot of the bed against the wall with my laptop—the same one Dad confiscated for two months after I came out because he found out I was using it to watch porn—and my guitar is propped along one of its legs. A bookshelf takes up the adjacent wall. My collection was larger last year, but our church had a book burning for *ungodly* books, so all my Dean Koontz and Michael Crichton books had to go for language alone, not counting the sex and evolution.

I bring my phone to life and finger through the notifications. Snaps and texts from Ian and Ty mainly, and a text from Rebekah, my sister. I check it. She wants to know if I like Conner or Layton as boy names. She's pregnant, and they don't even know the gender yet, but she's planning.

I don't care if she spells Conner with an E or an O like the douchebag at school, I'm not going for Conner. And Layton was our grandfather's name, so I get that one, but it's not really my type of name. Sounds old.

> *JACOB: Layton if its between those. What about Brennan?*

Brennan is my middle name. I think it would sound cool, but I'm ninety-nine percent sure she's not going for it, but that's sort of the point.

SKYLAR

I think I fucked up.

"You're riding with someone?" Kimberly stops wiping a glass plate dry. There's a hint of concern in her tone.

I nod and skew my mouth. *Yeah.*

What I don't say is that I'm wishing I'd told Seth not to pick me up this morning. I meant to. I battled it out in my head last night. Why do they want me to ride with them? Why do they want to be my friends? Are they planning to dump me on the road somewhere as a joke?

It's probably better just to avoid them, not get involved. But what if they're not like everyone else? What if maybe they're good people? But that's the problem—everyone sucks.

I told myself before falling asleep last night that I'd text Seth in the morning and tell him not to come. But I try not to use my phone once I'm in bed, and I was already under the covers. And I forgot to text him earlier, so now I'm stuck. I also laid my black and white plaid skirt on my desk before I went to bed—it's the only one I own and still fit into—but I didn't end up in it this morning either. So that makes it anxiety 2, Skylar 0.

"Who you riding with?" She goes back to wiping the plate.

"Seth and Imani," I let Siri tell her.

"Oh, your friends from…Sociology, right?" Kimberly faces me and leans against the kitchen counter.

Friends is pushing it.

I hadn't wanted to talk about them, but she wanted to know about my "friends", though I never once called them that. That's what she calls them. She has this grand idea I'm going to find people to get along with who won't backstab me. It's cute really, so I entertained her and told her about them.

"They sound nice." She walks over, abandoning the kitchen counter, and puts her hands on my shoulders. "You need to relax."

Relax? I look at her with the question in my eyes, and she smiles. It's warm and disarming. My eyes shoot away.

"Which one's driving?" Kimberly asks.

"Seth," Siri says.

"How long's he been driving?" she follows up.

I shrug. Hell if I know.

"How old is he?" It's beginning to sound like an interrogation.

What was that about relaxing?

Sixteen? I mouth.

My phone dings. Thank God. It's Imani.

IMANI: We're out front.

I look at Kimberly and mouth *I got to go* and point toward the front door just in case she didn't catch it. I grab my backpack on my way through the dining room and squeeze and release my fists to let off a little of the stress building in my chest and shoulders.

"Have fun! Tell Seth and Imani I said hey! And be careful," she calls as I walk out the front door. I turn and wave goodbye.

There's an older white Jetta in the driveway that wasn't there before. If Imani wasn't already hanging out the passenger window screaming, I might question who it is.

"Sky!" she screams. "Good morning!"

I'm sorry, but no one should be that chipper this early.

I raise my hand and wave with all the enthusiasm of a horse that just trekked the entire Sahara. Seth gets me. His eyes drag between Imani and me, head shaking.

"Hey man," he groans.

I swing open the back door and throw my pack on the seat before sliding in.

"Good morning, Mrs. Gray!" Imani yells.

Huh? I look over my shoulder, and Kimberly is waving from the porch.

"Morning, Imani," she calls back. And for a moment I wonder how Kimberly knew her name, but then I remember our conversation, as she tacks another name onto it. "Seth."

"Morning!" Seth yells out his window and then looks at me. "She knows my name?"

Imani looks back and grins. "You told your mom about us?"

I swear she's about to climb over the seat and grab my cheeks. And *Mom*? That's still weird.

I shrug. She did ask. What was I going to do? Lie and tell her no one talked to me, that these two didn't go out of their way to say hey?

Seth sighs and backs us out of the driveway. Imani keeps talking. I'm starting to expect that doesn't end.

"So every morning we go get coffee." Imani wiggles in her seat. "It's—"

"Not every morning." Seth glances at me in the rearview mirror and rolls his eyes.

"—this local place. Oh, and it's a cute little bookstore too. It's so adorable. You like books, right?"

I nod furiously. Her excitement is almost intoxicating. Although from the look on Seth's face, it seems you get used to it.

"How you like your coffee? Just straight coffee? Iced? Frappe?" She eyes me down as if the answer is important.

I let my mouth open, like something could come out, and shrug. Coffee wasn't something we really got in the orphanage, and none of my foster families volunteered any. So I don't really know.

"You don't know?" She's incredulous. Like it brought her whole world down.

I start typing, lip reading isn't going to get me far riding down a bumpy street with construction barriers lining the side of the road.

"I don't know. Never really had any. What do you get? And what's with all the construction?" Siri says.

"Not really sure. Dad says some big developer came in and bought most of downtown. It's been going on for a while." She frowns, like it's been a bother. Then she brightens. "My favorite is iced coffee. I love the caramel macchiato."

"Basic." It's the first thing Seth's said since interrupting earlier. He grins at me in the mirror.

"And proud of it." Imani bobs her head in the most overly sassy way possible.

We take the next left and Seth parks along the back of this little white house. Before us is a big black and white sign that reads *Editions Coffee Shop & Used Book Store*. There's something immediately welcoming about it, though I can't place what.

It's a quaint little building. And when we step inside it gets even better. It's charming and down to earth, lots of calming neutral colors, browns and grays and whites, wooden shelves painted white, and the scent of coffee in the air.

"Morning Imani, Seth," a woman's voice calls from the counter. She's plump, close to my height, and her hair is this deep green color. I'm guessing she's in her thirties, maybe late twenties. And the twang in her good morning says she's been around here all her life.

"Hey, Tina!" Imani replies, and pulls me to the register.

"Tina." Seth nods.

"Who's this cutie? Boyfriend?" the woman I now know as Tina asks, looking at me with a grin. I'm already getting the impression she could be a lot of fun. There's something mischievous about her.

"Nah," Imani giggles. "This is Skylar. He's our new friend from school."

"Nice to meet you, Skylar," Tina greets me.

"Nice to meet you," I type and let Siri tell her. The look on her face says it all.

"He can't talk," Seth explains.

"His phone does it for him," Imani picks up. "Sort of cool, right?"

Now that's something I've never heard before. She thinks my phone talking for me is cool?

"Hmm... That is neat." Tina smiles at me and nods. "So

what can I get for you?"

A few minutes later we're walking out with drinks in hand. I ended up with what Tina called a Witch's Brew Frappe, which seems like an awfully Halloween name for a drink in the middle of August. But she said it's basically a salted caramel frappe. I think for my first coffee, I did pretty great.

"Oh, what type of music do you like?" Seth asks before unlocking his car and getting in. "I forgot to ask."

My mind blooms with excitement. I've a few I just love. Or well, maybe *a few* isn't accurate, a ton is more like it. But type? That's a hard one. About the only things I don't listen to are rap and country.

"I like pop, a little punk rock, whatever's on the radio really," Siri translates as I keep typing. "My favorite is Myylo. His stuff is weird, but it's so good. And gay! Then it's Taylor Swift, Halsey, and Troye Sivan."

"Ooh! Halsey and Troye." Imani shoots me an excited look around her headrest. "Love 'em!"

"Uh… I think I have some Halsey," Seth considers, his finger swiping over his phone. "Yeah, here we go."

"Now or Never" comes over the speakers while Seth backs up and steers onto the road.

"What about The Weeknd? Ariana Grande?" Imani starts interrogating me.

I love Ariana, I mean, what self-respecting person doesn't like Ariana? I nod but type out a message so I'm not misunderstood. "Yes! Love her! Don't know the other."

By the time I get my words out, Seth is pulling into the school lot and searching for a spot. I see an open one just ahead, but Seth must have his eyes on another because he drives past it.

"I'm going to change that," Imani says, grinning.

"I'm so sorry," Seth apologizes, and I smile, my stomach shaking with laughter they'll not hear.

"Shut up, bitch." Imani slaps his shoulder.

I shake my head, and my eyes land on Jacob on the sidewalk. He's walking with the same guy he was eating lunch with yesterday. And before I look away, this tall brown-haired guy in a navy tank top shows up and shoves him. I can't hear what's going on but from the looks on their faces, they didn't compliment Jacob's black button-up.

"God, not again," Imani groans.

Again?

JACOB

"Get out of my way, fag!" is all I hear before a shoulder rams my chest.

That's when I see him. Well, Blake *and* Bexley, the indominable power couple in every way. He's star of the basketball team, she's captain of the volleyball team. He has the prototypical brown hair, green eyes, male model look, and she has the female model walk, even if she's too short for it, plus the British accent from her family. And speaking of family, they're both rich *and* total cunts. They were meant for each other.

"What's your problem?" I scream once I get my footing. Others might cower, but just because I'm an easy target doesn't mean I will.

"You," Blake snarls. "You're in my way."

"Then watch where you're going and it won't be a problem, asshole," I counter.

I can feel Ian staring me down. He's probably begging me to shut up, but I'm not looking to find out.

"Jac—" Ian starts, but Blake's voice growls over him.

"Who the fuck you think you are?"

"Not backing down to you, that's who!" I yell.

I imagine him stepping back, confused and surprised by the comeback. I see him looking for support and not finding any, typical bully, always needing validation from everyone around him. But it's *all* in my head. Instead, his lips form a sneer and his eyes grow slender.

"Fuck you, fag!" He thrusts forward, open hands rushing toward me.

I try to dodge, but I'm too slow. His palms connect with my shoulders and my body tumbles backward like a damn rag doll. My ass hits the sidewalk first. Then my back and elbows slam the concrete, and the pain screams through my limbs.

I yelp. God, I literally yelp!

"Stay down." Blake spits in my direction, missing, and then scoops an arm around Bexley and takes off. The pump in his step causes my blood to boil, and my pulse shoots the pain up my veins even harder.

"Really, Jacob?" Ian offers his hand and pulls me to my feet. He's looking at me like I'm stupid.

"Really." I roll my eyes. God, I hate them. Like, does he seriously have nothing better to do?

"You're bleeding," Ian says like it's an everyday occurrence.

I raise my arm, and sure enough there's blood seeping from my elbow below my sleeve. It's not that bad, just a scrape. Good thing I wear black.

"Have I said how much I hate them lately?" I ask, shaking my head and coughing. "Because I hate them."

"At least twice this week." Ian grins. "He's just afraid you're going to steal Bexley."

I eye Ian. It's definitely something Ian would say. It makes no sense.

"Really? Steal Bexley?" I laugh. "That's the best you got?"

SKYLAR

SUNDAY, AUGUST 18

"It's great to meet you, Skylar. Hope to see you next Sunday." The pastor shakes my hand.

He isn't what I think of when I think of a pastor. He's not old or bearded or stern. He *might* be in his forties, and not once during the service did he appear angry or mean behind the slim wooden pulpit.

I nod at him and follow Bob and Kimberly out the double doors and into the rain. Bob pops an umbrella open for Kimberly, and I open my own. It's pouring. Water rushes along the edge of the curb and gathers at the drains, splashing my shoes and dampening my socks. The umbrella only helps so much before I jump in the back seat.

"What did you think?" Bob turns in his seat.

They know my misgivings about church. My experience has been less than amazing, to put it simply. My last foster parents, the Grants, were *very* religious. For the year I was with them, we went to every service: Sunday morning, Sunday night, and Wednesday night, plus anything else that happened to be going on. That was also the year I came out. I don't know why I chose then. I'd known for a year, maybe more, before getting stuck with them. But that's when I did it. Talk about bad timing.

At first they wanted me to go to therapy with their pastor, and when the state wouldn't let them do that, they just berated me every day. They'd make me sit and read the Bible for an hour, the parts that say I'm an "abomination", and the Romans Road about how I was going to die and go to Hell *because* I'm an "abomination", unless I changed. Every chance they had to use a slur, they took it. Every time anything gay came on TV, they complained. Finally, I got Mrs. Johnson, my Family Services agent, to get me pulled from the home for abuse.

So, yeah. My understanding of church and religion isn't what you might call good. And honestly, I don't know what I really think of God. I hated Him while I was with the Grants. Every second He was the root of my problems, my pain. If it weren't for Him, I'd thought every day, people wouldn't be this mean. They wouldn't try to change me. Maybe they'd try to understand me.

But this church, it was sort of nice. I mean, the music was dated and boring, but the people were nice. If this is how God meant it to be, then maybe He's not such a bad guy after all.

"It was nice," I have Siri tell them. I'll critique the music later.

Kimberly sat me down a few days ago to talk about it before going. Seems the pianist is a lesbian, and there are a few gay couples in the congregation. I confirmed that today. I might have searched the pews to find them. And sure enough, they were there. A short dirty-blonde guy and an equally short brunette with long, drawn features and his arm draped over the other's shoulder. Husbands. Here, in church.

"Good." Kimberly smiles back as the car pulls away, rain pelting the windshield. "I told you it wasn't so bad."

I nod. I don't know what type of church it was, I didn't pay attention to the sign and no one said. A good one, maybe?

"Does the pastor always dress like that?" It's the one question that's been burning in my mind since he got up to preach.

I'm used to them dressing to the nines. Suit and tie, dress slacks, perfectly combed hair. But this pastor, uh…Pastor Dane, was in a tieless white button-up and jeans.

"Pretty much. Sometimes he wears a tie, but usually not," she tells me. "It's relaxed. We believe it's the heart that matters, not the dress."

I think about it and start typing. "The Grants' pastor said how we dress reflects our dedication to God. He was always in a suit and tie. But he was mean."

"How we dress can say a lot of things about us," Bob says and pauses to consider his words. "But I think when we put too much emphasis on it, it just becomes a show, a mask. If we're not careful it'll hide who we really are, even from ourselves, just like it can show who we are. That's why we don't get all dressed up. We're not putting on a mask for God, we're coming to Him as we are."

Now that makes sense. What we wear isn't that important. It's what's on the inside.

"I like that."

"Oh, before I forget," Kimberly pops up, interrupting the moment. "Your dad and I are throwing you a sixteenth birthday party."

Her eyes brighten like *she* just won the lottery, but I think maybe it's me. A birthday party? For me? I don't remember the last time I had my own birthday party. I really don't remember.

"We want you to invite your friends," Bob picks up as if Kimberly hadn't just totally switched topics.

I just keep looking between them with this look that's begging them to tell me they're joking. And friends? What friends? I guess Imani and Seth count. But that still feels foreign. There's actually someone I'd maybe, just maybe, call a friend. And there's two of them. *And* I'm getting a birthday party? What is happening?

Really? I mouth. I'm too excited to type. They nod excitedly, but Bob keeps his eyes on the road.

"Your birthday is on Friday, so we're having it then," she reminds me. I'd almost forgotten it was coming. It never really mattered much. "Just invite your friends and let us know who's coming so we can have enough food."

I can't believe this is happening.

JACOB
MONDAY, AUGUST 19

I don't know if it's the constant sweat-soaked bodies or the building itself. But the auxiliary gym always stinks.

That's what's going through my head in the changing room since it's awkward as fuck. I have to think about something. Skylar not talking just makes it weird. I tried talking to him some last week, but he has to get his phone out, and I don't know, but it seems sort of rude to make him do that while he's changing. I mean, he's cute, so I sort of want to talk to him, but I'm also a little nervous. Which is so not me.

He just has this innocent little vibe, and honestly, a dump truck that would make anyone jealous. And the leggings don't help any. I'm just glad I'm usually ahead of him in class so it's not distracting me the entire time.

I keep wondering what it's like not talking. Like right now, the silence is screwing with my head, so I can't even imagine what it's like not being able to speak. That's torment.

"Are you really in a band?" a British voice questions. I twist around to see who it is. Wow, okay. It's Skylar. Obviously.

He's in one of the changing stalls. I think he's weirded out changing in front of others. I used to be, especially before I came out. It was like every guy in the room knew I was gay, even when they didn't. It felt like if I even remotely looked at anyone, they'd beat my ass. But Skylar, I'm not sure why he does it, and it's not really something I plan on asking.

"Uh, yeah." I shrug.

Siri comes back with another question. "You and your friends?"

"Yeah, we started it freshman year, it's called The Nevermore," I tell him, trying to keep it short and sweet. How did he know about that? Don't worry about it.

I shrug and allow the silence to scooch back in.

"What type of band?" He keeps the questions coming as I pull on a pair of black jeans.

"Cover band mostly. Sort of emo rock fusion type of thing, a little pop here and there," I explain.

We don't have any of our own music, though I did try last year. Didn't work out too well. I kept hitting mental roadblocks. I think Eric has a few songs, but nothing we've ever tried.

"Cool," Siri says over the stall door, and it gets quiet again.

Half a minute later the latch clicks and I hear Skylar's feet padding the floor. I pull my shirt on and turn to tell him bye, I figure he's leav–

I stumble back a step. Like, it isn't bad, it's super fucking adorable, but it's *the* last thing I expect.

"U-u-uh," I stutter.

Skylar's standing in the open stall in a white collared button-up under a black long-sleeve shirt, with the most adorable black and white plaid skirt hanging just above his knees. My eyes stick in place on the bit of thigh peeking under the edge before I jerk my gaze back up.

He's grinning nervously. I don't know if it's because of the way my stupid self looked at him or if he's trying to gauge just how bad an idea wearing a skirt is. And it's probably not the best idea, even if he does look good in it.

"You weren't…uh…wearing that earlier," is the only thing I can think to say other than *God, you look good*, which is the last thing I'd say. My arms and fingers swing erratically, pointing at the skirt, as if he didn't know it was on his body.

He raises his phone. I hadn't even noticed it in his hand.

"I brought it with me," Siri explains. And it's both eerie and cool how he looks at me, mouth unmoving, while his words are spoken. "Wasn't sure how people would react, and I didn't want Bob or Kimberly talking me out of it."

That makes sense. I don't know his parents, I'm assuming that's who Bob and Kimberly are, but the *people* part, yeah. People around here are going to have a field day with this in the *least* wonderful way possible.

"Yeah. Not sure you're going to like that part," I tell him. I'm just being honest. "But *I* like it."

Yeah, I shouldn't have said that last bit. I don't even think he knows I'm gay, but I doubt… Oh wait. Is he? I mean, he's wearing a skirt. Wait, no. That doesn't mean anything. But could it? No. Now I'm just reaching.

He grins and flicks his eyes to the ground and starts saying something. His lips are moving, but I, being pathetic, can't read them. I shake my head in confusion.

"Uh… Sorry, but I can't read lips. Remember?" I remind him.

He forms a big O with his mouth and starts to type.

"My bad," his phone says. "What about the school?"

Good question. A lot of the teachers are progressive. If ninety-five percent of the English Department wouldn't go out and *buy* him a skirt, I'd honestly be surprised.

"I don't know," I tell him. "I think you should worry more about the students."

He purses his lips and huffs. I can imagine the looks he's going to get. Either he's really stupid or he's got nerves of steel under that unassuming little smile.

SKYLAR

MONDAY, AUGUST 19

You'd think I was a superstar the way the girls across the lunch line are whispering and staring me down while I stack my plate with fries. I swear every eye is on me.

And Jacob was right. We've got some work to do.

The moment the bell rang it was on. I don't think I've heard that many *what the fucks* in a five-minute stretch in my life, most of them not intended for me to hear, while others, yeah, they wanted me to hear. At least they don't assume I'm deaf. Positive, right?

The insults and catcalls veiled in thick sarcasm haven't failed either. Now it's not just bot boy — that started up Friday — which has picked up well enough. I imagine the rumors of me being gay have already begun, which is sort of funny, seeing that I am.

But I admit I've second-guessed putting this skirt on a few hundred times. It's stupid. It shouldn't be a big deal. I'm just hoping this town isn't so backward that I get lynched before the day is over. This type of thing wasn't really frowned upon up in Vermont, not in the schools at least, or maybe it was just too cold most the time for me to want to wear a skirt.

Just ignore them, I keep telling myself, shuffling to the cashier lady at the end of the line and paying for my lunch. Even she gives me a weird look, brow raised in disapproval when she hands over my change.

In fairness, I've had a few girls compliment the selection. Seems black and white plaid was a good choice, as if I had anything else that fit. And there was that semi-cute guy who whispered to me in the hall that I was cute without actually looking at me. So that was nice.

Focus, Skylar. Focus on your goal. You have to invite Imani and Seth to your party. Even that's weird. I'm going to have a birthday party, like a real deal, balloons and cake birthday party. And I'm inviting friends. It's a lot right now. I'm not sure which is more surprising — getting a birthday party or having people I think, just maybe, I can actually call friends.

And I'm about to find out. Being the weird new transfer student didn't worry them. The fact that I'm defective and can't talk didn't bother them. Finding out I was gay didn't even register on the shock scale. But maybe me wearing a skirt will be drawing the line just too far. I always end up finding that line, and it's not like I'm trying. It just doesn't usually take this long.

"What the—" some tall blonde-headed guy in a DC t-shirt and khaki shorts yells. Oh look, even the nerds are getting on board.

"He's a fag too?" someone else screams so the entire cafeteria can hear. Then a "Skirts are for girls, you faggot," and "Someone's a little sus", as if it's a bad thing.

I take a deep breath. I can call myself all of those things, and others like me can too, and it doesn't matter, it's even funny. But when it's someone like these assholes who say it with such disgust, it scales up my spine like a tarantula. It burrows deep into my bones and takes up residence, eating away from the inside. I remember the pastor up north telling me that feeling is my conscience telling me I'm being sinful, that inside I know it's wrong and disgusting to be gay. But that's not what it is. That's not it at all.

I'm not the most courageous person, not by a long shot, but maybe a little stupid courage is what I need more of. At least that's what I tell myself whenever I decide to wear a skirt. It's stupid. It's a little thing. It doesn't matter in the grand scheme. But it does.

"Dayum, bot boy's a pretty little fag," a gravelly voice haunts my ears. I shouldn't, but I turn and immediately my heart sinks. It's him. That douche that bullied Jacob in the parking lot. Blake, I think that's what Imani called him.

I turn and keep moving. There's no way I'm stopping for him. A few tables away I spot Imani and Seth, their eyes searching the crowd for whatever's causing all the disturbance. My eyes lock with Seth's first, and I think it registers. He's out of his seat in a second, and then Imani. Just a few more feet.

"You *are* a fag, aren't you?" Blake sounds proud of himself, like he's honored to out me.

Surprise, asshole, I've been out for years.

I stop, standing between a set of full tables, and twist around just to shrug. Like who cares if I am? No one.

"Oh God, he is," his girl laughs. Bex-something? "Another one. They just keep coming."

"I bet they do," Blake laughs. Wow, he thinks he's a real

hoot.

"That's disgusting." Bexley mock pukes.

"You wearing anything under that skirt?" Blake's voice drools out of his mouth in faux sensuality.

I hate every fucking syllable, every exaggerated word, every second his mouth moves. And for a moment I wish he'd drop dead right here and now, and do the world a favor.

"Sure hope so," his girl says. "Don't want to confirm you have no balls."

"Probably right," Blake agrees.

To hell with this. I'm not standing here and dealing with this. Not a chance.

I swivel around, sending my skirt swirling. And as I'm turning, I catch Blake's hand at the edge of my vision, sweeping toward my skirt. But before he makes contact another hand sails into its path and grabs his wrist in a deadlock. I stop and turn around when the person, who is definitely not Seth, starts to speak.

"Keep your hands to yourself, asshole," Jacob growls. Green eyes boring into Blake, but it doesn't faze him.

"Get your homo hands off me." Blake wrenches away. He shakes his arm like he's disgusted Jacob would even think to touch him. Hypocrite much?

"Keep your hands off him then," Jacob bites back.

"Whatcha going to do about it?" Blake steps closer, chest puffed inches from Jacob. "Huh? Is he your bitch or something? You fags will fuck anything, and I didn't even touch him."

Jacob shuffles his feet as Seth and Imani come up and form a line between me and Blake and his girl.

"What's y'all's problem?" Imani throws her hands up.

"His dick hasn't grown since middle school," Jacob answers without breaking eye contact with Blake. If it weren't for the adrenaline pumping through my veins, I'm certain I'd be laughing.

Blake shoves forward, knocking Jacob back an inch, but he quickly gets his ground again. "Nasty fu—"

"What's going on here?" a solid voice bellows in the open space. My eyes dart to the right. A teacher? Maybe. He struts our way, long face drawn tight. The top of his pale head is slick, encircled in a crown of thin gray. "I asked what's going on here?"

"He's harassing Skylar," Imani jumps in before Blake can get a word in.

He looks at Blake with one eyebrow raised. The blonde's demeanor changes from bad dude to innocent in a heartbeat. Then the man finds me and *literally* looks me up and down, and I swear he does a double take.

"Is this true?" he asks Blake.

"Of course not." Blake bops his shoulders like it's *the* most absurd thing in the world. Bullying? Not him.

"Excuse me?" Imani leans back and crosses her arms.

"He tried to grab Skylar's a...butt, Coach Bass!" Jacob faces the man, who's apparently a coach. Yay. Points for Blake. "That's not okay."

"Blake?" Coach Bass stares the basketball player down.

"Seriously, Coach? God, no!" Blake lies, he bald face lies like it's the most true thing he's ever said.

But the most infuriating part about it all is that as usual, I'm left depending on others to stand up for me. But *unlike* usual, there are people here, actually defending me.

"Blake, we'll talk about this during class." Coach Bass eyes him down and then waves him off. Blake flashes his despicable perfect grin at me just before turning and leaving in victory.

"You're just going to let him go?" Imani throws her hands up.

"What does he expect when he comes dressed like that?" Coach Bass waves his hand in front of me.

My eyes spring open. What the hell? Imani, Seth, and Jacob are all thinking the same thing from the look on their faces.

"What?!" Imani and Jacob both blurt.

"Look, uh…" Coach Bass points at me, searching for a name I can't give him.

"Skylar," Jacob angrily slings my name out.

"Can Skylar here not speak for himself?" Coach Bass asks. First, that's just rude, not to mention that chauvinistic crap you just threw out, and two, no, I can't.

"He's actually nonverbal," Seth speaks up, though he sounds sort of unsure.

"Nonverbal?" There's confusion in the coach's eyes.

"He can't talk." Each word juts from Imani's lips. She's really holding back.

"Okay," he says, stressing the O. "Well, Skylar, I'm going to need you to change into something more appropriate."

"What's wrong with what he's got on?" Imani almost jumps in front of me. I like this girl.

"We do have a dress code, and this," he waves his hand in front of me again as if I'm this shining example of what not to wear, "isn't in the dress code."

"Why not? It's not too short." Imani isn't giving up. And she's right. I made certain of it in case this very thing happened.

"Boys can't wear skirts to school," Coach Bass says dryly.

"Says who?" Imani asks.

Part of me wants to tap her on the shoulder and tell her it's okay. I don't need her getting in trouble on my behalf. The other part likes seeing her stand up to the patriarchy.

My eyes dart between her, Seth, and Jacob, who are both staring at Imani wide-eyed.

"The dress code," Coach repeats.

"Well, if it does, that's messed up," Imani huffs.

There's no mention of gender in the school's policy. Nowhere, nada. But there is this little piece about admin having the right to determine if anything is prohibited based on it being *distracting*, which is total vague bullshit.

"I don't make the rules," Coach Bass says, then fixes his stare on me. "Do you have anything else to wear?"

I don't want to change. I shouldn't have to. I huff and hand my tray to Seth, who takes it even though he seems shaken by the fact that I gave it to him, and pull out my phone.

"Yeah, but this isn't against the dress code," I let Siri tell him.

"Listen, kid, I'm not arguing with you." Coach Bass rolls his eyes again. He's so over us. Actually, no, I think he was over us the moment he saw me. "It's either change into something acceptable—you can call your parents to bring you some clothes if you have to—or it's detention. Your choice."

"This is insane." Jacob shuffles, his eyes darting all over

the place. "Like really?"

"Really," Coach says as blandly as possible.

"I'll change," I type and let my phone give in for me. Whatever. No point in getting detention yet.

JACOB
MONDAY, AUGUST 19

"This is so wrong." Imani hasn't stopped complaining since Skylar left to change. "It's *so* sexist."

I keep nodding. She's said it a few times. I've never really talked to her or Seth, we're not in the same clique. But seeing her in action makes me wonder why not.

"Yeah, it is," I say.

I'm waiting for Skylar to get back. That was some real shit, and I just think I need to make sure he's good.

"Isn't it a little weird though?" Ian says.

"Weird?" I eye him, trying to give him a chance to rethink it before I answer. If there's one thing I've learned since coming out, it's that unlearning all the baseless *norms* takes time, and he needs more time. It even took me a while to build up the nerve to paint my nails.

"You know, just not…" Ian stops short and poses a question instead. "I mean, you wouldn't wear one, right?"

Imani's eyes slap me, beaming with expectation. I avoid them and glance at the entrance to the bathroom where Skylar is changing instead. I don't know why I care. The boy's straight. Wearing a skirt means nothing, even if way back in my head I'm thinking it. But no.

I should leave.

"Maybe, I don't know. Not really my thing." I won't lie, it's crossed my mind before, but I don't think I'd look good in a dress. Others though, yeah. "But I do like a cute boy in a skirt."

Ian's and Seth's mugs gawk at me in surprise. Imani is practically gleeful. I bet her mind is going wild right now, and it suddenly hits me why.

"I'm not saying Skylar, just…you know…in general." I curtail the enthusiasm. Sure, he's hella cute in it, but I didn't mean to make that jump. Like, damn, guys.

"But maybe?" Imani gives me the side-eye, grinning wildly.

"That's not what I said." I fight the urge to cough, putting my finger in the air as if it helps make the point.

"So why you sticking around?" She prods her tongue between sparkling teeth. "Huh?"

I pause to keep myself from blurting something stupid. It's *not* like she's insinuating. He was getting bullied, and I hate that shit. I deal with it enough that I'm not standing by and watching someone else get it. That's it.

"Just want to make sure he's okay. Those guys are jerks." I shrug.

"Ah-huh…" She won't stop grinning.

Ian's on my right still, looking on in amusement, unconvinced. I show him my middle finger, and he giggles. They all do.

It gets quiet in our little huddle at the edge of the cafeteria for a moment. No one knows what else to say, so we glance awkwardly at each other while we wait. I check the bathroom entrance a few more times, but there's still no Skylar.

Imani breaks the silence.

"I heard your dad's running for Congress or something," she says.

Please stop reminding me, people.

"Yeah," I huff.

"You don't seem excited," Seth comments.

"Have you met his dad?" Ian points at me.

"He's not totally bad," I say. "I don't really want to talk about it. It's annoying enough he's running."

"Got it," Imani says and actually drops it.

It's all I hear about at home, and today everyone's been asking about it.

At the edge of my vision Skylar finally walks out of the bathroom, back in his black shorts. He squints when he sees me standing with the others. Yeah, I should have left.

"Sorry, Sky," Imani says. "That was some seriously sexist junk. And I know it's not in the dress code."

Skylar shrugs and mouths something I can't make out, but I guess she can.

"See, not in the dress code." She purses her lips knowingly.

"You okay?" I wedge my way in.

He nods and smiles, but his eyes jerk away.

"Sorry about that." I apologize even though it wasn't my fault. He deserves an apology and I know he'll never get it from the people he should. "Blake's the worst. And Bexley—"

"God, Bexley is a bitch," Imani talks over me. I grin and let her.

"Hot though," Ian gives his two cents.

"She's his perfect match," I tell him, rolling my eyes at Ian.

Skylar shrugs and blows out a heavy breath. I guess that's easier than typing.

"They're horrible. They feed off making our lives miserable," Seth chimes in. I'd almost forgotten he was here. He's so quiet, not to mention thin. Almost makes me look beefy.

He's right though. The scab on my elbow is a testament to that.

"Well, uh…just stay out of his way and you should be good," I say, but I don't know why. That won't work. I swear Blake has a nose for finding us. "See ya later."

SKYLAR

MONDAY, AUGUST 19

"You work at the bowling alley?" Siri asks for me.

"Yeah," Seth says, his eyes on the road.

I can see my house a few driveways ahead. But I can't tell if anyone's home. Unlike half our neighbors, we use the garage.

"He started last year," Imani says.

"No, I didn't." Seth smirks. "I didn't turn sixteen until January. I started in March."

Imani looks at me between the front seats, lips sucked in, eyes wide and rolling.

"My bad," she says. "Seems like forever ago."

I giggle…well, I smile and pantomime it. I feel like I'm forgetting something though. It's one of those annoying feelings. The type that eats at the back of your mind. Like you know there was something you were supposed to do, or maybe not do, but what? God, I hate it.

"Well it hasn't been." Seth pulls into my driveway.

I get out, but before I start off I remember what I'd meant to mention. My birthday party. I'm supposed to invite them. I reel around and tap the back of Seth's car before he can take off. This was supposed to happen at lunch. I was going to ask then, but with all that went down, and then Jacob sitting with us after, I failed.

Yeah, Jacob sat with us. It was weird.

"You good?" Seth rolls down his window.

Imani, with absolutely no perception of personal space, sprawls across the car, over Seth's lap, and juts her head out the window next to him. He glances at her in amusement and huffs.

I start to mouth the question but stop myself.

"My birthday is Friday," my phone drones with zero percent of the simultaneous enthusiasm and dread I'm feeling. What if they say no? "I'm having a party. Would you two come?"

"Yes! Yes! Yes!" Imani screams. The sound is near ear-piercing. Poor Seth.

"Uh…" Seth shakes away the flash bang in his ear. "Yeah!"

Thank you, I move my lips and sign it without thinking. And with that I wave, unable to stop smiling, and run inside.

They said yes!

I want to tell Kimberly, but just in case the school called, I shoot down the hall and start up the stairs. Then the negative thoughts invade. They'll probably decide they don't want to come before Friday. There's plenty of time for that, and chances are they'll stop talking to me outright by then too. What if Kimberly and Bob hate that I wore a skirt to school? They acted cool about it, but the Grants seemed cool before I had to move in with them too.

I slow, taking each step carefully. I think I hear Kimberly in the kitchen. Just a few more steps and I'll be safe in my room.

"Skylar." My name comes reaching up for me. I freeze, shoulders drooping. "Is that you?"

That's sort of a weird question to ask from two rooms away. I can't answer. And if it wasn't me, do you really want to be screaming?

I start back downstairs anyway, sighing in the hope this goes over well. She meets me halfway, and I give her a guilty as hell half grin. I'd be a horrible liar. She's not said a thing and I'm already breaking.

"The school called." She leans against the large doorway by one of her fake trees. She explained when I first arrived that she'd wanted plants in the house, but she killed everything she brought in, so fake it is. I don't move. Maybe it was about something else. "They said you wore a skirt to school today. Thought you had those shorts on when you left."

What do I say? I'm not going to lie, that's pointless.

I'm sorry. I didn't know if you'd let me. I bring my hand up to my face and sign, moving my mouth at the same time.

"Skylar," her voice is sweet but tinged with disappointment, "of course we would have let you."

You're not mad?

"No, silly," Kimberly giggles. She walks over and places a hand on my shoulder and part of me wants to drop from under her palm, but I don't. I've got to get used to that. "You don't need to hide that from us. Your school, though, they're not too excited about it."

I can tell. I shrug, pushing an unruly brown strand from my eyes. *What did they say?*

I feel like I'm intruding to ask, but I do it anyway.

"Just that it wasn't 'in line with the school dress code.'" She throws up some air quotes and produces a mock authoritative voice. "I told them they were wrong. But they're using that little catchall part in the code about it being 'distracting.'"

It basically gives them full reign to make anything against the dress code without the code being overtly sexist.

"I told them it's not 'distracting' and if they make you change again, they'll be talking to our lawyer." The grin in her voice becomes mischievous.

What? I mouth.

"Yeah, let them try it," she insists. "Of course, we have to get a lawyer first, but they don't know that."

I don't know what to say. This isn't the response I expected. I mean, I knew they didn't mind, generally speaking, but this? It's awesome.

"With that said," she takes her hand off my shoulder and pokes her pointer finger in the air, "let's hold off on wearing any more skirts for a week or so. Give your dad and me some time to talk to a lawyer and work things out just in case."

I think I can do that. A week isn't bad. I nod vigorously. I can do that.

Thank you! Was that all they said though? *Did they say…*

I stop. No. I don't want to talk about that asshole. Why did I even bring it up?

"Did they what?" Kimberly asks.

Nothing, I say.

It's nothing.

SKYLAR

TUESDAY, AUGUST 20

Why's Jacob at our table again?

I stop in the middle of the lunchroom when I see him. I'm getting enough looks as it is, and I don't need more, so I start moving again.

"Sky!" Imani yells, startling Seth, while I'm still two tables away.

I grin and throw a quick glance and smile at Jacob and Ian before putting my tray down. I get two tenuous grins back. I feel that. There needs to be someone between us, so I take the seat next to Seth, putting him between Ian and me.

"No skirt today?" Imani whines, like it's this major disappointment.

I shake my head. What *I* want to know is why Jacob and Ian are sitting with us. Sure, we're all outcasts, but they're a different type of outcast. We're nerds, the weird kids. But Jacob and maybe Ian—I can't really tell yet, he doesn't seem the dark type—are eboy rocker outcasts. They're the type most people see as different, but a cool sort of different, like it's trendy. *We're* not trendy.

"So yeah, we're going to cover it tonight," Ian says,

continuing whatever was being said before I arrived.

"Cool." Seth bobs his head.

What are they covering? A car? Someone's drink tab? Probably not. That one sounds illegal.

"A song, we're doing a cover of one tonight." Jacob must have seen the confusion on my face. "Five Finger Death Punch?"

I squint. More confusion. Five finger what the hell?

"It's a band, like a *really* cool band." Ian leans over the table.

You know who that is? I mouth to Seth. Ian and Jacob look as confused now as I was a second ago.

"Nope," Seth admits.

I didn't think so. *I might not have known you for years, but I've been in your car enough to know you don't know* any *of the bands Jacob and Ian play.*

"Same." Imani raises her hand in defeat.

"None of y'all?" Jacob asks.

I shake my head. I'm guessing it's rock because I haven't a clue.

"They're so good." Jacob deflates into his chair. "You'll have to listen to our cover. It'll be on YouTube."

He's looking at me. It's almost like he's *only* talking to me, and God, I like it and hate it at the same time. But I can't do eye contact like that, not with him. He's too hot. Like too hot to be sitting with us. That white hair and those bright green eyes. It's too much for this table.

I glance at him quickly enough to say, *Maybe. What's your YouTube?*

He squints and grimaces. "Sorry, didn't catch that."

Right. He can't read lips.

"He said, maybe. And what's your YouTube," Imani translates and then winks at me.

"If you text me, I can send you a link," Jacob suggests.

"Let me give you his number?" Imani eyes Jacob. Guess I don't get a say in this.

"He's already got it," Jacob says.

Her gaze darts to me and she raises an eyebrow, pooching her lips accusingly.

What? I have his number?

"I gave it to you when you first got here, remember?" He tilts his head.

Oh, my lips form an O. *That's right. So if I had questions I could ask you.*

I'd forgotten. Hopefully that's enough to get Imani off my tail. I can see her being the type to take it as an indication of something more that's *not* there. There's *no* chance of that.

Jacob twitches in confusion, and Imani translates again.

"He said he remembers now." It's not exact, and it's leaving out some key clues that were meant more for her anyway. It works I think, but then she gives me a look that says she's not buying it.

"Do you sing?" I have Siri ask so I don't have to use my translator this time, and send him the text right after. Imani keeps staring me down.

"Not really. I mean I can, but I'm mainly backup vocals," Jacob says. "But I play the guitar. Ian plays the drums."

"Eric's lead vocals and guitar," Ian picks up.

"Eric is like a more filled-out version of Seth," Imani says, and my eyes go straight to Seth, who's looking on in awe. "But with better hair and voice."

"Excuse me?" Seth tilts his head.

"What?" She shrugs.

"Okay," Jacob strings it out, "not how I'd have said it, but..."

"So you think I'm cute too then?" Seth questions Imani.

"Huh?" Ian looks confused, eyes jumping between the two.

"Didn't say that." Imani is all grins.

"You always say Eric is." Seth raises his brow.

Okay, I just want this to end. It's getting awkward.

"Cool. Guitar?" I have Siri ask, anything to get off this train. "I wanted to play when I was younger."

"Yeah, I've played since I was ten." Jacob nods, eyes lingering on Imani for a second longer before finding me again. "Started off playing acoustic at church, and now I play electric, superstrat. Lead guitar."

I don't know what superstrat means, but it sounds cool.

"I could never," Seth speaks up, still eyeing Imani. "Too much coordination."

Jacob and Imani laugh, but I think it's for different reasons.

"Sure you could," Jacob says.

"Nah, coordination isn't his thing," Imani steps in. Seth shoots her a death glare, but then sidelines it with a grunt. Satisfied with her dig, Imani turns to me. "What do you want for your birthday?"

That's not what I expected. Once I rebound, I shrug. I don't know. I've definitely thought about it, but they don't need to get me anything. AirPods and Apple Watches are a little expensive.

Nothing. It'll be cool enough having them over at an actual birthday party. I'm still stoked about that.

"Your birthday's coming up?" Jacob's voice comes a little higher than a second ago.

I nod, and Imani takes over.

"He'll be sixteen. Friday, right?" She looks at me for confirmation and I bow my head. "He's having a party."

And there she goes again.

"Oh that's soon!" Jacob's excited, which is sort of cool. Then his face goes all pouty. "Guess only the cool kids are invited."

"You want to come?" I make my phone ask faster than I can think. It's one of the downfalls of typing fast.

Sometimes having to type my thoughts helps filter out the stupid, but something didn't click this time. Not quickly enough, at least. I can't have him around. He's too hot to be around, and oddly really nice, and that's just going to make me think shit I don't need to.

"I was just kidding, sorry! I didn't mean to… Sorry." His mouth moves fast.

But now the invitation is out there, and I'd feel like a real genuine asshole if I took it back.

I type into my phone again and double down on my mistake. "No, seriously. You want to?"

"Uh, sure," Jacob coughs. I think he sees my predicament, but like me, he's stuck.

"Ian? You want to come?" my phone asks. While I'm digging my grave, I might just as well dig it for all of us.

JACOB
TUESDAY, AUGUST 20

The notes flow through my fingers with each pluck of the strings. Music pours from the amplifier, and the beat echoes off the walls of Ian's garage.

I look up long enough to glance at Ian's phone set on a tripod below the open garage door. Filming our covers was Eric's idea, but he's running late. It's just me on the lead guitar and Ian on the drums for the moment. It isn't the same, but it works.

And my mind is going full speed again. It's Skylar. It needs to stop, but it's all Skylar. His little short self, big hazel eyes that I think are more green than brown, and little hands. He's just cute. Like, too cute.

I miss my chord and the music screeches to a halt as I jerk my hand away.

"Fuck," I whisper. I've got to focus.

"What the hell?" Ian stops pounding the drums.

"My bad," I sigh.

"You good?" Ian asks, but then he digs. "Is it Skylar?"

I spin around and give him my what-the-hell look.

"Where is Eric?" I change topics. I'm not doing this game.

"Late." He states the obvious.

"Why though?" I ask.

I'd cut Eric off the week I came out. That week had been full of losing people, so it just seemed like another body on the stack when he didn't seem to really get it when I came out. It hit harder, but maybe that's why I cut him off so quick. He texted me some stupid gay meme a few days later and apologized. We've been great since. It was just a hiccup. But he better get his ass here quick for practice, or it's going to be more than a hiccup.

Ian shrugs. "He's always late."

That much is true.

"So is it Skylar?" Ian prods again.

"Why would it be about him?" I bite.

He shrugs and smiles like he knows something funny that I don't.

"He's not bad looking, if you're into guys, and now we're sitting with him at lunch." Ian lays it out.

"Huh? No!" I know exactly where he's going with this train of thought, right off the deep end. If Skylar were gay, *maybe*, but he's not. A few rumors started by the superbly unreliable Blake and Bexley mean nothing. Usually it means the opposite is true. "He's not gay. Blake will say anything."

"Nah, he's gay." Ian nods.

"Assume much? Even if he is, it'd be weird." I look away and fiddle with the guitar strings, sending a low bass note into the air.

"Why would it be weird?" Ian scrunches his face.

"He can't talk. And I can't read lips. I mean..." Immediately I feel bad for saying it. It's an excuse, and a bad one at that. But it *is* weird. I don't think I could, even if I did want to. I double down on how *not* gay he is to cover for my stupidity. "But he's straight, so it's dumb to even talk about it. So stop."

While I'm talking Eric pulls up and parks along the edge of the road and starts walking up the driveway with his guitar in hand.

"You know for a gay, your gaydar is broke as shit," Ian says. "He's so…" And he does the limp wrist thing.

I roll my eyes.

"Sort of rude," I tell him. "Just because he wore a dress doesn't mean he's gay. I *don't* wear them, am I straight?"

"You did have us fooled." He eyes me.

I try not to, but I laugh.

"Fuck you," I snicker.

"What you have us fooled on?" Eric hangs his guitar around his neck and scrunches his brow.

"That he was straight," Ian reminds him.

"Oh, yeah," Eric laughs.

"But *he's* not," I try again, ignoring them.

"Not trying to be rude, but how do I say this in a way you can't deny?" Ian looks around the unfinished ceiling of beams and exposed insulation, mumbling something to himself. His eyes brighten and out it comes. "The boy craves dick up his—"

"Woah! Okay! Stop right there." I throw my hands up, letting the guitar hang haphazardly from the strap around my shoulder. I cough. Just don't think about it, but of course I am now. Damn you, Ian.

"You're *so* red." Ian laughs and doubles over his drum set. "You're so into him."

"He's not even gay!" I say one more time.

"We talking about Skylar?" Eric tries to catch up.

"Yep." Ian smiles.

"Oh, yeah, he's so gay." Eric smirks.

"No he's not, Ted!" I try again.

"Uh, yeah he is," Eric comes back, but he's not done. "And you're definitely into him."

"No! I…I'm not. Just stop. It's not happening," I blurt.

But what if he *is* gay?

No. Stop. It's just a rumor.

SKYLAR

FRIDAY, AUGUST 23

I know it's them before Seth knocks on the door.

"Skylar!" Imani yells the moment the door swings open, and Seth jumps, nearly losing the shiny gift bag in his hands.

"Really?" He side-eyes her, but we're already laughing. Well she's laughing, and I'm shaking and smiling.

I wave them in. This is the first time they've been in my house. I mean, the Grays' house, but I guess that's my house too. Right?

They take off their shoes and line them up with the others next to the door. We're all trouncing around in our socks, adults too. And I've met too many new people tonight. Some familiar ones are needed. My brain's overloaded right now.

All of a sudden I have three aunts and two uncles, and as if that wasn't enough, I also have grandparents now. It's a lot to acclimate to, but they all seem really nice. That one, I think her name is Robin, was a bit over the top, but that's okay. She kept giving me hugs and saying how glad she was that my parents, my new parents, found me and all this stuff.

Thanks for coming, I say, and before I can move, Imani hugs me. Uh… Okay.

"Happy birthday, Sky!" she tells me again.

It's at least the fourth time today. She got two in during lunch, and one during Sociology. Actually, make that five. She also got one in when they picked me up for school this morning, and that's not counting the texts she sent. Birthdays are a big thing to her.

I grin. The reality of this, of having a party for *me*, is starting to sink in. Like, this is actually happening. It's not just in my head.

Kimberly had the living room and kitchen strewn with red and blue balloons before I got home, and there's this big banner of individually connected letters behind the dining room table that reads *HAPPY BIRTHDAY SKY*. And then there's the massive rectangular cake with sixteen candles, rows of cupcakes, bowls of chips, platters of veggies and dip, and I'm pretty sure there's ice cream waiting in the kitchen. And what for? Me.

I said no presents. I slouch, trying to act annoyed.

"Uh, no," Imani counters. "I'm not showing up to a birthday party without a present."

"It's from both of us," Seth adds. "She's broke."

Imani punches him and he puts on a good show, acting like it hurt his soul. I shake my head and motion for them to follow me into the dining room where everyone else is. On our way I glance back at the front door. Wonder when Jacob's going to get here? The party is about to start.

"You two must be Imani and Seth," Bob says before I can introduce them.

"That's us," Imani answers, grinning.

"Yes, sir." Seth nods. He's nervous. I would be too if I were at his house instead meeting his family.

"They're the ones who pick up Skylar in the morning," Kimberly says as she walks up. She's seen me out the door every morning, and the *goodbyes* and *have a good day at school* between them have become a ritual.

"Well, thank you." Bob pats Seth on the shoulder. "Skylar tells me you work at the bowling alley."

"Yes, sir." Seth nods. It's almost robotic.

Bob wanted to know all about my *friends* a few nights ago. It's weird how much he and Kimberly want me to talk to them. I didn't think parents did that shit. But *they* do.

I come up behind Seth and throw my arm over his shoulder. It's not something I'd normally do, but I can detect an uncomfortable person when I see one. It's usually me. Seth's eyes dart to me and I can see relief flooding out.

I tug him to follow, and before Bob can ask anything else, the three of us are rounding the dining room table and I've got them standing next to their assigned seats. Yeah, Kimberly decided where everyone was sitting yesterday. She's really on top of the planning thing.

My place is at the head of the table, right behind the cake. Seth's and Imani's seats are to my right, and then it's *family* after that, with Bob and Kimberly at the other end of the table. Oh, and Jacob's supposed to be in the seat on my left. But it looks like that chair's going to be empty.

"All right, everyone take your seats so we can wish the birthday boy a happy birthday!" Kimberly yells over the noise.

My eyes shoot toward the living room as if maybe a certain boy might come walking through, but it doesn't happen.

"You good?" Imani whispers.

I nod quickly. Yeah. All good. I'm not disappointed that a dreamy boy from school who said he'd be here isn't. Not me. Never. I knew he wouldn't come anyway. All of this, this is enough.

"Here comes the embarrassing part," one of my new uncles whispers in my ear in passing. Gary, I think. He looks exactly like Bob, his twin, like literally.

"Skylar." Bob taps a fork against a glass of sweet tea, something I still don't get. "Your mom and I are so glad you're here. From the day we first met you we knew you were special. And it didn't take long to know one day you'd be a part of this family."

"I knew the day we met you." Kimberly elbows Bob, which gets a laugh out of everyone.

I'm already wanting to lock my eyes on the table and not look at anyone, but that just seems rude, even if this *is* unbearable. *Uncle Gary, you were right.*

"Of course, honey." Bob shrugs. "So today we—"

A knock comes at the door. All heads turn.

"Hold that thought." Bob puts a finger up and heads to the front door. I want to get up and see who it is, but I don't.

The door clicks open and muffled voices reach the kitchen, followed by footsteps. First comes Bob and then Mr. Dreamy, white hair and all. The corners of my mouth shoot up when he sees me, but a thud against my calf dims my smile. My eyes shoot to Imani. She's grinning wide, teeth shining and proud. I glare at her as Bob tells Jacob where to sit and he ends up next to me.

"Sorry for being late," he leans over and whispers, his face too close to mine. My breath catches in my throat, and I manage to release it when he leans back.

It's okay, I say. But dammit, he can't read lips. Whatever.

"As I was saying," Bob starts up again. And I'm just hoping it's about to end. "Happy birthday, Skylar!"

Thank God!

Kimberly pulls her phone up and I know it's about to get worse.

"Everyone ready to sing?" she shrills.

A round of cheers sound off, and she starts singing. I pull into myself as the rest join in — everyone, my new parents, my new family, my new friends. Even Jacob.

* * *

Music plays from my TV, intermingling with our voices, well, their voices. This all feels so unusual, but in a good sort of way. They haven't left yet, and they could have. My mind is still trying to wrap itself around that concept.

We had cake and chips and ice cream and all the things I'd imagined you would at a birthday. There are bits of glitter still stuck on Jacob's black t-shirt and clinging to Imani's bouncy curls. Seth's still wearing the little cone-shaped party hat he strapped on after they sang happy birthday to me. He didn't notice it sitting next to his plate until then. The singing was *beyond* embarrassing, but still neat in this weird way. Imani chatted with one of my new aunts and knows her better than I do now. Oh, and the presents. There were so many. I didn't expect all this. It's almost too much.

A literal bike and AirPods from Kimberly and Bob.

Forty bucks from aunt number one and Uncle Gary.

A massive set of Star Wars Legos from aunt number two.

Another thirty dollars from aunt and uncle number three.

A massive box of hardback fantasy novels from my new grandparents, plus fifty bucks.

A super cute black skirt with a white stripe along the bottom from Imani and Seth.

And it was all for me. They all came for me, and they're all still here. It's unreal, even if I can't remember half their names. Like it's everything I can do not to happy cry right now in the middle of my room with them. But I'm not going to be that guy.

"You should try on the skirt," Imani suggests. But it's obvious she really wants me to.

Why not? Plus it'll let me get away for a second to process everything on my own. I nod and snatch it from my desk where I'd laid it next to my new AirPods when we came here to escape the adults. I put a finger up to say *one minute* before jogging off to the bathroom.

Before I slip out of my shorts, I stare into the mirror at the only person I've ever been able to trust, the only person who ever gave a fuck about me—well, most of the time. Is this family? Do I really have friends now? All these people I didn't know a month ago. Are they? A tear slips from the edge of my eye, but I'm smiling. I can't stop smiling.

Stop it, Sky! They're waiting on you. I take a breath and let this weird, new, cool feeling float up my spine.

Let's do this. I slip out of my shorts and into my birthday present and check myself out in the mirror. I love it. It's so cute. The pleated black fabric hangs effortlessly from my waist, ending just above my knees. I sway my hips and let it swing. My legs don't look too bad in this. Maybe should shave though.

Hm… I wonder. Pinching the bottom of my shirt, I fold it in on itself a few times, raising it a couple inches above my waist to show my stomach. I do a couple stances to see how it looks. I like it, but the mirror is the only place getting this style.

I let my shirt back down and jog back to the bedroom. Their faces light up when I walk in. Imani gasps, squealing something indecipherable and starts jumping. Seth grins and shakes his head, I think mainly because of Imani's display. Jacob looks stunned, but in a good way, I think, which gets me all flustered and my cheeks warm up.

"You look amazing!" Imani keeps squealing. "I love it. I love it. I love it."

Thanks, I tell her, squeezing my arms to my sides and skewing my lips, trying to focus on her.

"It does look good," Jacob says smoothly, like he says it to all the boys. He likes it.

I take a seat on the bed next to Imani and smooth out the skirt. I don't think I'll be getting over how much I like it anytime soon.

"So you like it?" Imani searches my eyes for any hint of deceit.

I love it, I assure her, signing it to make it obvious.

"She'll be asking you that for days," Seth sighs.

I'm getting the vibe that she does this with every gift. She did great though.

I did say no gifts though, I tell them. They really didn't need to get me anything. It wasn't expected, and I sort of hate they felt that they needed to, even if I really do love it.

"Already been over this. Me showing up to my friend's birthday party without a gift." Imani reels her head back. "No thank you!"

We all laugh. It's definitely an Imani thing to say. I've not even known her that long, and I can tell that.

"You play video games much?" Jacob asks out of the blue, and when I look up, he nods toward the PlayStation below my TV.

I shrug and tilt my head, trying to convey something close to *not really* without having to type it out. He seems to get it, but I get my phone out to be sure.

A British voice starts up, "I didn't have that until last week and never had one to myself long enough to get into it."

"Oh." Jacob's face droops. "Sorry, I didn't—"

No, I mouth and sign. I don't know why I sign, except maybe to get his attention, it's not like he can understand it. I type my next words, "It's okay. I'm more an outdoor person anyway. Thinking about trying out for the track and tennis teams next semester."

"I love tennis." Imani sits up. "We should go to the park and play sometime."

That would be great, I say.

"I could never play for school though." Imani shivers. "That's too much for me. I'll beat your ass, but I don't want a coach screaming at me."

I giggle deep in my chest along with the others. Coaches can be intense, but competing, like really competing, is next level. I just have to keep to single person or dual competition sports since I can't exactly communicate with a team. Sort of sucks. I'd like to play volleyball or something, but it presents a challenge.

"I'm on the school swim team. I think I mentioned that before. But yeah, outdoor sports are a no-go for me." Jacob laughs to himself, palms up in defeat. "I burn."

With skin as pale as his, I believe it. It's almost that vampire-white color. Okay, it's not that pale—that's more Ian—but he's definitely fair-skinned.

"You look like you would." Imani says what we're all unwilling to. Seth even gives her a WTF look.

"You're not wrong," Jacob says, smiling.

"Basketball, JV team." Seth says it like it's some sort of stat.

"I went to a few of your games last year," Jacob pipes in, but the looks he gets make him rebound. "Not like to watch you. There was another guy I was…sort of…crushing on. You know, before…"

"Ooh, who was it?" Seth leans in.

I'm honestly surprised. I wouldn't have pegged Seth as the type to care, but here we are.

"He's straight, it was stupid." Jacob brushes it off and switches topics. "You ever think about wrestling?"

He's looking right at me. Eyes bright and green, white hair hanging over his right eye.

"Like right now?" Imani eyes him.

"No, no!" Jacob's eyes go wide. "Like for school."

"Haha! The thought had crossed my mind," I let Siri admit. But I'd probably be horrible at it. I'm not exactly sturdy or strong, but I can't deny the appeal.

"Now *that's* a gay sport," Seth comments.

"He's not wrong." Imani sticks her tongue out. Her hair bounces, drooping in curls around her soft cheeks.

"It's basically a bunch of dudes grabbing each other's butts," Seth laughs. "Tell me I'm wrong."

I start typing immediately. "Why else you think I've thought about it? Have some cute boy grab my butt? Please!"

The look on Jacob's face is priceless. His green eyes blink wide and his mouth drops open a second.

"Wait, what? You're..." Jacob snaps his mouth shut. "I'm sorry. I didn't mean—"

I shrug and give him my best smile. It doesn't bother me. But something about the way he asks it spikes a jolt of adrenaline inside me. It was cute, nervous.

I start to type, to tell him yeah, but Imani steps in. "Of course he's gay."

When I meet her gaze, she's looking at me like she just did me a favor. That's not how I was planning on saying it, so I cock my head and give a look that screams *really*, not because I'm mad, because I'm not, but like what?

She smirks and grabs a pillow faster than I can move and swings it into my chest. I fall back, not expecting its squishy mass to have that much force.

I scramble for another pillow. I've five of them: two regular bed pillows, two decorative ones that I don't get what the point is, and of course my massive black body pillow with the *Jurassic Park* logo stamped in the middle. The little decorative ones are closer though.

But before I can grab one, Seth gets his hands on one instead and goes after Imani. While he's swinging, I wrap my finger around the other and let loose. I connect with Imani's thigh. And suddenly I hear Jacob yell, "Incoming!" just before the *Jurassic Park* logo slaps me in the face.

Five minutes later we're a mass of exhausted red faces, sore bodies, and ruffled pillows scattered about my room. I sprawl back on the floor to catch my breath. Imani drops on the bed next to Seth, and Jacob sags over my desk chair.

"I'm going to have bruises in the morning." Seth examines his forearm and then pushes Imani off the edge of the bed.

"What the—" Imani yelps, nearly falling on top of me, but I slide to the right just in time. "Fu— I mean, darn you, Seth."

My stomach jumps with silent laughter. Jacob and Seth make up for my quiet, laughing at her near slip. She gives Seth both her middle fingers and gets to her feet.

"You two are special." Jacob shakes his head and stands up. "I gotta go though."

He's leaving? It can't be later than eight, maybe eight thirty. And I can't type quick enough to ask why. But I shouldn't ask, that would just be weird. So I stretch my arm up toward him, hand outstretched, silently asking him to help me off the floor. He slips his hand around mine, and before he can yank me to my feet, the feeling of his soft hand clasped to mine rushes through my chest. He lets go when I'm back on my feet and I stumble back a little, trying to ignore the fact that he just touched my hand. Yep, ignore that.

Where's my phone? I dart my eyes around the room. I can't tell him bye without it! Not really, at least. He sees me searching, "You looking for this?"

I look up and he's holding my phone out for me. I take it and start typing, "I'll walk you out."

It's stupid. But I want to. And I'm not going to justify it, even if he's perfectly capable of walking himself downstairs and out the front door. If he did manage to somehow get lost between here and there, I'm sure Kimberly or Bob could help, but I want to. I like that he's here, and as pointless as it is, I want to see him a little longer.

"Okay." He shrugs.

If he only knew how crazy gorgeous I think he is. How I've almost memorized the way his pure white hair hangs over his right eye, bright green bursting between strands; the arch of his eyebrows and the way his cheekbones rise sharply over a hard-cut jaw; the pale pink of his lips. Actually, come to think about it, he'd probably think I was crazy and be disgusted someone like me thought any of that.

I bury that last thought and jut my head toward the door and lead the way.

"Bye, Jacob!" Imani calls, winking at me just before I look away.

"See ya." Seth waves.

"See y'all at school Monday," Jacob says and then follows me.

I lead us down the stairs and into the living room. I'm not sure if I'm supposed to tell Kimberly and Bob he's leaving. Like, I don't know birthday protocol. Does he just leave?

Before I can make a decision, Kimberly sees us and comes over.

"You leaving, Jacob?" She smiles.

"Yes, ma'am." He nods. "Thanks for allowing me over."

"Thanks for coming. I'm sure Skylar loved having you here," she says. "Have a nice night."

If she only knew how much. I giggle inside. I'm going to have to bury this one eventually like I always do when I crush on a guy though.

"You too, Mrs. Gray and Mr. Gray." Jacob leans around her and waves at Bob.

With that I take him to the front door and walk outside, letting the door shut behind us. What am I thinking? Why did I let the door shut? That's just weird. I just made it weird.

Jacob looks down and shuffles his feet.

It's late, but it's still hot out. Has been all week.

Don't make it weird, Sky!

Thanks for coming, I tell him, but he just looks at me like he doesn't have a clue. *He can't read lips, Sky!* And it's dark.

"Can't read lips, remember?" He laughs. "Sorry, I'm pathetic."

"No, you're not," Siri says after I type it. "Thanks for coming."

"Yeah, it was fun," he says, then dips his head again. "Sorry I didn't bring a present."

I shake my head vigorously.

"No!" I make Siri shout, even though it doesn't really sound like a shout, like I'd be doing right now if I could. "I said not to. Don't worry about it. You can just owe me."

I throw that last part in as a joke. But there's a fifty-fifty chance he won't catch it since I can't really make sarcasm evident over my phone. God, I hate not being able to talk.

Jacob tilts his head and the reflection of the porch light in his eyes glints with an idea. I swear for a moment I can almost see the comet's reflection.

"Actually," Jacob extends his arm toward me. It looks like he's going for my hand, but in the end it's wishful thinking. He just points at me. "You want to go to a concert?"

I squint. Did he just ask me to a concert? I'm not sure what to say. I think I put him on the spot, and I don't think he caught the sarcasm. Does he feel guilty? I scramble my finger across my phone.

"You don't owe me, I was just kidding. It's okay," my phone answers. *Dammit, Skylar, way to go.*

"No, it's good. I've got an extra ticket. It's this coming Wednesday," he explains. "Would you want to?"

I have questions, but I think it's best not to ask them. Like, what concert, mainly. Then why do you have an extra ticket? Am I taking it from someone else? What type of music?

"My friend has a ticket he's trying to get rid of." He waves the thought away. "It's me and three others. You don't know them."

"Ian?" I type into my phone. I know Ian.

"Nah, he hates this band," Jacob laughs.

Jacob and three other people I don't know. A band Ian hates. Sounds like a nightmare and anxiety waiting to happen.

Without letting myself think further, I nod.

"That a yes?" Jacob smiles.

"Yes," I have my phone confirm, and I'm all smiles, as much as I wish I could stop.

"All right." He steps backward off the porch and the shadows envelop him. I'm already wishing I could see his eyes again. "We'll figure it all out next week."

Then he's off to his car at the edge of the road, and I'm standing at my front door wondering what I just did.

JACOB

FRIDAY, AUGUST 23

What have I done?

Hands gripping the steering wheel, I stare at the Toyota symbol in the center. Did I just ask him to go to the concert? There's no way. Did I?

Oh my God, I did.

What the hell was I thinking? A concert? Can I take it back? No.

And I didn't technically have to leave just yet. But things started getting weird. Not like he was weird or Seth or Imani were weird. I just started feeling odd. And I don't know why. So I said I needed to go. And then I do this.

I check my phone to distract myself. There's a text from Ian.

IAN: How's the party? ::middle finger::

He complained all day that he had to work while I was going to a party. It's not like it was a raver or anything.

JACOB: Was fun. ::Middle finger:: U about off?

And now I have to get that ticket before Tyler sells it. He's been trying to for a month now. His other friend, Bryce I think, decided he didn't want to go. Why did I do this?

I start up the car and head toward the theater. It's too late to go anywhere else around here. Even Charlotte closes down after nine. And even *if* Ian's not off, I can still hang around and bug him as long as Zara isn't there.

Headlights glare past and lips flash in my mind. But not just any. Skylar's. The subtle pout of his lower lip, thick, and this vibrant pink. I clamp my mouth shut. I wanted to kiss them, I *want* to.

I try to shake it, but just like on his front porch, I can't. Back there I had a reason, I was supposed to read them, which I failed at miserably. It's hard for me period, but even more tonight. I'm glad he used his phone. I couldn't have stood looking at his mouth any longer.

He's too cute. And tonight he has to go and confirm he likes boys. I swear my stomach dropped when I heard it. Like, I suspected, but he does!

Doesn't really help me though. I'm that ghostly pale—like I haven't seen the sun since birth—pole that everyone jokes about and no one really wants to date. He's looking for someone with a little meat on their bones.

I pull the car into one of the angled spaces across from the theater and shut off the engine. *Focus on something else.* I check my messages again—there's another from Ian and a few TikTok messages, probably Ian too, or maybe Tyler.

IAN: Nah. Have to clean up after the last showing. ::crying face::

A giggle traps in my throat and I send him a quick reply.

JACOB: Sucks to be u. ::laughing face:: Im here. Coming to bug u.

The little bubbles start burping at the bottom of the screen, but I pocket my phone before he can reply. Ian will be glad to know he was right about Skylar. And he's going to be real surprised Skylar's going to the concert. I can only imag—

Oh God! No! Please don't let Skylar think I just asked him on a date!

SKYLAR

SATURDAY, AUGUST 24

The sun hits differently when you've been stuck hundreds of feet below ground inside tiny caverns for an hour. I blink away the glare and loosen my jacket. It's not exactly warm out here, but whatever it is, it's better than the forty-something degrees the tour guide said it was in the caverns.

"I feel bad for tall people in there," Bob sighs, hunkering over, palm pressed against his back. "I had to duck half the time."

"So did I," Kimberly laughs.

I didn't. Well, okay, I think I ducked once, but it might have been more because the guide said something about ducking than actually *needing* to.

I follow them into the Linville Caverns gift shop. It's this little woodsy room filled with cute and mostly useless trinkets that I'm afraid to even check the prices. The first thing my eyes catch is a smoky-gray quartz carved in the shape of a horse. I've never ridden one, probably never will, but I used to love them. I was the kid who read every book about horses I could find, *Black Beauty*, the Black Stallion books, and obsessed over them in movies. But I don't know, being thrown around and stuck in the group home so long I think I let go of it.

"You like that?" Kimberly sidles next to me, putting an arm over my shoulder.

I nod, looking up to her long enough to smile. It's not like I need it. And honestly, it's probably a little childish for a newly minted sixteen-year-old, so I put it down and move on. They have a little of everything. Rocks and walking canes made of wood from the surrounding forest, refrigerator magnets hailing *Linville Caverns* and *Blue Ridge Parkway* in bold letters, nasty transparent candies in all colors on sticks with scorpions and crickets inside them, and tons of necklaces. And so many cups and keychains.

Kimberly picks up something next to the walking canes, I think it's a magnet, and then comes back over to me.

"You want anything?" she asks.

I shake my head. They bought me a bike for my birthday and AirPods, and now we're here for the caverns and a hike. I'm good.

She smiles and heads off to the register with Bob, and a few minutes later we're back in the car. Next stop Linville Falls. It's like a package deal. Well, not really, it's all separate, but Bob said you can't do the falls without the caverns.

Bob pulls the car onto the tiny curving road. Trees guard the roadside, obscuring the nearby drop-offs. We're on the top of a mountain.

"It's pretty up here," I have Siri tell them from the back seat.

"You should see it in a few months when the leaves fall," Bob says, looking at me briefly in the rearview mirror.

"You might not be all that awed by it." Kimberly twists to

see me. It makes me think of Imani, just older, polar opposite skin, and her hair is this shoulder-length, straight and flowy mix of light browns and blondes. Okay, other than the pep in her shoulders, I guess she's not that much like Imani. "I've seen the pictures of Vermont in autumn. It looks beautiful. It's sort of like that here."

"I'm sure it's nice," Siri assures her. It's weird, but I like that she knows that about Vermont. It's this little thing about me, but she knows.

But I honestly can't wait to see what it's like here in the fall. Vermont is nice and all, I mean I've seen it, obviously, but I don't remember a lot of good up there, so this has to be better.

"And..." Kimberly wrangles something from her bag of gift shop goodies and hangs her closed hand over the back seat for me. I squint, putting my hand out and opening my palm. "You seemed to like this."

A smile spans my face when the little quartz horse drops into my palm. I don't know why, but it makes me happy. It's just a little horse, a kid's thing, but it does. I purse my lips to one side and grin before mouthing *thank you*. I honestly love it. It's like this weird little happy thing.

"So you've never been on a hike?" Bob asks.

"Nope," Siri replies for me. It's one of the things I told them I wanted to do before they adopted me. And I can't wait for my first. "I'm excited."

My phone buzzes and buzzes and the little green notifications start jumping on the screen. Looks like I finally got signal. Imani's name jumps on the screen over and over again and then Jacob's.

"There are a few waterfalls, and they're gorgeous," Bob

explains. I'm listening, but my attention is split between the real world and my phone.

IMANI: Nervous for ur date with Jacob? ::crazy face::

IMANI: Don't ignore me bitch! ::crying face::

IMANI: OH! Never mind. Forgot about ur trip. No signal sucks!

IMANI: Y do u AND Seth have to be out of reach at the same time?!?!? ::facepalm::

You'd think we had been friends for years and she was going through separation anxiety. I giggle inside. She's a mess.

SKYLAR: Calm TF down. ::crying face:: ::facepalm:: And what date? I know of no date.

She's been on my ass about it, and she refuses to call it anything but a date. But Jacob doesn't want to go on an actual date with someone broken like me, and I'm not talking about emotionally or mentally. I still can't figure out why he asked in the first place. I was so excited I didn't even stop to think why, and now it sort of puts a pit in my stomach. He probably felt bad for the whole present thing. But I swear I meant it when I said no presents. I didn't expect them. I mean, I've done without them for years.

Or maybe it was just one of those social things. He saw everyone else do something and thinks he looks bad because he didn't do it too, and that's why he asked. Dammit. Here I am again making people feel bad for me. And only doing shit for me because I'm messed up. He's probably regretting it so bad right now. Guess I could make up some excuse why I can't go.

"You okay back there?" Kimberly knocks me out of my blank stare into nowhere.

I blink away the stupor and try to remember what we were

talking about. The hike, waterfalls, the view.

"Good," I sort of make Siri lie, but not really. "Just excited."

I want to send another text to Imani telling her my new revelation, but I doubt she'd think the same. Instead, I reluctantly open the text from Jacob. Bet he texted to say he actually doesn't have a spare ticket after all or that his other friend decided to go. I roll my eyes before the message pops up.

JACOB: nothing,nowhere.

For a second I'm really confused. What the hell does that mean? Should that be one word? What? Then I read my text before where I asked what band we're going to see Wednesday. Hold up. That's a band?

SKYLAR: Never heard of them. What type of music?

"Here we are," Bob calls from the front as the car hits a bump and pulls into a small parking area. It's busy here. Cars take up most of the available spots, and groups are scattered about the lot and heading up the path.

A minute later we're walking a few car lengths behind another family and the vehicles and civilization disappear behind us. It's just us, a bunch of strangers, trees, rocks, dirt, plants and a cloud-dotted blue sky where the trees don't obscure them.

My phone dings.

JACOB: Sad boy music with a beat? ::shrug::

He doesn't even know how to categorize the music he listens to?

SKYLAR: You're the musician. Shouldn't you know? ::laughing face::

"Skylar," Bob gets my attention. "Don't want to be *that* dad, but can we turn off the cell signal? Let's make this just a family thing."

I slump my shoulders and fight the urge to breathe heavy. Like I get it, but really? I want to get to know them. I do. They've been so good to me, but what if Jacob texts back? Don't you realize there's a hot boy texting me?

But it's only a few hours, Sky.

I force a smile and switch off my phone's signal, cutting me off from the outside world. It's not like I don't still have my phone. I have the important part, the part that lets me talk. I'm going to need that.

"Thanks, bud," Bob says. "Here we go."

I nod to let him know it's okay. *Just don't think about how much you want to talk to him. Just don't.*

According to the sign at the start of the trail at the visitor's center, it's between a 0.5 mile and 0.9 mile hike depending on the trail you take. No one's said which we're going on yet. I'm sort of hoping for the last one.

"Which trail are we taking?" I have Siri ask.

"We can do them all if you want," Kimberly says, then gives her own suggestion. "But I think the best views are at Chimney View and Erwins View."

"How about we check out Chimney first, then the others?" Bob says.

"Works for me," I type.

Ahead of us there's another family, a mom and her two daughters, I think. They're talking away, the cadence of their voices falling back on us without the actual words, just faint noise among the chirps, the whistling of wind through the branches, and the distant trickling of water.

"Your friends seem really nice," Kimberly says out of the blue.

I think about it a second. They are. Which is weird and sort of great.

"I like them," my phone says with all the emotion of a bored cow. "Imani's crazy, but in a good way. Seth is quiet, but he's nice."

"She seems like a talker," Bob says, then backtracks a little. "I'm not saying that's a bad thing."

"You're not wrong!" I type. "She makes up for everything Seth doesn't say."

That gets a few laughs, and honestly, something about it just gets me. Like, why did they want me? And how is this real? I'm in the middle of the woods, on a hike like I've always wanted, with two people who *chose me*. It's hard to wrap my head around, and I keep waiting to wake up in the orphanage, like it's some fairy tale, some fleeting dream.

"Sounds like your mom," Bob side-eyes me and grins mischievously.

"Hey now," Kimberly chides him. "I'm not that bad."

"So she says." Bob keeps walking. "And to think she talks less now."

I pull my lower lip in and bite in surprise. He's going to get himself the couch if he isn't careful.

Mom waves her hand dismissively. "And you were no Prince Charming."

"Not how I remember it." Bob puffs his chest.

The family ahead of us takes a left at the upcoming fork where a wooden sign announces the *Upper Falls*.

Bob leads us to the right, while I dart my eyes between the two of them, waiting for what's going to happen next. This is getting exciting.

Kimberly looks at him crazily and shakes her head, laughing between heavy breaths. "You *would* think that."

The next quarter mile I learn a bunch about them. And it's great, because so far it's been them learning about me, them asking me questions.

They both went to different elementary schools but ended up at the same high school a few years apart, the same school I'm at now. Bob was on the football team, Kimberly was a shy underclassman who didn't do sports or clubs or anything. But Dad had his eye on her from the start of her freshman year. Kimberly debated that one a little, but Bob brushed it off.

She said she hadn't given Bob much thought until a few weeks into the semester when his twin brother, Gary, asked her out. She said yes but ended up running into Bob later that day and he acted like he'd never talked to her. He hadn't, and it made her really mad so she didn't talk to either of them for a week until she realized there were two of them. By then Gary had moved on to some cheerleader named Tammy. It took another couple months before Bob asked her out.

"The girls were obsessed with him," Kimberly says of Bob. His hair was longer back then, fuller, from her description. "But he asked me out. Then there were times he got on my last nerve and was sort of stalkerish, but it all worked out."

"I was never stalkerish," Bob shoots back, playfully squeezing his arm around her waist. "I was in love."

The whole interaction just makes me feel all fuzzy inside. Like I want that. I want someone to look at me the way Bob is

EVERY WORD YOU NEVER SAID

looking at her. It's so simple, but everything is in that look and the way they joke back and forth, jabbing playfully at each other.

"So Bob's a stalker, got it." I keep it going on my phone. "That's what I'm taking from this."

They laugh, taking a left at the next fork to Chimney View. The roiling of the water gets louder. It transforms from this distant trickle into thunder the closer we get.

"See, he gets it." Kimberly smiles at me.

It goes on like this the rest of the walk until we arrive at the viewing area. Kimberly went to the beach over the summer before Bob's senior year when they broke up for a little. Bob followed her there to try to win her back but made her furious instead. Then he managed to win her back just before homecoming.

The viewing area opens up past the trees and finally the sounds make sense. It's so high. The water crests the edge on the opposite side of the gorge, dropping in a brilliant display of pure white, plummeting and plummeting until it crashes into the pool below in an explosion of noise, water, and mist. It's beautiful.

I mouth *wow* as if words could actually break through my lips, but I don't care. This view, it's amazing.

"Stunning, isn't it?" Kimberly pats my back.

I crane my neck around and up to look at her and then Bob, nodding excitedly.

Gorgeous, I move my mouth.

I could sit up here for hours and not grow tired of the view. The sound of the water. The feeling of the cool breeze blended with the fall's mist. The chirp of birds and gentle cracking of limbs. The sun on my face and blue sky and puffy clouds above.

I take it all in one breath at a time.

"Sky." Bob gets my attention.

I look up to him and smile.

"I want you to know we're here for you," he starts. Usually this type of start would worry me or get my flight response going, but it doesn't. "Your mom and I want you to know that if you want to wear skirts or dresses, if you want to wear makeup or paint your nails, anything like that, it's okay. If that's what you want, we've got your back, and we'll root you on. We love you. None of that stuff matters."

Something in my chest flips. Something I've rarely felt. It's weird but amazing at the same time. It feels good. *This* feels good. I feel comfortable, and it's been so long since I've been able to say that.

JACOB

I put down my book for at least the fifth time to check a TikTok Ian sent. If I had restraint, I'd ignore them, or even better, not look at my phone, but I don't.

The video starts and I stare in dumbstruck wonder. The things he sends. It's this tiny squirrel shoving nuts in its mouth. I swear it's got at least six in there, its cheeks are pooching out like balloons. Oh wait, no, make that seven, nope, eight.

I sigh and go back to my book. It's an alien invasion story. Can't say it's what I expected, but I'm liking it.

My door is closed, but it does little to muffle the shrill screams of my little nephews and nieces and the conversations from the living room mixed with some talk show. My brothers and sister come over for lunch most Sundays after church with their eight kids and then stick around between services. Sometimes, like today, they stay up and talk, other weeks I'll find them all unconscious in whatever chair they chose, taking their Sunday nap.

All my siblings are older. I wasn't exactly planned. Mom and Dad were "done" having kids, and boom, here I came.

Their mistake. Rebekah's the closest in age to me, but she's still nine years older, she's twenty-six. She's also pregnant with her first kid, has a boyfriend my parents aren't fond of—but won't say it to his face—and besides me, she's the only liberal in the family.

Samuel is next. He's twenty-eight, the quiet self-righteous type who won't start a fight but he'll sure join one. He got divorced earlier this year when his wife cheated on him with a pastor in the area. My family was angrier about the divorce than his wife cheating. And maybe it's low, but now when he tries saying anything about me being gay or doing gay stuff, I nonchalantly bring up the divorce. He also looks the most like Dad. Blue eyes, rounder face, even the receding hairline.

Josiah is thirty-one. Weirdly, I've spent more time around him than Samuel, but that's only because he's more understanding. He hates it when the family talks politics, which my dad, Samuel, and Luke are constantly on about, and he might not say it, but I don't think he's as conservative as the rest of them. I know his wife isn't, even if she is annoying. She jumps on my side during half the fights, while Josiah just huffs and frowns. He's got two little girls, Natalie and Natasha. I think they're eleven and seven.

Then there's Luke. He's the oldest, thirty-three, and easily the most stubborn. He went to a local Bible college and was ordained before I got out of middle school. My dad was so proud. I remember it. I wasn't out then, but I just knew in my heart that I'd never see the man look at me like that. Luke's been married as far back as I can remember, and he's responsible for my other five nephews and nieces: Jonas, Micah, Hannah, Timothy, and Elizabeth.

Christmas gets expensive around here, one more reason I'm not looking forward to adulting.

So yeah, they're all out there, probably talking about Dad's campaign or something FOX is telling them to be mad about while I try to read. I'm not allowed to work on Sundays, even with the theater open. Dad won't allow it. Wednesday nights are off-limits too. I have to be at church, and since Ian's working and Eric's on a mini vacation with his family, I decided to take the day to relax, plus I usually game online with Tyler between services.

Hold up. That squirrel TikTok. I close my eyes and sigh. Ian wasn't just sending a cute little squirrel video after all. It was a gay joke. I cough to myself as it sinks in, the squirrel stuffing his face with nuts.

"Wow, Ian," I say to no one.

I have to send it to Tyler. He and Aidan would get a real kick out of it. I open SnapChat and send them the link. Ooh! And Skylar. Hmm… Maybe not. But he'd think it's funny too, right?

Only one way to find out.

I open our text conversation and send him the link with a little message.

JACOB: LMK if u get it. ::laughing face::

I try to get back in my book, but my phone dings. That was quick.

SKYLAR: Got it.

There's no way he had time to watch it.

JACOB: No ::laughing face:: Like what its about. ::facepalm::

Okay, maybe my message was a little unclear, but still. I shake my head.

SKYLAR: Oh... ::facepalm:: Give me a little.

Take as long as your little brain needs. I laugh to an empty room. Tyler just sent a Snap asking if I'm ready to play *Overwatch*. It's not my favorite game anymore, but that's the main thing he plays so it's our Sunday ritual. It doesn't look like I'm reading anymore.

I mark my spot and drop the book on the table, then get connected to Tyler on the PlayStation.

"Hey, Ty!" I say once the microphone connects.

"Jacob," he calls back. "Before we get started, I just have to say, I had the best time last night. A and I went up on the mountain and watched Breegge. It was perfect."

A is his boyfriend, Aidan. And Breegge is the comet everyone in the world is talking about right now. It's huge. Ty's been sort of obsessed with it, and now he's obsessed with Aidan.

"That's awesome!" I congratulate him while clicking the game logo on the screen. "What did y'all do?"

"We just watched the comet." Ty's voice jumps a note. There's definitely more there.

"Ah, is that it?" I accuse him, laughing.

He laughs back, but he's not budging.

"Maybe," he says.

The game starts up and I select my main, Moira, and Tyler locks in Mercy.

"Is Aidan joining?" I ask.

"Nah," Ty says. "He's with me today, so—"

"Hey, Jacob!" Aidan's muffled voice screams into the mic that I assume is on Ty's face.

"Hey, Aidan!" I yell back.

"Jacob says hey," Tyler relays.

My phone dings, and I see a text from Skylar. Oh! I need to tell them about Sky before the concert.

"Oh, you still have that extra ticket for the concert?" I ask. I keep forgetting to find out.

"Yeah, you want it?" Ty asks jokingly.

"Yep," I say.

"Really?" Tyler sounds surprised.

"Yeah, I have a new friend I want to bring," I tell him. *Want to bring?* Yeah, that's right. "Name's Skylar."

"New friend?" Tyler asks.

"Yes, *friend*," I emphasize. "Just a friend."

"Okay," Ty drags it out. "Ticket's yours."

"Thanks, I'll send you the money tonight," I say, and then a thought hits me. "And also, he can't talk. Like literally can't talk. He uses his phone to talk. Just so you know."

"Oh, okay," Tyler says as the game timer counts down to the beginning of the match. "Sounds good. Can't wait to meet your *friend*."

I can feel the air quotes in his voice, but I don't say anything. I just roll my eyes and watch the timer tick down. Guess I'll be checking that text after the match.

4... 3... 2... 1...

ATTACK.

SKYLAR

It's cute, but it's too short.

I pull at the hems, trying to make each skirt's bottom edge go down a few inches. But then their waists aren't high enough. I don't know why I thought they'd be any longer now than they were two weeks ago.

It just sucks I never wore them outside of my room back when they fit. They're really cute. At least I've grown a little I guess, even if I am still short as hell.

Oh well, it doesn't go that great with the horizontally striped white and black top I'm wearing anyway. I huff and pull the skirt off, folding it before putting it away. Oh wait!

I twist around and head for the laundry hamper next to the door. It's where I left it yesterday after Kimberly handed it off to me in the hallway and asked that I hang them up. I didn't get that far. I dig through the clean clothes and finally find it. The skirt Imani and Seth gave me for my birthday.

I rush to the mirror—already behind and Seth will be here at any moment—and slip into the cutest black skirt. It fits, and the bottom edge sits perfectly above my kneecaps.

I check me out. It's not like anyone cares what I look like, but it's not bad. I jut my hip out and strike a pose. Bad bitch. Oh my God, no. Anything but that, even if there is something about wearing it that puts me on top of the world, especially knowing how the school is. Time to challenge the patriarchy!

Beep! Beep!

A car horn blares outside at the same instant my phone dings.

IMANI: We're here.

SKYLAR: Be right out.

Taking one last glance at my new outfit, I do one last twirl and sling my pack over my shoulder before heading downstairs. I find Kimberly...I mean Mom—I'm trying—in the kitchen nibbling on a box of Cheez-Its.

I look at her and move my lips so I don't have to text it, *I'm off to school. Bye.*

"Hold up." She slips around the bar, grabbing an oversized plastic sandwich container on her way. She holds it out for me to take. "Here's a little snack for you and your friends. Have a good day, honey."

I grin and nod. She made us a snack?

Thanks, and I head out the door.

"Hiya!" Imani yells before I get to the car.

"'Bout time." Seth cranes his neck out the window.

I shrug and jump in the back seat.

"What's that?" Imani asks while I'm typing.

"Snacks. Mom sent them," Siri says. I had almost typed *Kimberly*, but I backspaced it before letting it go.

"Snacks?! What type of snacks?" Seth glances at the container as he looks out the back window and reverses.

Good question. I shrug and open it, releasing a small cloud

of steam and a temporal smack of heat. Oh my God! Yes! I love these things. Orange cinnamon rolls.

My mouth forms into an O, and I'd be oohing if I could. Instead I stop and smile, holding the container up for Imani to get one. She grabs one of the sticky rolls of goodness and doesn't waste time. Mom made these for Dad and me yesterday before church and I couldn't get over them! Like they're amazing. Guess she could tell I liked them.

"What about me?" Seth whines.

"You're driving," Imani says matter-of-factly.

"So?" He shrugs. "I've got two hands."

"Yeah, for the steering wheel, bud." She's smiling so big. It's obvious she loves teasing him, and to be honest, I sort of think she likes him, but that's another thing.

"Just give me one." Seth's eyes roll in the rearview mirror.

I pass the container and Imani helps him get the last roll.

"Like the skirt." Imani twists back around and nods approvingly. "Whoever got you that has great taste. That top though, it's all right."

I'm hit with two reactions at once. Like, of course you like it, you got it for me.

"What's wrong with the top?" Siri asks.

"Just a lot of stripes." Imani tilts her head. I think she notices my shift in demeanor, because hers changes quick. "But it looks great! Just not what I would have chosen, but still cute!"

What would you have chosen? I don't bother typing since she's turned completely around in her seat, probably sitting on her knees. Not the best idea in a moving car.

"Maybe a white sweatshirt—" she rattles off.

"It's the middle of summer," Seth interjects.

He slows the car at a crosswalk. The school's just around the corner. The closer we get the more tension grows in my stomach. Like I want to do this. I should be able to, but I also know people suck.

" — or a white tee with something cute on it." Imani doesn't lose a beat. "Or a cute black crop top and some black knee highs. Yes! A crop top!"

I'm not trying to get in trouble that bad! I tell her. I'm pushing it enough in a skirt. A crop top would really push their poor little eyes over the edge. I don't think the girls are even allowed to wear those *now*.

"Just a thought." She shrugs and slides back in her seat as Seth pulls us into the parking lot and we get out.

"Don't listen to her," Seth says.

"You're supposed to be on my side, and I wasn't saying for school." Imani eyes him as she gets out of the car. "I was meaning, like, for his date tomorrow."

I glare at her. Seth does the same, but the look is stunned humor. I just hope no one else heard. I'm already getting glares. All eyes on my skirt and legs.

"It was just a thought." Imani grins.

I type furiously and hit play even though I'm already one point behind. "Stop it! It's not like that."

We burst through the front doors and start upstairs. I catch the tail end of someone throwing the F word — not fuck — around just far enough away to think they're out of earshot.

"Sure it isn't." She grins.

On the landing Imani stops and spins around to face us before taking off to History. "Catch you next period, Seth. I'll see you at lunch."

"Put some pants on," some boy with a regulation-style haircut, blue jeans, and a black tee with a pathetic rebel flag stamped across it yells.

After you burn that flag is what comes to mind, but I don't.

"Shove it, Daniel." Imani stops long enough to yell at him before taking off.

I wasn't going to say anything, but that works. I wave her off and find Seth staring angrily in Daniel's direction. The boy is still eyeing me, but the smug look on his face is just annoyed, and he disappears in the crowd.

"She gives no fucks," he laughs. "And she's intense sometimes."

I get the first part, but the second… What?

He laughs and nods toward the doors leading into the English Department. I follow.

"The Jacob thing," he reminds me.

Ah, that. The thing that doesn't exist.

"It's just because she likes you."

Huh? Likes me? But then it clicks. Friends. It's still hard to process that these two are still hanging around. Like, I think I actually have friends.

A moment later we swing into Mrs. Sangster's room, English. And I don't make it past the first row of desks before she calls my name.

"Skylar." Her voice is old and high.

I stop in my tracks, lock eyes with Seth and get that knowing look back.

"Good luck," he sighs, and I spin around.

"Yes, ma'am?" Siri asks when I stop at her desk. Her face

is wrinkled, cheeks pudgy and aged, green eyes set deep behind thin-rimmed spectacles.

"I'm afraid I can't let you wear that in my classroom." She feigns regret, but I can feel the repulsion in her voice. Definitely not one of the cool, younger, gay-loving English teachers. "Do you have any other clothes you can change into?"

"No," I type, and then a thought comes. I do have my tights downstairs in my locker, for dance. They're pants, right? I type out a new message while she waits, "I have some tights in my locker."

It's sarcasm, but she probably wouldn't catch it even if I had a voice.

"Not acceptable, mister," she growls. "Go into the hallway and call your parents. Have them bring you something more appropriate. I'll go with you."

I don't know if it's the *I'll go with you* or the pompous *something more appropriate* part, but nah, I've had it. I type away.

"No," Siri says abruptly. "This isn't against dress code."

"Excuse me," Mrs. Sangster reels back, eyes wide. "It wasn't a request."

"No," I have my phone repeat.

"Go to the office, right now!" She waddles back to her desk and picks up the phone, already dialing something. "You'll be in ISS today."

* * *

Five more minutes of this hell.

I stare at the clock. The second hand is taking forever. It's one of those that doesn't tick between seconds, it glides, smoothly, excruciatingly slow.

My "assignment" is done. Has been for an hour. And talk about trash. Both the paper and the topic. I don't know if it's always the same, unless maybe you're a repeat, but it was to write at least a one-thousand-word paper on *Who do you think you are*. Like, what?

I spent all one thousand words explaining how sexist the school staff and admin are instead, and how it's not in the dress code. Because that's what it is. It's people applying imaginary societal norms on others. I made sure to use that phrase a few times, oh, and "The Patriarchy."

There are two other guys in here. Neither of whom I've spoken to. I mean, technically we're not supposed to speak to each other anyway. But considering how Chew Boy— something about the way he sprawls in his chair, holding his jaw off-kilter, and the worn circle in his jean pocket tells me he does snuff—keeps looking at me says if I did speak to him, I'd get hate-crimed on the spot. And Sleepy—the only time I've seen him awake has been when the teacher on duty wakes him—seems like an ass, if I'm being honest.

"Here's your phone." The teacher hands my lifeline over. I snatch it from thick calloused hands and refrain from glaring at him.

Honestly, it baffles me that they took it. I know it's detention, it's supposed to be silent, but it's literally my voice. And I almost had a mini-panic attack when the first teacher took it. That dead look in the man's eyes. I shiver.

The bell rings, but instead of moving I check my phone. Now that it's in my hands I feel more myself, even stuck in this stuffy room.

IMANI: *Fuck the patriarchy! ::angry face:: ISS?! Seriously?*

I giggle. Seth must have told her.

There's a few Instagram and TikTok notifications, and then a text from Mom. Guess he told her too.

MOM: *Proud of you. Can't believe they gave you ISS! They'll be getting a call from our lawyer.*

Ooh. A little fight the system, maybe? I send Mom a quick reply.

SKYLAR: *I'm out now. Thanks.*

Before I can get to the next message, from Jacob, which might have just lightened my mood, another from Imani dings in.

IMANI: *You out of jail yet? ::surprise face:: We're at the car.*

SKYLAR: *OMW!*

I throw my pack over my shoulder and practically run out the door, skirt flapping like a *fuck you* to ISS.

"About time," Seth huffs when I'm a few feet from his car.

"How was hell?" Imani hangs half out the window.

I blow my lips out in a dramatic sigh as I jump in the back seat. I go to type a reply, but I see Jacob's text again. Ah, let's check that first.

"So?" Imani asks. Guess I'm taking too long. She'll have to wait just a second though. I put a finger up for her to wait. "Well then."

JACOB: *Where r u? Class about to start.*

JACOB: *U okay?*

JACOB: *Seth just told me. ISS? ::eye roll::*

I notice Imani peeking over the back seat and I hide my screen. This is the last thing I need her seeing. She'll be on about it the rest of the evening, blowing it up into something it isn't.

I wish it *was* what it isn't. And I mean it is sort of adorable that he asked if I was okay. I can imagine, right?

"It was boring. Really, really, boring," I finally have Siri tell her. "Not much to tell."

JACOB

WEDNESDAY, AUGUST 28

"That one's not so bad," Skylar's phone pops off, and I try not to take it personally.

We're sitting in overflow parking at The Music Factory. I didn't want to be late and be forced to the rear of the venue, so we're early. We *will* be up front for the god of whatever genre Joe technically sings.

"Not bad?" I eye him. Nothing by Joe is bad.

Skylar shrugs.

"Okay, fuck you." I give him my most disgusted look.

He's been offending my music taste since he got in the car. I started him off with my favorite, "Nevermore," and he just looked at me like he didn't know what to say when it went off. Like, what?

He grimaces, cheek bunching under his right eye, making the brown and green bursts fight to be seen between slitted lids. God, I can't hate that, so I laugh. Plus, I'm not one hundred percent sure if he hates it all or not. He's been bobbing his head the entire time and when he does hate on it, it seems sort of exaggerated, like maybe he's kidding. It's just hard to tell with the British voice doing all the talking.

"We got to work on your music," I tell him. "And good luck tonight, because this is what you're getting all night."

"Fuck," his phone blurts without an ounce of emotion. But I can see it on his face. The amused grin between pink lips and the way the lines form around his mouth.

Stop being so cute!

Remember, Jacob, this is just a concert, a fun night with friends. *This is not a date. Don't get it in your head as something else.*

My phone dings.

TYLER: We're here.

Time to go! And they know not to insinuate that Skylar's my date. Especially after Tyler joked about it yesterday online.

JACOB: Meet u there.

"They're here. Let's go," I tell Sky and get out without checking to make sure he heard me.

I wait for him to shut the door and catch up before heading down the gravel parking lot toward the venue. It hits me again, for like the millionth time since I invited him, the absurdity of asking someone who can't talk to a concert. I don't think I'd want to go if I couldn't scream every lyric. That's part of the concert experience, right? It's about singing your heart out without caring what anyone else thinks.

But maybe not. I really hope not, because if there's one thing I've discovered over the past few days, it's that I really want Sky to enjoy this. Like I really want him to. It's almost as important to me as the concert itself, almost.

And he even lied to his parents to come. He told me when I picked him up. They never said he couldn't, but he never asked, so he told them he was sick when they left earlier for dinner before church so he could "stay home and sleep."

I'm not sure how all of this is going to play out, because he's got an 11 p.m. curfew, and we're not making it home before eleven. Plus, it's sort of a weak-ass excuse if you ask me.

Guess I'll be helping him sneak in tonight, somehow. He said he has experience with that, which is actually sort of intriguing.

I'm skipping church too. It's a quarter past seven now, and I've already got the expected texts from Dad and Mom asking where I'm at. I'm just ignoring them. I let it settle in that I'd be grounded for at least a few days back when I bought the tickets. It's worth it.

Ahead we round the bend by an office complex and The Music Factory comes into view, and so does the line. Damn. I thought we were early enough to avoid that.

"That's a lot longer than I expected," I tell Skylar.

"That's really long." His eyes are bugged out, adding emotion to Siri's unfazed translation. I think I see dread setting in.

"Yeah," I sigh. "Let me find out where the others are."

JACOB: Y'all in line?

It only takes a second to get a response.

"How long does it take to get in?" Skylar's phone asks before I can check the message.

"Depends." I shrug. "Shouldn't be that long."

I don't really know. And is it really a lie, if you don't know for sure?

TYLER: Yeah. Near back.

"Come on, they're in line," I tell him. "Ready to meet my *other* friends?"

I ask more for me than I do for him. I've never met them in

person, but we've been friends online—although I've never spoken to Kallie before—a good year at least.

He shrugs. I take that as a yes and take off.

I search the line. No one looks familiar yet. I'm looking for an average height brown-eyed Latine guy, his tall, lanky, messy-haired, green-eyed boyfriend, and their Skylar-height BFF who I've only seen a few Snaps of. I should have asked what they're wearing.

"Jacob!" a familiar voice yells a few car lengths down the line.

"Ty!" I yell back and switch into a jog. Oh my God, it's Tyler! It's literally Tyler! And Aidan! And the infamous Kallie!

It's crazy. He's not just a Snap picture or a voice on my PlayStation. It's actually him and them. Even that untamed mop on Ty's head. It's not that bad, but I like to give him a hard time about it.

I run up and wrap him in a hug. It's like meeting an old friend I haven't seen in ages. I pull back, and immediately Aidan grabs me up into another hug.

"A!" I sort of scream. I've heard so much about him, even before he started playing video games with us.

"Hey." Aidan smiles and steps back. "It's great to finally meet you."

"You too," I say.

"And this is Kallie." Ty points to the short girl with the big blue eyes next to them. "You've heard plenty about her."

"Uh, yeah. A lot." I make it sound more ominous than it is. Ty thinks the world of her. He gives her absolute grief, but he loves her to death.

"Great." She rolls her eyes. "Another one of you to deal with."

Her scowl transforms into a smile and she giggles. Yeah, just like he said.

"Nice to meet you. And this is my friend Skylar." I turn and put a hand on Skylar's shoulder. The moment my fingers meet fabric I have to fight not to yank them back. I didn't mean to touch him.

"Good to meet you, Skylar!" Tyler smiles.

Skylar nods and grins, and none of them bat an eye that he doesn't speak. I guess Tyler did his job.

"Jacob said you transferred from up north," Aidan says. I still find it hard to believe he's the older one between Ty and Aidan, he just looks younger.

Skylar nods again but gets his phone out and starts to type.

"Vermont," Siri says, and then keeps going. "It's a lot warmer down here."

They laugh, and that seems to make Skylar happy.

"Oh my! Your thing is British!" Tyler sounds amazed and excited. I roll my eyes, but Skylar seems to appreciate it. "That's so cool. I couldn't do the cold up there. And this one isn't up there, so nope."

It's adorable, and a little cringe, how he wraps his arms around Aidan and snuggles him. Okay, cringe. Definitely cringe.

"You get dragged into this against your will too?" Kallie asks Skylar while Tyler and Aidan have their moment. My eyes dart to Skylar, and I have to soften my glance at the last moment. What is he going to say? Why do I even care?

"You too?" his phone asks, and he rolls his eyes.

"Yes," Kallie huffs. "Their music sucks. I'm just being a good friend."

"Our music taste sucks? Who in this group listens to oldies?" Tyler scowls at her.

Skylar glances at me and grins before his phone spits out the rest. "Nah. He didn't have to drag me. But oldies?"

"Uh, yeah." Kallie acts offended, then nods toward the entrance which is finally in view. "You like this stuff?"

"Didn't say that," Skylar's phone says.

"That hurt, deep," I whine, giving him a pouty lip. He laughs, which gets the others going. "Well you better enjoy it, because I think we're both getting grounded."

SKYLAR

WEDNESDAY, AUGUST 28

I swear I didn't like the music in Jacob's car, but in there, with the bass vibrating through every sinew of my body and the crowd jumping and singing and the lights flashing, it was amazing!

"He sang 'Letdown'." Tyler's in another world as we leave, tailing a group of guys double our age outside. "I can die happy."

It's well after eleven, and I'm so hoping I don't get grounded for this. I don't know if Mom and Dad do that kind of thing, but I'm hoping not. I kept checking my phone during the concert, but I haven't gotten a text yet. So I'm guessing, hoping, they think I'm asleep in my room still.

"And 'Vacanter', or 'Vacanter.'" Jacob says it differently each time. The first time it's like Va-CAnter and the second it's more like VAy-Cunter. It's funny, but the look in his eye is absolute euphoria.

Tyler shrugs. "Not a clue, not sure why there's an -er anyway."

"Doesn't matter, it was fucking awesome!" Jacob is jumping, like literally. "He didn't sing 'Nevermore,' but I'll make it. He was so awesome!"

"Y'all are losers." Kallie rolls her eyes. She's eyeing me like I'm supposed to be on the same page. "But y'all cute."

"We've got to go." Aidan wraps an arm around Tyler's waist and kisses his cheek. "You and Kallie got a two-hour drive and school in the morning."

"So do you," Tyler kisses him back.

"But no two-hour drive," Aidan corrects him, then looks at us. "We'll see y'all later?"

He's looking at me as if I'm supposed to answer. I don't know. I mean, they were fun and all, but that's a Jacob question. I give him a timid smile and then look to Jacob with a look that hopefully says, *Answer the man.*

"Of course," Jacob says. "You're living in the university area now, right?"

"Yep." Aidan nods.

"Maybe we can hang out sometime," Jacob suggests.

"As long as you don't try stealing my boyfriend, I'm okay with that," Tyler laughs. "We do have to go though."

They go in for a goodbye hug, and before I know what's happening Tyler's hugging me and then Aidan. Kallie looks at me for a second. Something tells me she knows I'm not really into the hugging thing and then she hugs me too with this huge grin. I smile back, shaking my head, and her smile just gets bigger. I like her.

* * *

It's nearly midnight, and still not a single text from Mom or Dad. I'm not sure how to take that. When I left I thought they'd end up blowing up my phone. I knew I'd feel horrible about it, but now I'm feeling something different.

Like, they're not even mad? Worried? Nothing?

"Do you think Joe's cute?" Jacob interrupts my thoughts and steers us off the interstate.

That came from way out in right field, or maybe it's left field. I don't know, I don't play football. But cute? And who's Joe again?

"Joe?" Siri asks.

"The singer." Jacob scrunches his brow.

Ah. Him. I think back on the concert. It was dark, but he was lit up. There was something rough about his features, but the sad boy vibe suited him.

"Not sure I'd say cute," my phone explains. "More cool. Maybe bad-ass?"

"Was that a question?" Jacob takes a quick glance at me and then back at the road.

Yes. It was a question. And yes, I know, my phone doesn't always make it sound like one.

"Yeah," Siri confirms.

We come to a red light and Jacob looks at me. It's like he's searching me.

"That a good thing?" he asks.

I shrug and nod.

"I like the sad boy vibe. You think he's cute?" I, well, my phone, asks.

"Sort of, but he's not really my type." Jacob shrugs and starts back down the road when the light changes.

The takeoff presses me against the seat. I swear he thinks every green light starts a zero-to-sixty speed test or that the mom-van next to us wants to race.

"What's your type?" I ask once I'm no longer stuck to my seat. I hold my finger over the Talk button for a moment, debating how stupid a question it is. But I want to know, and this is sort of the perfect time to ask without it being weird. I mean, he brought it up. I add another question. "Tyler?" and hit Talk.

"Uh…" he stumbles and coughs. "No. Not really. I mean, he's kinda cute, but no. I go more for the cute guys."

He shrugs, his pale cheeks blooming crimson under each passing streetlamp. Someone gets nervous on this subject. And it makes his hotness both hot and cute at the same time.

"Like Aidan?" my phone asks. I'm reaching. Aidan's more tan than me and taller, but he's still shorter than Jacob and more the cute type, I think. "Like Tyler's boyfriend?"

"No! No!" Jacob yelps, glancing at me for a second. Worry is all over his face, like he just made a big mistake. "I didn't say that. He's cute and all, but I don't like him. I'd never do that to Tyler. Hell, I wouldn't date him even if Ty broke up with him. That'd just be dirty."

Oh my God. I'm trying so hard to hold back the grin that's screaming in my chest to be let loose. He's actually cute when he's flustered!

We hit my street while Jacob continues his damage control.

"So no, but I guess he's like, you know, my type. Cute, shorter than me, but that's not a must…a bottom." He manages to push back his embarrassment with that last qualification.

Oh. The crazy part is he thinks he's just being funny and TMI, but I'm over here mentally throwing my hand in the air as tribute. Unfortunately the only things that have ever been inside me weren't attached to a guy, and I bet I'd like it a lot more if it were.

"How do you know Aidan's a bottom?" I can't believe I'm asking this, but if it keeps him flustered, I'm here for it.

"I'm friends with his boyfriend." Jacob eyes me like it's obvious. Most of the blush has faded now and he's back in control. "I mean, he doesn't tell me everything, obviously. Just enough to know."

I let my mouth form a big O and nod slowly. Makes sense, I guess. The car slows, and ahead my house comes into view.

"So how you doing this?" Jacob nods toward my place. I think he's just trying to change subjects. I'll give him a pass.

I type out my plan. It's probably not the best plan. I could see me getting hurt, but it's all I've got.

"I'm going to climb up one of the columns holding up the roof over the porch and go in through my bedroom window on the second floor," my phone lays it out. At least it's simple.

He looks at me and raises both eyebrows.

"Really?" He brakes to a stop a block from my house.

I shrug. *Got a better plan?*

"What?" His face skews.

"Sorry," I type. "Got a better plan?"

He thinks on it for a second.

"Nope." He shakes his head and gets out of the car with a sigh.

Huh? I get out too and squint at him.

"What? I'm helping." He shrugs. "You've got short legs. You can't get up those columns on your own."

First, excuse the fuck me? Second, really? And third, he's got a point.

He laughs, way too proud of himself, and takes off. I groan
and take off after him. It's muggy, and it looks like it rained
while we were gone. The street is wet and the glow from the
streetlamps glistens off the grass.

We're almost to my house, and I'm fighting off the desire
to ask if he thinks I'm cute. I really want him to. I know he
doesn't. No one finds the defective guy cute. They
accommodate them, deal with them to not come off as
assholes, tell them they're good or adorable, but they don't
really think it. So I don't ask. Okay, that's not the only reason
I don't ask. I don't want to make him—or me—uncomfortable.
He's been so nice tonight, and it'd just be rude.

"When we get there, I'll boost you up to the roof and help
until you can climb up," he explains his plan.

"You sure you can lift me?" Siri asks, and I smirk.

"Calling me weak?" Jacob side-eyes me.

I shake my head and stick out my tongue so he knows I
was joking. He laughs and does this snorting thing.

"Oh my God, no." Jacob covers his face and waves his
hand in front of me. "You didn't hear that!"

My eyes go bright and excited. Oh, I did. I definitely heard
it. And if I could laugh I'd be losing it right now. Hell, I'm
barreled over anyway, holding my stomach while sounds try
to escape, but it's just pathetic wheezing I wish would stop.

He gives me his middle finger, and that just makes it
worse. I fight to stay on my feet and get my composure back,
but he's laughing too. It takes a solid minute for us to get back
to normal.

"Let's do this," I type.

"Got it." He purses his lips and leans forward like he's

prepping for a race. "Nice and quiet."

I crinkle my brow, and he shrugs, then takes off through the grass. We don't want to take the driveway, and walking past the living room window is a big no-go. But the moment my feet hit the grass, I wish we had. It's damp and mushy. My feet sink with each step, and I just know I'm going to get mud everywhere.

We cross the walking path and I step between the bushes in front of the porch, feet dipping into the mulch. Jacob shimmies in after. His chest brushes my arm, and I jerk back. *Breathe, Sky.*

"You ready?" He squats and forms a platform with his hands, holding it like two inches off the ground, all grins.

I cock my head to the side and give him a look that could kill. He giggles and brings his hands up just below my waist. I give him a sarcastic smile and plant my muddy shoe into his palms.

"Ugh," he groans, frowning at me.

I grin in triumph. Payback's a bitch.

He rolls his eyes and starts counting down.

"Three…" I lean forward and grasp the wooden column. "Two…" I fix my eyes on the tin roof. Oh no. Tin roof. It's going to be so slick. This is such a bad idea. "One…"

"Hey!" a deep voice shouts from the porch.

Jacob's hands falter and part, and he stumbles. I'd just begun to push down, expecting there to be support, but instead I fall forward, smashing into him. We topple and I land flat on top of him. My face is buried in his stomach, just above his waist. I wrangle my arms around, grasping for anything solid, but it's mostly chunks of wet mulch and dirt.

Finally I plant my hands on hard ground and push myself off, while he scrambles to get himself off the ground.

"Skylar." It's Dad. But I don't hear the anger I'd expected. It's not happy, like he's welcoming me home from school, but it's not stern either.

I force a grin, my lip and shoulders twitching, mulch and mud caking my side. Jacob pops up, using the porch railing to ground himself.

"Mr. Gray." He nods quickly, trying to get his breath.

"Jacob," Dad says slowly. He looks at me. "We've been waiting on you, Skylar."

I look away and nod.

"Jacob, you should get on home," Dad says.

"Yes, sir." Jacob nods again.

Our eyes meet for a moment, and I think he's saying sorry, but he really shouldn't be. This is my fault. I should have had a better plan. Or maybe just shouldn't have left. But I had so much fun. But yeah, sorry.

"Good night, Mr. Gray." Jacob steps out of the flower bed and starts down the walkway backward. He nods at me one last time before turning and practically jogging down the street. "Night, Sky."

Did he just tell me good night?

SKYLAR

THURSDAY, AUGUST 29

"Did you kiss him?" Imani reaches across the table. I swear she's about to crawl over. "No, he kissed you?"

NO! Stop it.

She's just now getting caught up at lunch. She was running behind this morning, so she didn't ride to school with us. And I refused to fill her in last night no matter how much she begged.

"Why not? He's hot." Imani looks at me like I'm such an idiot.

It wasn't a date, I say again, then type out the rest. "I did find out his type though."

I bounce my brow and grin.

"Oh?" Imani sits up straight. I've got her attention. As if I hadn't already.

"Here we go," Seth groans.

"Tell." She elbows Seth.

Before I can type, Jacob and Ian take up the seats around us. Jacob sits straight across from me and grins. Imani's looking at me suspiciously, while I try to be calm. I walked up from Dance with Jacob, but he had to go find Ian before getting

in the lunch line as usual, which gave me just enough time to
defuse Imani. I thought, at least.

"How's it going?" he asks.

"Good," Seth says.

"Better than last—" Imani starts, but I kick her under the
table. "Uh... Better than it could be."

"Ah." Jacob's brow scrunches. "I guess a certain someone
could be in ISS again."

"Give it a week," Ian blurts, lips pulled into a tight amused
grin.

Jacob gives him a disappointed look.

"What?" Ian drops his burger and puts his hands up.

"He's not wrong," Seth steps in.

I cock my head and give him my best WTF look.

"I mean, he's not." Seth's voice goes up an octave. "Just
wait. The next time you wear a skirt or a dress, they're going
to throw you in the slammer again."

"It's sort of true." Imani nods.

The sucky part is they're probably dead-on. And I'd really
like to not sit in that stuffy room all day again.

"So," Imani blurts, "Sky was just telling us about last
night."

"Oh yeah?" Jacob leans back and smirks.

I don't know what he's thinking, but whatever it is,
apparently it's amusing.

"Did he tell you about getting caught sneaking into his
house?" he asks.

I've thought about it a lot. For a few reasons. And I swear
it gets funnier the more it runs through my brain. I'm about to
let him bolt me onto the roof. Dad comes out, distracts us, and

we end up sloshing around in the wet mulch. I tracked so much dirt in the house after that.

"Not yet." Imani looks at me like I've been holding back.

Can't help you were late, I mouth.

She gives me a blank stare. I huff and type it out.

"If you hadn't been late this morning, you'd know already."

Imani looks in her purse and pulls out a clear bluish crystal.

"You better be glad I have my aquamarine with me, Sky." She grins and rubs it between her fingers.

I don't know what that means.

Seth shakes his head and laughs.

"So what happened?" she asks.

I look at Jacob. "You want to tell? It'd be easier."

"Sure." He grins and coughs likes he's about to recount this epic tale. "So, Sky had this great idea that he was going to climb on the roof and get in through his bedroom window. And I was going to help. You know, boost him up there. But it rained last night and everything was wet."

Seth's already heard this story, but he looks just as interested this time. Probably looking for any discrepancies. Imani leans over the table and stares.

"Well, I was counting down—and apparently his dad is standing behind us the entire time—and when I got to one his dad yells. It scared the shit out of me, so I let go of Sky's foot right when he put his weight down. Sky here falls and knocks me over, and ends up on top of me. Knocked the breath out of me." He smiles. I shrug. "We were covered in mud. Then *this* one had to do the walk of shame inside."

He forgot the part about him running away with his tail tucked between his legs, but I'll let that go.

"You fell on top of him?" Imani eyes me.

I nod and take a gulp of pop.

"I took you more for a bottom," Imani blurts.

My eyes bust open and liquid spews. I clutch my mouth, trying to keep more from shooting out. She didn't!

"Damn," Ian blurts, reeling over the table laughing.

"Imani!" Seth scolds, but he's grinning from ear to ear and gut laughing.

"Honestly, same," Jacob laughs, sucking in his top lip.

He locks his eyes on me and I want to die right here, right now. Why, Imani? Why?

I grin nervously but regain my composure. I'm going to kill them all. I swear it. My face is hot and wet now, not to mention the water spots on my shirt. I wipe some off my phone and type as fast as I can.

"I hate you all," Siri tells them with none of the intensity that's in my head. That gets them laughing harder. "Not talking about this."

"So you are?" Ian purses his lips like he's investigating.

"Ian." Jacob puts a hand out to say *enough*.

"Just asking," Ian says.

"What was your punishment?" Jacob turns the attention back on me. "I can't be the only one that got in trouble."

"You want me to be in trouble?" Siri asks, and I give him my best pouty eyes.

"I mean... No, but—" Jacob tries to rebound, but I put up a hand and shake my head, grinning.

"I'm not allowed to hang out with anyone after school, and

no WiFi until Sunday, they changed the password," I tell him.

It was way less than I expected, but I wasn't really sure what to expect either. Oh, and they also said I had to spend more time with them, which isn't really a punishment. I think that's why they changed the WiFi password.

"Okay, you officially suck." Jacob leans back and huffs. He holds up a hand and starts numbering off his sentence. "No car, no guitar, no phone, no PlayStation, and straight home after work and school, for a full hell-filled week."

Damn, I say. He nods, so I guess he understood.

"Oh! I found out why Mom and Dad didn't text or call to ask where I was," I type. "Apparently my phone tells them exactly where I'm at, and they didn't want to 'smother' me. And I forgot about the cameras outside. They saw you pick me up."

The camera part was a big God-you're-a-damn-idiot moment on my end. I knew about those, but it just didn't compute when I was planning. Oh, and Dad said he had to keep Mom from calling me.

Jacob groans with the rest of the table. "Wow. Okay. But I mean, they still seem pretty cool."

I shrug and give him a weak nod. He's right.

"*You* just need to stay on *top* of things next time." Imani looks at Jacob, head angled down, lips pooched.

His shoulders bounce and the others start rolling.

I give her my middle finger, but I can't deny it was good. Hell, I'm even laughing.

What they don't realize is, I spent all last night imagining what it would be like having him on top of me.

JACOB
THURSDAY, AUGUST 29

It's good I like to read. What the hell do book haters do when their parents ground them?

I turn the page. The main character is running through a house engulfed in this alien tentacle plant thing trying to find some kid she lost. It's intense.

Intense enough that when the buzzer on the old alarm clock Mom gave me goes off, I jump. I get up, trying and failing to not look at the empty space behind my bedroom door where my guitar usually sits.

Don't think about. Just get dressed.

I slide off the bed and change out of my school clothes and into my black and red uniform, then squeeze my feet into some old black sneakers. They're tight. It's about time I get a new pair, but I'm not asking Mom and Dad for them. I'm going to save up and get them myself, just like I'm going to save up and get my own car.

I start down the hall, wishing I could slip through the kitchen undetected. But without car privileges, Mom has to drive me.

The first thing I hear from the living room while I'm still

down the hall is "that queer boy at Brown." What the hell? I stop and angle my ear toward the living room and wait. Dad's loud enough that I don't need to get closer. Mom, on the other hand, is a little harder.

"What type of parent lets their *boy* wear *girls'* clothes? It's disgusting," Dad complains, his voice shivering with revulsion. "This is what happens when they take God out of the schools, Diane."

"Bruce, quieter, please," Mom begs him.

Oh, it's too late for that, Mom. My blood is boiling. That *queer boy* is *my* friend, and he's anything but disgusting. I plant my feet in place, refusing the urge to bust into the living room screaming. I don't need to get into this with Dad before work. He'll just make me late, even though he always tells me never to be late, but it'll be okay if he's arguing with me. I'm not giving him that.

"I have to do something," Dad says, and he doesn't get any quieter, just less aggressive. "The boy's parents got a lawyer involved and the school doesn't want to enforce the dress code. And the board's counsel is saying the code isn't explicit enough to stop him."

My eyes narrow. There's a pause.

"I'm going to propose a new dress code that addresses this. And makeup and nails, all of it," he says. "It has to stop."

"When are you going to announce it?" Mom asks.

"Announce it?" Dad sounds surprised.

A new dress code policy? Just to keep Skylar from wearing a skirt? How toxic do you have to be to do that? Oh yeah, my dad.

"Yeah." Her voice is tiny.

"It'll go on the agenda for the meeting we vote on it, but other than that we don't need the publicity," he says.

And there it is. He knows the backlash he'll get. So he's going to hide it.

"I still have to get with Craig to draft something up," Dad goes on. "This can be how we get Jacob to stop painting his nails too."

Okay, on that note, I'm done waiting. I'm not bringing the conversation up, but I need to get out of here before I do.

"I'm ready to go, Mom." I fast walk into the living room and look directly at her.

She looks at me like a ghost jumped from the hallway.

"Have a good day at work," Dad says as I rush past him, my lips zipped tight.

This is wrong. It's so damn wrong. How does he think this is okay? Oh yeah, he's blinded by his politics and messed up cultish faith. Someone has to do something. He can't be allowed to do this.

They can't railroad Sky like this. I've got to do something.

SKYLAR

FRIDAY, AUGUST 30

"I hate you both," Seth screams out the window.

"Love you too," Imani yells back as he reverses out the driveway.

I follow her down the walking path to the front door. We're at her place. My first time.

"You two have a weird relationship," Siri says as Imani opens the front door.

"Really?" She scrunches her face at me before going inside.

It's nice. Cozy. Black and white plaid blankets neatly draped over a recliner. Ornate pillows set on a white couch. And the floors are this ashen gray hardwood.

"Guess it's just an us thing." She shrugs.

A tall black man, who I'm assuming is her dad — she's never mentioned an older brother — comes around the corner. He smiles, a perfect match to Imani's glow.

"You must be Skylar." He holds out his hand.

I hesitate, then shake it, nodding. Okay, yeah, firm grip there.

"My Imi here seems quite smitten by you." His voice comes off like a badly produced eighteenth century movie.

Definitely more proper than Imani. But I'm more worried about what he said. My eyes dart to Imani in panic and I reel my hand back, still trying to play it cool. What?

"He's just being dumb." Imani's hands go to her waist, and she gives him this knowing glare. "Stop it."

"Wrong boy?" He squints and his voice comes back to the twenty-first century, but there's still an accent. She definitely didn't catch that.

"Or girl," she reminds him.

"Ah, yes." He nods, lower lip pooched. "Guess you're not the one?"

I shake my head vigorously and type away. "No, sir."

"No, no. None of that sir stuff here." Mr. Banks dismisses it entirely. "Just Zion. Imi *has* told me about you though. She doesn't talk to enough people to *have* a boyfriend or girlfriend," he laughs, nudging Imani, and then returns to me. "Although I'm not sure one could handle her."

"Where's Mom?" Imani rolls her eyes.

"Out getting groceries," he says.

I really like his voice.

"Good, she can get us coffee," Imani blurts.

"Better call her then," Mr. Banks says.

"Got it. Well, plans." She grabs my hand and yanks me down the hallway.

"Good meeting you, Skylar," Mr. Banks calls after us, and I nod as best I can while I'm being dragged away. "Door open!"

"He's gay!" Imani yells back. She takes a hard right into what I'm assuming is her room. There's a bed, after all.

"Don't care," her dad's voice calls back, and a huge smile

paints across my cheeks.

Imani rolls her eyes and huffs, "Hope you don't mind him seeing you in makeup."

Why would I mind? I want her to teach me how to do it so I can wear it in public, nothing extravagant though. Just to experiment a little.

Had I not been grounded the past few days we would have already done this. And when Imani asked if I could come today after school, I was certain the answer was no. But I texted Mom anyway and she said it was okay. So unless there's some unwritten rule I don't know about, I guess I'm ungrounded a day early.

"Sit here," Imani commands.

In the corner there's a little vanity. A large mirror on a swivel sits atop the cherry desk crowded with boxes and boxes of makeup. She's sitting on a smaller rolling chair, patting the cushion of a larger wooden one that matches the vanity.

I sit and take in the room while she rummages through bottles and brushes and things I don't recognize. Ooh! A bookshelf. It's small but packed. And the books look worn and used.

While I'm looking she starts her makeup tutorial, but I'm only half listening. For the most part, I follow. She's washed her face and is putting primer on, but I can already tell I'm going to need to go back over the steps. There's apparently a list.

My eye catches on a title. *Bhagavad Gita.* What is that? I type it in my phone, earning a glare from her, and hit Talk.

"What's the *Bhagavad Gita*?" I ask.

"It's Hindu scripture," she answers and starts back into

her makeup tutorial. "So now that the primer is on—"

"You're Hindu?" my phone asks. "Thought you were Wiccan."

"No," she laughs, dots of foundation on her cheek, chin and forehead. She starts brushing at the dots, pausing to answer. "I *am* Wiccan."

I'm confused. *Why a Hindu book then?*

My hands are moving again, signing. I grip them closed and remind myself that's not needed.

"It's like one of the books witches use. We don't have just one big book." She blends in some foundation, I think, and gets up to fetch it and two other books and comes back to the vanity. "Like these too. *The Four Agreements*, it's like our Bible on how to be good people. *The Wiccapedia*, well, we get a lot from it. Like spells and affirmations, stuff about moon phases and cleansing." She opens the last with a little more care. "And this is my *Book of Shadows*. It's sort of like a journal where I put my spells and thoughts."

A half grin creeps onto my face. She's serious about this. That's actually pretty cool.

"So you really do like spells and junk?" Siri asks.

"Not like you're thinking probably." She grins. "It's more like I hold a crystal or light some candles and say a few words, with intent, to ask for strength or calm or something like that."

She pulls a deep-green rock from the drawer of the vanity. It's solid and smooth with a smoky texture.

"Let's say I wanted to wish you luck." She shrugs. "Give me your hands."

I put my hands in front of her, palms up. She places the stone on my palm and closes my hands around it. It's cold to the touch. Imani closes her eyes, with her hands wrapped over mine.

"I wish you luck and fortune in the week to come," Imani says. Then she opens her eyes and shrugs. "That's it. We also call them affirmations, they're basically what Christians call prayers or blessings."

"Cool," my phone tells her. And it really is.

She opens my hand and takes the stone back, returning it to the drawer. Definitely not how I'd envisioned it.

When I think of a witch, I get visions of women in pointy black hats trying to drain the life out of some poor virgin for immortality. Not little Imani wishing me a good week. And if witches are real, and I guess they are, I definitely would prefer the Imani type. "So is Satan, like, you know, your God?"

"No, no, no." She waves and rolls her eyes. "That's what everyone thinks. We're *Pagan*, not Satanist. There *is* a difference."

"What do your parents say about it? Are they Wiccan?" I ask.

She sighs. "They're Christian. I don't think they really like it, but they don't try to stop me. They let me, do me. Which is cool, because being Wiccan is all about not condemning other people's beliefs, so it's nice that they don't condemn mine. Witches are actually pretty cool and normal."

I knew she was Wiccan. I remember her telling the class the first day of school, but I guess she just seemed so normal I sort of forgot.

"So enough about me. I'll talk about Wicca for hours, so…" She shimmies closer and puts her hands on my knees, looking me right in the eyes, forgetting about the makeup tutorial too.

"You like Jacob, don't you?"

I think my jaw drops because the mischief in her eyes grows. How do I answer? An outright no would be a lie. But thinking he's good-looking isn't the same as liking him, right? But do I have a crush on him? *Come on, Sky, don't be stupid, you know you do. How many times have you thought about those green eyes and that hair?* Too many times. But does that mean I like him?

No, I move my lips and shake my head. *Of course not.*

"You sure? Because you blush a lot when I bring him up." Imani purses her lips and giggles.

I cock my head and part my lips. Not fair.

Do you like Seth? I counter. The question's crossed my mind a few times, so what better time to ask than now?

"What? No!" Imani curls back in shock.

You sure? I ask.

"No, we're just friends," she says much too quickly. I can't say I'm buying it. "You do like Jacob though. I mean, he *is* cute."

There's definitely something there. But I drop it. And no, Jacob's not cute. Let's get it right. He's hot.

Slowly, I nod and teeter my head from side to side. If it's so obvious on my face, what's the point in denying it? Even if it is useless to entertain. I guess it's no more useless than thinking about my weekly TikTok crush.

"Nah, Jacob is hot." Siri bites the bullet and I dig my own grave.

"Well," she smiles, "he is gay... And you're gay... And I think he likes you too."

There she goes with thinking I like him again. Wait, hold

up. I put a hand up to stop her.

You think he likes me? I ask.

"Yeah." She shrugs as if it's obvious.

Wouldn't I have noticed if he did? And I definitely haven't. I shake my head and laugh, which is basically just spurts of air shooting from my nose.

"I think he does," she says again. "And I think you like him."

I shake my head.

But do I?

JACOB
MONDAY, SEPTEMBER 2

If I end up in jail today, it's because I'm about to kill a motherfucker. These people are testing my patience. You'd think none of them had seen a skirt, and the way they're talking to Sky is making my blood boil.

"Faggots," someone whispers.

I can feel it slung at us. I'm used to it from their pathetic little minds, but when it's aimed at him, it slices at my skin like a hundred paper cuts.

"ISS is looking real good about now," I whisper in Skylar's ear as we hit the top stair and venture into the lunch room. Maybe Dad would be proud of me if I beat the crap out of someone. Then again, once he figured out it was for the *queer boy* he's trying to screw over, probably not.

Skylar shakes his head and smiles. I'm learning that's like his laugh. "Just a thought. You good?"

I don't want to leave him, but Ian will have something to say if I'm not at his locker waiting when he gets down from second block. It's a ritual.

Skylar nods, and I take it as a yes. "K. See you in a sec."

I spin around on the balls of my feet and start down the

hall. The singular thought going through my head is *Oh my God that was stupid*. Why did I do that?

Today I'm even more worried for Skylar. Not only is he wearing a skirt again, his nails are painted a pale yellow too. They look great. It fits his vibe, more cuteness, courtesy of Imani's weekend nail salon, I hear. But it's also more for the idiots to pick on.

"Where you been?" Ian shouts from the other end of the hall.

I tilt my head and check my watch.

"I'm like a minute later than normal," I answer.

I turn to walk back down the hall, and Ian throws an arm over my shoulder. "You're not trading me in for Sky, are you?"

"Trading you in?" I squint at him. "You sound like some old used car. And no. I'm not 'trading you in' for Sky."

"You sure?" he digs.

"No. I mean yes," I correct. It's one of those tricky questions. "I'm good with a junker."

"So I'm the junker?" Ian reels back, a smile plastered on his face.

I let it hang as we weave through the crowd.

"You're no Ferrari." I shrug.

"Screw you," Ian laughs. "You can have your new little model."

"Why would I trade you in in the first place?" I ask and step into the back of the lunch line.

"Because you've got a crush on him." He drags it out.

"Even if I did, I wouldn't ditch you," I tell him. "I don't do that shit."

We go through the line in silence mostly, except when Ian elbows my arm while I'm trying to scoop fries onto my plate and I about dump half the tray on the floor. Lucky for me Ainsleigh caught it on the opposite side before it could careen off the rack.

"And here's your new model," Ian says before we get to the table.

"Hiya." Imani grins as I drop my plate and sit across from her. Skylar's next to her. "Sky says you liked his nails."

Did he? It's stupid, but I like that he told her.

"Yeah, they look great!" I tell her and my next words pop out before I think about them. "Yellow looks good on him."

"You hear that, Sky, yellow looks good on you," Imani nudges his shoulder. "Told you. He thought they'd be too much."

"No. They look great," I say. They do look great, but I shouldn't have said they looked good *on him*.

"New model," Ian whispers in my ear.

"Huh?" Imani asks, leaning over the table.

"Uh… Jacob's uh… He's working on a new model, I was just reminding him," Ian stutters.

I could kill you right now. I'm working on a new model? What new model? You could have just said, Oh nothing, I was just being stupid. No one would have questioned that.

Skylar's eyes light up a little, and he starts typing.

Before he can say anything Seth leans around Ian. "You do models?"

"Not really," I start, trying to figure out what to say as I go. "I'm just trying it out. It's nothing really."

My eyes switch from Seth to Ian. He's smiling stupidly. I

stare into his soul, lips sealed tight, a smile that says *I could punch you right now*.

"What type of model?" Sky's phone pulls my attention away from my idiot.

"It's a…a…" I struggle. What the hell is it? How should I know? Ian? I glance at him, hoping he'll get the idea to fix what he started, but he doesn't seem to. "You know…a…car."

My mind goes back to telling Ian I wouldn't trade him in. I've changed my mind. I'd even downgrade right now.

"I didn't know you did models," Imani says.

"Me either." I kick Ian under the table.

He yelps, and all eyes dart to him. He eyes me angrily.

"What type of car?" Skylar asks. He's way too interested in this, and I don't have the answers.

"Ferrari?" I ask. Why the hell would I ask?

"You don't know?" Seth sounds confused.

"No. I know. I just don't remember what *type* of Ferrari," I lie. God, I've got to change the subject or I'm going to end up having to buy a model. "Is Imani going to keep doing your nails?"

Sky nods, grinning at her. She seems excited about it.

"What color you doing next?" I ask. Anything to get the attention off my *model*.

I wait for him to type out his response. "Probably blue. Maybe black with little white dots like stars."

"Speaking of black," Imani looks at me and then down at my black nails. "You ever paint yours anything but black?"

"Nah," I shrug, "I really like it. Not sure anything else would fit me."

"You'd be surprised. I can always help you out there." She tilts her head and smiles.

"I don't know. I like black," I tell her.

"You should let her," Sky's phone says. I'm still not used to the mismatched British voice, but I'm getting there.

"Maybe. Maybe," I say. And it's a big maybe, but mainly no. So I switch topics again. "You not worried your teachers are going to give you a hard time again? Suspension and all that?"

Skylar starts typing, and the table gets quiet.

"I think crimson would look good," Imani breaks it.

"Sounds even darker than black." Ian frowns. "Like blood on your hands."

"Yeah, exactly." Imani grins.

"That could be cool," I admit. Sort of morbid, but I don't know. Maybe.

"No. I think they're all too scared to say or do anything now," Skylar's phone finally starts up. "My parents got a lawyer involved. If they try anything, then it's going to be a big issue."

Inside, something in my chest sinks. He's talking about the dress code. The one my dad is working to royally screw up for him for exactly the same reason. And no one has a clue he's doing it except my mom, the other school board members, and me.

"You good?" Imani looks at me.

"Uh, yeah." I snap back to reality. I hadn't even noticed I zoned out. "That's cool though. Good thing your parents are on top of it."

My parents are on top of it too. Why is everything always so messed up?

* * *

"We're taking care of the church lawn this weekend," Dad says, shoveling a forkful of Mom's homemade meatloaf to his mouth.

"Again?" Mom sighs. "I thought Dale signed up this week."

"He did," Dad says. "He called this morning. Got family coming in. I told him we'd cover it."

Thank God I'm working Saturday. They get stuck with it a lot. No one else wants to do it, and the church won't hire anyone.

"Sorry, honey," Dad says. "People put everything before serving."

Except him. He puts *serving*, well anything about the church, before *everything* else. It's annoying. I could have a once-in-a-lifetime opportunity and he'd miss it if someone else wouldn't mow the church lawn, or if it was the same time as church visitation, or overlapped a church service or event. And usually *I'd* have to miss it too. Sort of like when Christmas falls on a Sunday or Wednesday. Either the rest of the family postpones their Christmas plans or we miss the family get-togethers because hell if he's going to miss one little service. I mean a normal church would just move the service, but not ours.

"Did you see that article in *The Observer*?" Dad starts up. "It actually wasn't a total liberal hit piece."

"I did." Mom nods. She's not one for politics. She's more the type to be quiet, in the background. But she tries.

I don't want to hear about his campaign. I use my fork to draw lines in the ketchup that's fallen from my meatloaf before taking another bite. Why can't we talk about movies, or books, or music, or Skylar? Okay, maybe not Skylar. Just anything other than his campaign.

"They're calling me a religious freak like it's a bad thing though," Dad laughs. He wears the title proudly. "They focused a lot on my Traditional Family Pride Month proposal."

Oh God, that. One of his campaign proposals is to make the time between Thanksgiving and the end of the year Traditional Family Pride Month. First, that's more than a month, so it's already stupid. Second, he's just trying to create a Straight Pride Month without calling it that, which the paper saw right through. It's disgusting and amazing how they literally think they're oppressed for having their "values". It's even more demeaning knowing that he's proposing it and I have to exist in his family.

I finish off the last of my food. I'm about to get up when Dad says something that sparks my interest.

"We finally finished writing the new dress code proposal. Craig and Janet did most of the research since I was held up with the campaign, but I double-checked it and counsel says it should hold up," Dad says.

It's all I can do not to scream. Instead, I squeeze my fist and act disinterested, scooping and moving the ketchup that's left on my plate. I want to hear this conversation.

"We're proposing it Monday," he tells us and pulls a piece of paper from the stack next to his plate. He never stops working. "It'll pass easily."

My eyes lock on the paper, and I sigh as quietly as I can. I need a copy of that. But how do I do that without Dad asking questions? I excuse myself from the table. *Think, Jacob.*

Halfway down the hall, I hear Mom and Dad getting up and dishes clinking in the sink. My mind is stuck on that proposal, that piece of paper. He's not going to tell anyone about it, then he's going to ram it through the school board and boom, it's over for anyone who doesn't subscribe to his outdated church dress standards. There has to be something, some case that says no, he can't do that. I mean there's logic and basic human decency, but that ain't going to work here.

This is so unfair to Skylar.

I slink into my room, facing my bed and the pile of clothes in the corner. People need to know about this, and they need to know before Monday. I could leak it. I could. I could do it. All I need is a picture.

I just have to snap a pic and send it out to any paper or blog or website that'll listen. I can do that. I can make this a nightmare for him. An actual nightmare. I wiggle my fingers—oh my God, this could be something. I could literally stop this. I mean maybe, probably not, but it could throw a wrench in it at least, and the papers would eat it up. Maybe it'd be enough.

I turn around and take a deep breath. *Just walk out there like you're getting a snack—nothing wrong with grabbing a cookie after dinner—and take a picture. Just act normal. That's all you have to do. Easy.*

Blowing slowly, I release a breath and step down the hall. It feels longer than usual, like it's stretching longer and longer as if I'm in *The Matrix*. Finally, I reach the kitchen. Mom and Dad are in the living room with the TV going. They seem occupied. It sounds like a news channel, a bunch of people talking, and one of them sounds frustrated. Nope, that's Dad.

With the coast clear, I tiptoe to the dining room table. His stack of campaign junk is still there. I scan the first page. A position statement on gun rights. It might sound crazy to some, but I know my entire family — except Rebekah — would vote to keep their guns even if it meant screwing my equality. Makes me sort of sick thinking about it, so I move on to the next page. More position statements. One on how immigrants are stealing our jobs, another claiming Democrats are segregationist — like, really? — another on how evil the United Nations is. My eyes keep rolling like a lottery machine, which he also doesn't like. And then I find it.

I take a second to speed read it. And damn, it literally says "biological males" aren't allowed to wear clothes that are traditionally for "biological females" and lists a few, including skirts, dresses, high heels. I pat my palm to my face as I read the next part. It even prohibits guys from painting their nails or wearing makeup. Hell, some guys wear makeup to cover up acne, what about that?

Just take the damn picture, Jacob. I pull out my phone and snap a few to be certain I get a clear one. I take a deep breath.

Let the games begin.

SKYLAR

TUESDAY, SEPTEMBER 3

"Welcome back," the blonde girl at the register says when we walk through the coffee shop door and the little bell announces our entrance.

"Hiya, L.A., Odessa," Imani says.

"Hey," Seth echoes.

L.A.? That's her name?

"Hey." A thin woman with long dreads hanging over her shoulder joins in next to L.A. Odessa? I guess.

Before we walked in the shop, Imani had been going on about the project Mr. Clements assigned in American History. Something about research and a presentation on women's suffrage, which she had to explain means women's voting rights. Although it sounds like there was a lot of suffering too.

"This is our new friend, Skylar." Imani introduces me, and I nod. "He can't talk."

L.A. looks at Odessa, confusion written on both of their faces. Seth jumps in without delay. "Like literally. He can't. He has to use his phone."

I hold up my phone and press a quick greeting. "Hey."

This would be so much easier if Tina was here again today.

"Oh." L.A.'s mouth hangs while she takes it in.

"Well don't just stand there," Odessa laughs. That's when I notice the tattoos going up her arm. It's not quite a sleeve, but it's close. There are flowers, this '40s era pin-up girl in a red bikini, a painter's palette, and the words *Find Your Song* encircled in butterflies. All arranged in this patchwork of color that just works.

"Uh, sorry. What can I get you?" L.A. jerks back to reality.

After our orders are in, Imani takes off without us. I think she's looking for stuff for her project.

"Looking for anything specific?" I have Siri ask once we catch up.

"Not really. Anything about voting way back then," she says.

"Something tells me you ain't finding that here. Most of their history section is like military stuff," Seth tells her, and from a brief look, I have to agree. It is a used bookstore after all.

"Yeah," she huffs. "Maybe something fantasy then."

"What happened to voting rights?" Seth side-eyes me.

"Fantasy *is* more interesting," I have my phone chime in. And that means I can check out some books too.

Imani shoots across the foyer into another room. Little chalk plates announce *Fantasy*, *Sci-fi*, and *Thrillers* above the shelves. I run my finger along the spines, names and titles skirting by announcing this book or that. I'd read all of them if I could, but there's not enough time in the day, especially with homework.

"You see the posters for Homecoming?" Imani asks. I can't tell if she's talking to me or Seth or both.

No one answers. I saw them. It's coming up in October. But I didn't read the details. It's probably not something I'll be going to.

"No?" Imani stops and stares at us both.

"Oh, yeah." Seth nods furiously. "Saw them."

I nod too. *Yeah.*

"We should go, the three of us." Imani leans against one of the shelves. "We could rent some cool car, dress up all fancy, and go to the dance. We don't have to go to the game. I'm assuming you can dance, right? I mean, you are taking dance."

I nod. *Sort of.*

The idea of going to a school dance rockets my anxiety into high gear. I'm not sure if it's dancing in front of the entire school, all the people—who mostly hate me—or that people expect you to have a date for Homecoming that causes my skin to crawl more. And I definitely won't have a date.

"I can't." Seth puts up a hand like he's waiting to be called on.

"You'll be fine. I can teach you." Imani dismisses it.

"You gonna teach me?" Seth squints at her. "I've known you my whole life and I've never seen you dance. Not once."

"I can dance," she sasses him.

"Okay." Seth looks at me questioningly. "Still not sure I *want* to go to Homecoming. The populars will be out in force and twice as assholish. Plus no one's going to rent a car to a bunch of sixteen-year-olds."

What he said, I mouth to Imani.

She moans, "You two are no fun. Come on! You know what, no. Take your time. Think about it."

Seth and I look at each other at the same time. His eyelids

raise, that look that says *sure I'll "think" about it.* But if he's thinking the same thing, he's already put it so far in the back of his mind it'll never come back up.

The L.A. girl saves us from further dance talk by bringing our drinks. A girl I don't know is helping her. She's this tiny thing, like my height, with long black hair. She hands Seth his drink and smiles sillily before running off. I could be wrong, but I think she might have a thing for him, especially when Seth looks at me and literally says, "What?"

I shrug, then go back to searching the books. Covers that scream excitement and adventure, and some that make me wonder what they were thinking. And the smell. It makes my heart happy, the smell of old books, all in one place, close together, scenting the air with adventure and nostalgia.

My finger traces the spines as I get to the end of the room and cross through a doorway. So many books. And there's another room back here. I cross the hall and enter a tiny room set in the back of the shop. I stop when I see a boy.

Jacob? I mouth. But he's not looking.

His white hair drapes over his forehead, dangling above a book in his pale hands. I can't see his eyes. They're lost behind his hair, devouring whatever it is he's reading. And whatever it is, it's thick. I didn't take him for a book guy.

I kick the chair he's sitting in.

"What the…" The book jumps and his face shoots upward, slinging his hair in the air. It falls back over his face, but I can see his eyes now. "Sky! What are you doing here?"

JACOB
TUESDAY, SEPTEMBER 3

"Sky! What are you doing here?" I blurt.

Skylar mouths something, or starts to. He grins and shakes his head, then pulls out his phone.

"I'm here with Imani and Seth. We're just looking around," Siri explains while Sky looks at me. I hate to admit it, but I think I could look at those hazel eyes, that green with flecks of light brown, all day. "I didn't take you as a reader."

You didn't take me as a reader? All right now. Just because I'm in a band doesn't mean I don't read.

"Well…" I hold up my book. It's a new one. I finished the alien one last night, it was crazy. That twist. "I do."

He starts to say something without his phone again, forming an O with his lips and then frantically goes back to his phone. Imani and Seth come around the corner at the same time, but they're not as surprised to see me.

"Hey, Jacob." Seth waves casually.

"Whatcha reading?" Imani asks.

"It's called *The Last Astronaut.*" I show her the cover. It's got a woman's face inside a space helmet, looking all serious and worried. "It's supposed to be like one of the scariest space books, so…" I bounce my shoulders.

I'm always looking for a book that can actually get under my skin. Hope this one doesn't disappoint.

"Sorry," Sky's phone finally starts up. I think he was so nervous he had to rewrite his reply a few times. "I didn't mean to assume. I just didn't know. That's cool though. And space horror! So cool!"

"It's okay so far," I say, glancing at Imani, who's trying her best not to laugh. She can see just as easily that Sky's in damage control. "I need it to really scare the shit out of me. I love that type of thing."

We've talked a little about movies, and I keep thinking horror isn't his go-to. Or was it that he doesn't like the bloody stuff?

"You come here to read a lot?" Sky asks.

I find myself wishing I could hear his voice, like his actual voice, not his phone. As cute as he is, I bet it would be amazing.

"When I can. I'm just wasting time before work," I tell them. I'd rather stick around here and read than go home.

"Thought you were grounded still," Seth says.

"I am," I groan. But today is the last day. Tomorrow I'll be a free man again, or as free as a flaming eboy faggot in a super religious conservative house can be. "But it's less work for my mom if I stick around here between school and work. That way Ian doesn't have to take me home and she doesn't have to drive me to work. So they let this slide. It's all about how you make it sound and if it benefits them."

"Oh-h-h." Imani drags it out in fake awe. "Not sure I could pull that on my parents."

"Mine already ended my grounding," Skylar's phone says, and he's grinning. He knows what he's doing. Bitch.

He told me Saturday. He's got cool parents. But before I can say anything witty, Sandra walks around the corner. She must have just gotten here, I didn't see her when I arrived earlier.

"What do we have here?" she crows, arm propped on the doorway. "Someone new?"

My eyes dart to Skylar. He's waving awkwardly. Guess he hasn't met Sandra. She's the owner. And one of my favorite people, like ever. She's like another mom, but one who gets it. I sort of came out to her first.

"This is Skylar." Imani points before he can type anything out, then she points to Sandra. "Skylar, Sandra. She's the owner of the shop."

His eyes lift from his phone, then he presses a button. "Good to meet you. I don't have a voice, so I have to use this."

"You too, sweetie." She grins. I bet he's still getting used to our Southern ways. Wonder how many people in Vermont ever called him sweetie. "I hope you like the shop."

He nods and smiles.

"Good," Sandra says. "Well, I've got work to do. Let me know if y'all need anything."

"Thanks," a chorus of voices replies.

Sandra pauses and eyes me down, shaking her head, "One of these days, Jacob, you're just going to go *poof* in here. I know it."

The looks on the others' faces are priceless. Shock and confusion. If only I could know what's going through their minds. Skylar's got this what-the-fuck look on his face.

A laugh jumps in my throat and Sandra breaks character and joins me. "Y'all enjoy."

She walks away without explanation, leaving everyone staring me down for answer.

"It's this running joke because this is the quote, unquote Christian Room, and you now, I'm a fag, so I'm going to burst into flames back here one day," I tell them. Tina started it. I hadn't been out a full week and she found me back here, and it was the first thing out of her mouth. The looks on Imani and Seth's faces say they want to laugh but they're not sure they should, but Skylar's already grabbing his stomach, wheezing. "It's okay, we joke about it all the time."

Finally, they let themselves laugh. *Live a little, people.*

Imani drops into the only remaining chair in the room, and Seth and Skylar take up residence on opposing arms, like her bodyguards.

But now I'm struggling to keep my eyes up. I like Skylar's skirts, I really do, but they don't hug him like the shorts he's wearing right now. I pull my attention back up where it's supposed to be, trying to remember what we were talking about.

"You going to Homecoming?" Imani blurts.

For some reason my instinct is to look at Skylar. And it's such a stupid instinct. Why would I do that? Okay, I know exactly *why* I'd do that, but still.

When I saw the flyer today my first thought was to ask Skylar to go with me. And what a stupid thought it was. But I keep rolling our conversation after the concert about our *types* over and over in my head. I could be twisting it a little, but maybe.

I yank my gaze back to Imani. She's squinting now. That's not good.

"Uh, I don't know," I tell her. "I hadn't thought much about it."

Liar. Fucking liar. You've thought about it all day. I reposition my hips in the chair and swallow. *Say something, Jacob, and not anything stupid.*

"Are y'all?" I ask.

"Yeah." Imani straightens her back, a smile blooming across her face.

"Says who?" Seth looks down at her, incredulous, like she's springing this on him all at once. "You just brought it up. We didn't say we were."

"Of course we are. We just have to find a date for Sky," she says, and the look on Sky's face is just as surprised.

My lips turn up, and I manage to suppress most of the giggles building in my throat, but not all of them. Skylar's fingers are moving fast.

"What?" Skylar's phone speaks. "That isn't happening. No one's going to do that. I'll just go with you two, if I go."

"Don't say that." I jump in the moment his phone stops. "You'll find a date."

It's everything I can do to keep my stupid mouth from screaming *ME*. And who knows, maybe I *will* ask him. Probably not, because that means he could say no, but maybe.

He looks at me, lips skewed, shaking his head.

"Jacob's right, you can find a date," Imani backs me up. "We'll help."

"Maybe I don't want to go, or maybe I just want to go with you two," his phone spits out.

There it is. Even more confirmation he'd say no. He's not fond of the idea of the dance at all. But I thought he liked to dance. Oh, and he could wear a dress. I bet he'd be gorgeous in a… But the dress code. Dad's literally holding the vote on Monday!

My mood shifts, and my excitement turns to simmering anxiety, the permanent resident in my chest. That's not fair. It's a long shot, but maybe tomorrow's news can put a wrench in it long enough and he'll get to. Homecoming is what, the end of October? So like two months.

I tipped off the papers and TV stations last night and even got a few calls about it this morning. I told them everything I knew. I just made sure they knew they couldn't tell their source, *me*. If he knew I leaked it, I'd be grounded from everything until the day I move out.

"If that's what you want, then that's good too." I nod and look at Imani. Nothing wrong with going with friends. Maybe I'll go with him after all, just not as a date. Maybe Ian and I can tag along with them.

"Yeah, but we *are* going." She looks at Seth with eyes that say there is *no* other option.

He huffs and shakes his head, but it looks an awful lot like *whatever*.

"I gotta go," I say. My shift starts in fifteen minutes. "Time for work."

"At the theater?" Skylar's phone asks as I'm getting up. Before I can respond he's typing again. "Imani told me."

"Yeah," I giggle. "And yes, I can get y'all discounted tickets."

Seth does a little fist pump, and Imani and Skylar shake

their heads at him. I don't mind though.

"Bye," Siri says, echoed by Imani and Seth.

"See y'all later." I get up and start down the hall.

I clench my fists into tight balls and release. Tomorrow's either going to be really good or really bad. News is going to break, either in a little section no one reads and amount to nothing, or it'll blow the lid on my dad's ramrodding of the new dress code. Either way, it's going to be something.

JACOB

Dad's livid.

I'm not sure which article he read, but the local paper covered it, and they didn't appreciate his proposal. Neither did the Charlotte or Raleigh papers.

"Outdated conservatism", "a step too far", "homophobic", and "sexist dress standards" were just some of the phrases they used. It's put an extra bump in my step this morning. I despise mornings. Like, who in their right mind decided it was great to wake up at 7:00 a.m.? But today I could kiss someone, I'm so excited.

Now I just have to get out of the house without him questioning me. I pull the curtain back and check the driveway. Ian's already waiting outside in his old silver hatchback.

I sneak out of my room. But I stop—why the hell am I sneaking? They know I'm here. *You're making yourself look guilty. Just be normal.*

I try. But every step feels unnatural, guilty. At the end of the hall, I take a breath.

"How? Who would have talked to the papers?" Dad's still

going on.

"I don't know, Bruce," Mom says.

"They're going to want hearings now, you know they are," Dad says, like it's something bad.

I thought that's how government was supposed to work. Isn't it supposed to be for the people? That's what Mr. Roper said a few years ago in Civics, and that's what you say, Dad, in all your campaign speeches.

I could sneak through the kitchen, but I only do that when I'm taking Mom's car, so right now it'd make me look extra guilty. I take another deep breath and start through the living room, acting like it's just a normal conversation they're having and I'm not worried about it.

"Morning," I throw back as I keep walking.

"Jacob." My dad's voice is stern.

I freeze. *Act natural. Just act natural.* I turn around.

"You're ungrounded after school." He puts a finger up. "*After* school."

My chest loosens and the air I'd been holding pours out. What? Okay, I mean, that's actually pretty cool. It's only half a day early, but still.

Mom smiles and winks at me. Yep. It was her doing. Bet she's been trying for the past few days. I give her a half grin.

"Gotta go," I say, bolting out the front door.

"Come on! You're going to make us late, man." Ian yells the moment my feet hit our tiny excuse of a porch.

"I'm coming," I bite back and throw myself into the passenger seat. "You hear the news yet?"

"News? You have news?" Ian purses his lips and pulls us onto the road, the tiny engine roaring like it's about to burst.

"Yeah, but like in the papers," I try again.

"Do I look like a guy who reads the paper?" There's a crazy look on his face. "Was it on Insta?"

I roll my eyes. But, well, I don't normally read the paper either.

"I mean maybe, I don't know." I shrug. "Probably?"

He looks at me, eyes wider than before. "So? You going to tell me?"

"Oh, yeah." I unzip my pack. "I leaked Dad's dress code to the papers. And they're reporting on it from an *anonymous* source. They're actually doing it. And they hate it! Dad's not happy."

"Hell yeah! Stick it to them." Ian fist pumps. "Does he know it was you?"

"Hell no," I say and pull the skirt I bought from the local thrift shop yesterday from my pack. It's pleated, about knee-length, and all black, so it'll fit my vibe still.

I undo my shorts and start taking them off.

"What the hell, man?" Ian swerves. I grab the door handle for dear life and lock my eyes on him.

"What are—?" I yell.

"No, what are *you* doing?" His eyes are wide.

"I'm just changing," I say. Okay, yeah, I can see where this might have come off a little odd. I am sort of sitting in his car with my shorts around my ankles. I lift the skirt for him to see. "Into this. Calm down!"

"Uh… Homecoming ain't for another month, man," Ian jokes, but he's still side-eying me.

"It's not *for* Homecoming, it's a *protest*," I explain. "But just me, and maybe Sky if he happens to wear one today. So not really, but maybe."

"Ah," Ian sighs. "Right, 'cause that's how protests work. Absolutely no organization."

"Whatever," I say, unfolding the skirt and sliding it on, which is a lot harder to do buckled in a car than I thought it'd be. "They can't do this to him though."

"You mean anyone, right?" Ian gives me a sideways grin.

"Yeah, anyone." I nod vigorously. "It's messed up."

"You know you're getting grounded for this, right?" Ian says what I've been thinking since the second I bought the skirt. "And you're not even ungrounded yet."

"Actually, Dad said I'm ungrounded as soon as school is out today, so…" I tell him.

And yeah, I'm sort of horrified. I'm gay, everyone knows that, but I've never worn a skirt before—except that one time when I was like nine or something, but it was "cute" then—and this is a whole new ballgame for me.

"When did that happen?" he asks, pulling into the school parking lot.

"Like five minutes ago." I shrug.

"You're screwed," Ian laughs.

Yeah. My eyes lock onto the school, and suddenly this all seems like a really bad idea.

SKYLAR
WEDNESDAY, SEPTEMBER 4

"We're with you, Skylar," a brunette I've never spoken to shouts as she passes me up the stairs.

I'm headed to Dance, and I'm even more confused now than I was a minute ago. I swing around to say *what*, but one of the joys of my, uh…condition, is I can't. So she disappears into the crowd and I'm left wondering. I turn around and make my way down the last flight without an answer.

"If you want to protest, we've got your back," another girl says, then sprints off. What are we protesting? Like, what is happening?

When I turn, a shoulder bumps into mine.

"Hope they pass the new dress code," the boy who'd knocked into me, a thin guy, gamer-looking type, spats at me. Dress code?

What dress code? What is he talking about? What is happening?

I finally get away from it all, to the seclusion of the changing room and retrieve my tights and t-shirt. The door creaks open behind me.

"Morning, Sky," Jacob says before I turn around. And

when I do my eyes go wide.

He's in a skirt. I have to snap my mouth shut. I point at the skirt like he's supposed to understand and tilt my head. It's not how I'd normally think of him, but it's not bad. But why? I didn't take him for the type. I grab my phone from the bench and start typing. He's smiling.

"You're wondering why *I'm* wearing this?" he laughs.

I stop typing and nod.

"Have you not heard the news?" He squints as if it might be a bad thing.

"What news?" I type out instead.

"That'd be a no." He laughs again. "Well, uh… My dad, who's on the city school board, chair of the board actually, is proposing a new school dress code." Jacob pauses as if to gauge my response. If nothing else, some of the pieces are coming together now. "To keep you from wearing a skirt to school."

What? All because of me? A grown-ass man is proposing a whole new dress code because little ol' me wore a freaking skirt to school?

"And I might have sort of leaked it to the papers." Jacob purses his lips and looks away coyly, then back at me with a huge grin. "So, I thought I'd wear a skirt today in support…of you, I mean, opposing the new dress code."

Me? He's wearing a skirt for me? To support me? My cheeks heat up, and I can't look at him, so I look at his black skirt instead.

"Are you serious?" is what I have Siri ask, which now that I think about it, is sort of a stupid question.

"Yeah. He's sort of a super conservative and thinks boys in

skirts will destroy the fabric of the universe or something." Jacob bobs his head and throws his hands around, rolling his eyes. "He believes a lot of stupid shit. And he's running for Congress. Yay, us!"

I laugh at that. It's his dad, but Jacob sure doesn't seem to mind saying what he thinks.

"You're wearing the skirt to protest then?" my phone asks.

"Yeah." He shrugs, then gets his clothes from his locker and starts to slip the skirt off. I turn around.

"You think getting the media involved will help?" I have Siri ask.

"Dad was going to try to ram a vote through next week without anyone knowing. The board is nothing but Republicans," Jacob explains. "But now people know, so maybe it'll be harder. Maybe he'll have to delay the vote, and we can have a real protest or something."

A protest? All because I wore a skirt? I've got to be dreaming. This is insane.

"Thanks," I tell him. Not really sure what else to say.

He wore a skirt. For me?

JACOB
WEDNESDAY, SEPTEMBER 4

"They're not actually going to, right?" Seth leans across the table.

"Sounds like it." Ian is way too excited.

I pull up another meme and hold my phone up for them. It's some dude on a bike saying he's going into Area 51, and then the picture next to it is a bike in front of the moon with what looks like some creature in a basket on the handlebars, saying that's how he's leaving.

"Oh my God," Imani laughs. "What is that even?"

"I don't know," I laugh, but these people are crazy.

"Isn't that from some old movie?" Skylar's phone asks.

I shrug and look at the others, no one knows. Sky seems to be in thought.

"I think it is, some alien movie," Siri says.

The bell rings, and the conversation is over. I pocket my phone so a teacher doesn't confiscate it, and we're off.

"Stay down," I say to myself, grabbing the edges of my skirt and pulling down for the hundredth time. It's not short, but it feels like it's riding up.

"You should wear that more," Imani comments as she and

Seth head off. "Looks good."

"Probably not happening," I tell her and glance at Skylar.

His smile gets bigger, and I'm not entirely sure how to take that. Does he sense how uncomfortable I am?

"See ya," Imani yells, and the two take off.

I turn and walk the other direction with Skylar and Ian. They've got class together next and it's in the same hall as mine.

"How do you stand this thing?" I ask Skylar. "I feel like every move I make it's going to fly up and everyone's going to see my underwear."

He starts typing. And honestly, I don't know how he does it without falling up the stairs.

"Faggots." One of the good ol' boy types spits on his way past. It's Liam. Great, I know him. He goes to my church. Definitely getting grounded now.

"Maybe I like living on the edge," Skylar's phone distracts me. He's scowling at Liam until he sees me looking. "Not really. Unless you twirl around a ton, you don't have much to worry about though."

"Ah." I sigh. "I think I'll leave the skirts to you. You loo—"

My shoulder yanks back, and I stumble up a step.

"Put on some damn pants. You're not a girl," a boy says.

I don't know this one. I've seen him around a few times, typical, nothing special guy, brown hair, don't-give-a-fuck color eyes and a rod up his ass.

He throws up his hands like it's my fault *he* ran into me, and then turns around to the raucous laughter of his squad.

I turn to face Ian and Sky. "I hate people, men mostly, but people."

"Yeah, people suck," Ian agrees.

Skylar nods eagerly and mock pukes. I think he mouths *men*, but I can't tell for sure.

"See ya later," I tell Skylar. He and Ian are just about to head off in the opposite direction.

He waves.

"See you in fourth," I tell Ian.

They veer off and leave me to walk into English on my own. Mr. Pritchett smiles warmly at me. He's one of the cool teachers. Which basically means he lets us watch lots of movies. Somehow he always brings it back around to what we're learning. I don't know how he does it.

"Jacob." I hear Eric's voice.

I look his way. His brow is high, and his eyes are screaming *what the hell* as they scroll up and down my profile, but he's smiling. At least he's amused.

"Yeah." I drop into my usual desk next to him.

"*You* told the papers, didn't you?" Eric guesses on the first try.

"How'd you know?" I ask.

"It's you. That's so something you'd do," Eric laughs. "I knew the moment I read the first article. When they said an *anonymous* source, I was like, aka Jacob Brennan Walters."

"That's me," I laugh.

"I can't say it looks good on you though." He glances at my skirt and then back up at me. "But I also think you're an ugly fuck, so you know."

"Fuck you," I whisper. Mr. Pritchett is cool, but he's not cool enough to cuss around. I start to say I did it for Skylar, but I clamp my mouth shut on that one real quick.

"You wish," Eric slings back, his mouth open wide in victory.

"I hate you, Ted," I laugh.

"Eh." He shrugs, ignoring the nickname. Mr. Pritchett gets up. "You do know you're getting grounded for that though, right?"

"Yeah, I know," I sigh.

* * *

"You good?" Ian asks.

I'm sitting in his car, eyes locked on the front door of my house. I should go somewhere else. I am technically ungrounded at the moment.

"Yeah," I lie.

I'm nervous as hell. My mind is bouncing off my skull. Thoughts colliding and begging for dominance. Dad's going to kill me. No, he's not going to kill me. He's going to ground me for eternity, it'll be like literal hell on Earth. But what if he doesn't know? Maybe he thinks it was Debra Ledford, the least conservative Republican on the board. No, he knows better. Has he heard I wore a skirt? I hope not.

"Good luck?" Ian has the nerve to ask.

I yank my eyes from my house. "Really?"

He shrugs. "Yeah..."

"Thanks." I roll my eyes and pat at my legs to assure myself I changed back into pants.

"See you tomorrow," Ian says when I finally open the door and get out.

"Hopefully." I barely notice the word coming out of my mouth. The urge to jump back in is strong, but I deny it and start for the front door.

Maybe he's out. Maybe he's more worried about the papers. Maybe he won't give me a second thought. Or maybe he's asleep.

All hope comes crashing down when I walk through the door. He's in his recliner, eyes locked on me before I have a chance to cross the threshold. I tear my eyes away and try to act like nothing's up and make off for my room.

"Woah," Dad calls after me. "Where you off to?"

"My...my room," I stutter, freezing.

He sits and considers me a moment. It's like he's analyzing, waiting for me to say something stupid. Or rather something he thinks is stupid. He takes a long breath.

"You told the papers, didn't you?" he accuses me.

"What? Told them wha—" I play dumb, which *is* dumb, really dumb.

"Don't." He puts up a hand. "You told them about the dress code. Didn't you?"

I huff. Why am I hiding it? Yes. I told them. I sent them an image of it. I blew it wide open. Take that. But it doesn't come out that brazen.

"I did." I jut my chin. "They needed to know."

"Needed to know?" He looks incredulous. "And why is that? Why would they need to know?"

"Because you had no right to shove it through without people knowing." I gain a little confidence. "Not very Christian of you."

Okay, I wish I could reel that last part back in. The look on his face goes from aggravation to shock, then anger.

"I don't need *you* telling *me* what's *Christian* or not," Dad yells. "And you wore a dress to school today?!"

"I didn't wear a dress," I correct him, which I realize after the fact isn't the smartest choice, "it was a skirt."

"Skirt, dress. It doesn't matter. You *don't* wear girls' clothes. No son of mine wears skirts. You hear me?" His voice becomes aggressive. I fight the need to correct him again despite the pit growing in my stomach. "You're not a girl. You're not gay. You're just confused. That's all it is, Jacob. You'll see. You're just looking for attention. And you know, I'm this close to making you quit your job. Half the movies they play are just liberal brainwashing anyway."

"No!" I scream. He can't do that. My job is my only hope of getting a car, it's my only hope of being free from all this shit. "You can't do that."

"Oh yes I can," he says. "As long as you live in my house, you'll live by my rules. And if you can't, you'll find somewhere else."

Somewhere else? Is he threatening to kick me out? Like what the fuck?

"You would... You..." I choke on my words.

Tears well up in my eyes. How could he say that? Like all he cares about is that I'm this perfect little version of his Christian son. Not that I'm simply his son. Where is all that *love others* stuff they preach?

"If you can't listen. And it's not me doing it, it's you, Jacob." He doesn't hesitate to shift the blame.

I wish Mom was here. Maybe she'd stop him. Maybe. No, she wouldn't. She'd just stand there, crying probably.

"All I've ever wanted was for you to love *me* for *me*, and you can't even do that," I scream through my tears. "That's all

I want. Why can't you do that?"

I don't know where the words are coming from, but they're coming. And I'm not taking them back.

"I love my son. But this person you've become, that's not my son." He bites deep. "You're being something ungodly and wrong. You're not my Jacob."

SKYLAR
WEDNESDAY, SEPTEMBER 4

The wind brushes my cheek. It's all that's keeping me from sweating as I pedal down some random street. I've made it past downtown and into a neighborhood I've not ventured into before.

And you know, for the middle of a city, if you can call Kannapolis a city, there are a lot of trees. It's more like a forest with houses than a housing development with trees.

I couldn't stick around the house after school, and Seth had to work, and Imani's busy with her project. So I took off on my bike after Mom calmed down a little. She heard about the dress code thing, like everyone else in town, and she's furious. She was going on and on about how they were going to fight it. Something about lawyers and protests. I nodded and smiled the entire time. I'm glad, I am. But it's still so weird having someone who's really going to be there for me, but she was on high alert, and I just needed some air.

It's all settling in. What I caused. Me, little me. Like, how did I cause this much of a fuss? All I did was wear a freaking skirt, and people lost their goddamn minds.

Everything in my life is always a fight. I swear, nothing

can ever be easy, ever. The only difference is I have people on my side this time. Which is weird. Really weird.

I pedal faster. It's hot and the wind isn't kicking enough. It picks up the quicker I ride, and God, it feels good.

Turning the corner, I go down another street I don't know. I think that makes two right turns off the main road. If that's wrong I'll have to use GPS, it'll just be harder to ride and navigate with my phone in hand.

But something catches my eye. There's someone cradled against the trunk of a massive tree between a pair of old houses. I squint to get a better look. The sun in my face makes it difficult, so I slow down as I get closer. Whoever it is, they're bent over and their face is buried in their hands.

Wait. That's the same collared gray tee Jacob had on at school. And the shoes, I swear they're the same adidas!

I skid to a stop. The tire screeches against the sidewalk, and Jacob's head whips up. His eyes are wet, tears streaming down his cheeks.

Jacob! I mouth, but it's useless. I drop my bike on the curb and jog up to him and kneel a few feet away. I know I wouldn't want someone getting up in my space when I'm like that, so I don't.

"Sky?" he mumbles, whipping at his face and refusing to look at me.

I get my phone and start typing. "You okay?"

"Yeah," he says much too quick.

I can't *talk*, I'm not *stupid*. But now doesn't seem like the time to joke.

"Jacob, what's wrong?" I have Siri ask again. "Is it your dad?"

Jacob looks away and fixes his eyes on the grass under his feet. It was the only thing I could think of. I hear he's strict, the religious type I'm used to. I wait.

"Yeah," he says after a minute, eyes stuck on the grass.

I wait for more, but he doesn't speak. What do I do? I look around us. There's a house to either side and a few across the street. A silver hatchback zooms by, and an elderly woman is walking her dog past my bike. She doesn't seem to notice us. Something in my head says to leave, but I can't. I won't leave him here like this.

Why don't you— I start to mouth it but stop and type instead. "Why don't you walk with me? You can keep me company."

I try to make it sound like it's about me so it doesn't sound like I'm petting a hurt dog. I hate it when people do that. He looks up and meets my eyes. I blink to steady myself. How can something so vibrant and green and beautiful be so sullen and sad, yet strike me so hard? I fight back a knot in my throat and my own tears. I hate seeing people cry.

Jacob shrugs, biting nervously at his lips, and swallows. He gets up. I'm not sure what's happening, but I get up too. Is he taking me up on my offer? Hoping I don't look like an idiot, I lead him toward my bike. He follows. Okay, so he is. When we get to the curb I pick up my bike and start walking. For the first few minutes he doesn't say a word, and I leave it that way. He's hurting. I'm not going to push him.

He keeps sniffling, and I have to keep taking deep breaths to stay calm. How could anyone do something to make him feel like this? How fucked up is that?

"He knew it was me," Jacob finally says. It's just above a

whisper, and his voice is hoarse. "He knew."

I nod and give him a concerned grin. I thought he'd said his dad would probably figure it out. I guess I didn't really think about what that would mean for him. I didn't expect this.

"He threatened to kick me out and to make me quit my job," he goes on, talking quicker now. "He can't do that, I need my job. It's the only way I'm getting out of this damn town. I need my job."

I keep nodding. It feels so pathetic, just nodding, nodding, nodding. I want to tell him I get it. But I can't type worth shit and push this bike at the same time, so I stop and prop it against my hip while I type.

"I don't mean to be an ass, but could you push my bike so I can talk?" Siri asks. I point at my phone to make sure he understands.

"Oh… Uh, sure." He wipes some tears away and takes the bike. "And he's going to make me go back to *counseling* with our pastor."

"Counseling?" Siri asks. With his pastor? Not that. My foster parents had me in that when I came out before I reported them. It's torture, pure and simple.

"Yeah. If they had the money they'd send me off to one of those pray the gay away places, but he's using it all on his campaign, thankfully, I guess," Jacob spits. He pauses to take a breath. "He said I'm not his son, not while I'm gay. Like, how stupid is that?"

I've heard of the places he's talking about, the camps. I think they were outlawed where I come from, but maybe not here. I wouldn't be surprised.

"I'm sorry," I say. I am. I know how it feels. To want your dad or mom to love you. I've not told anyone down here much about my family, but he needs to know he's not alone, so I start typing. "I get it. My parents, my real parents, hated me. I don't remember much about them. I was seven I think when the state took me away from them, but I remember them hitting me and screaming at me because I couldn't talk after I got sick. The foster homes weren't any better. They didn't beat me, but they always ended up sending me back to the group home. The last ones were mean. They tried to make me go to church counseling when I came out, but I reported them."

"Oh." The word hangs from his lip.

"Yeah," Siri says. My last foster parents sound a lot like Jacob's family. But my real parents, there's part of me that misses them, which is weird, because I don't remember much about them except the beatings. I only have flashes of what they look like in my mind. No pictures, no good memories. Most of what I feel toward them is anger. "I know how it feels."

"Wish I had parents like your new ones. I wish I could get new parents like that," he says.

I wince.

"No, you don't," I type and send it. "At least you know your family. And you've got Ian too. Getting passed around like a piece of clothing, like some hand-me-down…it sucks. I am glad I'm with the Grays now though. They're pretty great, but still."

He nods, and it gets quiet again. I swipe at the sweat building on my forehead. The wind's died down and the shade from the arching trees isn't enough. I chance looking at him. It's not like other times when I'd admire his face or when his shirt comes up a little and I manage to glimpse a little stomach. It's not like that all. I see something different here.

He's like me. He's broken, hurting. This, all of this, is not what I expected, it's not the idea of him I had in my head. It makes him more real to me. And honestly, it makes him beautiful. He's trying so hard to be himself. All he wants is for the people he loves to love him back as he is. I get that. And I'll never get the chance to have that. My real parents are never coming back, and I guess that's best. They probably don't even know where I'm at, probably don't care.

"You know, I don't know how to ride a bike," Jacob confesses, and then his shoulders slump. "God, why'd I just admit that. So lame."

"Nah, that's not lame," I let Siri assure him. But honestly, I'm shook. Like, how do you reach seventeen, or however old he is, and not know how to ride a bike? "You never tried?"

"No, I tried. When I was younger. My, uh, dad…" He pauses to cough. His face has dried up for the most part. "He tried. But I wrecked when he was teaching me and tore up my arm. I refused to try after that, and he just stopped trying."

Oh. I can't imagine. Riding a bike is like freedom. It's just you and the bicycle, on your own, doing whatever you want. It's sort of great.

I nod, nibbling at my bottom lip while I debate the words I'm typing into my phone before pressing Talk.

"Want me to teach you?" Siri asks.

I look him dead in the eye, refusing to appear unsure. I want him to say yes. Not going to lie, I want a reason to hang around.

"Uh…" His lips twitch into an almost smile and then dim into embarrassment. "Maybe. It's stupid. I'm almost eighteen and I can't ride a damn bike."

"It's not stupid," I tell him. It's unusual, but not stupid.

"You sure?" he asks, but there's so much reservation in his voice.

"Nothing stupid about it." I double down, I just wish Siri had a little more conviction in his voice.

"No, not that." A laugh breaks through and even a tiny smile. He looks away and shakes his head. And honestly, seeing that is everything. "Teaching me to ride."

Oh! That! My lips form a massive O, and I slap my palm to my forehead, which gets an even bigger laugh.

"It went right over my head. Yes! Of course! I'd love to," Siri tells him.

"Now?" Jacob nods toward my bike.

I nod and step up to the bike. Am I seriously about to teach Jacob to ride a bike?

SKYLAR
SATURDAY, SEPTEMBER 7

Everyone's busy. Except me. Of course.

Seth has an early shift at the bowling alley and Imani's out with her mom birthday shopping for her little brother, who I still haven't met. She calls him the "little shit", but I'm pretty sure she likes him.

Mom's at a ladies' meeting at church, and I think they're cleaning after. Apparently all the ladies get together for breakfast once a month and do a deep clean so the church can focus its funds on helping the community. And Dad was working on his Sunday school outline for tomorrow when I walked into the kitchen to get some lunch—he teaches the College & Career Class every other week.

So I took my bike out for a spin. It's cloudy, but at least the sun isn't beating my skin and the wind's light. I pedal quicker and the wind slaps harder.

Oh, I got Jacob to accept my follow request on Instagram. I texted him last night and told him he *had* to let me follow him. I mean, we're friends now, right? But I also think I get why his account is private. I don't think he wants his parents to find it.

It's mostly normal, and definitely fits the guy I know. Comic and video game memes and stills, most of which I don't recognize, the occasional selfie with Ian and Eric, pictures of his band, The Nevermore, playing in dimly lit venues. And then there's the less frequent, but very notable, thirst trap. At least that's what I'm calling them, and I'm here for it. There's nothing shirtless—I went through all of them to see—but plenty of half-unbuttoned shirts, which is enough for me. He's a lot more comfortable on Insta.

I take a right and cross the railroad tracks into downtown and past Veterans Park with its cool waterfall display. The music in my AirPods drowns out the "city" sounds. The theater comes up on my left, and I spy through the ticket booth window, but it's no one I know.

I hang the next turn and end up in Research Park, which is basically a bunch of oversized brick buildings that are so obviously newer than the rest. My tires glide over the new path encircling the campus. I don't know where I'm heading.

I make a wide circle around a woman and her cute pitch-black dog—I think it's what they call a Schnoodle—then take the next street. Trees hang over the road here like a green patchwork canopy, and the shade is more than welcome. I slow down, taking the bumpy sidewalk at a leisurely pace. Tree roots shoot past neatly manicured lawns and burrow their way under concrete, causing it to bow and bust.

It's quieter here. The sound of car engines and work equipment beeping and whirring is dim, almost gone until a tiny green car straight out of the nineties comes flying by. It sounds wound up tight and as it passes, the ruckus whirs to a deep hum and disappears altogether.

Down the street a new noise emerges. I squint. Music?

I pedal harder. It gets louder, more like a roar and crash. The bass clears up first, then guitar. Is there a concert out here? In the middle of a neighborhood?

I pass two more houses before I reach the source, and I stop when two guys and their instruments come into view inside a mostly empty garage. Ian and Jacob. I laugh to myself and watch from the road for a moment. Crazy I'd find him again, and not even in the same neighborhood. It's not my type of music, and nothing like the concert Jacob took me to. It's harder, much harder.

Bass quakes the ground. Jacob strums the guitar strapped around his chest, and the notes fly from the amplifiers. It's good. It's actually good. Then it crashes to a screeching halt, and I flinch at the harsh squeal.

"Sky?" Jacob spots me.

I've been caught. I grin as big as I can and pedal up to their set.

"What are you doing over here?" Jacob asks, letting his guitar hang loose at his side. It looks dangerous to me, but it's his guitar. He can be as careless with it as he likes.

"You live over here?" Ian asks.

I go to open my mouth but remember how useless that'll be. Waving at Ian, I take my phone out.

"No. Just riding around before I go to the coffee shop," I type. "You two are good."

"Thought you didn't like rock." Ian cocks his head and hammers out a volley of notes.

"He doesn't," Jacob answers for me.

"Not my favorite," Siri explains, "but I can deal with it."

"He can deal with it," Jacob swings around and shakes his head at Ian. "You hear that? Such hatefulness. I mean really."

My fingers fly over my phone, but I keep messing up. I get it right finally and hit Talk. "You know, like I'll listen to it. Just not usually voluntarily."

"Is that supposed to be better?" Ian asks.

I shrug. Guess not.

"Did you say you're going to the coffee shop?" Jacob suddenly forgets I don't like their music.

I nod.

"Mind if I come?" he asks.

Uh, I... My mind races. I wasn't expecting this. Hell, I wasn't expecting to see him again until Monday. And yes! Please! But no, I can't say it like that. So instead I keep it cool and force myself to type slowly.

"You sure you don't need more practice?" Siri answers with a question.

"I can't tell if you're being sarcastic or serious." Jacob eyes me, but he's grinning.

"He definitely needs more practice." Ian throws it out there. "A lot more."

"No one asked you," Jacob yells back without taking his eyes off me, waiting for me to break.

I can't do it anymore. A smile paints across my lips and I start typing.

"Sarcastic. This stupid thing makes sarcasm impossible," I tell him.

Jacob cocks his head and gives me the middle finger, but the smile on his face betrays him. Behind him Ian rolls his eyes and huffs.

"I'm borrowing your bike." Jacob races into the back of the garage and places his guitar carefully on a stand along the back wall.

"You don't ride bikes. Hell, you don't know how." Ian gives him the most incredulous look.

"Do now." Jacob beams. Ian's face radiates with confusion. "Sky taught me the other day."

"Sky taught..." Ian starts rambling and it becomes a blur of whispered words. But Jacob's smiling so I guess it's just Ian being Ian. "And Eric's going to flip if we don't get this right. That gig is coming up!"

"So?" Jacob asks again, ignoring everything Ian said.

"Don't scratch my bike," Ian huffs.

"Thanks, man! We can practice more later, or maybe tomorrow." Jacob grabs the bike and rolls out next to me. "Ready?"

JACOB

"You like romance? Like romance books?" I ask. Skylar's definitely the softboy type, but I try not to make assumptions.

He slides the book back on the shelf. I didn't see the title, but the cover wasn't spaceships and monsters. More like two guys holding hands, which is also a surprise to find in a little bookstore in a tiny conservative town, but not here, not in Sandra's shop.

Sky nods nervously. Did that come off judgey? I didn't mean to! He's typing, but I want to make sure he isn't offended.

"That's cool, I like them too." I do damage control. It's not a lie. I do. They're just not my go-to. I prefer scary shit, the type of thing that'll get my heart pumping.

"I do," his phone says. "They're the only way I'm ever going to experience it, you know?"

"Romance?" I squint. Why would he say that?

He nods and shrugs, picking up another.

"You'll get a romance story." I cough. It sounds cheesy as hell, but I'd sort of like to give him one. But I don't know how to say that. And it's weird to think about. Like, he can't talk.

That weirded me out just weeks ago. Now it's this normal part of life.

A puff of air huffs from Skylar's nose and his lips skew. I don't think he believes it. He starts typing, and I'm eagerly waiting to hear what he has to say.

"You like your job at the theater?" isn't what I expected.

"Uh… Yeah, I guess." Guess he didn't want to continue down romance road. "Most of the time. Free movies and all. You should come sometime. I can get you discounted tickets, remember?"

"Cool," his phone spits out. That was quick. I wonder if he has like a list of quick replies on there. "I'll see if I can get Imani and Seth to go sometime."

"That'd be cool." I nod and sip my iced latte. I've a question burning in my head. It's been there a few weeks now, and I think maybe it's all right to ask finally. But I hold on to it a little longer. Instead, I eye him suspiciously. "You looking for a job?"

"Are they hiring?" His eyes widen before his phone can speak, the little green dino swinging from the case.

"I don't know, maybe," I tell him. I don't even know why I said it. Like, I haven't a clue. But it'd be cool if he worked with Ian and me, right? "Want me to check?"

"Sure," his phone comes back. "Not really looking. But I might."

"Okay." I nod.

A minute passes and neither of us says anything. I act like I'm looking at books too, but I honestly couldn't tell you a single one I've looked at.

I'm going to do it. I'm going to ask.

"Hey, so," I start, which is anything but a good start. It's like screaming, *I'm about to ask you a scary question*, or *brace yourself, this is about to get awkward*. But I can't stop now. "Have you ever been able to talk or were you born…mute?"

There it is. I asked! I put the question out there, and it's not as scary as it was a minute ago. He's smiling at me like he knows it's been eating at me, and starts typing.

"Yes. A long time ago. And I prefer 'nonverbal'," he explains. "But it's okay. Not a big deal."

"I'm sorry, and you don't have to explain. I shouldn't have asked," I apologize.

He smiles and leans against the bookshelf, his eyes going back to his phone. I allow mine to linger on his brilliant brown and green irises for just a moment, short enough he hopefully doesn't notice.

"It's okay," Siri, Skylar, says. "I could talk until I was like five, I think. I don't remember it. It's what the doctors and orphanage told me. I don't ever remember talking. I don't have a clue what my voice sounds like, or sounded like. I got sick, real bad laryngitis, and it developed into something called muscle tension dysphonia, which basically means my vocal cords are screwed up."

The words carry no emotion, no cadence beyond what his phone's cold British accent allows. But I can still hear it, somehow, somewhere deep in the deadpan words. He doesn't ever remember talking? He doesn't know what his own voice sounds like? If it were me it'd be resentment, anger. I wouldn't want to repeat it to anyone if I were in his shoes.

"I'm sorry." It comes out quiet. I don't know what I expected. But it wasn't this. I didn't expect to feel like this about it.

"It's okay. I just wish I knew what my voice sounded like," his phone tells me. I'm about to say I'm sorry again because stupid me doesn't know what to say now that I've opened this up, but he types something out real quick. "So the dress code policy is getting a vote Monday, right?"

"Uh…yeah," I react, not expecting that to come up. I swallow back this heavy feeling in my throat and refocus on the question. "Yeah, they're trying, at least. The local Pride group is planning a protest outside the school board, big signs, bunch of e-mails, and they're making calls too."

I would make calls, but I know all the board members, and when I say it's pointless, I mean it's pointless. None of them are going to listen to the gay son of the chairman of the very board they're on.

"Yeah, I e-mailed them all," Skylar's phone says. I don't know why, but it surprises me.

"Even my dad?" My eyes fly open. "How'd that go?"

"He hasn't responded." Skylar shrugs.

"Figures."

SKYLAR

MONDAY, SEPTEMBER 9

Mr. Walters kept his promise. Jacob's plan worked.

"Come on, Skylar." Mom taps my shoulder. I think the atmosphere is getting to her.

Jacob said his dad originally had no plan to hold a public forum. He'd only planned to rush a vote tonight. But he had a change of heart. He did what he promised the papers this morning instead, what he claimed to have planned the entire time. They set a day for a public forum in the school gymnasium in October.

I follow Mom and Dad outside. The chants have died out, but the protestors still line both sides of the path under the bright blanket of the street lamps. On the right are my people. Their signs proclaiming *WHAT ABOUT ACCEPTANCE* and *CLOTHES HAVE NO GENDER* now hang at their sides, parading away from the building. On the opposite side are the *DRESSES ARE FOR GIRLS*, *BRING BACK REAL MEN*, and *DEUTERONOMY 22:5 BOYS IN GIRLS CLOTHES IS AN ABOMINATION*. Oh, and my favorite *STAND UP FOR RELIGIOUS FREEDOM*. Like, what? How stupid can you get? How is me wearing the skirt I literally have on right now hurting your religious freedom? What about my freedom?

I swear they live to feel like they're oppressed and not the oppressors. I roll my eyes and walk the path between them, their glares taunting me.

"You need to turn to God, young man," some gray-bearded guy in the crowd yells, pointing and shaking his hand. "Repent of your demonic ways and be saved."

My face scrunches. Demonic? Dad puts a hand on my back and urges me forward. The other side erupts.

"Big man, heckling a kid," an equally old guy on the other side yells.

"It also says love thy neighbor," a woman about Mom's age counters, her long brown hair flipping over her shoulder.

"God is not mocked," the old religious guy screams back. He sounds so angry.

"Being gay is a sin. Stop letting the devil confuse you," a boy from my school joins in. I didn't even know this was about being gay. I thought it was about boys wearing skirts, but I guess it's all the same to them. "Or you're going to hell."

"Come on," Dad urges.

We slip past and start up the sidewalk.

"This is ridiculous," Mom complains. "All that for a dress code. Really? He's just a kid, and they're out here screaming at him."

"They're not real Christians, honey," Dad reassures her and then looks at me. "That's not what real Christianity looks like, Skylar. I promise you that. That's just hate and fear."

I nod, but I don't know. That's the only side of religion I've ever seen, except at my new church. It's different there.

"We have a chance, right?" I have my phone ask. There's a

forum set up, so that's good, right?

"Of course." Mom smiles, but there's reservation in her voice.

Jacob hadn't bothered to cover his doubt at lunch today. He straight up told me not to get my hopes up, that we should still fight it, but not to hope too much. And to be honest, the tiny hope that had lodged itself in my chest is shifting and cracking. I remind myself it doesn't technically hurt me not to wear a skirt to school. It's stupid though. It shouldn't matter. Hell, this shouldn't even be an issue. It's like some fight out of the damn dark ages. No, wait. They all wore dresses back then, didn't they? So that doesn't even work.

And I'd thought about wearing a dress, like a full-on dress, to Homecoming if I went. Not like I'm going, but still, I'd thought about it.

We cross the parking lot and I slip in the back seat.

"We're going to fight this, Skylar," Dad assures me.

I nod at him in the rearview mirror, then pull out my phone. Jacob might like to know what happened. It's exactly what he said, but whatever. I type out a quick text.

SKYLAR: Your dad set up a forum at the school on October 10. It hasn't passed yet. ::shrug::

JACOB

MONDAY, SEPTEMBER 9

My phone buzzes in my pocket. It's slow tonight. It's always slow on Monday nights.

"You really think J.J. Abrams can fix how badly Johnson screwed up the last one?" Ian casts a doubting glare at me, leaning against the popcorn machine.

We just watched the trailer for the new *Star Wars* movie on his phone, and now Ian's in full geek mode. I can deal with it, but sci-fi just isn't my shit.

"He did it with *The Force Awakens*." I shrug, checking my phone. The buzz was a text from Sky.

"I guess. But how is he going to make it all make sense?" Ian keeps going.

I let it hang while I open the text. Ian hates it when I do this, but I've been waiting for this all evening. What did my dad do? And is Sky okay? I mean, I'm sure he's okay, but you know.

SKYLAR: Your dad set up a forum at the school on October 10. It hasn't passed yet. ::shrug::

Dad kept his word. I mean that makes sense. He's not a liar, even if he was trying to be underhanded about the whole deal.

JACOB: Thats good! No church dress code...yet!

"Skylar?" Ian asks, and I nod. "How'd the board meeting go?"

I'm glad he's asking. Politics has never interested Ian much, about as much as it has me. I just got stuck with it because of Dad. But he knows this one's important to me.

"Sounds like it went okay. They scheduled a forum instead of voting on it," I tell him. "I've got to figure out something else to help stop it."

"You've done a lot already," Ian says before a lady distracts him at the register for a refill.

Have I? But it's my dad who's screwing shit up. And he's messing it up for Skylar and who knows who else.

"You leaked it to the papers." Ian makes it sound like this big thing, but is it? "And don't say that's not big. Because it is. Had you not, you know your dad would be ramming the new dress code through just as hard as you want to—"

"Don't, just don't." I throw up a hand and cough, but a laugh betrays me. "Dirty fuck."

"You've thought worse," Ian says, grinning.

My brow raises. Denying it would be a lie.

"The point is, you've done a lot. Hell, you're grounded again already," he reminds me.

Oh yeah. Dad decided I'm grounded until Saturday for the whole paper spy informant thing and wearing a skirt to school. It's the same rules as the last time, so I hung out at the coffee shop between school and work today. He was going for a month, but Mom managed to calm him down and got most of my sentence commuted. But I had to take off my nail polish too. It was the single term for the deal.

"Yeah, yeah, I know." I wave my hands in the air. "I just want to stop it from happening."

And now that it's almost time for me to get off work, I don't want to go home. Maybe by some miracle he'll be worn out and in bed early and I'll be able to skip out on the drama. Please God, if you can grant me one thing, just give me this.

My phone buzzes again.

SKYLAR: Fingers crossed.

JACOB: Got ur back!

"I know," Ian says. "I'll help."

That's not what I was expecting.

"Really?" I lock on to him.

"Sure. Just don't ask me to wear a dress, okay?" He grimaces. "That's my limit."

"But you'd be cute in a—"

"No, just no." He puts a hand up, smiling.

I nod. And suddenly a thought pops into my head.

Sky uses sign language, right? I roll back through my memories. Today at lunch when he and Imani got one of her stones out and did a chant because Sky was nervous. Nope. This weekend at the coffee shop. Nope. Further back. His birthday party. Wait. I think he did. I think.

Hell, why am I thinking so hard on this? Just ask.

JACOB: U know sign language?

"You wouldn't know if Sky knows sign language, would you?" I ask Ian. It's worth a shot. He does have third block with him.

"Uh… I don't know… Maybe?" Ian shrugs.

"Well, you're absolutely no help." I roll my eyes.

"Thank you," Ian laughs, and my phone buzzes in my hand.

SKYLAR: Yeah, why?

JACOB: Just wondering.

SKYLAR

THURSDAY, SEPTEMBER 12

This week has been crazy and I sort of just want it to be over. Everyone keeps talking about me like I'm either this icon or a drag on society. To some I'm pioneering the way for inclusion, and to others I'm everything that's wrong with boys today.

And Blake came by our lunch table yesterday and didn't leave until Jacob and Seth almost got detention. Bexley was showing how much of a bitch she could be. Slamming her hand on the table and telling me how I'm not a real man. Suddenly I became the ugliest and stupidest person in the school, the "ugly little bitch that's too stupid to even talk" were Blake's words.

I had to beg Jacob and Seth to sit down. I don't need both of them in trouble over people as dumb as those two. They just wanted a show, to get under my skin, an excuse to cause trouble.

The number of times I've been called the f-slur skyrocketed too. Like, people need to get a more original insult.

I pedal past the research institute's brick buildings and onto a familiar street where the trees shield me from the sun and their branches intermingle over the road. Julia Michaels plays through my headphones, sending me down the street with her smooth voice in my ears.

I switch into a driveway, trying to tell myself I didn't mean to come here, but I'm lying to myself. Especially now that the reason I came isn't even here.

I pull out my headphones as Ian waves.

"Hey, Sky," he yells, but my eyes are on Eric. I've not officially met him yet.

I nod, looking around the equipment, hoping maybe I just missed him. But Jacob's still grounded. I don't know why I thought he'd be here.

"This is Skylar," Ian tells Eric.

Eric eyes me a second. His wavy hair droops over his forehead, and his blue eyes are sort of cold. He steps forward, small arms swaying. He's even taller than Jacob, so I'm really looking up to him.

"Hey, I'm Eric—"

"Ted, his name is Ted," Ian interrupts him.

"Eric," he repeats. "I'm Jacob's *other* friend," he tells me, rolling his eyes. A smile spreads across his face, making big dimples in his cheeks. I nod and put on a grin. Is it Eric or Ted? "I've heard about you."

Who hasn't at this point? I wish they hadn't.

"Hey," I have Siri say. "Good to meet you. Jacob's still grounded?"

It's one of those stupid questions you ask when you don't have anything else to say. The type you know the answer to.

"Yeah." Ian shrugs. "Rest in peace, poor friend."

I grimace at him, but he laughs.

"Sorry," I tell them.

"For what?" Eric asks.

"For him getting grounded," my phone explains. "It's my fault."

Eric and Ian break into laughter. Eric's making a real show of it, leaning over and slapping his legs.

"You've got lots to learn," Eric says between laughs. "He's always getting grounded. His dad's insane, like I swear the man lives to ground him."

"He really does," Ian agrees.

"That's sort of horrible," I have my phone say. I knew his dad was a bit much, but this sounds next level.

"You just have to know his parents," Eric answers.

"Have you texted him?" Ian asks out of nowhere.

"Why?" I type. He's grounded. He can't text, he doesn't even have his phone. Plus, I'm not that worried about it. Really!

"I think he'd like it if you did." Ian raises an eyebrow and smiles at me. Eric rolls his eyes, but he's laughing as he nods in agreement.

I can feel my cheeks heating up. They have to be mistaken. I'm positive he couldn't care less if I texted him. Or wait... No, they're just saying he'd like to hear from a friend. *God, Skylar, shut your damn mind up!*

"But I thought he didn't have his phone," I type.

"Nah, his mom gave it back to him," Eric tells me. "He just Snapped me a lovely middle finger like ten minutes ago."

My body shakes a little with a laugh.

"You should text him," Ian says with a smile.

I shrug and type. "Maybe. I'm going to go. Enjoy your

practice."

Which translated means yes, I definitely will, but I have to leave first so I don't look too eager.

"See ya," Ian says as I pull my bike back onto the sidewalk.

"Good meeting you," Eric throws back.

I wave and take off.

A thought crosses my mind as I pedal past the house. If he got his phone back, and they're so determined he'd like to hear from me, why wouldn't he just text me? It's a valid question, right? I think on it a moment but decide it's stupid. There could be a million reasons.

Once I'm a few blocks away from Ian's place I brake to a stop and pull out my phone. It feels different opening his message thread for some reason. I stare at the tiny digital keyboard. What do I say? How is it so hard to think of something to say?

Finally, my fingers start tapping the screen.

SKYLAR: Heard you got your phone back.

JACOB

FRIDAY, SEPTEMBER 13

Rain pelts the windshield. It's warm, which means it's going to be humid when it stops, and I hate humidity. It gets up in everything and feels miserable.

"When you getting your own car again?" Ian asks, steering us down the road.

"One day," I groan. It's one of those subjects I don't have an answer for. But I'm seriously trying. Cars are expensive, plus the gas, and the insurance, and what if it messes up? And I don't want just anything. "I want to save up like two thousand or something, you know? Get something at least half decent."

If I had a car, I could do my own thing. I wouldn't be asking Mom for hers or bumming rides from Ian and Eric. I could just go wherever, whenever. Maybe I'd drive over to Sky's and pick him up and take him somewhere. The thought makes me nervous. The problem there is getting the nerve to be like *hey, want to go somewhere with me* and it not sounding like a date, because, well, that's exactly what I want, but he probably doesn't.

"You think you're getting something *half decent* for two

grand?" Ian doesn't sound convinced. The car bounces over a pothole and his eyes shoot back to the road.

"Life, Ian, I choose life." I grip the door handle.

"Shut up!" he snaps. "It's going to take you forever to get two grand from the theater."

"Why you think I still don't have a car?" I complain.

"Good point." Ian nods. I think he forgot to finish combing today, the black mop on his head is messier than usual. But I'm not mentioning it.

I check my phone. The screen's blank. Not going to lie, I was hoping Sky might text or Snap me. We talked a good deal last night, well, texted.

I had nothing better to do stuck at home. But it wasn't so bad. We even exchanged music. It sort of became a mini intro to music class. I listened to his pop stuff, and he gave my rock a chance. I still can't say Ariana Grande is my thing, but he had a few good ones. Oh, and Skylar's favorite, Myylo! It's so different from what I'm used to, quirky, blunt, but I can't lie. I liked it. Like, enough that I convinced Ian and Eric to do a cover or two.

Skylar liked the calmer songs I sent him, but not much else. At least he's honest, right? He'd already heard some Blackbear, so there was a little common ground.

"You think Sky drove by your place yesterday looking for me?" I pop the question, half wishing I'd left it in my head. "No, don't answer that."

"Uh, yeah. Why else would he?" Ian eyes me like I'm stupid.

I can't withhold the grin that sprawls across my lips. But I keep reminding myself it doesn't mean anything. He likes to see Imani too, but it's not like *that*. Calm down.

"You really like him, don't you?" Ian asks out of nowhere.

At first I don't answer. I glance at Ian and then out the passenger window. Rains splats on the glass, streaking horizontally. Hell, I started practicing sign language this week. And why? For *him*, so I could talk to him. So it'd be easier to talk to him. And what's been on my brain twenty-four seven lately? Him.

I shrug, pursing my lips.

"Maybe."

SKYLAR

FRIDAY, SEPTEMBER 13

"Here." Imani pulls out a small purple chunk of crystal, striated with bands of browns and grays. "We're going to preempt people's shit today."

I hold out my hands and Imani places the stone or crystal—I don't really know which—in my hand.

"What're we doing?" Jacob leans over the table.

"It's a charoite stone. I think I'm saying that right." Imani shrugs, folding my hands over it and wrapping them in her own. "It helps with peace and wisdom. And gives you a better state of mind to deal with people, like you know, Bexley."

"Ah," Jacob sighs.

If it'll help, I tell her.

"Even voodoo shit?" Ian pipes in from the corner of the table.

I catch Jacob giving him a look, but I focus on Imani. She isn't fazed. I don't understand witch stuff, but from all I've learned the past weeks, it's not like people think. It's more about peace and kindness than any Christian I know, except my parents, of course. They're like cool Christians.

And today's the first day since the board meeting that I'm

wearing a skirt. So I'll take it.

"Okay." Imani breathes out and back in and closes her eyes. "I diminish all feelings of fear, doubt, and anxiety around you. May you absorb all the enthusiasm and joy the day ahead may provide."

"Thanks," I type once her hands open and she takes the stone back. "And speaking of the devil."

"Devil, witchcraft." Ian laughs, but everyone at the table glares at him. "Sorry. Not funny."

I nod toward Bexley and Blake. They see us too, but just glare instead of approaching. Good. I don't want to test Imani's stone just yet.

"It's okay," Imani tells Ian. "Wrong, but still."

"Nah, I'm sorry." Ian droops his head over the table. "It's just…different, I guess. I know —"

"It's okay, really. I get it. If I know you, you've been taught it's devil worship," she tells him. Most people would get bent out of shape had someone said that about their faith. But she doesn't. She's calm about it. "Just do better?"

Ian's eyes widen, like he doesn't know if it was a cut down or genuine request, but he softens. "Yeah."

There's a moment of tension at the table. No one knows what to say next. So much for peace, but I guess that *was* mainly for me and the bullies.

"You want to go to the shop tomorrow?" Jacob turns to me.

The shop? Me? I think he's talking about the coffee shop, but I could be wrong, so I ask.

"Like the coffee shop? The bookstore?" my phone asks.

"Yeah, what other shop would you go to?" He smiles.

"Walmart, sandwich shop, tool shop—" Seth tries, but Imani cuts him off.

"Just stop," she laughs.

I smile at Seth. He tries. He really does try.

"Aren't we practicing tomorrow?" Ian speaks up. I think a nerve just got hit.

"Yeah, but not until five," Jacob reminds him.

Ian nods, mulling it over. Guess it checks out because he shrugs.

"Sure," I type and hit Talk. Why not?

"Great!" Jacob grins.

I swear his cheeks turn a light shade of pink. But I've been wrong before.

JACOB
SATURDAY, SEPTEMBER 14

JACOB: U still want to go to the shop?

We planned on ten, but I want to be sure he hasn't changed his mind. People do that sometimes.

I slip on a pair of shorts and scowl at my plain nails. The black has become so much of a staple that they look weird without any polish. *Just remember, you don't want to get grounded again. Not just yet, at least.*

My phone dings.

SKYLAR: YES! ::smiling face::

JACOB: OMW then!

I make sure I have everything, which is basically that I'm wearing clothes and have my phone and wallet. On the way through the kitchen, I snatch Mom's keys off the counter.

"Where you off to all smiley?" Mom catches me before I can escape.

"The coffee shop." I turn and lean against the counter. I can't stop smiling. "Gonna go read."

"All right." She smiles back. "You're definitely my only child who enjoys reading that much. You *didn't* get that from me."

"Then who?" I throw it back and head for the door.

Mom starts to answer. I know who she's thinking, but I don't stop for her to say it. I don't want to hear it. I shouldn't have asked.

Five minutes later, almost on the dot, I pull up at Skylar's and turn down my music. Don't need his parents thinking I'm one of those teens, even if I sort of am.

So, do I get out and walk to the door? Or is that more of a date thing? Because this isn't a date. Definitely not a date. This is just two guys hanging out, totally platonic. That's it. And if going up to the door makes it look like a date, then that's a no. But if I don't, will his parents think I'm rude?

The front door swings open, saving me from the decision, and Skylar trots out in the cutest black skirt. I think it's the one Imani got him, but I could be wrong. He's so cute. He waves, and I wave back as his dad walks out behind him and follows Skylar up to my car.

Skylar opens the passenger door, and the first thought that hits me is *dammit, I was supposed to open it for him*, immediately followed by *no, Jacob, it's not a date!*

"Hey," I say once he's in, and he nods. I have to remind myself that he's not being rude, he just can't say it back. I should know that by now.

"Hey, Jacob." His dad, Mr. Gray, props his arms on the open passenger window, looking at me across the cutest boy in North Carolina. I turn the music all the way off right as someone starts screaming the F word. *Why me?* He puts on a sly grin, and Skylar shoots his eyes to the floor. "I hadn't a chance to thank you yet."

"Thank me?" I don't understand, especially now.

"For standing up for Skylar," he tells me. I look at Sky. His lips are skewed nervously, and he tilts his head, glancing at me and shrugging naively. Then his dad continues, "At school with this Blake fellow, and the whole dress code thing. It took a lot of courage to tell the papers. And you're giving us a chance to stop it. Thanks."

"Uh... Y-you're welcome, Mr. Gray," I stutter. It needed to be done, and as for the bullies, that's not happening while I'm around, not to Sky. "You don't need to thank me though."

"Well, I am." Mr. Gray grins and steps away from the car. "Be careful with my son now. You two have fun."

Skylar huffs and shakes his head. I'm about to respond, and Mr. Gray is in the process of turning when he stops and laughs. "And it's just Bob. None of this Mr. Gray junk, please."

"Okay, Mr.... I mean Bob. Bye." I wave and put the car in reverse before I can mess up again.

His dad waves as we roll back onto the road and I put it in drive. It's so weird seeing a dad like that. He walked out the door with Skylar in a skirt like it was the most normal thing in the world. I mean it should be. But I can't imagine my dad doing that.

"How's it going?" I ask Sky.

His fingers tap on his phone, and I wait for the response. Suddenly this spike of doubt hits me. This is sort of awkward, waiting for a response. But it always is. Why is it only hitting me now?

"Good," Siri announces. "So been looking forward to the shop. I need coffee so bad right now. And I'm getting a new book this time."

The feeling passes the moment Siri translates his written

words into the air. And it's like it never was.

"Same. Except I brought a book with me," I tell him. It seemed like a bad idea to bring a book at first. It's sort of a backup plan in case things get awkward and quiet. Gotta be prepared. Plus, he might think this is more than it is if I expect him to talk the entire time.

"What are you reading?" his phone asks after a few seconds.

I wonder what it would be like to sign instead of using his phone. I've been practicing with YouTube videos. And I think I've got some of it down, but it's harder than I thought it'd be. I was looking up how to describe Skylar, and shy was the word I wanted to use. Well, I have to be real careful, because if I pull my hand away from my face too far, I could be calling him a prostitute. Like, what?

"*The Last Astronaut*," I tell him.

His face skews and he taps out a quick reply.

"Still?"

"All right, bitch, I'm a slow reader. Calm it down," I fight back, laughing a little extra just to make sure he knows I'm joking.

He shakes his head as I pull into the shop parking lot and take the only available spot. It's busy for 10:00 a.m. I get out without waiting, pausing long enough for him to follow before walking up the ramp and immersing myself in the smell of old books and coffee.

"Good morning, Jacob," Sandra yells when I walk around the corner, and then she notices Skylar, "and Skylar! This is early for y'all!"

She's looking right at me on that last part. Wow, just call

me out. I don't have an answer for that.

"Just woke up early," I lie, sort of. I did, just not for no reason, but I'm *not* explaining.

We order drinks and spend a few minutes browsing until Skylar chooses a book called *Warcross*. He said it's like this future super high tech alternate reality story. Sounds interesting, but probably too sci-fi-ish for my taste. We go back into the Christian Room — it's just quieter back here — and plop into the two big comfy green chairs.

"So you don't like *Star Wars* or *Star Trek*?" Skylar's phone asks.

"Like?" I grimace. "I mean, that depends. *Star Wars* is a bit much. Too unbelievable. *Star Trek?* Which one you talking about?"

He thinks about it a moment, green-brown eyes scaling the plain ceiling. His lips are pooched out in thought. A decision is made and he starts typing.

"The new ones?" he asks.

"I can deal with those. But honestly, they're still not my thing," I admit. Like they're cool, at times. But the whole space thing and aliens, I don't know, it's just too out there for me most of the time. "Definitely can't do the old ones."

He rolls his eyes and huffs, and Siri condemns me, "So uncultured. Laughing emoji."

Oh my God, he made Siri talk out an emoji again. I laugh and shake my head. So cringe.

"Really? Laughing emoji?" I roll my eyes. I'm about to say *just laugh*, but I stop myself. He doesn't really laugh. Not like we do. I mean he does, but there's no sound, just air, or this sort of wheezing sound.

He shrugs, and the conversation keeps going. I guess sci-fi is a favorite of his. By the time I'm halfway done with my drink he's already listed off at least six shows and movies along with why I should give them a chance. I've only seen one of them.

"Have you seen *Covenant*, the new one?" I ask.

"Of course, I just had to cover my eyes a few times," his phone tells me.

"Makes sense, it's bloody as," and I mouth *fuck* so I don't say it in the middle of the Christian Room. Sky's not a blood and guts fan. He said he has to look away when it gets too nasty, especially anything involving eyes or sawing off body parts.

"Yeah. How about we read some?" Skylar suggests.

Read? My instinct is to ask if I said something wrong. Does he not want to talk anymore? Did I do something? But I hold back the urge. We did come to a coffee shop that has books, and he did pick out a new one.

"Yeah, of course." I nod and pick up the book I brought.

Sky does the same and at once his eyes are lost inside it. I linger a second longer, admiring the way his jaw angles into his chin and his pink lips pooch while he studies the page.

Something stirs in my chest, and I yank my eyes away. *Read, Jacob.*

SKYLAR

SATURDAY, SEPTEMBER 14

My eyes dart from one end of the page to the next without catching a single word. I'm not reading. Not yet, at least.

I'm loving everything about being here with Jacob. The ride here, even if Dad made it sound like I was going on a date. I wish. Browsing the books, seeing what Jacob's hand gravitated toward—mostly horror and techno-thrillers. And sitting here talking, it's just…nice.

I keep reminding myself that just because he's gay too and he's talking to me doesn't mean he likes me. Gays can be friends too, it's not impossible. It's like Imani and Seth, he's straight, and she likes everyone, but they're not a thing.

That's why I asked to read. I needed to calm my nerves, to get my mind and chest—I refuse to say heart, it's not that— back in line. I wanted to keep talking, I really did, but my mind was going every which way.

I let my eyes slink to my right, landing on his hand. His fingers are long and thin and pale. They look so soft. My mind wanders, creating a fantasy of those fingers slipping around mine, gripping my hand. I force myself to breathe. I've never held another boy's hand, not like that. And I've never kissed a boy — well, anyone. I dare a quick glance at his face, and my eyes lock on his lips. And a glance is all it takes to pull in every detail.

They're thin but perfect. Pale pink. They blend perfectly with his complexion. And those freckles making a bridge over his nose from cheek to cheek. Oh my God!

Read. Focus. But my mind still can't recognize a word my eyes glide over. Instead, I wonder what it would be like to kiss him, what it would feel like. Is there a world in which he'd ever look at me as more than a friend, where he could see me as more than the handicapped kid? But it's all a dream, a fantasy, the same ones I've been dwelling on a lot more than I should lately.

"Jacob?" A new voice enters the room, and I almost jump.

He's around our age, maybe more on Jacob's side, dressed in a plaid button-up with the top few buttons undone. His squarish jaw is a few shades darker than Jacob's, and his eyes are this magnificent steel gray. He's rather good-looking, and it's stupid, but I feel bad for thinking that next to Jacob. Yeah, really stupid.

"Noah? What are you doing here?" A smile springs across Jacob's face and he jumps up, dropping his book in his chair.

They both jump forward and wrap each other in a hug. Without thinking I twitch back. Does Jacob have a boyfriend? No! It can't be. He would have said something about him, right?

"Just back for the weekend," Noah says. "How've you been? Your dad's been all over the news."

My head snaps between them. It's like I'm not here, and I'm not completely fond of it.

"I've been great, minus all that," Jacob laughs. "Yeah, he's running for Congress."

Jacob rolls his eyes, and Noah shakes his head.

"I heard about that too," Noah says.

"Oh." Jacob's eyes snap onto me. "I'm sorry. Skylar, meet Noah Andrews. Noah, meet Skylar Gray. He's my new friend! Moved down from Vermont."

Skylar *Gray*. Instinct is to correct him, it's Skylar *Rice*, but nope, it's not. It's Gray. I like how he didn't mention my adoption in the move. What I don't like, as accurate as it technically is, is that I'm introduced as his new friend. It's like a confirmation that my fantasy world will never come true.

I stand.

"Good to meet you, Skylar." Noah smiles and envelops me in a hug of my own.

At first I stand stoic, like a statue, not sure what to do, but I realize I'm coming off like a scared asshole and give him a quick hug before backing away. I don't say anything, like I even could, and he doesn't seem to balk at it.

"Noah was on the swim team with me before he graduated and left us last year," Jacob side-eyes him, "and went off to State."

I nod and grin. I still don't see Jacob as a swimmer, like the competitive type. The season hasn't started yet, so maybe when he's actually doing it that'll change in my head.

"This one's a fish, I swear. Always ahead of me." Noah laughs, and I join in with the typical head bobbing in place of laughter.

"Oh, sorry, I about forgot." Jacob looks at me like he made a mistake. "Sky doesn't talk. Okay, like he actually talks a lot, just not from his mouth."

I know what he's saying, but I don't think he fully thought that one through. That phrase is usually reserved for another orifice, not nonverbalism. I purse my lips and eye him with this comical gaze.

"Uh…" Noah groans, unsure what to say.

"No, that's not what I meant! Swear it. God, no." Jacob flies into damage control. "No, I meant like with his phone, not his…uh…you know, uh… Oh God, I'm going to shut up."

My hand clutches my stomach, and I barrel over. I might not be able to laugh like everyone else, but that doesn't stop the awkward wheezing noise that comes out of me. I get my composure. Noah looks like he's not sure what to do. I pick up my phone from the chair and start typing.

"I literally can't talk. I don't have a voice. I talk through my phone… A lot, apparently." I glare at Jacob when my phone reads that last part out.

He chews his lip! Don't do that, it makes you even hotter, and I can't handle that!

"Not like *too* much," Jacob apologizes, like he thinks I'm actually irritated.

"Gotcha." Noah scrunches his forehead. "Jacob never did have a way with words."

Oh! Burn, Jacob. I look directly at him and laugh.

"I know. It's okay though. I don't give a, you know," I have Siri say, opting not to say the F word because I can't exactly tell Siri to whisper it.

"Mind if I sit with y'all?" Noah laughs.

"Sure," Jacob says.

I, on the other hand, I'm not so sure I want this new guy

sticking around. Nothing against him, he seems like a nice guy, but I don't know him, and I wanted to spend the time with Jacob, even if he doesn't see it that way.

Noah pulls over the little wooden chair in the corner and takes a seat. He leans back and raises a book to his lap. I hadn't noticed the book earlier.

"Random, but Noah," Jacob's looking at me, "is the reason I came out over the summer."

Really? I shoot my gaze from Jacob to the unassuming boy across from us. And it's like Jacob can see the question in my eyes.

"Yeah, he…" But he stops and turns to Noah. "Stop me if I'm overstepping."

"You're good." Noah motions.

"'Kay. So Noah came out last year while I was still horrified," Jacob tells me. "He went through a lot, but he made it, and if Noah could do it, I knew I could."

Jacob shrugs, but there's something somber there I don't think I'm getting. But it's still sort of awesome. And now I know Noah's gay too, and the whole hug thing earlier hits even deeper. Were they… Or are they?

"You would have on your own eventually. You're not exactly the go-along-to-get-along type," Noah giggles. Then he focuses on me and points at my skirt. "You wouldn't happen to be the guy at Brown Jacob's dad got his feelings all hurt over, would you?"

A grin immediately jumps across my face. That's the first time I've heard it put like that, but yeah. I guess I am.

I nod furiously and type, "That's me."

"It's all his fault," Jacob laughs. He gives me an approving smile, but his eyes jump down to my skirt for a second. "Who knew a skirt could cause so much trouble? He's cute in it though. Uh… Like in a purely…uh, objective way, of course."

Noah's brow rises, as does mine. I let it shoot through my head, wrapping his words around all the things in my mind. He said it because I happen to be another guy and he likes guys, but that's it. Or maybe it's not just that, maybe it's just me, maybe he thinks I'm actually cute, that I, Skylar Gray, am cute. Or he's just a typical gay and sees the skirt as easy access. He did just glance at my skirt. Ugh. It's probably the last. That's probably the only reason I'm here.

"Yeah… People get all weird about us gays doing anything. Wearing skirts, painting our nails, swimming, speaking…existing." Noah's voice trails off and I'm caught up in a sudden sadness in his eyes. "It sucks, and it doesn't make *any* sense."

It's not that bad. It's just a skirt. I mean, yeah, it sucks, but the way Noah's talking makes it sound so much worse. But there's something else in his face, something hurt and distant that I can't quite pinpoint.

I turn my attention to Jacob, hoping there will be some answer there, but even his pale upturned lips have drooped into a frown and the electricity behind his eyes dulls.

"They're holding a public forum to debate it though," I have Siri jump into the quiet. I don't understand what's happening, but I feel like I need to fix it, and I don't know how else other than to talk. "We get to fight back."

"I heard," Noah says slowly, taking a deep breath. A put-on smile rises across his lips and he lets out the breath. "I'm thinking about coming."

"You should. We need every voice we can get, and..." Jacob goes quiet again but starts back up with purpose. "They can't ignore you. But only if you're okay with it."

Now I'm one hundred percent lost, but the tension in the air tells me it's something difficult, something I probably shouldn't pry into.

"It'd be great if you could come," I type out, keeping a hopeful smile on.

Jacob's phone dings, and when he looks at it, his eyes go wide.

"God," Jacob says nervously, "I'm late. I'm supposed to be at Ian's right now for practice!"

Oops! He'd told me about that, but I didn't think to keep track of it. Guess he hadn't either. I laugh at him, not with, because it's sort of funny, and Noah actually joins in.

"Sorry Noah, but we've got to go," he apologizes.

"All good." Noah nods and before I can type anything, Jacob's up and walking.

So I nod and wave instead, which Noah seems to understand. He seems like a nice guy.

He just better not be anything more to Jacob than a friend.

JACOB
TUESDAY, SEPTEMBER 17

Open Mic night was a success, mostly. The crowd applauded us at least, despite my mess up.

We were on our third cover, a song from Hands Like Houses. Eric started his tap countdown, and I might have started playing our last song. It worked out though, the crowd thought it was funny.

"Bucket list?" I spout the words after taking a lick from my cone of vanilla ice cream.

Lips purse and eyes wander around the picnic table outside the ice cream shop. It's dark and the wind is light. Cars slog by on the little road slicing through downtown. The sky's clear but the streetlamps along the strip drown out the stars.

"Skydiving!" Eric spurts. "I've always wanted to go skydiving. And meet Maria Brink!"

I shake my head. Makes sense. He's had a huge crush on her since we discovered her band a few years ago.

Seth speaks up next, which is a real surprise. I really want to know what's on Sky's list, but it'd be rude not to ask the whole group. I glance at him, but then refocus on Seth.

"I want to go to Star Wars Land," Seth says, and I think

he's talking about the Disney park. They'd have to drag me in. "And then maybe… Attend a rodeo."

"A rodeo?" Imani's eyes scream *what the hell.*

"Yeah. Just looks fun, but I'm not sure I could do all the rednecks," he laughs.

"You're doing that one on your own," Imani tells him. "I'm not getting hate-crimed for that."

"And you?" I'm laughing but still manage to ask her.

"I don't know," she shrugs. "Not really thought about it. Maybe visit Rome or Greece?"

"Greece would be so cool," Ian chimes in. "That's on my list too. I want to see the temples."

"Yes! Stand where the gods stood." Imani sticks her tongue out.

"Or where they thought they did, at least." Ian shrugs. "Then maybe bungee jumping and drive a car over one hundred miles per hour!"

All dangerous shit. But I'm not surprised.

"Let's just make sure I'm not in the car when you do that," I beg.

He shrugs.

"What about you?" I look at Sky.

He's been sitting patiently, nodding and laughing in his own way. And it's been everything I can manage not to completely ignore the others to ask him.

"See the northern lights. Go to a Myylo concert," Skylar's phone lists. "Skinny dipping, maybe. Go to Finland." Did he just say skinny dipping? I shake my head and laugh, but there's more. "And write a love letter, but that's corny."

Corny? What? Why? He can write me one any day! He just

doesn't know it.

Skylar's eyes light up. "I can strike off my main bucket list item though. A family."

Sighs slip around the picnic table. And I have to hold back a verbal *aw*, even though my mouth forms a little O. Part of me wants to tell him how lucky he is. His new parents seem really cool. I'm still sort of jealous.

"We better be included in that, bitch." Imani destroys the moment. "We're your family too."

The biggest grin I've seen yet slides across Skylar's face, and for a moment he locks eyes with me.

"Definitely," his phone says all astute-like, while Skylar nods coyly.

Something in my chest warms at the thought that he thinks of us as family. But something else is stirring, a longing, a desire, a wanting to be even more than that.

I've got to keep this in check.

JACOB
WEDNESDAY, SEPTEMBER 18

It's quiet at home as it usually is after Sunday morning service except for the mumbles tunnelling down the hallway. Exactly where I'm headed now, even while my feet beg to go the other direction.

I've sat in my room long enough practicing sign language, and I can't stop wanting to reason with Dad. I keep telling myself no, it's useless. But I want to change his mind. I want to see the light click in his eyes and for him to be like, *you know, you're right*.

So here I am standing in the doorway of the living room, swallowing back the unease. Dad's lounging on his recliner, lost in one of the *Bourne* movies. I distract myself by thinking how two-faced it is. He rails on how words like damn and fuck and shit and hell are bad, but those movies are full of them.

I force my legs to carry me forward and plop down on the couch. It's on one of the action scenes right now, so I'm going to wait for it to calm down. I'm going to do this. But after ten minutes it hits me that this movie is basically one big action scene. I sigh and clench and unclench my fists. Just do it.

"Is this *Supremacy*?" I ask, because I'm too pathetic to do what I came to do.

"No, *Identity*, the first one," Dad says without breaking eye contact with the TV.

I don't know what I'm doing, this is stupid. He's too lost in his movie anyway. I sit a minute longer, angry with myself, and then get up and make a break for my room.

But before I can make it to the hall, I stop. I throw my head back and huff. He can't hear me, the volume is too loud. I swing around and cast my voice over the TV before I can stop myself.

"Is there anything that could get you to pull the new dress code? Anything?" I try. My feet are stone on the carpet.

The volume goes down and Dad swivels the recliner.

"Yeah," is not what I was expecting, but Dad doesn't disappoint. "Revival. If we finally had a real revival sweep in this country, I wouldn't need the new dress code."

It's all I can do not to roll my eyes. Really? I swear that's his answer for all of society's problems, that or *if people would get saved*, like it's actually that simple. Hell, churches can't even agree.

"I mean like is there anything someone can say to convince you?" I try again.

"No. It's against nature, against what the Bible says," he goes on. Not sure what else I expected him to say. "Boys have no business dressing like girls or doing girl things."

"You do realize pants are a newer invention, right?" I throw out my new fact. I did some Googling before church when I got the idea stuck in my head to confront him. "Pants were considered clothes for barbarians by the Greeks and Romans. They were basically just for horse riding."

"No, you're just letting that rewritten history get in your head," Dad dismisses me. Which seems a little weird for the chair of the local board of education. "Which of your teachers told you that?"

"None of them," I tell him. I seriously think he'd hunt a teacher down to get them fired if they taught us that. "I looked it up myself."

"I see," he sighs.

"Jesus didn't wear pants," I try again.

"Don't be twisting scripture, Jacob," Dad's voice curls. "He wasn't wearing women's clothes."

"It was a dress." I squint in disbelief. "Clothes change, society changes. It's all relative. Clothes don't have a gender, Dad. It's just a modern societal construct."

"You're trying to throw around big words too much." Dad shakes his head and grabs the remote. "The Bible says it's wrong and that's all I need to know. Boys shouldn't wear girls' clothes. And no, I'm not pulling the proposal, and I better never find out you're wearing a dress again as long as you live in my house. This conversation is over."

"Yeah, nice talk," I blurt and jog down the hall.

His answer for everything is the Bible this, the Bible that, and nine times out of ten it's something you can't do. It's rarely the parts where Jesus said to love others and not judge.

And he wonders why it's so hard for me to listen.

SKYLAR

This mall is huge and way too busy. I don't like it.

Imani grabs my hand and pulls me into one of those stores with the fancy wedding and prom dresses hanging in the windows. The type none of us can afford. And like, who pays a lot for Homecoming outfits anyway? It's not like it's prom.

Plus, I'm not going. So I don't need to be here. But try explaining that to Imani. I mentioned it to Seth and he was just like, *yeah, don't, just don't.*

"Aw! Look at this one." It begins.

She pulls on the waist of, I swear, the first dress she sees. It's white, with sequin striping down the neck in two thin lines that merge at a much too thin waist above a long straight bottom. It's pretty, but it screams *I'm getting married*, not *I'm at a high school dance*.

I nod. Even if I were going to Homecoming—and I'm not—I don't have a date, and there's no way I'm getting one. And I'm not asking Mom and Dad for money for a dress.

"What about this one?" Imani pulls a pink dress off the rack that'd probably come just above her knees.

I shrug and type, "It's okay. I don't really see you in pink though."

"Not for me silly, you!" She looks at me like I'm crazy.

I point at myself and return the look.

"Yeah," she repeats, and I look at Seth. His eyes go wide, begging not be brought into the conversation.

"Nah," Siri tells her. Pink isn't for me either. "If it were me, it'd be like black or green or maybe a red color. And longer than that."

"It's no shorter than your skirts," Imani says and puts the dress back on the rack.

"Yeah," I start typing. "But if we're going for fancy, I want it long."

And not fluffy, and that pink dress was borderline fluffy at the bottom too.

"Eh." She waves it off. "We'll figure something out."

I'm about to protest when my phone buzzes.

JACOB: Heard ur going to homecoming.

My eyes lock on Imani's face. She's sorting through another rack when she notices my look and squints.

"What?"

Nothing, I mouth and answer Jacob's text instead.

SKYLAR: Maybe. Doubtful. Imani's determined I'm going with her and Seth.

But I feel like he already knows that, and I'm positive I know who told him.

JACOB: Threesome!

I close my eyes and laugh. Wow! Okay. It's funny though. Definitely not *that* type of threesome. I don't want anywhere near that.

SKYLAR: ::puke face:: ::crying laughing face::

"Who you talking to?" Imani leans over my phone.

I yank it back and eye her down, mouthing, *rude*.

"Jacob?" She grins.

"Probably," Seth joins in, and I shoot him a glare. He shrugs and breaks eye contact.

"You really should be going to Homecoming with him, not us, you know," she remarks, as if I hadn't thought about it a million times.

It's not happening. The only way I'm going to Homecoming is with her and Seth. No one else is going to ask me unless it's a cruel prank, and honestly, I don't know anyone other than Jacob I'd say yes to anyway. And I'd say yes a hundred times to him.

"No!" I make Siri yell, intentionally turning up the volume. "Not happening. Nope!"

She scowls and slides back a step. Her hands go to the next rack and she pulls a green dress from it like she'd had her eye on it the entire time.

"He'd love this on you." Imani grins knowingly.

She holds it up for me to see. It's actually beautiful. Bottle green, velvety, simple. There are no shoulders, just tiny sleeves that wrap around the arms. I imagine what it might look like on me. The bottom would easily go to my feet. I'd probably need it hemmed up a little, and I'd have to have the slit running all the way up to the thigh sewn up some, maybe. But what am I thinking? I'm not getting a dress in here. Money doesn't grow on trees.

I sigh. *It is gorgeous.*

"I love the color. Hunter green." She examines it.

I squint. Uh, no.

"That's bottle green," I have Siri correct her.

"No, it's hunter green," Imani reiterates.

No. It's not. Definitely bottle green, I say.

"Nah." She looks to Seth for backup.

"Hell no, I'm not getting into this." He steps back, hands up in surrender. "Y'all can battle this out yourselves."

"Either way, you can wear this to Homecoming with Jacob," Imani says again.

Why is she so determined?

No! I try again, and then type it out. "Not happening."

"Why not?" Seth, to my surprise, asks.

I sigh as I type up my reason. "He doesn't like me like that. No guy likes me like that. No one wants to take bot boy to the dance."

"I'm not gay, but I'd take you if I were," Seth tries.

Imani jerks her head in a resolute nod, proud of her BFF.

"That's easy to say when you're not gay," Siri tells him. I sort of hate it when people say shit like that. I know they mean well, but it's hollow. It's easy to say when you'll never have to confront the choice. "But you're also not a dick, so there's that too."

Seth slouches. Maybe that was a little harsh of me. He was trying to be nice.

"Jacob's not a dick either." Imani doesn't lose a beat. "He's sort of brash, but he's not a dick."

"It doesn't matter," I type. And it really doesn't. "I'm not asking him. I'm way too scared to do that. And he's not going to ask me."

"So you *would* go with him?" Imani grins.

My lips skew to the side and I grin. *Yeah.*

My phone dings, and my eyes shoot to my hand.

"God, you *do* have it bad." Imani sticks out her tongue playfully and jumps like it's some big victory.

Bitch, I say, but that just makes her laugh more.

"We've got to take you to the theater." She suddenly changes topic. What? "Have you seen the new *IT* movie?"

Uh… What? *No*, I say.

"You need the Gem experience," she says. There something's going on here. The gears behind her dark eyes are spinning much too hard. "We're going to the movies tonight."

JACOB

I'm taking him on a date. Or, well, I'm going to. A real one too. Not one of these let's-go-to-the-coffee-shop-but-let's-not-call-it-a-date dates again, a real one.

But how?

"My ticket?" The man on the opposite side of the glass squints.

"Oh, right." I snatch the ticket and pass it through the little opening. "Enjoy your show."

The line spans down the sidewalk. It does this every Friday for the seven o'clock showing. And lucky me got ticket duty. A couple steps up and I try to focus. Greet them, let them tell me they want a ticket like I don't already know, and what show as if I don't know that too, take their money and give them a ticket. Over and over.

And between each sale my mind drifts back to his unruly cocoa-brown hair and the way it fell in his face after we raced bikes to the shop, those hazel eyes that are more green than brown, the way his thick lips purse when he's unsure, and how his nose doesn't quite reach above my shoulders.

I mindlessly take the next order, and the next. Skylar's

been on my mind a lot. Enough that Ian gives me that look anytime I daydream, and Eric noticed it during Open Mic night. And I didn't even tell him that's why I played the wrong song.

The line comes to an end a few minutes after seven, and I'm left with only my thoughts again. A dangerous place, at least that's what I tell Ian and Eric.

I've made a point of being careful about how much I texted Sky the last few days. I want to every second, but there's this voice in the back of my head that tells me I might be reading him wrong and it'll just drive him away. I think he likes me, maybe. There's something about the looks he gives me at lunch when we're all talking, or when he sees me in the morning before Dance. It's this nervous smile, almost a flinch. It's tiny, but maybe. And I swear it felt like he was staring at *me* during our set at the Open Mic night. But then again, I was probably imagining that too.

But how could he look at me and think to himself: *Now there's a man. I want to be on that.* My ears are weird, they stick out too far. And I'm too skinny. I look like a starved child, and my skin is ghost white.

Yeah! I nod to myself, stopping so I don't look odd to the two girls rushing the booth and asking for a ticket. I put on a fake grin and send them on their way.

You know what? It doesn't matter. I'm going to do it. I'm going to ask Skylar on a date the next time I see him. I'm not backing out. I'm doing it!

If he says no I'll just save money, right? It'll be fine. Yeah, I'll be devastated and embarrassed beyond repair, but I'll be okay.

The next time I see Skylar, I'm going to walk up and say —

"Three tickets, please." A familiar female voice grabs my attention and my eyes sweep upward.

I freeze like a frightened deer. Three faces stare back at me, and in the middle, there he is.

"You okay?" Seth scrunches his forehead.

My eyes are locked on Skylar. He grins. It's the softest, the cutest grin I've ever seen.

"Sorry, you scared me." I relax just enough to get the words out.

Skylar cocks his head and eyes me curiously, that grin still on his lips.

"You usually freeze up like some helpless goat when people ask for tickets?" Imani squints, then raises her left brow. "That'd be horrible in a break-in situation."

"Uh... I... It's just..." I stumble. The words refuse to come to my mouth, hell, they're not even coming to my brain. My eyes bounce between Imani, Skylar, Seth, and then back again. I close and open my fist on my bouncing leg. Then my eyes catch Skylar again, and all at once a whole-ass word train bursts through the retaining wall without a single stutter. "Can I take you out tomorrow?"

The whole world goes silent. Even the passing car seems silent, insignificant, as I will myself to act cool. *You didn't just make the worst decision ever. Timing sucked, but that's okay.*

Imani's eyes spring open, and her mouth drops in this massive smile. Seth's head bounces forward and the first sound I hear is his voice making this "Ooooh!" noise. But the weird part is that Sky's lips don't flip, the edges don't suddenly slump into a frown, and his eyes don't dull into annoyance. No, the left side of his mouth rises even higher than before, and the first sound I hear is spurts of air shooting from his nose, laughter. Then his eyes dart away nervously, but quickly find me again.

"Shut up, fool!" Imani reaches around Skylar and slaps Seth on the back of the head and the tension falls away. Then she looks at me. "So like with a bullet or on a date?"

"Uh… What? Oh! On… On…" The stuttering comes back and I want to punch something so bad right now, but I've dug this grave, so I'll be damned if I stop digging. "On a date."

"Yes!" Imani yells. Skylar jumps, still unable to get a word in.

I don't know what to say to that. I think I'm supposed to wait on Skylar.

"He didn't ask you, bitch." Seth eyes her down.

"I know." She does this sassy thing where she bobs her head from side to side. "Sky?"

Finally, Skylar locks his eyes on me. They're browner than usual tonight. His cheeks are red. How'd I miss that?

He starts nodding furiously, with a smile that tugs as far as his lips can reach.

"Okay, uh…yeah…" I don't know what to say next. Should I ask where he wants to go, or what time? Do I ask what to wear? I'm shaking now. I mean, I've been shaking, but now it's different. I cough, grounding myself, and try again. "Sounds awesome. How about I text you after your movie and we can figure it out."

Skylar mouths something, and I'm just assuming it's a yes of some kind, because he's still smiling and nodding.

"He said, 'sounds good,'" Imani translates. Guess she saw

the confusion loud and clear.

Seth is shaking his head and laughing.

"Great." I about snap my neck, I nod so hard. Oh no, their movie. I tap furiously on my screen and pass their tickets under the glass to Imani. "No previews, you might want to hurry. You're late."

I can't wipe the smile off my face as they slink around the booth. I did it. I actually did it. Skylar's eyes linger on me a second longer as they go around the booth, and I smile at him. Then he's gone, and I'm by myself again.

"I'm going on a date," I say to no one. My first date ever. With Skylar. I shake my head. I can't believe this.

I'm going on a date.

SKYLAR
SATURDAY, SEPTEMBER 21

My nerves are shot. I've been pacing my bedroom the past hour. Mom's checked on me at least four times. Seems my footsteps aren't that light.

"Would you stop that?" Imani falls back onto my bed.

I shrug and plop my butt next to her. I want to scream. What am I doing? Am I insane? Why did I say yes to Jacob last night? Now I have to go! I'm not saying that's a bad thing. It's exactly what I want, but now I'm terrified. What if he decides I'm no fun? What if I say something stupid, something too cheesy, and he gets weirded out? There are so many things that could go wrong. And what if he wants to kiss? That's what scares me the most.

I've never kissed anyone before, I tell Imani, but my eyes are glued to the little quartz horse figurine Mom got me up at the caverns. I'm not saying that and looking at her. No way.

"You've never kissed anyone?" she repeats. "Really?"

I nod crazily, hopelessly. What if he tries to kiss me? I've watched enough porn to know how it's done, but actually doing it… Oh God!

"It's okay, you're just panicking. Calm down." She

changes gears. "You'll figure it out, and it's definitely cool to kiss on the first date."

I check my phone. He's supposed to be here at seven. It's *6:57 p.m.*

I catch my reflection in the phone screen, so I check my hair one more time. I didn't do anything different with it, I just want to make sure it looks okay. It's always a mess.

"It's also okay to do other things..." And she slips something from her pocket and places it in my palm.

As soon as I see the square plastic wrapping on my fingers, I jerk my hand back and it plummets to the ground, skittering along the carpet. My face goes pale and my eyes jerk to the door. What if Mom comes back and it's there! I jump up and sweep the condom off the floor and throw it into Imani's lap.

I don't need that. I beam at her and wipe my palms on my tan short-shorts.

She's rolling, literally, one hand grasping her stomach, the other wrapped around her little "gift". She laughs and laughs, and finally calms.

"You might." She shimmies her head. "Got to be safe. No—"

I put my hand up to stop her. *It's okay. Thank you. But I don't want... I mean... You know?*

"I don't know, do I?" Imani squints at me. "You do or you don't want him to fuck you?"

My head bounces back. Like, what?

Who said he'd be doing the fucking? I gasp, tiny wisps of air and noise escaping between my lips.

Imani tilts her head and her eyes say it all before she speaks.

"You going to make me lay out my reasons? 'Cause I will." She sits upright, ready to give her dissertation on my sexuality.

I stop her. I don't need her being completely right out loud.

Okay. I put my hand up. I roll my eyes and shake my head.

Tires scratch against pavement outside and my eyes bolt to Imani and we freeze. She smiles first, and I can't help but do it too. We burst out laughing, and I'm up, springing for the window. I pull the shade away and there he is. Every glorious inch of eboy.

He's here! My mouth moves wildly, excited.

"Bet he's as excited as you are," Imani says. She pulls out a stone and puts it in my hand. "I wish you a successful date, my friend."

The doorbell rings and I nod thankfully.

"Sky, your *date* is here," Mom yells up the stairs.

Even she's teasing me.

"He's coming," Imani yells down for me and then grabs my shoulders. She locks her dark brown eyes on mine. "You are a bad bitch. Repeat after me. I'm a bad…" She stops and shakes her head, huffing. I was already beginning to giggle, but that just sealed the deal. I try to be serious when she starts back up. "Sorry, don't repeat after me, obviously. But! You are a bad bitch. You're going to have a great time! Jacob's the lucky one taking *you* on a date. Remember that!"

I'm a bad bitch, I mouth her mantra. That's right. I'm a bad bitch, and tonight is going to be great!

"That's right." Imani nods aggressively. "Now get your ass down there. He's waiting on you."

I turn and start down the stairs. Imani's on my heels as I hurry down, slowing a few steps from the landing to take a breath.

"Breathe, that's right," Imani whispers behind me.

Not helping, I look back quick enough to mouth.

"Bad bitch," she whispers in my ear, but I'm actively ignoring her now.

I let out the breath and turn the corner into the living room. There he is, standing next to Mom. And wow, he's not in all black. Okay, he's still got a lot of black on, but his half-unbuttoned shirt is white. He's a mix of dress and casual, and there's something sexy about the way some of his chest is showing.

"Hey." Jacob smiles. He's beautiful.

Hey, I mouth, nodding nervously before I remember I need to move my feet if I plan on walking out the door with him.

"Hey, Im." Jacob casts a nod past me as I come up next to him.

"Hiya." She waves back, all smiles, like a proud mother.

"You ready to go?" Jacob asks.

I nod, and he starts for the door and I follow.

"Y'all have fun, and be careful," Mom calls after us.

I'd completely forgotten she was in the room. That's bad. I kick myself for that one. I smile at her, and suddenly the urge to hug her burrows itself into my chest. I don't know what it is, but I just need to. I put a finger up to let Jacob know to wait, and then run up to Mom and wrap her in a hug.

She's surprised. I can tell because she doesn't wrap her arms around me immediately. It has to sink in first. I let go and look her in the eye. *Thank you.*

Mom nods and smiles warmly. "Have fun."

JACOB

SATURDAY, SEPTEMBER 21

The fair was a good idea. Skylar hasn't stopped laughing and smiling. I think it's put a permanent bright spot in my dark little heart.

Neon lights flash and fizzle against a darkening sky. Screams and cheers and the sound of metal rides whooshing and clanking fill the air, and the cool breeze is perfect.

We're in line for the Hurler. I'd usually refuse, but I can't let him think I'm a wuss. Watching it though, I'm reminded why I never ride it when Ian or Eric beg. It's this death contraption where two people sit in a metal box with only a flimsy bar over their waist to keep them from flying out while it slings you around a central axis, and if that wasn't bad enough, the box you're in spins too, knocking you from one end of the compartment to the other.

I swallow back the nerves gathering in my throat.

"I can't believe I'm about to ride this thing," I whisper.

"Why?" Skylar's phone questions.

Oh, sweet Sky, so innocent of my fears. And why did you have to hear that?

What if the bar flings open mid-ride and we go flying into

the barricade? What if the center axis spins one too many times and unscrews itself? What if the tired people who put the ride together four thousand times failed to tighten the bolt that holds our box on?

"Reasons." I give him a nervous grin. "But I'm doing it!"

He shakes his head and giggles in his chest before moving his lips. I focus hard, which is difficult because the more I focus, the less I see the words and the more I just see his lips moving. And that gets other feelings going in my chest.

He must see the concentration in my eyes, because he stops and types instead, "You don't have to. We can ride something else."

"No, you wanted to ride this one." I forbid it. "You're insane, but still."

He laughs, and at that most fortunate moment, the attendant lets us in.

"Here we go," I huff, and wave Sky ahead of me. You know, being the gentleman, or maybe just delaying the inevitable.

Sky rushes forward, claiming the first car he comes to. I slide in next to him and pull the bar in and latch it closed. I pull and push it a few times to make sure it's locked tight, then smile sheepishly at Sky.

You good? he asks, pocketing his phone so it doesn't go flying out until we do, not before.

I nod, but I think my face is betraying me. I press against the lame excuse for padding and barricade myself against the wall. Maybe that'll help. Sky taps me.

Can I? he says, and points next to me.

"Uh...y-yeah," I stutter. We're going to be plastered together anyway, so best to get it over with. And I'm not complaining.

He slides closer, smiling as he presses against me. I grin but look away quick. We're going to be body-to-body, smushed against each other this entire ride. The blood rushes to my face. I might actually like this ride.

My eyes shoot down and without thinking, they lock onto his leg. He's wearing these cute tan shorts that ride up his thigh, exposing his soft knees. I was surprised when he came downstairs in them instead of a skirt. I'd sort of hoped he'd wear a skirt, but I kept quiet about it.

"Just curious," I start. I think we've got a minute before the ride threatens our lives. "Why'd you not wear a skirt?"

Sorry. He frowns.

"No! Don't be sorry. I didn't mean it like that," I tell him. Leave it to me to sound disappointed on the first date. *Dammit, Jacob.*

I wanted to, he says, hands pointing at himself and moving about, eyes locked on me. His face is so close. I tell myself not to move. Otherwise I'm in danger of launching forward and kissing him. He starts talking again, but all I catch is *Didn't* and I miss the rest.

"I'm sorry, can you say that again?" I ask and pay better attention to what he's saying this time.

Didn't want to get hate-crimed, he says.

That's smart. The fair is a few small towns over out in the country, so even more of a country-boy mentality than K-Town.

Disappointed? He skews his cheeks.

"Hell no! I'm not disappointed! Never," I tell him. A part of my heart sinks, I don't want him to think like that. I throw in a little joke to, hopefully, lighten the mood and get my mind off his lips. "Just means I won't get to defend your honor tonight."

You can another day, he giggles.

I laugh and shake my head.

"We'll see how—" But my words are cut off when the car starts moving. I would keep talking but my mind just shot into overdrive.

Are the screws all tightened? Did they tighten them too much? Are they stripped? Is the car going to stay attached? What is that creaking noise? Should it sway like that?

Skylar's hand slides over mine, and he wiggles his fingers through the cracks between my fingers, threatening to lift my hand from my thigh where I'm gripping tight. He pulls until I let go and grip his hand. My head spins between the cold metal death we're trapped in and the warm comforting softness of his skin in my hand. It's a whir of contradictions.

He squeezes and I force myself to face him. His cheeks rise, causing his eyes to squint in the cutest way, even if our bodies are ricocheting from one end of the car to the other. And somehow it works. The tension in my chest loosens a little, just a little, but it's something. Then suddenly the car shoots the other direction. It spins and whirls and cartwheels.

For a second my mind screams, but it stops. This isn't so bad. My body smushes against Skylar and if I weren't so damned skinny, I'd worry I might crush him. The car jerks the other way and our bodies fling to the opposite edge. I manage a glance at his face. He's beaming, excited. I think to put my arm around him, but I'm afraid to move it.

* * *

"I've read some messed up stories about mazes." I bump his shoulder with my elbow.

It's dark. And the sky is clear tonight. The moon hasn't shown itself yet, and stars fill the sky like diamonds on a sea of black. Across the corn field, the scream of fair rides and kids mixes in the distance with the click and hum of cicadas hiding in the corn.

I watch Skylar's mouth for a reply. But when his lips move, in the dark, it's so hard to follow. But I think I got it. If it weren't for the lightning bugs blinking here and there, lightly shedding their glow on his smooth cheeks, I doubt I could.

"Not cool?" I squint, repeating what I think he said.

Skylar nods excitedly and starts moving his lips again.

Wow! You got it, he says, and I got that too. I've done better tonight.

I laugh. "Don't know why it's so hard for me."

Skylar shrugs. It'd make it easier to talk to him if reading lips wasn't so hard for me, and God knows I like talking to him. I don't say anything for a moment. I let it hang there under the stars, feet patting down the straw and grass on the path. Corn stalks shoot high above our heads on all sides, casting swaying shadows on the trail.

I don't know how many turns we've made, and honestly, I've never been that good at mazes, so we could be a while in here. But I'm okay with that. As long as he's here, I'm happy with it.

"I uh…" I start and stop. I want to tell him I've been learning sign language. But that means I'll need to show him, and what if I get it wrong? But I say it anyway. "I've been teaching myself sign language."

His face twists to find me and his eyes shoot open over a smile. *Really?*

I nod. "Yeah, but I still don't know much. You know how good YouTube learning is."

He mouths something, but between the shadows jumping across his face, it being so dark anyway, and my general inability and ineptness, I miss it. I give him a confused gaze.

He tries again. *Show me.*

"Uh, okay. I'll try," I say.

What do I say? And how? I cough, trying to think of something to say. Hell, I'll just tell him my name. I practiced that one a lot.

"Here we go." I cough again. He smiles and steps back to give me some space. Not sure what that's about.

I bring my hand to my forehead with two fingers to say *hi*, I think, then pat my open hand on my chest and tap my fingers together in an X in front of me. Now's the hard part. Remembering the bloody alphabet. The first one's easy, I swoop my finger down and around and start spelling. Then A, and C, and O, and then the B. The B's the hardest for me.

Skylar tilts his head and squints. He starts signing, but I focus hard on his lips. I catch most of it.

Was that supposed to be a B?

"Yeah." I smile stupidly. "My fingers just don't make that shape. I swear I can't get my thumb to bend that far."

I throw my hand over my face and shake my head. His fingers peel under and pull my hand away.

He's smiling and giggling. I wish it was just a little brighter so I could really see his face. His eyes are stunning regardless, but I want to see every detail.

You did…good. It'll take time, he says and starts walking, but stops again. *Thank you.*

There's something sweet and warm in his eyes when he says it. I have to fight back the prickly sensation at the base of my neck. I smile back, not sure what else to say, and definitely not sure how to sign it. I swear I've learned more than how to say my name, but right now that's all I've got.

He starts to mouth something else when behind us something ruffles in the corn, and Skylar comes off his feet. He clears the ground a good few inches and spins to face the noise. But when his feet make contact again, he's nearly on top of me. His arms press against me, and his hand jerks back and clamps onto mine.

Instinctively, I squeeze and pull him closer. My eyes dart between him and where the noise came from. It comes again, but this time there's laughter, and before Skylar can squeeze any harder a boy and girl about our ages shove the stalks aside and stumble into the clearing. Skylar's hand springs open and he steps a safe distance away.

I want to reach out and pull him back. I want that jolt of electricity from him wrapping his fingers in mine. I want to feel that again.

"You two lost?" the boy throws his voice around with a slur. He stumbles, and his girl isn't doing any better. "I figure if we just keep heading this way, we'll get out eventually."

"Oh." I nod as he takes the girl's hand and leads her straight across the opening and into the corn on the opposite side. When he's gone, I turn back to Skylar, eyes wide and a hysterical smile across my face. I break down at the same instant he does, bent over laughing, coughing and trying to get my breath.

"Like what the?" I say.

Skylar's nodding, and his lips are moving. I think he's saying *Yeah, really!*

"Scared the hell out of you," I say when I finally gather myself.

Skylar stands up straight and eyes me like I've just insulted him.

"No... I, uh... I'm sorry, I didn't..." I stumble, but he puts a hand up and stops me.

He looks me in the eyes, making sure I'm watching so I can read his lips. I wonder if he's blushing. It's too dark to tell.

It's okay. Promise. It did.

"Nothing wrong with that," I tell him.

I debate the words that are in my head, whether to speak them. But I'm done debating it. I hold out my hand, palm up, fingers loose and waiting. It's like in the movies when the prince holds his hand out for the girl at the ball, except it's not a movie, and we're in a corn maze, and my mouth is moving before my mind can keep up.

"If it helps any, you can hold my hand," I say.

It immediately gets awkward. Skylar looks at my hand and pauses. I've made a mistake. Why do I do this shit? But then the consideration on his face morphs into a smile. He reaches out and takes my hand, and then looks me in the eye.

I can't hold back the smile screaming all over my face. Electricity pulses up my arm, and I squeeze his hand. He bites at his lip. God, he's got to stop doing that. I force myself to start walking. Focus on the here and now, the straw and grass beneath our feet, the flickering lightning bugs, the thick stalks of fresh corn rising from the ground and soaring feet above me and another foot above Skylar.

For a few steps neither of us talks. I almost break the silence but decide he probably doesn't really care about how I slaughtered Tyler in *Overwatch* last night. He's not into gaming. I keep walking, trying hard not to think about his hand in mine. But I can't. His skin is so soft, and his fingers fit perfectly between my own, like they were meant to be there. I know that's cheesy, but it feels like it.

"Wanna play a game?" I blurt. It sounds childish. We're in the middle of a corn maze, on a date, and I ask if he wants to play a game like we're ten.

He nods and squeezes my hand.

"How about two truths and a lie?" I suggest. To be honest, I looked up what games were good on dates, and this was one of the few that didn't involve alcohol or dares. "You know, like tell me two true things and one lie and I have to guess the lie."

The only thing is I didn't know I'd be holding his hand while we played it. I figured he'd have his phone and let Siri do the talking, but I don't plan on letting go for that.

He nods again.

"I'll start," I say and look up at the stars to think of my first truths and a lie. "Okay. Got it. I'm claustrophobic. I'm on the school swim team. And my favorite color is green."

Skylar shakes his head at me. *That's too easy.*

"Oh really?" I ask.

Yeah, your favorite color is black. He shrugs.

"Okay yeah, that was easy." I'll give him that. "I am claustrophobic. Tight spaces suck. And elevators, they're like tiny death boxes."

Skylar looks at me like I'm crazy. *Don't think I've ever heard of an elevator accident.*

"They happen," I tell him. "I read about this couple that drowned in one during a rainstorm, and this other where the floor broke open and these two teenagers fell down six stories."

His eyes widen and his lips tighten.

"Not good date talk, huh?" I ask. There I go letting my mouth get away. "How about you go now?"

Skylar grins and looks me in the eye. He stares at me for a full half minute, thinking of his three things, I assume, before his mouth begins to move.

My favorite color is yellow, pale yellow. I want to go to college for architecture. And I snuck out of my foster parents' house when I was twelve in the middle of the night to get a Snickers bar.

I hold my gaze, looking him dead in the eyes. Okay, it could either be the color or the major. The sneaking out one is definitely true. What is his favorite color? What does he usually wear? Everything. He's not like me and my monochromatic wardrobe.

"Your favorite color isn't pale yellow?" I scrunch my cheeks.

Immediately he shakes his head, and I groan.

No, I want to major in psychology, he says. *I love yellow.*

"Well, at least I knew the sneaking out one had to be true. That was way too specific," I laugh.

Skylar nods and his hand shakes in mine as he laughs.

Your turn, he says.

"Will you dance with me?" I blurt.

I know it's not two truths and a lie, but it's what came to my mind. I don't know where from either. Like I wasn't thinking it a second ago, but now it's planted in my mind.

We've danced in the same room every day since school started. But not once have we danced together. I've watched him move, hitting each beat and every step, missing a few here and there. But I've never danced *with* him, eyes locked, holding him.

That's what I want.

He doesn't say anything, he doesn't move his lips to answer. Instead, he turns to face me and steps closer. I smile slowly and move a pace closer. There are mere inches between us.

I take a breath and slide my arm under his, and carefully, slowly, pull him closer. At the same time his hand finds mine in the air, and our bodies meet. I swallow, fighting back a cough, and give him a nervous grin. God, I hope he doesn't see how nervous I am.

My feet move, and then his. Our bodies sway together, moving to the chirp and hum of nature, the buzz of cicadas, the singing of grasshoppers and birds, the creaking of branches in the distance. My eyes are fastened to his big, deep eyes, painted in stars and the gentle flash of lightning bugs. I might not be able to see the hues of green and brown, but I know them.

I don't know how long we're like this. It could be seconds or hours, there's no difference in my head, but I don't want it to end. But does he want it as much as me? I fight back the doubt and hug him tighter, swaying with my face so close to his. His eyes divert, looking down, and his lips part for a moment, allowing his tongue to lick at their soft surface. I let out a stuttered breath, hoping to God he doesn't notice. I want to kiss him so bad.

I'm going to do it. I'm going to kiss him. I try not to make it obvious, but then again, maybe I should, but I don't know. When his eyes meet mine again, there's a spark in them, and I can't wait any longer. I move forward, my lips parting, and pull his body against me. My palm caresses his cheek just as our lips touch. Sparks ignite in my mind, and the faint taste of something sweet I can't place explodes on my tongue. I pull away, nerves banging at the back of my mind, screaming that I shouldn't have stopped.

When I step back Skylar's eyes are stuck on me, surprised.

"I'm sorr—" I try to apologize, but before I can finish the word, Skylar presses his entire body into me.

His lips lock onto mine and my knees go weak. The sweetness shoots through my mouth, sinking into every part of my brain. Then his lips part, and without thinking I match him bit by bit until our tongues touch, and something new I can't explain surges through me. If I were to glow with how much I want him right now, I'd be brighter than the sun.

SKYLAR

"Someone's happy." Imani twists around like she does every morning when I slip in the back seat.

This morning is different though. It's the Monday after my first date ever, and I haven't come off the high yet. It's all I thought about all weekend. From the time Jacob left my house Saturday night, to church yesterday morning, during every moment I tried to read, going to bed last night, and getting ready this morning.

I nod harder than usual. No point in hiding it. *Talk slowly,* I remind myself. She isn't going to be able to understand if my lips are flying.

Yeah, I tell her. *A little bit.*

"Uh. Obvious." Seth grins and pulls onto the road.

"So? Spill it." Imani slumps desperately.

I told her *all* about it over text Saturday night, but she told me then, she needed to hear it in person. Which doesn't make a lot of sense to me, since she isn't going to *hear* anything from me. I shrug and start anyway.

He took me to the fair. You know that, I tell her. I'm not repeating everything, so I give her the abridged version. It's frustrating not being able to blurt it all out when it all wants to just spill out. You would think I'd have gotten used to it by now, but no. Something about seeing others get to, I guess. *I won a stuffed animal bear. And I made him ride all the rides, but I think he was scared of a few. Then we went through a corn maze, and we danced.*

Imani's eyes watch me intently, catching every word. Her eyes squint and widen, she's so into the story.

"And?" she pries.

I know what she's digging for. I smile, tilting my head and pursing my lips.

He kissed me, I tell her. The blood rushes to my cheeks. I'm not sure that will ever change. It was amazing. His lips were perfect. *Then I kissed him. And he kissed me good night when he dropped me off at home.*

I push my shoulders up, squeezing them close to my body and grinning. After the corn maze, once we *finally* got out, which took longer than he expected, we sat in his car and talked until he had to get me home. I made him sing for me. He's convinced he's not that good, but I love his voice.

"Aw!" Imani sighs. "So sweet! In the corn maze! I bet that was *so* romantic."

It was, except when people interrupted, I tell her. I leave off the part about them scaring me. She doesn't need to know that part.

"Interrupted? Like…" she prods.

No! I push her arm off the edge of the seat, but I'm blushing. That was it. Just kisses! *But we've been Snapping a lot more!*

"So you're boyfriends?" She sticks out her tongue.

I've asked myself the same question a lot. Are we? I mean, I think we are. I want to be. But we never really said it. But is that something you say? Like, hey, you want to be my boyfriend? Or does that just happen? We did kiss, and I can't think of anything but him. And he says he feels the same. So I think. So that's what I tell her.

I guess.

JACOB

"Did Imani interrogate you?" I ask.

Sky's in the stall changing. Part of me wishes he'd change out here, but I don't push it. I don't want to come off like *that*.

A few seconds later his phone starts talking. It's weird how I've gotten used to the delay.

"Of course she did!" Siri says, and I imagine the duh look in his hazel eyes. I bet he's rolling them too. "I told her all about it Saturday night, but she had to hear it again."

"That's sort of awesome though," I tell him. Not to complain, Ian and Eric are happy for me, but if Skylar had been a girl, they'd have had a lot more questions. "She's pretty great."

"She's awesome. Eccentric," Sky's phone says.

The stall latch clicks and the door swings open. Skylar walks out in tan short shorts and a graphic tee with an unbuttoned pink Hawaiian button-up draped over his shoulders. His eyes widen the slightest when he sees me, stuck just below my neck on my bare chest. I freeze. I hope I'm not too skinny for him.

Don't think about that.

"I like the tee." I nod at his shirt, signing my first two words. I don't know how to say tee. I also don't have a clue who My Chemical Romance is, but it looks cool. It has this massive spider silhouette over the name. "Who is that anyway?"

I pull a white V-neck tank top over my head. It's got a pink pentagram front and center. Dad hates it. And honestly, that's the only reason I got it. I don't give a hell about pentagrams.

Sky shrugs and signs while he moves his lips. *Don't know. Thought it looked cool.*

"Really?" I close my eyes and feign disappointment. "You're wearing a shirt about some…thing you don't know anything about?"

He nods slowly, putting his fist up, bobbing it up and down. I think that means yes. Gah, he's so cute. I shake my head and step up to him, leaving only a few inches.

"You're so cute today." I grin mischievously. His eyes dart away and his bright white teeth chew at his lips. I lean in and peck at his mouth. "Really cute."

I lean down and kiss him again, but I don't pull away. Our lips linger, but this isn't the place. So reluctantly I stop.

"Walk you to lunch?" I ask, as if I don't every day.

He puts his hand up and bobs it again.

"That mean yes, right?" I squint.

He does it again, then starts to laugh. He pulls his phone out and types. "Yes. It means yes. Laughing face emoji."

"And there you go again with the emojis." I roll my eyes, but I'm laughing. "Come on."

Skylar grabs my hand as I start toward the door. Two thoughts jump into my head. God, I love how his hands feels, and I'm not sure this is a good idea. My nerves fly every which way, and before I decide what's best, I'm already talking.

"Maybe not here, not yet." I look at our hands.

His eyes dim a little, but he lets go. Suddenly my hand feels stone cold, and my chest caves. That look, the disappointment. *Why'd you have to say that! Why do you even care what anyone else thinks?* I don't, I really don't!

But it's too late. It's done, and I feel like such an ass.

SKYLAR

We arrive at the coffee shop in three cars. Seth and Imani park next to us, and Ian is with Eric in his old blue Honda with the faded roof in the next spot. I'm with Jacob.

He finally explained why they call Eric Ted on the way over. His last name is Bundy, so Ted Bundy! That's some dark humor. One of the most famous serial killers ever. Wow. Now I understand the glare Eric gives them every time they call him Ted.

"Just so you know," Imani starts up as we walk toward the entrance, "you might be with Jacob now, but we've still got first dibs on you."

I hope she didn't expect me to say no after he tried signing *Want to ride to the coffee shop with me,* but actually signed *Want to ride and make out with me* instead. Yeah, I had to just to give him hell for that.

Sure, I mouth, smiling brightly for her.

Inside we order, and Imani takes off to the enclosed porch to grab some seats. I'm sipping on my Witch's Brew when Sandra comes around the corner with Eric's and Imani's drinks.

"I've got one regular iced latte for Eric..." Sandra places the plastic cup in front of him.

"Ted," Ian coughs under his breath. Jacob snorts, and Eric's glance could kill.

She squints. I guess she doesn't know the joke. "And an iced caramel macchiato for Im."

"How do you drink that?" Seth peers at Eric.

"Just do," Eric's shoulders bounce.

"How's the skirt crusade going?" Sandra looks right at me.

I don't know what to say. It sort of slipped my mind. I've been focusing on Jacob so much lately that I almost forgot. I try to take a mental inventory. The last I heard the local Pride group is still making phone calls. They tried getting our local reps to oppose it, but Jacob says that's wasted effort.

"Waiting, I think," Siri tells her.

"It's a losing battle." Jacob frowns. "They're never going to listen to us. They know what they want already, believe me."

"Maybe not." Imani leans across the table.

"Nah, they do. Plus, it's not like we can run a full campaign against it," Jacob says.

"He's not entirely wrong," Sandra admits. She sighs, placing a hand on the back of my chair. "You do know Mr. Walters better than the rest of us."

It takes my mind a moment to connect that Mr. Walters is Jacob's dad.

"It must be hard living with him," Imani huffs.

Part of me wants to give her the stink eye. Like, it's his dad. But at the same time, they're not exactly buddy-buddy.

"Has its moments." Jacob half grins and his eyes dart away.

Sandra shifts behind me. She has the look of a mother, a friend, a sister who sees pain. Then something changes. She squints and purses her lips.

"But why not?" Sandra asks.

All eyes shift to her. Why not what?

"Why can't y'all campaign against it? Flyers and phone calls. All of it," she suggests, like it's so simple.

I scrunch my brow. Could we? I scan the table. Seth's left brow is raised like Spock when he's in deep thought. Imani's frowning. Ian and Eric are squinting at Jacob. And Jacob's looking at the table, but it looks like he's considering it.

"Maybe we can," Jacob finally speaks up. He repeats it, but louder, "Maybe we can. One of us could design a flyer. I bet I could get Concord Pride to help us. They are already, technically. We could put flyers all over the school. Get teachers to publicly oppose the new dress code."

I'm nodding before he gets halfway through. Just the way he says it, the growing determination in his voice, it drives me to agree, but maybe that's because I like him too.

"I could make the flyer," Seth offers, raising his hand.

Imani eyes his hand questioningly, and he drops it to the table.

"He could, he's *actually* good at that type of thing," Imani says.

"As fun as this is, I got to get to work," Ian apologizes as he gets up. "Let me know what you decide. I can put up flyers."

A smile finds its way across my face. I guess he's a good guy after all, not to say I thought he was a bad one. Just didn't see him as the type to get involved in something like this.

"And I'm his ride, so looks like I'm out too." Eric points and follows Ian.

"See you tomorrow." Ian waves.

As they leave and everyone waves, I start typing.

"We need a slogan," Siri announces. It needs to be something catchy.

"Ooh, yes!" Imani coos across from me.

"Great idea!" Jacob bumps me.

"Why didn't y'all think of doing this before?" Seth shrugs.

All eyes turn on him, even Sandra's. His head jerks between all of us and he slouches, settling on Imani. I think that might be a mistake.

"Did you think of it before?" Imani bobs her head, snapping sassily. He shakes his head. "No. *Didn't* think so."

A pent-up cough juts from my lips, and Jacob breaks down laughing. Imani finally breaks character and a tiny bit of relief floods Seth's face.

"You're brutal," Jacob says, then looks at me. "I like you."

I roll my eyes and start moving my lips and signing. *Our slogan needs to —* I stop. None of them know sign well enough for that, and I can't look at them all at the same time so they can read my lips. I type instead.

"It needs to be catchy," Siri tells them, but the moment it comes out my mind switches gears. *Does he really like me? Why? Of course he does. Stop it. You're being stupid.*

"Let's throw around some ideas," Jacob says. Imani and Seth seem to agree. I nod, trying to focus on the here and now instead of the shit my brain is throwing at me.

I glance at Sandra when she takes a seat where Ian had been a minute before.

"What? I'm helping," she says, grinning.

I smile. Jacob's eyes dart between us and then he grabs my hand on top of the table, where everyone can see, and squeezes it. A flurry runs up my arm, but it doesn't banish the thoughts in my head. *Please just go away. Let me be.*

"We're going to do this," he says. "We have to."

JACOB
WEDNESDAY, SEPTEMBER 25

I've been in my room the past half hour, bored as fuck, begging the clock to strike 3:30 p.m.

There's no time to read, and I can't concentrate. Not even enough time to play video games. I can't play guitar, my fingers are all fidgety. I tried, but I keep hitting the wrong chords.

It's not like I'm about to step on the moon, or I'm accepting a million-dollar check. I'm just excited. Having to wait half an hour to pick up Skylar is torment.

I throw my head back, slinging my back onto the bed and check my phone again. *3:27 p.m.* I *could* leave now, get there a few minutes early. But that might seem too excited. No. Just wait. The crazy part is I'm less anxious than I was the day I took him to the fair. I paced my room so much; made enough noise to get Mom's attention. When she asked what was up, I told her I was practicing a dance warm-up.

3:28 p.m.

You know what? To hell with it. I'm leaving. I want to see him, and I've only got until six thirty. I've got church tonight, and if I skip again, I think I'm seriously in danger of Dad storming into the theater and quitting my job *for* me. I can't afford that, literally.

I throw myself from the edge of the bed and walk as quick as I can without making a scene into the kitchen and swipe Mom's keys from the counter. It sounds like they're watching TV, so I head out the back door without a word, and before another minute passes, I'm on the road to Skylar's.

For the beginning of fall it's much too hot to have the windows down. Instead, they're up and the A/C's competing with Vic Fuentes belting the lyrics to "Caraphernelia". I take a right at the end of our street and fight the urge to shove the accelerator.

I really shouldn't be so excited. Everyone says teen relationships don't last anyway. And is it even a relationship? I think. I hope. You know what? Stop thinking about that.

I cross over the railroad tracks and go through downtown until I make my last right turn and Imani's house appears. Sky went home with her after school. She wanted some "Imani-Sky" time doing I have no clue what. I didn't bother asking. Didn't want to come off too attached.

I pull in her driveway. *Okay, breathe.* I'm about to reach for my door handle when Skylar and Imani emerge from the house's brick facade. He's wearing a new red and white plaid skirt, the same one he wore at school today.

"Don't tell him," Imani's voice whispers through the glass just as I turn the music down. Don't think I wasn't meant to hear that.

I roll down the passenger window. "Don't tell me what?"

"Nothing," she says with a smile.

Skylar shakes his head as he opens the door and slides into

the passenger seat. When he turns to look at me, my jaw drops before I catch it.

"Woah," I say. His eyes. She must have done his lashes and eyes. His lashes are darker than usual, and his eyelids have a blushed appearance. It makes his eyes pop.

He grins coyly, angling away and skewing his lips.

"You look great," I tell him.

"You're welcome," Imani says, to both of us, I think.

Skylar's lips move, but I can't read them. Luckily, he puts his hand to his mouth and lowers it. *Thank you.* I do know that one.

"Have fun." Imani waves and walks off backward.

"See ya." I wave back and reverse out the driveway. "You ready for some donuts?"

I'm taking him to our local donut shop. The type that makes everything from scratch and even fills them on the spot for you. Sky's in for a treat.

"Yes! Imani said they're to die for," Siri's voice takes over so I can keep my eyes on the road.

"Yeah, they're amazing," I laugh. "You said you like cake donuts, right?"

My tastes are simple. Chocolate covered filled with Bavarian crème, or the prototypical Oreo or Reese's, and they have them all!

"Yes. Especially blueberry or chocolate," his phone spits off.

Oh, he *is* in for a treat.

"What about red velvet?" I glance at him. His eyes light up, and that's all the answer I need. "You're going to like this place."

A few seconds pass, I think he's typing something else, and we bounce over new pavement. I swear they're *always* doing construction. It's annoying, especially when you can't tell which lines are the new ones.

"You really do look great, by the way," I blurt.

He stops typing and looks at me with his coy grin.

"Like, you're super cute, even without makeup. But like woah! Your eyes... I mean, like... Uh... Yeah." I lose track of my words and start coughing to try to mask my nerves. I don't think it's working.

Skylar smiles at me and shuffles in his seat. The silence is deafening while he types. I hope I didn't make him have to erase what he'd been typing. Oh my. I'm so sorry!

"Thanks," Siri says. I glance at him and nod, but his phone keeps talking. "You look handsome yourself."

My eyes blossom and suddenly my throat dries. No. No, he didn't just say that. I'm awkward and skinny and hell, half my attire is black. I'm wearing black jeans and an oversized black and white striped shirt that's much too thick for this weather right now.

"Nah, but thanks," I say. "You're the one people wanna see."

"Only because I'm a boy in a skirt," his phone blurts a few seconds later.

"No!" I nearly shout. "It's because you're so damn cute, and they're jealous you look so good in it."

He smiles, and we both go silent. A song I don't recall fills the void. Part of me can't believe I said it. It's true, but it's got my cheeks burning.

"You going to church tonight?" Skylar's phone breaks the

silence.

"Yeah," I sigh. I wish I wasn't. Then I could spend the whole evening with him. "Gotta keep my job."

I pull into the donut shop's parking lot before he finishes typing. He either isn't done yet, or he's just waiting to get inside first. We get out and I jump in front of him so I can open the glass door for him. Skylar stops for a second, then walks in ahead of me.

"You really think your dad will make you quit? Surely not," his phone asks as the door shuts behind me and all the goodies come into view.

"You just gotta know my dad," I groan, nodding toward the glass case filled with glorious donuts. "He would. He's diehard like that."

Sky's shoulders drop. He makes a fist at the center of his chest and motions clockwise in a circle. *Sorry.*

"It's okay." I shrug. "Let's order."

"What can I get for you?" the black lady behind the counter asks. I don't know her name but I've seen her here before.

I point at the Reese's donut. "Reese's, please."

"And your friend?" she asks.

My *friend*? No. He's more than that. And I'm going to ask him to Homecoming!

SKYLAR

THURSDAY, SEPTEMBER 26

"That's too retro," Imani complains.

She's not wrong. The image on Seth's computer makes me think of '80s album art, not a political flyer.

"Retro?" Seth eyes her. "How is that retro?"

Someone walking down the sidewalk draws my attention through the coffee shop's large windows overlooking Main Street. They're walking a tiny little shaggy brown doggie, so it's worth the distraction.

"Really? You don't think that looks retro?" she asks.

It's mostly faded colors, teal, rosy red, yellow, and this grayish-blue on a super light tan background, and the lettering screams old. It's definitely *not* the one.

"How about the next one," I have Siri suggest, and I take a sip of my frappe.

"Okay," Seth whines.

It's the third design so far, and it hasn't been good. They're not bad, just not right. This one though, it's simple, and it gets the point across. It proclaims CLOTHES HAVE NO GENDER in big bold white letters against a red background, and then STOP THE SEXIST DRESS CODE, CALL THE SCHOOL

BOARD in smaller black lettering along the bottom. The back side has all their phone numbers and names, with Bruce Walters at the top.

I slap my hands on the table. Seth jumps. His fingers skitter across the keyboard and a jumble of letters infiltrate the flyer.

"Ah!" he yelps.

I'm fighting between typing and laughing, but I manage it.

"Give the boy a heart attack, why don't you?" Sandra chimes in from the other end of the table.

I laugh at her between typing words. I hear she and some of the others have made it a sport to see who can scare him first when he's here. So I figure I'm in good company.

"That's the one," Siri says. "Minus all those extra letters."

"Not my fault." Seth shakes his head.

I sign and mouth *sorry*, but it was pretty great.

"I agree." Imani shakes her head spastically. "But is that really the best we've got for a slogan?"

"What else do you have?" Seth falls against his chair and crosses his arms over his chest.

I've been thinking about this one a lot. It needs to be catchy, but I don't know how people come up with cool phrases. All I've been able to come up with are gems like *Say No to Sexism, Resist the Board* — you know, like the Borg? — and *Not Your Problem*. So, unless Imani or Sandra has something better, it's about to be *Clothes Have No Gender*.

Imani bunches her cheeks and puffs out an aggravated breath as the shop's entry bell chimes. She goes to open her mouth, then stops. Sandra's expression is blank, then her lips pooch as if she might say something, and she stops too.

"I got nothing." Imani's head droops.

"What do you got nothing on?" My favorite voice draws my attention to the open doorway. Jacob!

My eyes brighten, I know it, and I don't care.

"This damn—" Imani's eyes lock onto Sandra like she's made a mistake, but Sandra shrugs. "This slogan. None of us have anything better."

"What's wrong with it? It gets the point across, right?" Jacob shrugs.

Maybe we're just overthinking it.

I sign, *You like it?* to Jacob, mouthing the words at the same time.

"Yeah, it's good," Jacob says.

Sandra's eyes land on Jacob. "You know sign now?"

"Just a little." He grins.

"He's doing great," my phone tells them. "Still needs practice though."

"Like I said, a little." Jacob rolls his eyes at me.

"I think we've decided on a design." Seth speaks up, twisting in his seat. "Might have to change the wording, but…"

Jacob leans over his shoulder, and I find myself wishing it was my shoulder. He's got his black skinny jeans on today, and that black tank top with the plunging sleeve holes that show half his side. I swallow when I accidentally let my eyes take a peek. *Face, Skylar, face.*

"Simple." Jacob shrugs.

"You don't like it?" Seth's shoulders droop again.

"Nah, I do," Jacob says, but I can't read him. I think he does, but he's looking at it very seriously. "It's good."

"Okay…" Seth says.

"So—" Jacob starts to talk, his eyes locking on me, but Imani cuts him off.

"See, it's good." Imani cocks her head sassily at Seth. "So much better than the first one. What were you trying to imitate with those, the Coca-Cola logo?"

Seth's hands fan out in defense. Jacob looks like he really wants to say something, but he doesn't.

"No!" Seth gets defensive. "Coca-Cola? Really? You just don't understand graphic design."

"I don't understand graphic design? Of course I don't understand graphic design. But that?" Imani is smiling the entire time.

"It wasn't that bad," Seth tries.

"I'm sure it wasn't that bad," Jacob chimes in, and Imani looks at him like he's crazy.

"Okay, guys, let's not get into it," Sandra breaks in. I think she gets that it's just a Seth-Imani thing, but I could be wrong.

"Thank you," Seth says and gives Imani a set of take-that-bitch eyes. She rolls hers, and I catch a tiny grin on Seth's face. Yeah, he knew what was happening.

"So, uh," Jacob stutters, his gaze locking on me and then dropping to the floor and back again. "I've got to get to work, but I uh…"

He steps around Imani's chair so that he's right next to me. I twist around and prop my arm on the wood to face him, looking up into his bright greens. Something has him fidgety, and it's adorable in his perpetually hot way.

For some reason I reach out and take his hand. He looks down at our hands, and his finger brushes against my palm sending a flurry up my arm.

"Sky," he looks me in the eyes and pauses, "will you go to the Homecoming dance with me?"

Gasps jump around the table, and although I'm not looking, I know all eyes are on me. But I don't have to think about my answer. I'd almost forgotten about the dance with everything else happening, but there's no question.

I nod furiously! Screaming, *YES!* through silent lips.

Of course I will!

JACOB

FRIDAY, SEPTEMBER 27

Mom's car needs an alignment or a rotation or something. Maybe new brakes. I don't know. But it's been shimmying a lot lately. And I really don't want a wheel to go flying off.

"Where do you want to travel? Like overseas," Sky's phone asks.

I glance at him and grunt like I'm in deep thought. It's not a question I've thought much about. There's no doubt when I have the chance I'm getting out of the house, but I've always thought more in terms of the next city or somewhere in the mountains, not out of the country.

I used to plan on running away, back before I came out. Back when I thought Dad would kick me out anyway. He didn't, but sometimes I think it might have been better. I'd settled on Asheville. My family always complains how liberal they are, so it can't be all that bad, plus it's in the mountains.

"I don't know," I admit. The tires hit a pothole and the car jolts. "Maybe Germany. They talk cool there."

Skylar's fingers start typing again with the same little fingers that minutes ago were tacking up flyers around school. He and I took the language arts halls while Seth and Imani filled the science wing. And Ian just sent a Snap of the flyers he left at the local library. Eric's supposed to be dropping some off at the shops downtown.

"Talk cool? That's why?" Sky's phone asks.

Without looking, I nod and attempt to defend my choice. "Yeah, why not?"

He puts his palms out in resignation and starts typing again.

"I want to go to Finland, or maybe Denmark," Siri says.

Finland? Denmark? Of all the places, I'd never thought of those. I can't say I knew Finland was an actual place, to be honest.

"Why? What's there?" I ask. I was expecting something more like Greece or Spain, or maybe Australia. Actually, I should have said Australia.

"Finland is the happiest place on Earth, and Denmark is the second," Sky's phone states in its British accent. I glance at him to remind myself I'm not listening to the National Geographic Channel. "They're consistently ranked the highest. And I hear Denmark is beautiful. I just want to be somewhere that happy."

What do I say to that?

I take the next right and pull into his driveway. I have to say something. But what?

"Are you not happy?" is what comes out. *Why aren't you happy?*

I park the car and twist in my seat to face him. His eyes look down and then back up, finding me and smiling.

He motions *yes* with his fist, and then types some more.

"Now, maybe. It was always just so messed up before. I

used to read all about Denmark, I think I want to go there more. There's this castle called Kronborg Slot that has this statue of a famous Viking that's supposed to save them during Ragnarok. And they have this rune stone thing I've heard is cool."

"Ragnarok, like in *Thor*?" I ask.

He starts typing furiously. "Sort of, but no. It's Viking mythology or something."

If it has something to do with Thor, count me in. Who knows, maybe I will. Maybe *we* will?

"Sounds cool. Maybe you'll get to go one day," I tell him. "Mind if I come inside? I've like half an hour before I need to be gone for work."

He smiles, and while he types I let my eyes linger up and down his t-shirt. Is it bad that I want to cuddle and wrap myself up in him?

"Yeah. I meant to tell you that Mom and Dad want to talk to you anyway." He shrugs. I squint.

What?

"Talk to me? Am I in trouble?" I ask, half grinning, half holding my breath.

He shakes his head, bunching his nose up and laughing silently. I let out my half breath and get out the car.

"So, like what do they want to talk about?" I ask.

He shrugs, but he's grinning too big for me to believe that. I don't question it further though. At least I'll get to see him longer.

I open his front door and let him go in first.

"Look at that gentleman," a woman's voice comes from inside.

"Hey, Mrs. Gray." I try to sound confident even though my insides are starting to turn.

There's about a ninety percent chance I know what's about to go down. The you're-dating-our-son-so-here-are-the-ground-rules talk, or something like that. At least I can't imagine them giving me the Judge talk. That's what my dad gave Rebekah's boyfriend the first time he met him. The basics are that he owns a Judge pistol—the type that fires forty-five caliber pistol rounds and shotgun shells—and it would be waiting on him if he got her home too late or tried anything "funny". Medieval shit bordering on a criminal threat, typical conservative dad stuff.

"Jacob," Bob says...I think it's Bob.

That's what Sky usually calls him. Actually wait up a second there. I glance at Skylar. He hasn't called him Bob in a while.

"Bob," I reply. It feels weird using his first name, but that's what he told me to do.

"Glad you came. Did Sky tell you we wanted to talk with you?" he asks.

I glance at Skylar and nod. He's got a skewed grin plastered across those perfect lips. *You little shit, about to sacrifice me to the parents.* I restrain a laugh, straightening my posture and nodding to Mr. Gray. "Yes, sir."

"Good. Come sit." Mrs. Gray waves me over to the gray leather loveseat set next to the couch in a large L.

I do as I'm told and drop into the seat. Skylar starts off for the stairs, like he's going to get away. Hold the fuck up!

"Where you going?" Mr. Gray calls after him.

Ha! Take that, bitch! He catches my stare when he turns

around. His eyes narrow, and I'm beaming victory right back at him. He makes the walk back, half defeated, half amused, and sits next to me, making certain to leave a good foot between.

"This isn't going to be bad, we promise." Mrs. Gray looks between us.

"This isn't that type of talk." His dad grins. "We just wanted to sit you down since you're dating Skylar and go over some ground rules. Nothing scary."

I nod. Nothing scary? Then why are my nerves on edge and my fists clenched?

"First, curfew. Skylar's curfew is eleven. Please try to have him back by then. If you're a few minutes late it's not a big deal, just let us know ahead of time." Mr. Gray waits for us to acknowledge, so I nod. "Second, Skylar's our son. And if you're going to date him, we expect you to respect him—"

Oh no! Here it comes. I brace for it.

"—so as long as you don't do anything to hurt him, we're good. I'm not going to threaten you with something scary. Just know you'll answer to me if you hurt him."

I release the air stuck in my lungs. That was surprisingly painless, so much better than I'd expected. Sort of like Dad's Judge talk, without the threat of death.

"And one last thing." His mom leans forward, her sandy-blonde hair falling over her eye. She pulls it back. "We also know that boys will be boys, and no matter how much we might say not to, you two are going to do what you want."

What is happening now? She reaches in her pocket and pulls out a handful of little plastic square packages. I swallow and stiffen. Really?

"Just be safe," she says and hands *me* the condoms. Why me?

I look down at my hand. There are at least six, maybe more, of the brightly colored packages in my palm. I swallow again. What the hell? I've never seen one in real life before, and I've damn well never held one. I close my fist around them and shove them in my pocket. What do I say?

"Uh... Yeah, I mean... Yes, ma'am," I stutter, trying my best to look her in the eye. But she, Skylar's *mom*, literally just handed me a stash of condoms and said to *be safe*.

"Oh! And one more thing." She jumps from the sofa and prances off into the other room.

One more thing?

Wonder if I took off now, could I make it to the front door before Bob catches me? *Stop being stupid.* My parents would never have said half of that, and especially not the condom bit. It would have been more like, *If you so much as kiss my daughter* — 'cause they'll never talk to Sky or admit I'm dating a boy — *I'll knock your head against a brick wall*. Not, *Hey, we know you're going to mess around, so at least wear this condom when you fuck our son.*

While we wait Mr. Gray nods nervously. "You into any sports?"

"Uh, yeah. Swim team," I stutter, still processing everything. I'm about to tell him I'm in a band, but I decide against it. Instead, I go with, "I play the guitar too."

Internally, I'm screaming. He didn't ask. Why did you say that?

"That's great. I used to play acoustic back in college," Mr. Gray starts up, leaning back to get more comfortable. He crosses one leg over the other, creasing his slate slacks. I don't know what he does for a living, but he looks like a businessman. Skylar tilts his head. I don't think he'd heard this either. "Benji, Conner, and I played at bars around campus for extra cash back then. I can't tell you how many girls—"

"Is he boring you with his college stories?" Mrs. Gray saves us, coming around the corner with a black gift bag. I glance at Skylar. He looks like he wanted to hear more.

"Nah, not at all," I say. But thank you!

"They were enjoying it." Mr. Gray shrugs. "Not all my stories are boring."

"Tell that to anyone who has to listen to them," Mrs. Gray says.

She takes a seat next to her husband and places the bag on the coffee table, pushing it toward Skylar. "Skylar told us you asked him to Homecoming. That's so sweet. You two are going to be a cute couple. But," she puts a finger up and points to the bag while eyeing Skylar, "you need a great outfit. And your friend Imani might have gone with me to the mall to pick one out for you. She says you liked it."

My attention darts to Skylar. His eyes are wide, and his lips start to part. They begin to move, forming a word. But I can't tell which. His eyes dart between the bag and his parents, and he keeps mouthing something I can't read.

"Yes," his mom keeps saying. "Open it."

Sky leans forward and starts pillaging through the white tissue paper. When his hands come out, he's holding something green and silky. His mouth drops. I'm guessing it's a skirt or something, but I can't tell. He drops it to the sofa and races Mr. and Mrs. Gray with a hug before I get a glance of it.

"Why don't you try it on?" Mr. Gray says.

"What is it?" I finally ask once they stop hugging and Sky's back at the couch scooping it up, his eyes wet.

In answer, he holds it up and lets the bottle-green fabric topple down to reveal a long dress. They got him a dress for Homecoming. My mouth parts in surprise.

Oh God, I bet he'll look beautiful in it.

SKYLAR

FRIDAY, SEPTEMBER 27

I can't believe they got it. Imani. You sly bitch.

It's beautiful. Well, other than needing to be shortened a few inches, courtesy of my short self. But it fits perfectly around my thighs and waist.

Jacob seemed to like it too. His jaw dropped a little when I walked out and spun around in the living room. And how much that made my day, even more than the dress, sort of scares me, but that's a good thing. Right?

He's waiting in my room right now. I asked him to stay a little longer. I know he has to get to work, but he has a few minutes. I take one final glance at myself in the mirror, double-checking how the dress fits around my chest and arms, yet leaving my shoulders bare. I sigh happily and slip out of it and back into a pair of soft white shorts and a simple black tee.

Folding the dress over my arm, I unlock the bathroom door and head to my bedroom where the door is standing half ajar. Mom and Dad's only requirement for him to be in my room was that the door stay open and that they may or may not come check on us at any time.

I push past the door and Jacob's sitting on my bed. On my

bed. Something else. Think about something else! He sees me immediately and a smile slips across his lips.

Did you like the dress? I ask, signing at the same time while trying to balance it on my arm. But my mind begs me to ask if he really likes me. I push it aside and try to focus.

He pauses, eyes squinting, dividing his focus between my lips and hands. That might have been a little much to ask him to translate. Oops.

"You asked if I liked the dress?" Jacob asks.

I nod and bounce my fist. He got it!

"Duh! Of course!" he practically yells, his brow crinkling as if to ask how crazy I must be to ask. "You look great in anything! But…"

But?

"Don't kill me for saying this." Jacob shifts and skews his mouth nervously. "But, well… Uh… Your uh…uh… Your butt looks great in it."

Immediately he looks away, eyes darting to the floor. He coughs, and he's not the only nervous one now.

I can feel the heat rushing into my cheeks, probably blossoming my face in red. I twist around to hide it and put the dress away. While he can't see I open my mouth wide and bite at my lip to try and calm myself. He likes my butt! It seems like such a weird thing to be excited about, but he likes something about me. I mean he must, he's dating me, but before he's just told me I'm cute. This is something more.

I suck in a breath of courage and turn around and drop next to him on the bed. I wrap my fingers in his hand and when my eyes land on him I can tell he's nervous.

So you like my butt? I mouth it slowly.

"Uh…" His eyes dart away and then back up at me and away again. "Yeah. Hope that's okay. Maybe I shouldn't have said it. I say too much sometimes."

I shake my head furiously.

Tell me! I move my lips. *It makes me feel good.*

And now I'm looking away. Did I just admit that? To him?

"Oh… O-okay," he stutters, and before I can respond his lips are on mine, and his hands are exploring my cheekbone.

He pulls back, and his eyes drift to the open door. Mom and Dad said they don't mind kissing as long as we're not making out on top of each other in the living room in front of them basically. But I think he's still nervous. I don't really know his family, but from what I've heard this is foreign to him. He's probably waiting for my dad to jump around the doorframe and scream, *I got you!*

Neither of us speaks for a moment, but it's not really awkward. It's peaceful. Usually silence isn't peaceful, even for someone like me who lives in it for the most part, but it is right now.

"I have to figure out what I'm wearing to Homecoming." His eyes widen. "Can't have you looking all hot and I show up in some basic-ass button-up."

I nod. Yeah, he needs to turn eyes. I mean, he will anyway, but he needs an outfit that'll make it that much more.

"You think I should go basic or something colorful?" he asks.

Colorful? Him? I laugh silently, my eyes closing and air jutting from my nose. When my eyes open he's looking at me with this incredulous smile.

"What?" he says, and even signs it.

Colorful? You? I say, moving my hands and pointing at him. *Really?*

"I can do colors. I just don't." He shrugs.

Stick to black, I tell him.

"Really?" he asks.

I'm not sure if it's confirmation or if he isn't sure what I said, but either way I nod.

"If that's what you want," he tilts his head and pecks me on the lips before continuing, "then that's what I'll do."

Oh! And some eye makeup, like Imani did to me, I bet his eyes would look amazing with mascara! *You could have Imani do your eyes!*

"I caught Imani and eyes," he says. "I'm trying. I promise. This sign language stuff is hard though."

I giggle. It's second nature for me. Instead of trying again I retrieve my phone and have Siri say it. "You should have Imani do your eyes. Like black lashes. It'll make them longer. And maybe some black eye shadow? I think it'd be hot. I mean…hotter. You're already hot."

Jacob's lips skew to the left, and he straightens his collar.

"Uh… Thanks." He almost questions it but doesn't. He better take it! "Maybe. I've never worn makeup. Oh my God, Dad would freak! He can't even stand my nails."

I look to his plain nails. His Dad is still being a pain about that, so he hasn't painted them lately. I like them black. I start typing.

"He's going to flip if he finds out you're taking *me* to the dance either way," I remind him.

"Good point. So it's a maybe." Jacob points at me and nods. He checks his watch. "I've only got a few more minutes.

Ugh! I don't want to go to work."

I want to be the clingy boyfriend that tells him to call in, but I refuse to be that guy. Nope. Not doing it. Not yet at least.

"Can I ask you a weird... Sort of... Well really actually, a personal question?" Jacob pulls his bottom lip in. He's nervous about whatever it is he wants to ask.

A really personal question? I think about it. It could be anything. That's a good question, should I? Instinct is to say yes, shoot, what do I have to hide. I've told him about most of my trauma anyway.

I nod slowly, eyes squinting.

"So uh... You ever had sex?" His eyes lock on mine. His arms stiffen and his fingers go rigid around mine. He's nervous, but he's trying not to appear that way.

Sex? Somehow that's not what I was expecting. I don't know what I was expecting actually, just not that. But it's sort of a relief, somehow. And the answer is a resounding no. Who's going to mess around with the defective kid? They just want to make fun of him.

I shake my head slowly, twisting my lips and shrugging.

"That's okay." His voice jumps back, higher than before. "I shouldn't have asked though. Sorry."

He pulls his hand away and burrows his fingers between his thighs. A cough works its way up his throat. It's adorable how nervous that little question makes him. I've been thinking about sex too, not going to lie. But it's sweet that he'd want to be so careful. I pull my phone out and start typing.

"It's okay. I don't mind. What about you?" Siri asks for me, and I reach for his hand. I put my palm on his wrist and look at him, asking with my eyes for his hand again.

Jacob grins and pulls his hand from its hiding spot and gives it to me.

"Nah." He shrugs, like it's a mark of inadequacy.

"That's okay," my phone assures him. He grins a little more, clearing his throat again. He does that a lot when he's nervous. I stare at the next words on my screen. I probably shouldn't say this, but what teen hasn't said something stupid. "Maybe we'll be each other's first."

His eyes go wide, and his hands tighten for a split second.

"I... Uh..." Jacob stutters. It's crazy how he goes from so hot to adorable as fuck in a moment. "Yeah. Maybe."

I'm not sure that means yes, he wants me to be, or that it's cool that I'd think that. I'm going to imagine he wants me to be. But I don't know what to do now. How do you follow that up?

Awkward silence, I guess. Very awkward silence.

But I'm not letting go of his hand until he has to leave. I'll just stroke the fluffy comforter I'm sitting on with my other hand, trying to think of anything but that, but sex keeps jumping into the center of my focus. Like, I'm not stupid. I know how it works. The internet teaches a lot. My mind flashes with images like those, just with Jacob and me instead, and I have to stop. Stuff is already moving between my legs and I don't need that right now.

"Uh..." Jacob starts to talk, but he stops. Instead, he smiles at me, lips held tightly together.

I flash a smile back. I swear we could joke about this with anyone else and it wouldn't matter. Like I could joke about Imani wanting to mess with that Jen girl she thinks is so hot and it wouldn't faze me. But this? This is so different. I like him, and I want him.

"You ever done *anything*?" he finally asks, or more like spurts the words out as quick as he can.

I shake my head again. It's not like the guys at the orphanage were friendly, and even the assholes weren't *that* type of asshole. Maybe I'm lucky in that.

"You?" I have my phone ask.

"Nah." He shrugs. And that sort of surprises me. But I think he's a lot less outgoing than he comes off too. "You want to try some?"

My eyes dart to him, eyes locked together. He's nervous. Yes! I want to. I want to feel his hands on me. I want to feel him on me. But I don't know that right now is the time. And I don't know if it's just my nerves or that Mom and Dad are just downstairs.

I shake my head slowly and immediately start moving my mouth.

Not now. I want to. I really do, just not now, I tell him, speaking slowly so he catches every word, my hands moving just in case he can catch any of the signs. *Mom and Dad are here.*

"Oh yeah." He smiles, sucking in a quick relieved breath. I think it's partly that it's over, and partly that I didn't run him out of my room. "I'm sorry. I shouldn't have asked."

There he goes apologizing again. He needs to stop that.

Stop saying sorry, I demand, hands moving in circle. *It's okay.*

JACOB

SATURDAY, SEPTEMBER 28

Why did I volunteer to be up before eleven on a Saturday?

"One, two, three, go." Ian taps his drumsticks on each count and we start playing on cue.

Ian has work at two, and Eric was insistent we practice today, that's why. I try blinking the sleep from my eyes with each beat. But it's not working.

We're playing an older Mayday Parade song. It's part of our old emo music list. Eric wants to mix it up for the show in Charlotte, the one we've yet to be confirmed for.

When I hit my last note, I let my guitar fall to my side and reach for my phone. Before I can see the screen Ian opens his mouth.

"Can you focus?" Ian complains.

"I am focused." I turn to face him, flicking my gaze back to Eric for support. He steps back.

"You keep checking your phone," Ian huffs.

"So?" I shrug and reposition the black beanie I put on this morning. It's finally getting colder.

"You're distracted. And you keep missing notes," he says. Okay, he might have something there, but it's early and my fingers haven't fully come to life yet. "I promise Sky can wait an hour. We're here to practice."

"What?" I curl my brow. What's his problem? "What's wrong with me checking my texts?"

"You've been on your phone between every song. It's slowing us down." He rolls his eyes.

"Really?" I look to Eric.

"I mean, yeah." Eric shrugs.

I roll my eyes. "Seriously, guys?"

"Seriously," Eric bites back.

"Oh yeah? What's the real problem?" This is stupid. I'm here. I'm playing. And my mistakes have nothing to do with checking my damn phone.

At first he doesn't respond, he just grunts. But something builds behind his eyes—frustration. Seriously?

"You're not around as much, and when you are, all you talk about is Sky this, Sky that," Ian complains. "I know you like him, but…"

His voice trails off. Wow.

"You're mad I didn't hang out with you Thursday? Is that it?" It's not like I completely ignore him.

"No. It's not that. He's all I hear about now," Ian goes on. "And right now, you'd rather not be here. Right?"

"Right now, with you complaining? Yeah, no," I bite back.

"Come on," Eric steps in. "But he does have a boyfriend now. You can't tell me you wouldn't totally ditch us if you got a girlfriend. Like, if that ever happens."

Boyfriend?

"Hey now!" Ian snaps. "I'm just not in the mood for that. I could—"

"That's not what your browser history says, man," Eric counters, and a laugh busts from my gut.

"Nice try, I delete my browser history." Ian wags his shoulders like he just mounted the hill and won the battle.

"My point exactly." Eric smiles even bigger.

My mind is still reeling from Eric calling Sky my boyfriend. Are we? That seems like a big step. But is it really a question? We were talking about sex last night and now I'm worried about someone calling him my boyfriend?

"Look, I'm sorry," I jump in — one, to stop my mind from running rampant with this new contradiction, and two, because maybe Ian has a tiny point. Plus I might be a little fussy because I wanted to sleep more this morning. "I'll try to focus more, but I really like him. It's sort of weird, but I do."

"We know." Eric shakes his head and pats my shoulder. "You couldn't deceive anyone. Hell, I could tell before you took him on a date."

"He's right." Ian agrees.

"I hate you both."

SKYLAR

SATURDAY, SEPTEMBER 28

Jacob's car is in my driveway when I pedal up. He gets out and my eyes magnetize to his bare stomach. He's wearing the gray tank he cropped last week. Damn. I can't hold back the grin when I stop and type the code to get into the garage, trying not to stare.

"Hey, cutie," he says.

He's never called me that before. He's called me cute in conversation, but never like that. I like it.

I look back, blushing, and give him a smile. I put my hands together and sign, *How are you?* The wheels spin behind his eyes as he translates.

"I got *you*. That one's easy. Uh…" He laughs. "Was it *how are you*?"

I nod enthusiastically. He got it! He's been doing good lately, really good.

"In that case, I'm good. Work was crazy," he says, but my eyes keep dropping to his slim stomach. Those effortless pale abs. I pull my eyes up and lead him inside the garage. "I think everyone in town waited to go to the movies until tonight."

When his mouth stops moving I take my opportunity. I

bounce to the tips of my toes and kiss him and kiss him and kiss him. I don't want to stop.

"Well, hey there," Jacob catches his breath and smiles. "Good to see you too."

I laugh, the air whistling awkwardly from my throat. He looks around the empty garage. It's lined with boxes and clear crates of I have no clue what, and then there's the yard equipment in the far corner. But no cars.

"Where are your parents?" He cocks his head.

They're out, I tell him. *They won't be back until late.*

"Oh?" He eyes me mischievously. "So what you're saying is we can make out all evening?"

I'm blushing again. That or the other thing we talked about last night. I bite at my lip and nod, even though my insides are a mess of excitement and nerves.

"I mean, you know, I'm not saying we have to, just a… You know, an idea," he starts to stutter. There he goes speeding from hot to adorable in an instant with all those nerves.

I lead him inside and through the kitchen, stopping long enough to ask if he wants something to drink. He shakes his head and I head straight for the stairs and my room. It's as I left it this afternoon. Posters on every wall, plus a new string of pictures I had printed of Imani, Seth, and myself from the past two months hanging over my nightstand, and there's even a few of Jacob and me now.

"Ooh, I'm on your wall," he says, pointing.

It's the one I took of him the day he learned to ride a bike. We weren't a *thing* then, but I thought it was something that needed to be captured, so I snapped a picture when he was coming back toward me. I wasn't sure how he'd react, but he seems to like it.

"Our first date." He points to another one of us like it's been ages. It's outside, at the end of the corn maze that took us way too long to get out of. The night of our first kiss. "I love it!"

I can't wipe away my smile. He even signed the words; sure, it was a little exaggerated, but he's learning. I take a seat on the edge of my bed, and he's quick to follow. His bare arm brushes my shoulder. I like it when he wears tank tops. He's not buff, but he's not as puny as he thinks either. And his arms look just strong enough to pin me down.

"Ian got butt hurt today about me spending time with you," he says. Suddenly my mood drops a notch, guilt filling the space. He must see it in my eyes. "No, no. It's okay. He gets it now. He's just used to us always hanging out. Just the trio. Not the trio, plus you, plus Imani and Seth."

Oh. Okay, I say. I don't want to get in the way. Oh no! Am I getting in the way?

"It's really okay, Sky, I promise." He throws an arm over my shoulder and squeezes me. "We talked it over. He's good. Ted even understood."

That brings a smile to my face. *You mean Eric?*

"Nah, Ted." He grins, motioning his hand in front of us dramatically, "Eric 'Ted' Bundy."

I roll my eyes. And when they settle I'm looking at his thigh covered in skin-tight black jeans, wishing they weren't there. An urge to grab his leg and slide my hand north surges through my head, but I resist.

"Why you so stiff?" Jacob shakes me playfully, his eyes

never leaving mine.

I shake my head. *I'm not stiff.*

Of course, it's a lie. But I'm not telling him the thoughts running through my head, the things I've imagined him doing to me. They're too much to be spoken, and we texted about it last night anyway. What we thought we wanted, how to be safe when the time came. And I think both of us were thinking sooner rather than later.

"Sure." He stretches it out. "Let's loosen you up a bit."

He leans over and slowly begins kissing me. It works. My whole body goes slack, and I melt into him, our lips fusing into one. The taste of his tongue invades my senses in this way I can't explain. Happiness. Exhilaration. Excitement. And horniness, which is why I made certain to wear my baggier pants. If I hadn't, he'd be able to see exactly how excited he's making me right now.

His hand reaches for my face, rubbing my cheek and down my neck. I put my worries aside and push myself closer, sliding my hand onto his stomach. I've never touched him like this, fingers against bare skin. He twitches and I start to pull back, but he grabs my hand and presses it back to his skin. He stops kissing me long enough to look into my eyes.

He's about to say something, but I slide my hand up his shirt and push him back. He falls against my bed, and I slide on top of him and wrap my arms around him, pressing our bodies together. He rolls, pinning me underneath him.

"Oh wow," he blurts. What? Did I do something wrong? "Someone's uh...you know."

I tilt my head, confused. He looks down and I follow his gaze to my crotch. I look back up and meet his eyes. He's smiling hard. I don't know what to say, so I just shrug and give him a mischievous grin. I go to pull him back down, but he stops me.

"Are you...uh..." he starts but stops. "Like, you want to?"

I nod with everything that's in me. Yes. I want it. I want it all.

"Are you sure? I don't want to—" he starts.

It's the sweetest thing, and honestly, it makes my body burn hotter for him. But I shove a finger against his lips.

I want this, I mouth between breaths.

The concern in his face morphs into desire and he falls on top of me.

His lips press against mine, our breaths intermingling. I grip his waist and slide my fingers under his shirt, gliding over the smooth contours of his back. It's like there's nothing else. Just us. Just our bodies, our hands, our mouths. And that's all I want.

His shirt comes off, and then mine. I yank him back to me, not wanting our mouths apart for a moment longer, and gasp when our bare chests touch and his hand explores my skin.

"Are you sure?" He stops again, asking between breaths.

I can see in his eyes how much he wants me to say yes, but the man inside him wants me to be at ease.

Did you bring a condom? I ask.

"Yeah." He grins and produces one from his pocket.

I nod vigorously. He's going to need it. That's the other thing we talked about last night. Imani was right. I think I'm a bottom. Guess we're about to find out.

He kisses me again. His lips move down, pecking my chin and then my neck. Oh my God, I never expected it to feel this good. His tongue slides down my skin, and my back arches under his weight, my mouth open wide in pleasure. His hand slides down my stomach and begins exploring my pants. He finds what he's looking for and his fingers squeeze. His touch forces a gasp of air from my mouth, and my body is aflame, rioting.

I want nothing more than to know more. To know how he can make me feel when he explores more. To know how I can make him feel.

He opens his eyes and I grin at him. My stomach rises and falls rapidly. And his lips drop back to my neck and start making a trail south. First my chest, then my stomach. Every touch absolute euphoria. I shove my head against the bed and close my eyes as I feel a tug at my pants.

I glance down and meet Jacob's hungry gaze.

"Are you sure?" he asks one more time.

Yes, I nod. *Yes.*

SKYLAR

SUNDAY, SEPTEMBER 29

It's still dark when my eyes peel open. What time is it?

I roll over, attempting to keep my eyes closed while not falling onto the floor, trying to find my phone on the nightstand. It can't be past eight. My window's still dark except the hard light of the streetlamp outside.

My hand fumbles until I find it, and it blares to life in my face. I squint long enough to make out the numbers.

7:13 a.m.

Why am I up at seven?

I lie back, staring at the inside of my eyelids, but my brain starts up anyway. And I hate what it whispers.

He doesn't like you. He's just using you. Everyone always does. You're just a defective toy to him.

Stop it! Stop! I twist and turn, like it'll rid the thought from my head. Like it'll dislodge the words from my mind and expel my fear. He does like me! He does!

But what if he doesn't? Has he just been trying to get me in bed? No! Stop it.

I bring my phone to life again and tap the text message icon to bring up our thread.

JACOB: I'm home.

JACOB: Ur literally the most beautiful boy on the planet! ::hug face:: ::kissy face::

SKYLAR: No I'm not! Stop it! ::pouty face::

JACOB: Yes u are! U stop it! ::kissy face:: Ur gorgeous.

SKYLAR: No! ::facepalm::

JACOB: YES!! ::eye roll:

SKYLAR: I can do this all night!

And we did for at least half an hour before he had to go to bed.

JACOB: Tired. Church in the morning. Gotta go to bed.

SKYLAR: Okay. Thanks for tonight. You were amazing. ::devil face::

JACOB: ::surprise face:: Ur the naughty one. That mouth. ::devil face:: ::crying laughing face::

SKYLAR: ::facepalm:: ::surprised face::

JACOB: ::crazy face:: Can't wait to see you again. ::kissy face::

SKYLAR: You too! ::kissy face::

JACOB: Night babe ::kissy face::

SKYLAR: Night! ::pouty face:: ::hug face:: ::kissy face::

I might have gone a little overboard on the emojis on that last message, but when he called me babe, I almost cried. And reading it again, I almost cry again. He does like me. I squeeze my fists and bunch my shoulders up and squeal inside.

He really does like me.

JACOB

I'm waiting in the hall for Sky. It's our new tradition. After first block we meet by the water fountain and walk to dance together. My foot taps the worn carpet, and I crane over the crowd looking for him.

Finally a hand pops over the torrent of bodies and there he is. Every perfect, beautiful inch of his short self.

"Sky!" I wrap him in a hug.

Then without delay I do what I've been waiting for all morning. I reach for his hand. Everyone knows we're talking anyway, and why should we hide it?

"How was English?" I ask.

He shrugs and shakes his outspread hand.

I squeeze closer to him to get through the crowd. No one wants to move, and everyone's in a hurry. I clamp my hand tighter around his and pull us through, winding between standing groups and running bodies. Traffic lightens at the stairs and I slow, letting Sky come up next to me. I still can't believe—

Something, a body, wedges between us. Hands shoving us apart. My fingers loosen, so as not to hurt Sky, and I stumble away, but my eyes immediately dart back to Skylar.

He looks as confused as I am. But it takes no time to realize what happened. Blake spins around, walking backward long enough to yell at us.

"No one wants to see y'all fags holding hands," he spits.

"What the hell, man?" I yell, but he's done a one-eighty and disappears into the sea of bodies before I can get it out.

A few voices call him out, telling him to chill. Which is new.

But I have other worries. I rush back to Skylar. He's looking down at his hand like it's dirty. I scoop it up and squeeze.

"You okay?" I ask, searching his eyes when they find me again. He nods. "You have to ignore him. He's just an asshole."

Skylar nods, but there's something else in his eyes. Worry?

"Hey, look at me, Sky," I beg him, and raise our intertwined fingers for him to see. "I'm not letting go."

The green in his eyes sparkles between the flecks of brown, and he nods.

"Let's get downstairs," I tell him.

We take the stairs down two more levels and dump into the arts section. It might smell like dirty laundry down here, but it's less crowded, so I'll take it.

Skylar tugs at my hand, and I stop. He's tilting his head toward one of the bulletin boards with school announcements on it, like weekly news, sports events, a Homecoming Dance flyer. There *was* one of our *Clothes Have No Gender* flyers too, but it's gone. Or rather most of it.

Someone tore it from the board, leaving only the top

quarter where the tack held it in place. I hate people. Have I said how much I hate people?

"People are stupid," I comment as Skylar digs in his pack for another flyer. "If they don't like it, they should just make their own flyers, not fuck with ours."

Skylar's nodding as he replaces the flyer, then shrugs at me.

"We're going to win this!" I tell him.

But if I'm honest, I don't really believe it. I wish I did. The board made up its mind weeks ago. Does that make me a liar? Am I lying to him? Suddenly I feel disgusting, dirty. But how could I ever tell him to give up? That seems just as wrong.

I've told him it's not in our favor, and I hope that's enough. He wants to fight it. He wants to take it to the end. And I can't help but stand with him.

SKYLAR
WEDNESDAY, OCTOBER 2

Things have been great! Even school seems a little better. And it's all because of him.

I still can't wrap my head around it all. It seems like this straw house that's bound to come falling down. But I'm going to live in it until it does, until every last piece is wilted and gone, and there's no way to rebuild it. I've never had this before. I've never felt this type of... Joy? Happiness? I don't even know what to call it. It's just awesome!

I saw him in the hall between Civics and Sociology. Jacob's Chemistry classroom is just down the hall from my fourth block. It's good for everyone else that I can't scream and yell, because I want to every time I see him. And he's wearing his cropped shirt again. I'm honestly surprised he hasn't got dress coded yet. I mean that is sort of the school's thing.

A nudge knocks me from my daydreaming.

"You still with us?" Imani whispers across the empty row between our desks.

Yeah, I mouth, darting my eye around the room to see if anyone else noticed me zoning out.

"—teaches that a person's beliefs, their values, and their

practices can, or rather should, be understood," Mr. Dennard drones on about something, "based on that person's culture."

What should be based on their culture? I squint. Okay, maybe I'm not with you. I've been like this the whole period.

"Liar," Imani grins. "Wanna go bowling after your boy goes to work tonight?"

Seth's looking now, his lips pursed, eyes begging us to shut up. I don't think he wants to get called out by Mr. Dennard a third time this week.

My boy, I think to myself. A spurt of energy and euphoria shoots through my chest. My boy.

I give her a nod. I'm going to lose, no question, but I'll go for that.

I check my phone again. Thirty seconds until I get to see him. We're going for a walk after school. Twenty-five seconds. He has work after, so we're going to spend the half hour he's got between walking around the larger-than-life Earnhardt statue in the middle of downtown. He's apparently a local celebrity. Ten seconds. It's not my favorite spot, but it's nice, and Jacob will be there. Five seconds. Come on!

I can feel Imani staring me down, so I look, and she is. I roll my eyes at her and smile.

Three. Two. One. The bell rings and I only wait long enough to jump from my seat so that I'm not the first to move.

"Wait for us!" Imani calls out dramatically.

I've not taken a step yet, just stood up. I eye her and move my lips slow enough to be read, *Fine. Waiting on your slow ass.*

"Salty." Imani shoulders her pack.

"Damn, you're in a hurry." Seth maneuvers around the desks and comes between us.

Come on, I say. I don't have long and I don't want to waste it.

They grin knowingly and follow me into the hallway. Immediately my eyes go into search mode, jumping from face to face, looking for those perfect green eyes, pale skin, and that platinum-blonde hair. No one else at Brown has hair like it. His eyes light up when they land on me, and it sends a flood of dopamine up and down my body.

It's hard, but I refrain from sprinting. Finally he's in front of me, wrapping his arms around me and pecking me on the cheek. A faint "ew" nags at my ear from somewhere in the crowd, but I shrug it off as my hand finds its way into his.

"Ready for a walk?" Jacob leans into me and we start down the hall.

I nod eagerly.

"You two coming?" Jacob looks around me at Seth and Imani.

We're making a sort of wall as we make for the exit, four strong.

"To walk?" Seth eyes him stupidly.

Imani skews her lips and grunts.

"Take that as a no." Jacob laughs and returns his attention to me. "Guess it's just us."

I love you two! If I were telepathic that's what I'd be sending to Seth and Imani right this moment. I don't care if it's mainly because neither of them thinks walking is fun, at least part of it's because they know I'm excited to spend time with Jacob alone.

I nod again and smile. But before we go I've got to pee. I stop them and put a hand up, signing and moving my lips at the same time.

Hold on. I'm going to the bathroom first. I think they understand. They're nodding at least, so I start back the direction we came. The bathrooms are just a few doors down.

Jacob starts to walk with me but thinks twice about it and stays next to Imani. He says something I can't hear as I disappear around the corner and find a stall. It's quiet until a group of voices crowd the space, echoing off the walls. Someone doesn't have an inside voice.

I zip up and open the stall door. Lovely. It's Blake and some guy I don't know. Their eyes lock on me when the stall door squeaks. I freeze and a forced grin pulls back at my cheeks before I go to wash my hands.

"Well, well," Blake starts, his feet plopping against the tile floor. "I hear you think you're going to Homecoming with Jacob."

No, I *am* going with Jacob. How is it a question?

I nod, glancing at him long enough to acknowledge it. He settles next to me, planting his butt against the next open sink and crosses his arms. The other guy is practically on my ass, puffing his big square chest and grunting.

"You really think he's going to take you?" he asks, punching at Blake like it's hilarious.

Of course he is. *Jacob* asked *me* to go. I nod, raising my brow to give them a little more assurance of my confidence, and dry off my hands.

"What was that? I didn't catch it. You don't know?" Blake feigns concern and steps closer.

Something about his general presence makes me anxious, like this pit in my chest that grows the longer he's standing there, eyes boring into me no matter how playful he comes off. And now this. It always comes back to this.

He knows what I said. I'm not stupid. This isn't the first time I've had shitheads like him act stupid to feed their own empty heads.

I force another smile, let out a breath, and try to push my way between them. But I only manage a step when Blake throws his long arm out and catches me around the chest, his hand grabbing my shoulder.

"Is bot boy having trouble talking?" Blake puts on a pouty face, his voice whining.

I swallow back the urge to knee his micro penis and pea balls. It takes a lot, but I remind myself that while I might not be pretty, I'd be a whole lot uglier with a black eye and a broken nose.

"Cat got your tongue?" His friend jumps a step closer. I refuse to look up.

"Jacob doesn't want to take you," Blake tries again. "You're just the only option."

That's not true! He likes me. I know he does! And there *are* other options. There are at least three other gay guys in my grade and his. I've not met them, but that's what Imani's told me.

"You can't even talk. You're all like…" He keeps going, but I'm not going to let him get in my head with his piss-poor British accent. "Oh Jacob, will you please fucketh me? Please! I want it up the arse."

That does it. Who the hell gave them the right? I'm a person like anyone else. I try to push between them, but Blake holds me back.

"You ain't going to the dance with Jacob. And you sure ain't going in a dress. They're not going to let you do that," nameless boy snarls.

"We don't go for that shit here," Blake says, "you little retard."

Nope. Can't do this anymore. I feel a ball welling up inside my chest. I hold it down and force my way through them into the hallway. My eyes catch Imani and Seth, then land on Jacob. Years of practice kick in and I mask up everything I felt in the bathroom. Leaving it behind me. But I can't quite look at him the same. Does he really want to take me to Homecoming? Am I being stupid to think he does?

"You ready?" Jacob grins.

Stop it. You're just overthinking. And why the hell would I let anything Blake says mean anything? He's just an asshole.

I nod forcefully.

Let's go.

* * *

"What's up?" Imani asks. Her black skin is radiant even on my phone. And those curls.

I've been dying to talk to her since we left school, privately, that is. My head hasn't stopped churning out thoughts, and I don't like it.

Does Jacob actually like me? I get right to the point, making an effort to move my lips slowly.

Please tell me it's all in my head! I've never had anyone like me, not like this, and until I moved here, I've never *really* had friends. Not real ones. This is all still so new to me and sudden.

"What?" Her mouth skews, but it's not an I-didn't-catch-that what, it's disbelief. "Why would you ask that?"

And do I really like him? Oh my God! What if he's just the first person who's shown interest and I just flung myself at him because he gave me attention? Am I that pathetic?

I drop on my bed and let the camera refocus so she can read my lips. I'm not telling her about this afternoon in the bathroom. I'm pathetic enough as it is, and I don't need that type of sympathy.

Just wondering, I lie.

"Just wondering, huh?" Imani's eyes pierce through my screen and right into my mind. "You're doing that doubting thing again, aren't you?"

I roll my eyes. How does she know me like this?

I shrug. *Maybe.*

"So yes," she huffs. Her hair falls over her dark eyes and she pushes it away. "He likes you. He *really* likes you. Isn't it obvious? I knew weeks before he asked you on a date."

Did he tell you? The query snaps from my lips.

"Nah!" A giggle reaches through the phone and settles my nerves a little. "I could see it in his face. You're the only one he really wanted to talk to. I mean, at first it was annoying because he just wanted to be around you, and it felt like we were just there, but nah. He likes you. And he's actually a pretty good guy, I think."

That helps a little. Maybe I saw some of that, but didn't at the same time. I remember thinking he was looking at me longer than he should, but I refused to read anything into it. But does that really mean anything?

You sure it's not just because I'm one of the few gay guys at

Brown? I ask. It's a bit of an accusation that a certain ass put in my mind, but it stands to be asked.

"Nah again," Imani laughs. "Why you all worked up about this?"

I choose my next words a little more carefully. It's not like she doesn't know, I told her the night it happened, but it still seems like an intensely private thing to me.

You don't think he just wanted me for... I pause. *Sex?*

"No!" she blurts. Mom and Dad probably heard that in the living room. My eyes jump open, but it puts a grin on my face. "Have you talked to him about this?"

No! I shake my head vigorously.

How would I even start that conversation? Hey Jacob, did you talk to me just to screw me? Hell no!

Then my mind goes a little deeper and I ask a question before thinking it through. *Does he love me? Shouldn't you love someone before you...you know?*

"Do *you* love *him*?" She throws the question back at me, and it hits square in my chest.

Do I? I've only known him for what, a month and a half? And we've only been friendly really for the last month. Is that long enough to fall in love with someone?

I shrug, and my right cheek rises like it always does when I'm unsure.

"Then can you expect him to love you yet?" Imani comes back, sounding all wise and shit. I sort of hate it. "Sex doesn't mean you love him or that he loves you. People just do that. It's sort of weird, actually. But it doesn't mean he's using you. Maybe you should think about why *you* did it."

She smiles nervously. Maybe she's right. Maybe I'm just

overthinking it, and he does like me, maybe that is possible. And I know better on the sex thing. That was a stupid question, even if deep inside I want it to mean that.

But are we boyfriends? Like, I don't really know, I tell her.

I think we are. But neither of us has said it. And somehow in my head it's the next level, it's like making it all real. But I don't know. And now that I'm thinking about it, maybe that's what's eating at me.

"I don't know. Are you?" she asks. That's not the answer I wanted. "Look, Sky. You have to ask *him* that. As far as I'm concerned, you two are dating, and that makes you boyfriends, but I know everyone has different takes on that, so yeah. Ask him."

Ask him. That's harder though. But maybe she's right.

JACOB
THURSDAY, OCTOBER 3

"I'm going to be sore tonight," I laugh. But it falls flat.

Skylar's been weird today. Distant. He looks at me after a second and grins, like he finally heard it.

"You did great!" I tell him.

We're finally doing some choreographed dances. It took some convincing, but Mrs. Lockerman finally gave in last week and we started the first one today. It's harder than I expected to dance like Britney.

It's been awkward in the changing room. Quiet. Something is up, and I don't know why or what. I start undressing like normal, anything to distract. But I can't.

"You okay, Sky?" I ask, trying to keep my eyes off his stomach when his shirt comes off.

He nods, and I think he mouths *I'm good*, but I'm not sure. His eyes are distant when he looks at me. Just don't think about it. It's nothing.

"Want to go rock climbing Saturday?" I throw the question out.

I was looking up hiking types of things you can do around here or near Charlotte. It's not my thing, but I know he likes the outdoors stuff, and apparently there's a rock-climbing spot at the Whitewater Center. They've also got kayaking and whitewater rafting, but that all seems a little too dangerous.

He looks at me, his eyes brightening a bit, and nods, but there's a shrug too. It's like a silent, bland "sure", and something in his eyes changes. They look up, and his lips twitch as he pulls on his shorts and slides into the white tee and pink button-up he had on before class. Then his eyes lock on me.

His hands start moving, faster than I can really translate, and I struggle to keep up with his lips as they move.

Do you love me? is what I think he said.

W-What?

"Do I love you?" I repeat, partly from shock and partly to be sure that's what he asked. Uh... I mean, maybe. I don't know. Love? I really like you, Sky, I do. But love? That's... I don't know if I know that yet. But I think so.

He nods vigorously. A nerve pinches in my stomach. Why are you asking me this? It's only been a few weeks. And shouldn't I just tell you that when I know? I can feel my mood changing and aggravation slipping in.

"I don't know," I tell him. It's honest. What if I don't really? What if I'm wrong? I want to know before I say that. "But I like you! A lot! A *whole* lot!"

The spot between Skylar's eyes just above his nose bunches up and he purses his lips. Surely he can't expect more right now.

He brings a hand up above his eyebrow and closes it, then draws it back down toward his chest. He lets a breath out and starts over, making the same motion and drops his brow questioningly. I try to follow his lips but my focus is off, so instead I follow his hands. Using both hands, he taps his index fingers together in front of his stomach, interlocking them briefly before turning his hands and doing it again and swiping across his chest.

Boyfriend. Is he asking if we're boyfriends?

"Are we boyfriends?" I squint.

I think the answer is yes, but now that he's asking, I don't know. Isn't it just a word to say you're dating? Or is it something more? Does it mean you love them? Why is this suddenly so hard?

Skylar nods furiously, his eyes pouting. I want to scoop him up and hold him and tell him everything is going to be okay, but I can't even answer his question. It seems so simple when you hear everyone else say it, but now, it's just not. What if I don't like him as much as I think I do, and I say yes? What then? But I do like him a ton! I really do. But...

"Maybe. I mean... I think," I stutter, like some pathetic ass who can't make his mind up. I swore I wouldn't be this person, but I've never been in this position.

The pout in Skylar's eyes twists into sadness and something more, something darker. His mouth is moving, but I'm too flustered to keep up, and his hands and arms are a blur. It all seems like so much right now, and I step back.

He looks at me expectantly, like I should have caught all of it. But I didn't. I know he said something about us, but I don't know what. Frustration builds in his face and he pulls out his phone and starts tapping at the screen. With each tap, my heart jumps. Am I ruining everything?

"Skylar, I really like you, I hope you know that, I ju—" I'm trying, but his phone starts up.

"If we're not boyfriends, what are we doing?" Siri asks, but my eyes are stuck on him. Glued to those hurting hazel wonders, wishing the tears forming at the edges would go away. "Why did we have sex if you don't love me?"

"I didn't say I don't love you, Sky." I jump back, needing him to understand. "I just don't know. It's only been like two weeks. Maybe I do, but I don't know."

"Are we boyfriends?" his phone questions again.

"I don't know," is what comes out, even though I want to scream yes. But something in my head won't let me.

Skylar shoots his index finger into the sky, twisting his hand, and then points at himself. His eyes pout angrily as he points at me and pounds his fist against his other hand with his little fingers splayed out into a V, hands trembling. Then he shoots his finger toward the sky again. His brow is furrowed, his face is angry and red. He throws up his hands, palms out, begging for an answer to a question I don't understand.

All I caught was *you* and *I*, and I think *why*. But I don't understand the rest. My mouth hangs open, not knowing what to say, how to respond. I don't know what's more frustrating right now, not knowing how to answer his questions or not being able to understand what he's asking.

"I'm sorry, I don't know," is what finally comes out.

He juts his middle finger toward me, and as suddenly as his finger flashes, he twists on his feet and runs out the door.

I meant I didn't know what he said, but it came out all wrong. What did he say? I can't even tell what he said for sure. How can I be a good boyfriend if I can't even understand him?

Maybe it's best I said what I did. Maybe.

But it doesn't feel right. My heart is screaming. The way his eyes pleaded feels like he pierced his hand through my chest and clutched my heart. And he's not letting go, no, he's gripping tighter and tighter, and my heart is suffocating. I drop to the bench and throw my face into my hands.

"What did you do?" I cry, tears seeping down my cheeks.

No! I'm not doing this. I was fine before him, and he can't just throw it all on me like that and expect answers. And this quick? This isn't some movie or a song where the boy meets the girl and immediately falls in love and they live happily ever after. I don't even know if that shit is real. This though, this is real life. And I don't know the answers. I know what I want. I want him. I like him. But I refuse to say something I don't mean before I know for sure, especially not that. And if he can't handle that maybe I don't, maybe I can't.

Maybe I rushed into all of this. Did I feel bad for him because he couldn't talk? No. Okay, that's stupid. No. Definitely not that. But did I rush in?

What I do know is I'm not going to beg him to understand. If he wants to talk about it like a normal person, then I will, but I won't beg.

This isn't my fault.

SKYLAR

How could I be so blind? Why did I think he was any different? All the sweet words, the cute looks. All for nothing. All just to dig a spike into my heart and twist it when I finally caught on.

I stomp up the stairs, fist clenched except to wipe at my face. I shouldn't be crying. This is stupid. I knew this was coming. I did. I told myself it was stupid to think he could like a defect like me. Impossible.

Where the stairs crest I dart toward the lunchroom and practically fall into my usual seat at an empty table. I drop my head on the table to cover my bloodshot eyes. Maybe they'll just think I'm tired.

He literally said he didn't know. How do you not know? What's so different about being boyfriends and what we're doing? What else would we have to do to make it real in his head? Does he think he has to see me every day? Move in with me? Screw me every day? Well, Jacob, you sure just fucked me over, just like everyone else.

"Sky?" Imani's voice questions.

I breathe and try to bat away some of the tears before

raising my head.

"You okay?" She steps forward, worry sketching her smooth features.

"Skylar?" Seth drops his tray on the table. "Who do I need to fuck up?"

I purse my lips. I don't want to talk about this. But it's not like I can say it was just a bad morning.

I shake my head as Imani takes the seat next to me and wraps an arm around me.

"What's going on?" she asks.

I swallow back a sob and find the courage to look her in the eyes. *Jacob.* I mouth.

"Jacob?" Seth's voice drops. "What the hell did he do?"

I shake my head. He didn't do anything like that. He just broke my heart.

Before I answer, my eyes wander away from Imani and to the entrance, where he should be walking up any moment. Maybe he'll come running through and apologize, tell me we are boyfriends, and make it all go away. I wait a second, but there's nothing.

"What happened, Sky?" she asks again.

He... I start but stop when Jacob appears at the entry and his eyes land on me. I don't look away. I let my face go cold and stare back. But he looks away and walks the other direction, disappearing down the hall. Guess that's that.

I pull out my phone. It'll be easier this way.

"I asked him if we were boyfriends," my phone tells them.

"Oh." Imani leans in, waiting for the answer.

"He said he didn't know. Like, what's not to know? We literally, you know," Siri reasons. My eyes plead with her to understand.

"Maybe he just needs more time," Imani says, but I'm typing before she finishes.

"What's so hard to know? What more do we have to do to be boyfriends?" I beg the question. I don't understand this gray area.

"But maybe he's scared," Seth says. "He did just come out this year."

Imani nods. They're on his side? What the hell?

I frown at them, eyes narrowing. *He doesn't love me. He was just using me like everyone always does.*

Imani's eyes follow my lips, catching my words. "Everyone doesn't use you, Sky." She points at herself and then nods toward Seth. "*We're* your friends. *We* love you!"

I give her a weak smile and drop my gaze to the table.

But do you?

JACOB

"Huh?" I jump.

"I asked if you've watched *Joker* yet," Ian tries again, standing next to the popcorn machine.

It started playing Thursday. I was planning to see it that night since I had the day off. I was going to take Sky. But...that didn't happen.

He's all I can think about. That much hasn't changed. It's just different thoughts.

The thrill of seeing him is still there, but it's cloaked by regret, this shadow of my own stupid fuck up. I can still remember the taste of his lips, but it's just a cruel imposter, a knockoff version behind my eyes. It's not real, and my mind keeps telling me I'll never feel that again.

And I still have to see him in Dance every day. That's been excruciating. He acts like I'm not there, and I'm too scared to say otherwise. But I don't think it'd matter. When he does seem to see me, it's cold. If it weren't for the hint of anger under his eyes, I'd say it was indifference, but I can see it. And I hate it.

I did that to him. Me! And why? Because I couldn't wrap

my head around one simple thing. The stupid fact that we were boyfriends. We were. It's just a title. That's it. And what's a title for? For the boy you care about. For the boy that cares about you. For the boy you spend your time with, thinking how great another tomorrow with him will be. For that boy you can't help but smile for. The way I see it now, we were boyfriends the moment I kissed him in the corn maze, hell, maybe even the moment we started dancing. That was when I saw completely past his imperfections to all that really mattered.

But my imperfections ruined it.

"Uh… No." I shrug back. He's staring at me. I took longer to answer than I think he liked, but he doesn't call me out.

"You want to tomorrow? We're both off," Ian suggests. And here I was thinking that meant he'd seen it already. "I can pick you up from church."

"I don't know." I shrug again. I should have said yes to Skylar. It keeps flashing through my mind, the moment I should have said it. I pull my eyes off the candy shelf. "Actually, yeah, let's do that."

"Awesome." Ian grins.

A lady emerges from the screening room and approaches the counter. Ian goes to see what she needs, but I put out my hand and wave him back. I have this. I need the distraction.

"What can I get you?" I ask.

She peers over my shoulder. Probably checking out the popcorn machine. Her hair is short on the side, like buzzed short, and the top is dyed crimson. I focus on that. I really like it. It's cool.

"Let me have a small popcorn." Her lips twitch, barely

smiling. No one smiles. "And a box of Reese's Pieces."

"Okay," I say and start to ring her up, but my fingers miss and I ring her up for two popcorns. I try to remove it and only make it worse. I clench my fists as a burning sensation climbs up my chest. "Come the…"

My eyes spring up to the woman. Her eyes lift, but I don't think it has anything to do with what just about came out of my mouth. I think it's because I'm being a total fuck up.

"Hey." Ian slides in next to me and starts deftly moving his hands over the keys, correcting my mistake. He whispers to me, "It's all good. I got it."

When the women leaves, Ian twists around and props against the counter. He smiles, but it's one of those okay-I've-got-to-do-something smiles.

"Jacob," he says and then pauses.

You don't have to say anything, Ian, I swear it. I know he hates this stuff.

"You know I don't do sappy stuff," he says, which actually makes me giggle a little. He smiles when he sees it and keeps talking. "But have you talked to Skylar since Thursday? At all?"

"Why?" I ask him. "He won't even *look* at me. He's not going to *talk* to me."

"Text him." Ian shrugs, like it's something I haven't thought about a million times.

"Nah." I shake my head and let my back fall against the popcorn machine. It shifts and makes a screeching noise, and for a second I think I busted the glass. I didn't. Thank God. That's the last thing I need.

"Maybe you should. It can't make things worse, right?"

Ian says, but can't it? "Not to knock on him, but he was expecting a lot. I've dated a few girls, and honestly, I don't think I've ever been 'in love' with any of them."

"I don't think that's the biggest part," I tell him. "It's the boyfriend thing. But *now* it doesn't matter."

"Why doesn't it matter now?" He squints, throwing up his hands like it's insane. "Of course it matters. Yeah, you're a little stupid sometimes, but you're *allowed* to *not* know. *And* change. So, yeah. It's okay. Text him!"

"I don't know," I say, but I'm already planning it in my head. I manage a smile. "And I might be stupid, but at least I'm not you."

"Asshole." He smiles.

I'm going to do it. I'm going to text him. I just don't know what to say yet.

SKYLAR

Laser lights flash in our faces and Billie Eilish is whispering loudly over the speakers. For a small-town bowling alley, this place is a lot cooler than I expected. I was thinking more like a stuffy old building with paper and pen scoring.

"You still trying out for the tennis team?" Seth asks from behind the counter, swiping hair from his face.

He's working, but that hasn't stopped him from hanging out with us. It's also the reason we haven't paid full price for a single thing tonight, and unfortunately why I'm on my second bowl of nachos.

"Yeah. When are they?" I let my phone carry the conversation. I can't expect Seth and Imani to read my lips in this lighting.

Seth looks at me crazily and then drifts to Imani.

"Hell if I know." He shrugs.

"Same," Imani says, but raises her phone, "but we can find out."

While she's searching and bowling balls slap against glossy lanes and the music blares into some rock anthem I don't know, my phone buzzes in my hand. Instinctively, my eyes gravitate to the little green bubble. Jacob.

I frown and drop it on the counter.

"Who was that?" Imani eyes me.

Mom, I mouth. Imani's not been completely on my side with all the Jacob shit, so I don't want to go there.

"You're ignoring your mom?" She throws her head back. "It's Jacob, isn't it?"

I look to Seth for backup. His eyes go wide. Come on, man. This, right here, isn't what I need right now, so I pick up my phone and swipe the message off the screen.

"What if it is?" Siri tells her, but it makes me seem dull and undetermined. It'll never come close to the shit burning in my chest, and it's infuriating. "I don't want to talk to him. He's like everyone else I've ever met. People either want nothing to do with me because I'm broken, or they only want me temporarily. No one sticks around for long, and most people just want a laugh or want to feel like they helped the disabled boy, and then they're out. Chances are you two will drop me eventually."

"Woah there! No! That's not going to happen." Seth's hands slap the counter and he cranes his long neck forward, motioning between himself and Imani. "I don't know about all these other people, but *we're* not those people. We're your friends, like it or not. We're like you."

Like me? Really? He must see the doubtful look on my face because he restarts.

"Not the talking thing." He rolls his eyes. "I'm—"

"Yeah, not that," Imani assures me.

"—talking about being an outcast. We're not trying to please anyone with who we are. We're the weird, nerdy, crazy," he nods toward Imani and grins stupidly, "people. Hell, I'm awkward as hell around people. I'm literally on the JV basketball team and don't talk to any of them. My best friend is pan and a witch. She's allergic to shellfish. And she's a witch."

"You said the witch thing twice." Imani shakes her head.

That brings a smile to my face. Yeah, they're sort of weird.

"I mean, you *are* a witch," he laughs. "Who else do you know that gets to call their BFF a witch and get away with it?"

I pooch my lips and nod, laughing silently. He's got a point there.

"At least check the text." Imani nudges me, shaking her head at Seth.

I don't want to. He couldn't even give me an answer in the locker room when I asked him why he fucked me. How do you not have an answer to that?

But whatever. I grunt and pick up my phone. I don't open the message, I can read it without bothering.

JACOB: Can we talk? Im sorry.

Ugh. My body seizes up for a second, but I push through it. Is he really sorry? Or does he just regret that he can't use me anymore?

"What'd he say?" Imani scoots closer, eyes wider than before.

I roll my eyes and type, "Says he's sorry. He wants to talk."

"Well?" Seth's expression is a picture of expectation.

"I don't want to talk to him," I relay through Siri. As far as I'm concerned Jacob can shove it. I have to protect myself. No one else will.

"Sky, he really does like—" Imani starts, but I throw up a

hand and shake my head.

I don't want to hear it.

The conversation comes to an end, and some rock song burrows in between us. Hell, it's probably something *he'd* like. Sounds like shit.

"So what are we doing about the forum?" Seth breaks the awkwardness.

I'd almost forgotten about it again. Hell, it's literally because of me, and I'm letting all this other shit get in the way. I should be focused on that. I should be fighting tooth and nail and not letting *him* get in the way.

"Isn't Concord Pride helping?" Imani asks. We don't have an actual Pride organization here, but the neighboring town does and they were excited to help when things started. Not to mention the state and Charlotte chapters too. "Aren't we supposed to be making phone calls with them after school next week?"

I nod and start typing. "Yeah. Well, you two. But they're also doing a protest outside during the forum, and we're making signs for that on Tuesday."

I can make signs. I can't make calls, so that has to be my contribution.

"I have to talk to people? On the phone?" Seth looks disgusted.

"You'll live." Imani rolls her eyes.

Maybe. Just maybe they won't leave me.

JACOB

"Did you get Eric's text?" Ian leans across the lunch table.

"Huh?" I grunt. "Oh yeah."

"He did it!" Ian literally wiggles.

Eric got us into the show in Charlotte. Which means he's going to want to start practicing even more.

I force a smile. "Yeah, it's great."

I try not to, but I glance to my right. Skylar's at his usual table with Imani and Seth. His back is to me and Seth's sitting across from him where I'd been the last few weeks, where I wish I was right now.

He hasn't responded yet. And either he turned off his read receipts or hasn't opened it.

"He wants to practice tonight," Ian says.

"I know." I got the same text. I swear I'm trying, but I know it doesn't look like it, so I try again. "How many songs are we doing?"

"Don't know." Ian goes back to his phone and starts typing something. "I'll see if he knows."

"I just have to be gone by six, 'kay?" I tell him.

"But I thought you were off tonight." Ian looks confused.

His fingers stop for a moment, then start back up.

"I am." I nod, coughing. "But I've got to be at Trinity in Concord around six thirty. I'm helping to make signs for the protest."

"Oh," Ian sighs, confusion lighting his face. "I thought you were doing that with… You know."

He doesn't say Skylar's name. He knows it's sort of a trigger right now.

"I was, but I'm still going," I tell him. "It's not just for him. Still need to fight it."

"Sorry, you're right." Ian smiles. "I'm going too then."

"Huh?" I squint. I mean, he was going originally, but I don't expect him to now. They need to practice. I mean, *we* need to practice, but they can do without me for one night.

But he's typing on his phone, so he doesn't answer right away. Instead my phone dings, and a message from Ian comes through our group text. When he looks up, I eye him like he's insane. I'm sitting right here.

IAN: We need 2 wrap up practice by 6.

My look changes to confusion.

ERIC: Huh?

IAN: WERE volunteering with Jacob 2 make signs for the protest.

"There should have been an apostrophe in that 'were', just saying," I point out.

Ian gives me the middle finger as bubbles pop up under his last text.

"Like you use proper grammar in text." He smirks.

ERIC: K deal.

I can't say I was expecting this.

SKYLAR

TUESDAY, OCTOBER 8

"Look at mine." Imani's practically jumping.

I stop shading the A on my sign in bright red and take a look at her sign. I shake my head.

IF GOD HATES BOYS IN SKIRTS, THEN WHY ARE THEY SO CUTE?

Really? I mouth.

"Yeah!" she laughs.

Seth couldn't come. He's working tonight. Something about one of his co-workers calling out.

My sign's more colorful than Imani's, but it's not as funny. I go back to shading after I lean back and reread the outline.

IF ME WEARING A SKIRT OFFENDS YOU, MAYBE YOU'RE THE SNOWFLAKE.

Mine's probably going to make them more mad than anything, but it'll work. And of course, I'll be wearing a skirt at the protest, so double trigger. They're going to hate it, but that *is* sort of the problem.

"Speaking of cute—" Imani's eyes raise toward the entrance into the church fellowship hall.

I follow her gaze and immediately regret it. My eyes lock

with Jacob's, and my mood shifts downward along with the edges of my lips. He smiles and waves. No. We're not doing this. I divert my eyes.

"Stop being mean." Imani slaps my shoulder.

I squint evilly at her. I'm not the mean one. The mean one just walked in.

With a grunt I go back to coloring my sign, but suddenly there aren't enough people in the room. It was fine before that there were only a handful of us. Imani, me, this super nice blonde-haired woman and her wife, two girls about our age I've never met but apparently go to Brown too, and Ransom. He's in my Civics class. I hadn't spoken to him before today, but apparently he's supportive. Maybe he's gay or bi or pan or non-binary? Or maybe he's just an ally. I don't know, and I'm not asking. I don't need anyone thinking I'm hitting on them, so I'm not taking that chance.

Before Jacob and his crew walked in, us seven felt like plenty. Now it feels like there aren't enough people to cushion me from his presence. I'm not going to be an ass if he gets too close, but I'm not talking to him either. Wow. Did I just find a positive to not having a voice? I roll my eyes. Isn't that ironic?

I'm not mean, I tell Imani, but she rolls her eyes and gets up.

"Hey Jacob." She glances at me out of the corner of her eye. I huff and look away. "Ian, Eric. Thanks for coming! We're just making signs. Y'all helping?"

"Yeah," Jacob says. And I hate how much I like the sound of that one word. I don't want to like it, but maybe there are some things I can't just stop liking all at once.

I chance a look. He's walking over to the stack of oversized posters with Imani. Ian and Eric trail behind like lost puppies.

Why do you have to be so hot and fucked up at the same time? But I mean, he is here. He didn't have to come. But he did, and even though I don't want to find myself wanting him to look at me, wanting to look into those green eyes and feel their electricity again, here I am.

Be strong, Sky. Be strong.

JACOB

Sometimes I wonder if Rebekah and her husband come to church just for me. Just so I'm not alone in this room, despite the seventy or eighty others rummaging from pew to pew with some dire prayer request, the latest gossip, or talk of what ungodly member of society they *witnessed* to since Sunday. I swear I'm in a cult.

"Y'all are moving?" I ask.

She's been going on about cute little houses up in the foothills ever since she found out she was pregnant six months ago. But I honestly thought it was just talk. Surely she isn't going to move off and leave me here with Mom and Dad. I can't bike a hundred miles, and Mom isn't going to let me take her car all the way up the mountain without taking her *and* Dad.

"Maybe," Rebekah nods slowly, holding her protruding stomach. "Nathan's family is up that way. And it's really nice up there. And North," that's going to be my nephew's name, "will have more yard to play in."

And you'd have an excuse to not come to church here. Just say it, Rebekah, I know you're thinking it. I think it all the time!

"But you can't leave me here." I grip her arm, and give her my best puppy eyes. It's half joking, the other half pure horror. I lower my voice to whisper, "Take me with you."

She laughs and chances a glance at Mom to be sure she isn't paying attention, then leans in like what she has to say is a big secret.

"How are things with Skylar?" she asks. I don't think my frown is what she expected. "What happened?"

"It's a long story." I shrug. I was doing half decent not thinking about him. I was miserable enough being here, but now I'm miserable because I'm here and thinking about him. Thanks, sis. "But *we're* not anymore."

"What?" She gets even quieter. Her green eyes—they're just like mine—are concerned.

What do I tell her? Sure, she's the cool sister, and the only sibling I've told about him. But how do I tell my sister I lost my virginity to him but couldn't admit he was my boyfriend and that's why he blew up on me and dumped me. Oh my God! He dumped me! How did that just hit me? My shoulders slump, and I say the best thing I can think of.

"It just ended. He got mad, and—"

Mrs. McKee steps in like I'm not even there and starts talking *at* my sister. "Rebekah, have you thought any more about helping this weekend?"

How rude! But thank you. I don't know what she's talking about and honestly don't care, but right now, if it means I don't have to explain more, I'm going to accept it. Rebekah grimaces at me and raises her brow. It's a look that screams *this conversation isn't over*. She puts on a smile and turns her attention to Mrs. McKee. Yeah, sorry, I'm not saving you from that.

Without my only bastion of hope in this place, except maybe my brother-in-law, I'm left staring around the building. I wish the Evans family hadn't left after what happened to Parker. They might have been just like my family before, but I think they'd understand me now. That's why they left after all.

My eyes land on the splintery wooden cross hanging against a rock-covered wall above the baptistry. It's always struck me as ironic that we hold the cross as the symbol of our faith. It's like we couldn't come up with anything better. I mean, it's like your kid being murdered by a gunman, and then putting plaques and pendants of the gun that shot him everywhere. Seems a bit morbid to me.

And on cue, my mind asks the same question it does every time I look at that cross. Why do I have to be gay? Why couldn't you have made me straight, God? If it's so wrong, why couldn't I have been given the choice, because I tell you right now, it wasn't. I don't want this. I never did. And honestly, every person in this building who thinks I woke up one day and chose this, that I chose to be ridiculed by them, to be looked down on by them, hated by them, is a fucking moron.

I clench my fists and divert my eyes. But at least I have a voice. Sky. He doesn't even have that. He's stuck in a world of silence.

Stop thinking about him. It's like he keeps creeping into my mind and then he's stuck there, and I start feeling shit I don't want to feel.

"Looks like you chipped a nail." Rebekah pulls my attention away.

"Huh?" Did she just say something about my nails?

I painted them again last night, black as always. The look on Dad's face when he saw them before Sunday school was priceless, and there's sure to be some consequences, but I wasn't thinking about that last night. I got all up in my feels and it got my mind off of it, off of *him*.

"Your nail." She points to my finger. It's chipped at the edge. Dammit, I don't remember doing that! "Might want to fix that when you get home."

She brings her finger up to her lips and shushes me with a smile.

"Uh, okay," I manage to get out right before the pastor starts the service.

I zone out. It's just announcements. Actually, I zone out for most of it, well, all of it, if I can manage. I'm just here because of Dad. But then something piques my interest. Is he talking about... Oh God!

"We need everyone who can to be at the school board forum tomorrow evening," Pastor Spencer starts. And here we go. "I've told you before how the devil likes to creep in slowly to poison the minds of our children and get them away from God. And I'm telling you that's what's happening right now, right here in our own town and in our schools."

Oh, just get on with it, man. You hate that a boy looks better in a skirt than you ever will in pants.

"We need to show up and support our school board. This dress code policy shouldn't even be needed. It's common sense that men shouldn't wear women's clothing, but the world is determined to pollute our kids' minds," Pastor rants, his voice cutting in and out with huffs of indignation. "The Bible is clear. And *we* must make it clear that we will not accept this ungodly agenda to normalize sin and homosexuality in our schools."

What the hell does this have to do with homos? This has nothing to do with us homos! Which, by the way, is sitting right here in front of you, mister. I'm so tired of hearing this stupid shit.

"The gays are sure to be there protesting, so we need to be there fighting for what's right," he says and then does a rally call. "Who's with me?"

The church erupts in amens, and I deflate, air seeping from my lungs. I hate it here.

SKYLAR

I've never been involved in a protest before. So I'm not sure this is how it normally goes, but if it is, it's a lot louder than I expected.

In my mind I imagined two groups of people, both in a line, holding their signs and walking in circles, chanting unified slogans. There's nothing unified about this.

Sure, the anti-skirters are all gathered on the opposite edge of the sidewalk leading to the school gymnasium, and our side is congregated over here. But other than that? Nope. People are shouting from both sides, and it's almost impossible to distinguish one from the other. It's more like two miniature mobs than lines. At least we're chanting uplifting stuff over here. Half the other side is telling people they're going to hell and to man up.

I'm holding my *IF ME WEARING A SKIRT OFFENDS YOU, MAYBE YOU'RE THE SNOWFLAKE* sign above my head. Imani's pulling double duty since Seth's at work, hoisting her sign and the one she made for him. It has a picture of some random boy in a skirt—she'd threatened to use my picture on it, but I refuse to be plastered on a sign—with the question *Does it bother you THAT much?*

And the answer is yes. It's definitely yes. Because damn, are they angry.

This guy who's probably in his sixties, full head of gray hair and a bushy beard has a sign that simply reads *BE A MAN*. Another sways a black poster with yellow writing stating *Boys DON'T Wear Skirts*. The variety is insane, just as insane as the messages. There's one that proclaims *GOD HATES SIN*. Like, I get that, but I don't think He minds me wearing a cute skirt. The dude's even screaming it too. There's a bunch of printed ones being tossed around that say *This ISN'T Equality*, and an even more confusing *REPENT AND TURN TO CHRIST*.

At this point, I'm ready to be done with this and get inside. Plus Jacob's here. Don't get me wrong. I'm glad he came, that he's sticking to the fight, but I could really go for not having to look at his unfortunately nice face right now. Oh, and I saw Noah go in earlier.

A few minutes of this chaos pass and the time strikes 7:00 p.m. I keep my sign up as I start toward the gymnasium, expecting Imani to follow. We drop our signs in the lobby and file inside the gym. There are so many more people here than I thought there'd be. Like, I was hoping, but I didn't expect this type of turnout. Even the news stations are set up and waiting.

Imani passes me and leads me to a spot in the front row of bleachers where our parents are waiting. I sit next to Mom and she gives me a quick squeeze.

"All right, we'd like to get this meeting started," the man sitting at the center of a long black foldout table announces and smacks a gavel against a block of wood. The sound echoes in the big space, and people start to quiet. It's the school board, I guess. And one of them is you-know-who's dad. "I'm Bruce Walters." Yep, that's him. I haven't met his dad, but I'm assuming there's only one Walters on the board.

He keeps going. "We're here to listen to your concerns about the new school dress code proposal to ensure a safe and distraction-free environment for your students. We only have about an hour and a half, so in the interest of fairness and time, we have two mics setup at either end of the table."

My eyes gravitate to the left, finding a microphone atop a black stand, and on the opposite end there's another. I know I'm going to be at one of them in a moment, and even though I can't speak, I'm nervous as hell.

"The way we're going to work this is for those in favor of the proposed dress code policy to line up at the mic to your left, and for those opposed to line up at the mic to your right," he explains. So the one to my right. Got it. "This way we hear equally from each side. No, we might not be able to get through everyone, but we'll move back and forth between mics, with each individual getting a maximum of three minutes. We ask that you listen when your time is up and let the next person have the mic. All right, let's begin."

A hand prods my back. I twist to see it's Dad pushing me to get up. He's smiling as he gets to his feet. He said he wouldn't let me do this by myself, so he's going to speak too.

I get up but keep my eyes down. This isn't exactly my idea of a good time, so maybe if I just don't look around I won't feel so dizzy.

"We'll start over here," Mr. Walters—Jacob's dad–says. I

look up quickly enough to see him pointing to a man about my dad's age at the other mic.

"I don't have much to say," he begins, crouched over, leaning into the microphone. His voice strikes me. The accent is unusually harsh. "But we need this new dress code. If people gonna come to *our* schools, with *our* children, and try to use lawyers to scare *our* teachers from upholding a godly dress for boys *and* girls, we gotta do something. It's simple, really. The gay agenda is going to destroy our children if we don't do something. God didn't intend for no boy to wear girls' clothes. It's perverted." He walks back the bleachers.

My eyes pop. What? Perverted? You've got to be kidding me. And people in the crowd clap, they literally clap.

"Sorry, I forgot to mention this, but going forward," Mr. Walters speaks up from the table in front of us, "please state your name before you start."

"Larry Baker!" a voice yells from the bleachers. It's the guy who was just speaking. No one cares, Larry.

"Thank you, Mr. Baker," Mr. Walters laughs. "Let's continue."

I lean to my left, peeking at the line ahead of me. There are at least six people ahead of me, but I can't see who's about to speak.

"Hey, my name's Liam," a guy's voice starts up. I don't recognize the high tone as the words come quick and nervous. "Uh... The new dress code isn't necessary. Guys should be able to wear a skirt if they want. Vote against the new dress code."

The speaker steps away as if leaving but spins back around and shoves his face back in the mic. He practically yells,

"Clothes have no gender!" and then takes off for the bleachers.

Oh! I do know him. He smiles at me on his way back. I've passed him in the hall a few times, I think he might have said something to me once. Freshman, maybe.

Someone across the room starts up, and it turns into a rant. But at least this time they don't interject God. The attention switches to our side again, and a girl starts talking. She does good. More elaborate than Liam and less punctuated. It goes back and forth a few times until a familiar voice echoes through the gym when it comes back to us.

"My name's Noah Andrews, I graduated from A.L. Brown last semester. I want to speak against the new proposal."

It's Noah! I didn't see him go up. I lean around the line again, and there he is, hands crammed into his pockets.

"First, there is no gay agenda, except to be equal, to be loved for the people we are, which is no different from anyone else. And second, this isn't a 'gay' issue." He says what I've been thinking for weeks. "It isn't gay for a boy to wear a skirt or a dress. Straight guys wear skirts too, and paint their nails, wear makeup. Sometimes that's just how they feel more comfortable, or they just like it. Why does it hurt anyone if a boy wears a skirt to school, just like a girl? It doesn't. It hurts literally no one!"

Wow! Now I'm second-guessing everything I planned to say. He's basically hit all my points, and I'm one hundred percent certain it sounds better than my Siri translation is going to.

"But this new dress code is going to hurt people. You might not think it will, but it will." Noah pauses. I can't see him, but I can feel something tense building before he speaks

again. "Most of you don't know me, but you do know who
Parker Evans is. Or was. You know who he was. He
uh…he…he died earlier this year. He…" Noah's voice cracks,
but he doesn't stop. "The point is that…uh…it's these types of
rules that demonize people for being who they are and make
them see themselves as less than and other people as more
than. It hurts them inside, even if you can't see it *or* refuse to
see it. It damages them, their mental health, and can cause
them to hurt themselves because they don't see a way out, a
way of acceptance. And school should be a safe place for
everyone. This new dress code makes it less safe. So I urge you
to vote against the new dress code policy. Thank you."

The next speaker steps up, and I'm wondering how
anyone could follow that. There are still three people ahead of
me and my palms are already sweating. It doesn't help any
that I typed my *speech* out before we got here. It's one of the
tiniest perks of not having a voice. But I feel like I'm going to
repeat a lot of stuff. And I still hate talking in front of big
groups.

"I'm Pastor Kevin Spencer," the speaker starts. Oh, this
should be good. He's younger than I imagine for a pastor, no
gray hair yet, and he's tall. "I preach just down the road at the
Berea Baptist Church. And it's my job every Sunday and
Wednesday to get up and teach my flock what is good and
holy and acceptable in the eyes of our God. And this here is no
different. The media and those trying to stop this measure
want to say we Christians don't have a role in this, that faith
and God don't belong in the public schools, but they're wrong.
This is *our* community."

There they go again with the *our* mantra, claiming that this is only *their* community, that it's all about *their* kids. It's crazy how if they see you as different, they can just dismiss you. I wish he'd just stop there. We get the point.

"And we have a right to have our opinion heard and to protect our children from the influence of the ungodly. And it *is* ungodly for a boy to wear a girl's clothes. All this *clothes have no gender* junk is simply wrong. Clothes do have a gender," he asserts. I want to throw up, but I don't want to get that all over the diamond-pattern sweater vest and the white skirt I'm wearing. "Why do you think there's a *men's* section and a *women's* section in Walmart and Target? Why do you think the sizing is all different? Because we're different, and that's how God made us. He made us to be distinct. For women to be feminine and adorned with beauty. And for men to be men, to be masculine and keepers of the home."

Pastor Spencer straightens and laughs. "I'm sorry, I think I'm about to run over. So let me just end by saying, we need to pass the new dress code. We need to make it clear that in *our* schools, we listen to what God says about how to dress. We have to be an example for the areas around us."

We have to do what God says in the school? This isn't a church school! This is a public school. Let me repeat that, *public*! I force myself not to stare him down as he walks proudly back to the bleachers and the *amens* literally rattle through the building, and I have to wait for the next two speakers to finish up.

Finally it's my turn. My eyes lock on Mr. Walters and immediately I can see the lightly concealed disgust in his eyes when he sees what I'm wearing. I want to curl inside myself, to just disappear. What am I doing? Instead, I hold my phone up to the mic and push the button to let Siri start talking.

"Hello, my name's Skylar Gray," my phone starts up. The looks on the faces of the board members is a patchwork of confusion and boredom. Not sure if it's that my phone is talking for me or its British accent. "This whole dress code issue is sort of my fault. See, I just happen to like skirts and dresses. I feel comfortable in them. And I wore one to school when I transferred in at the beginning of the semester. And as they say, the rest is history. Now we're here."

I wish it would pause and let me look between the board members all dramatic-like before the next bit, even if it was corny, but Siri stops for no one.

"And it's sort of crazy that we are. You're looking to change the dress code just because I wore a skirt to school, and I keep wearing a skirt to school. Because somehow, you have this idea that it hurts you or distracts people. I don't see it. If anything it's more scary for me, because of all the people who look down on me just for wearing a skirt, because they believe it's bad, and so it's okay to bully me for it. Even proposing this new code puts people like me in danger, because it makes some think it's okay to bully us. And it's not. That's not promoting a safe space in school."

Eyes across the table dart away. I guess it at least hit home a little. Or maybe I'm totally off. But here comes the big part.

"School is where I'm supposed to go to learn. And yes, you can't have guys or girls running down the hall with their pants off. Plus, none of us want to see that anyway." I glimpse around on that one, and on cue a few laughs echo around the gym. Now it's time for a little history lesson. "And we have to remember that guys wore dresses a long time before they ever wore pants. Jesus wore a tunic, basically a dress. They wore big, long wigs back in the 1700s. They wore makeup. But they were still men. People wear clothes. It doesn't matter if you're a man or woman or something else, clothes are for everyone, and it's your job to keep our school from discriminating against people like me with illogical sexist dress standards. Please vote against the new dress code policy."

The moment my phone shuts up I twist around and start toward my seat. Imani's fists are pumping in the air and she's smiling like I just won the lottery. But my head jumps to what I probably shouldn't have said. The *illogical sexist* part probably wasn't the best method, considering my audience. Why did I say that? Dammit.

Just focus on Imani and sit down. Just sit down.

JACOB
THURSDAY, OCTOBER 10

This whole charade was a total waste of time. It didn't matter what anyone said. My dad and his council buddies already know exactly what they're doing.

If anything, some of the stuff said tonight may have sealed the deal. The moment Sky said *sexist* I know he lost my dad and at least half the others, even Councilwoman Ledford. Which is insane, because it's true, and any person with half a brain can see it.

Voices bounce off the gym's cinderblock walls now that the forum is over. Everyone's up and moving from person to person like at the end of a church service, and eyes flick across the aisle at the boys in skirts. There are a few, actually. Some I'd never expect, like Liam and Mr. Pritchett, my English teacher. And, of course, Skylar.

"You going to do it?" Ian asks.

I know Skylar sort of hates me, but I have to do something. So I'm going to try to talk to him.

"Yeah," I say, but I'm terrified.

He doesn't say anything back, and I'm not looking to see the   I-know-you're-going-to-fail-but-good-luck-anyway expression I'm sure is there. I put one foot in front of the other instead. That's the best way to do something, right? Just do it.

I weave through the crowd, words flying, which I try to ignore, because most of them seem to be saying stupid shit that makes me want to vomit or punch someone.

A moment later I'm standing behind Skylar, locked in place. I probably look like a fucking stalker. Imani's not noticed me yet, but the others are starting to. Liam eyes me weirdly, then smiles. Cover blown. Wait. Is Skylar talking to Liam?

Imani turns first, and her face transforms from confusion to a warm smile. At least someone likes me, because Skylar turns around and the smile disappears from his face in an instant.

"Hey, how's it going?" I blurt nervously.

He stares at me, his expression unchanging.

I bring my hands to my chest and sign *How are you?*

Heard you fine, he bites.

That's not what I meant! But I refuse to show him that I'm kicking myself for it. *Act like it doesn't faze you!*

"Congrats on getting here." I nod toward the gym and back where the mics are still standing. It's an accomplishment, even if it isn't going to work. "I hope it helps."

When he doesn't say anything back, Imani steps in.

"We hope so too." She smiles at me. "Insane how medieval some of these people are, right?"

"Right?" My voice raises an octave. "Just imagine if half of them knew you were a witch."

"Can you say Kannapolis Witch Trials?" Her brow raises, and she laughs.

Skylar's lips turn up a little, but the moment I open mine that tiny ray disappears. Okay, I get it, I screwed things up, but can you give me a break? You don't realize how bad I feel about it, or how much it hurts for me.

"You want to hang out?" I look him directly in the eyes. Maybe he'll be able to see how sorry I am and how badly I want him back.

Instead, his face scrunches up and he mouths something, but I don't catch it. Then, without so much as a gesture, he stomps off, disappearing into the crowd, leaving me with Imani and the others, all looking at me like I just lost a family member to cancer.

What the fuck? I'm trying! I take a breath and push the resentment back.

"Uh..." My eyes twitch between them. "Y'all have a good one."

"Jacob." Imani grabs my arm before I get more than a few steps. "He thinks everyone just uses him and throws him away. It's not *all* you. Give him some time."

Before I can respond, she twists around and takes off.

He thinks everyone just uses him? My mind goes back to the weeks I spent with him before it all fell apart, and my eyes light up with understanding. Did he take my uncertainty as a way out? I was scared. That's normal, right? But for him, did it really look like I was just going to throw him away? Oh my God!

"You good?" Ian shoves through the crowd. "You look like you saw a ghost."

"I think I did," I say without thinking.

"Uh..." Ian squints, his mouth hanging open, considering

what to say. I must sound crazy. "Guess he said no?"

"Would I be here if he hadn't?" I look at him stupidly.

"Sorry." He shrugs. "Someone's having a good day though."

"Huh?" I ask.

Ian nods behind me.

Dad.

He's in the corner with one of the news stations. I hope they're grilling him, but I also know him. He's still working every second of it to his advantage. And all this, the junk around this dress code, it all timed perfectly with the launch of his campaign. Tons of free press.

It's disgusting.

Why does everything seem to work in his favor? Why can't *I* get a break?

SKYLAR

I can't do this. I wanted to say yes so bad. But I can't. I can't just open myself back up so he can get what he wants and then be done with me again.

Instead, I do the only thing I know how. I run.

The night air bites at my legs and arms, and I shiver as goosebumps rise across my skin and images of green eyes and pure white hair flash behind my eyes. Stop haunting my mind! Leave me be! It's not fair. All I have are my thoughts, but they're all of him. Why do they all have to be of him?

I peer down the parking lot and my mind conjures up a memory. He's walking next to me with Ian's bike. I turn toward the school, but the memories keep colliding. We rush through those doors after the end-of-day bell. Then there's the first time I saw him in the office and he showed me around the school, and I rightfully thought he was a douchebag. Laughing at something stupid he said at lunch. I twist around, trying to find something that doesn't remind me of him. My eyes trail the road into downtown, but that's where he asked me on our first date, just over the tracks. And the field down the road with its tall grass conjures up the cornstalks we walked between under the stars. I swallow as I remember how it felt to hold his hand for the first time, and that first kiss.

"Skylar!" Imani's voice yanks me back to Earth.

I throw my head back.

"That was rude back there," she starts. I know she's been here for me, but she has this soft spot for Jacob.

I shut down. Nope, not having this. I turn around and start toward my parents' car. I can just barricade myself inside… Dammit. They have the keys, but that doesn't stop me from walking.

"Stop, Sky!" Imani raises her voice, and I freeze, like some sheep.

When I turn there's a trickle of people leaving the gymnasium, and a handful of eyes are on me now. I start moving my arms, as if she can read sign language, before moving my lips.

It was rude of him to fuck me over, I tell her.

"Sky, you're going to have slow down." Imani bunches her cheeks. "I know you're angry, but talk to me, slowly."

I suck in and exhale a big breath.

Why shouldn't I be rude? He fucked me over, I say again.

She catches it this time and scowls.

"Did he though?" Her tone softens, and she steps closer. "Did he? Are you sure you just weren't expecting something more? Or maybe you were *expecting* him to leave?"

Don't I have a right to expect more of the boy I like? Of the boy I can't get out of my head, even fucking now? And what's wrong with expecting people to leave? That's what they do. Every time. So no, I'm not answering that. Instead, I look away.

"Sky," her voice is calm and kind, "you still like him.

You're horrible at hiding it, even if you hate him right now too. And you know what? He *really* likes you, a lot. I swear, he's trying."

He's trying? What's that worth? Hell, one day she's going to leave me too.

So when are you going to leave me? I stare at her. *Everyone does. It's easier to leave first.*

"Sky…don't say that." Imani holds a hand up, then clamps it softly on my shoulder. "I'm not leaving you. I'm *here* for you. Just like you'd be here for me. You're my friend. I love you, Sky!"

I love you?

I shake my head. No. She can't. Just like he can't. No one can. If there's one thing I've learned through all these years of pain, it's that I'm unlovable. Period. In every way.

A tear slips from my eye, but I'm not doing that here, not in front of her. So I twist around and walk off.

I lock my eyes on the concrete and just walk and walk and walk. The light from the streetlamps comes and goes and I lose track of time. When I finally look up, I'm at the other end of the school. I check my six, and Imani hasn't followed. Guess I was right. I deviate from the sidewalk and trot through the grass until I reach the back of the building. It's damp back here, and the buzz of the streetlamps barely reaches me. I drop into a crouch and fall back against the brick wall.

Why is this my life? Why couldn't *I* have been like Imani or Seth? Why couldn't *I* have a voice and a family? Why am *I* always the last one, the one no one wants?

Jacob's electric eyes blaze in my mind, lighting up everything behind my eyelids. I squeeze my eyes tight, begging them to go away, but they refuse to leave. So I stare back, holding his gaze in my mind. Why can't I accept that maybe he does care?

Because he doesn't. That's why! He doesn't.

But what if he does? What if somehow, under all that indecision, he does?

And Imani! And Seth! And Mom and Dad!

I let my eyes open and throw my head back, tapping the wall and staring up at the sky. How could I ever think they don't care? Until I got here, I've never known anyone who treats me like them. Normal. Nothing unusual or special, just normal. It didn't faze any of them that I was different. And I just turned my back on Imani.

Damn you, Sky! Damn you!

I wipe the tears from my eyes and pull my phone out. There's a text from Imani. I don't know what it says, but it makes my chest shudder and the tears fall quicker just knowing it's there. I unlock my phone and read it.

IMANI: I'm around the corner. Not letting your dumb ass get sex-trafficked even if you are being a bitch. ::red heart::

Air bursts through my nose and I double over laughing. I type a reply and hit send.

SKYLAR: Sorry for running off. Everyone always leaves though and I'm always afraid you and Seth will too. ::eye roll:: Which is stupid, I know, but it's what I'm used to. Coming back now.

A ding echoes behind me, and I roll my eyes. She really is just around the corner. I stand up and start to walk, but before I can she jumps around the brick wall and pulls me into a big hug.

"We ain't going anywhere, Sky!"

JACOB
SATURDAY, OCTOBER 12

They say we all have a doppelganger, right? But shouldn't that asshole live like hundreds of miles away? I swear I just saw Sky's. And I didn't need that. Not at work.

He wasn't as cute, and he was taller by at least a few inches, and his hair wasn't as long. Okay, now that I think about it, he also didn't have that signature grin. Maybe he wasn't Sky's doppelganger. Maybe it's just me.

"Hello?!" someone shouts, yanking my attention from the floor. I look up to find an older lady with peppered hair cut close like M from the Bond movies hunched over the counter.

"Hey." I jump to attention and approach the counter where I'm supposed to be anyway. "What can I get you?"

She orders a bag of popcorn, like everyone does, and a Diet Coke. What is everyone's obsession with Coke? Ugh. I ring her up and she disappears back into the screening room.

My brain hops from her four-dollar snack to Homecoming. I talked to Ian and Eric about it last night. I'd rented my tux a few days before Skylar asked if I loved him. I'd planned on surprising him with it but forgot about it after that. So I need to use it, right? I convinced Ian to go with me, as friends obviously, something I had to reassure him of a few times, 'cause he's stupid like that. Eric asked why I just don't go instead. And the answer was simple. That suit set me back a good few weeks on getting a car, so I'm using it, *and* I want to see Skylar all dressed up and having a great time, even if it's not with me.

Neither of them understood that last part. Ian said if he'd been dumped, he'd want to egg their car and watch them cry. It's a funny thought, but not for Sky. I just can't think like that.

Eric said he can't stomach the idea of Homecoming. The only way he'd go is if they invited us to be the live band. And obviously, they didn't. Wouldn't that be cool though? Us, The Nevermore, playing on stage for the entire school?

I twitch as a thought hits me. Wait a damn minute. Imani. At the forum. What had she said when Sky ran off? *Give him some time*, right? Does she know something I don't? What if he's been talking about me? What if, maybe, he's just waiting, giving it time? It's stupid, like it's really stupid to think, but what if?

But Imani's the key. Maybe she'll talk to me. Of course I don't have her number! And I don't have her Snap! Hold up, I follow her on Insta. That's my chance!

I check to make sure no one's emerged from the screening room and with the coast clear I grab my phone, open Instagram, and start searching my *Following* list. Skylar used to be in here, but now I can't even search and find his profile. He literally blocked me the day things went to shit. Focus, Jacob! I find her picture and name and click to message her.

It's an empty thread. Dammit. Now I feel bad that this is the first message I'm sending her. We never talked before Sky.

We were in different worlds, and it made sense then. But now they're my people, I just didn't know it because everyone, aka me, sticks in their own lane. But I'm not backing out.

JACOB: Hey... I know ur Skys friend, but I need ur help. I rly like him...maybe more... Can I text you?

It isn't ten seconds later before the little bubbles start jumping on the screen and I get a response.

IMANI: Uh, yes!

JACOB: Can I get ur number? ::shrug::

She sends it and I immediately open a new text thread and type out my plea. But before I hit send, a stupid thought hits me. Why didn't I just ask on Insta? Wow. Whatever. I hit send.

JACOB: Hey! It's Jacob. So... How do I win him back?

JACOB

"I'm not dropping it," Dad shouts, bumping a stack of papers on the table to even them out before depositing them into a manila folder.

"Come on! It's not a real problem," I try.

The vote is in an hour. I'm making my last-ditch effort to stop it. The teen from Kannapolis trying to stop the school board from making a stupid 1860s America decision. God, it's pointless. I knew the moment it all started, but since when has that stopped me? Isn't everything pointless? So why not fight like hell the whole time?

"Oh but it is, Jacob. And no, I'm not stopping it." Dad jumps back, a new sternness in his eyes. "This is happening, no matter what you and your friends think. Adults have to make decisions, because you're all too young and immature to make the right ones."

"This has nothing to do with my age," I say, squinting. It's such an old argument. He throws it out half the time when we disagree. I'm just too young to understand. Well, guess what, I get to vote next year, so deal with it. I raise my voice a notch. "You have no right telling people what they can and can't wear!"

"You want your classmates coming to school naked next?" he posits, looking at me like he's just made some grand point.

Sure, we're all going to show up butt-ass naked because our dress code doesn't say boys can't wear skirts.

"That's absurd and you know it," I yell back.

"No, what's absurd is boys in skirts and nail polish." He scowls, glancing at my nails. I roll my eyes, and he starts up again. "I don't care if your gay little friend thinks he's a girl, God's not pleased with any of that, and we have a duty to stop it. We have—"

"My *gay* little friend doesn't think he's girl, he just likes to dress the way he likes to dress." I throw up my hands. What's so hard to understand about that? "It doesn't matter if you think God doesn't like it. We don't live in the United Christian States of America, we live in the United States, and last time I checked the first amendment's there for a reason."

"Exactly, and we're not letting the world tell us we can't have a voice," my dad comes back without losing a beat.

What? I'll never get this argument that somehow the very amendment that gives us freedom *of* religion and speech is somehow the one that gives people like my dad permission to force their religion on everyone else. Like, how?

My eyes flash wide, and I shake my head. "Seriously? Do you even understand the Constitution?"

"Of course I do." He shakes his head and picks up his briefcase. "And this conversation is over. I'm not dropping the proposal. It's too important, plus my campaign is riding on this now."

"What?" I question. Did he just bring his campaign into

this?

"I'm done, Jacob, you're going to make me late." He starts toward the door.

"Fine, just wait until I can vote," I yell after him. "I'll be the first person there to vote against you!"

He rolls his eyes and leaves without saying another word.

I hate it here. I hate it so much. All I want is some common sense, some reason, someone to listen to me even just a little, and not just be talked at and expected to fall in line.

My head drops and my eyes land on the black jeans I put on this morning before school. You know what? I don't give a fuck if I get grounded. Dad already hates me for every reason imaginable, we're going to lose this vote, and Skylar still won't talk to me, so who fucking cares? Why not give him something to get mad over?

I'm wearing a skirt to the vote tonight.

SKYLAR

Effectively immediately, the school dress code prohibits boys from wearing clothes *they* deem to be "traditionally" for girls. Because somehow that makes sense.

I guess we all knew this was how it was going to end. But it still hits like a rejection of me as a person. We lost. But somehow, it's also a weight off me, even if that means I have to deal with this for the next three years.

"Come on." Mom nudges me through the door and down the stairs from the board's tiny little building.

I glance toward the school, it's literally right beside the school board. I don't want to go tomorrow. Now I'm not just bot boy or the defect. I'm not just the fag who wears skirts. Now I'm the defective skirting-wearing fag that lost. I don't want to ever show my face there again.

"This isn't over, Sky," Dad says lightly, leading us up the hallway to the car.

Cameras flash, and suddenly a swarm of reporters, and by swarm I mean like four, bunch around us.

"Are you still going to wear skirts to school?" one of them asks, shoving a fat mic in front of my face. I stare back, squinting angrily at his bearded face.

"How do you feel about—" another starts, but my dad throws up a hand and pushes them back.

"Leave him alone. We're not answering any questions," he says.

That barely deters them, but we keep walking and eventually they stop. I look back to see if they've really given up, and I see Jacob standing at the entrance to the school board. My eyes lock on him, and he stares back. This huge part inside me wants to run to him and let him wrap me up and make me feel better. But I can't; there's no way to be *sure* he wasn't using me. I bury the feeling, but then his skirt flaps in the wind and it comes back. He's so getting grounded for that. But something about him standing up like that, even though we're not a thing, sends a happy chill through me.

"We're going to fight this," Dad reiterates.

JACOB
TUESDAY, OCTOBER 15

The car door slams shut and I drop my head to the steering wheel. A flutter drives up my back and my shoulders shiver before the heater can do its thing.

It's been one of those days. I'm exhausted, and I've done nothing except go to school and stand behind a counter handing people tickets all night. But I need a nap.

My phone dings.

IAN: Wanna go to Bojangles when I get off?

I grunt under a faint grin. That sounds pretty great, except they'll be closed before he gets off, and I want my bed. He thinks he's being sly, but I know what he's doing. I was a bore all evening. It had to be obvious I feel like shit. He's trying to be nice without sounding all fuzzy and heartfelt.

JACOB: Theyll be closed when u get off. Cookout?

I fall against my seat and sigh. Why not?

Everything sucks now, like even more than it did. Dad's on a high with the passage of the new dress code and the news channels are railing against it. Which means he gets more airtime, and somehow it's helped him. It's crazy.

And you-know-who still isn't talking to me. Oh, and it's

only three days until Homecoming. I doubt I'll want to go when the time comes, but Ian's still planning to go with me.

So yeah. Things suck. And I think I'm finally at the point of quitting on Sky. He doesn't care.

I pick my phone back up and send Imani a text.

JACOB: Still no reply. Think I'm going to stop. He hates me.

I huff and go to put the car in gear, but my phone dings before I have the chance. She's fast.

IMANI: NO! ::sad face:: Don't do that.

IMANI: After yesterday he's just mad.

So am I. But he had to see it coming. And how does that change what's going on between us, or rather what's not?

JACOB: Same. I live with the guy that did it.

IMANI: Ah... Yeah. ::sad face:: Could be worse.

JACOB: Worse? Nah.

JACOB: Don't think I can keep holding on to Sky. He doesn't want me.

IMANI: I think he does. Just too stubborn to admit it.

IMANI: What about homecoming?

What about it?

JACOB: Huh?

How is homecoming going to help anything?

IMANI: An idea just hit me. ::mind blown face::

JACOB: Don't. It's pointless.

IMANI: ::sad face::

SKYLAR
FRIDAY, OCTOBER 18

It's Homecoming day and I'm in detention. I might have tested the new dress code rules. It's safe to say they're following them strictly. My cute blue and white skirt was too much.

I sprawl back in the desk. I'm the only delinquent today, so there's not anyone to stare crazily at me this time. Just me, my offensive skirt, and Mr. Prescott, the unusually cute mid-twenty-something Biology teacher. I think he's been grading assignments since he got here at the beginning of second block. And the worst part is he's got the same bright green eyes Jacob does. So I've basically sat here an hour thinking about Jacob, as if that's different than the past three days.

But Mr. Prescott's eyes are only a faded facsimile of Jacob's raging greens at best. Maybe it's being stuck in here with me, or he's just tired of grading papers, but they don't have the same energy.

Two more minutes.

They only gave me detention for the first two blocks. I think they're treading lightly. But whatever. None of that matters. I'm in pants now anyway. I knew this was going to happen, so I brought them just in case, hoping it might spare me detention. Instead, it just lessened my tenure.

Finally, the bell rings and I'm off, sprinting out the door before Mr. Prescott has a chance to say anything. A few minutes later I'm at our table in the lunchroom.

"You ready for tonight?" Imani shimmies in her seat.

I drop my tray and nod. I am. I'm nervous as hell, but I am.

"I can't believe I'm actually getting you in a suit." She grins at Seth, and he rolls his eyes.

"And it'll be the last time," he assures her.

"No! You ain't coming to my wedding without one," she says.

"Wedding?" Seth scrunches his brow.

"Yes, wedding," Imani says.

Her eyes bore into him. I've not heard her talk much about her relationships, so I'm not sure how tender a topic it is. But I think there's something in there I'm missing.

"Yeah, yeah," Seth grumbles.

She shakes her head and turns to me.

"You wearing the dress tonight?" she asks, but there's reservation in her voice.

I nod. It's a stupid idea, but surely they won't turn me away from the dance. I mean, that's a step above class. But in case they do, I'm taking some church clothes.

"I don't think they're going to let you in like that," she says, reading my mind. "You were literally just in detention for a skirt."

"I'll have a change of clothes," I have Siri tell her.

She sighs and changes direction. "Have you talked to Jacob lately?"

I shake my head. I wish she'd stop asking. I know she likes him and thinks I made a mistake, but it's my mistake. But at the same time, I need her to be her relentless self. He hasn't tried to talk the past two days and it's sort of got me worried. Has he decided I'm not worth the effort? I know. I've ignored him. I'm an ass.

Honestly, if he walked up right now and asked me to go to the dance, I'd say yes and grab him up in a hug and never let go. But he's done with me, like I always knew would happen anyway. So I tuck the thought away before it threatens to bring me to tears like it did last night. In front of Imani, maybe Seth, is one thing, but in the middle of the school cafeteria with a quarter of the student body present, hell no.

"Would you say yes if he asked you to the dance again?" Seth asks, brushing his long brown hair back.

I eye him crazily. He's not the one I'd expect to ask, plus is he reading my thoughts or something? But I nod anyway, which earns a massive grin from Imani.

"Cool." Seth nods nervously.

Okay? I look to Imani for some clue, but her eyes drift behind me.

"Hey, Sky."

Jacob?

JACOB

He's smiling when he turns, but then his face goes slack. Guess that's my answer.

"Uh… See you at the dance tonight," is not what I'd planned to say when I started across the cafeteria with Ian on my back. "Hope you have a great time!"

I was *going* to ask him to the dance again, but the look on his face shattered the words I had planned. I don't think this is what Imani had planned when she told me what I should do. Seth looks as lost as usual, but Skylar, he permits me a tiny smile and nods. Before I leave he forms his hand into what looks like the rock-n-roll hand gesture and waves it between us.

You too.

I smile and take off. He signed to me. I know it means nothing, but that was our thing. I mean, it wasn't our thing. But it sort of was. I'm the *only one* he signs with. None of the others know ASL. So even if it wasn't our thing, it felt like it.

But now I'm embarrassed. I failed. So I lead Ian around the corner and upstairs. I don't know where I'm going, but we'll figure that out.

"So that went well," Ian mumbles as we hit the landing

and I finally decide where I'm going. The library. It's quieter, and we can hide in some dark corner. "Did Imani have anything to help?"

"Yeah, for me to ask him to go to the dance again," I tell him, "like I just failed to do."

"Ah," Ian sighs. "Definitely failed. Like epically."

"Not helping." I roll my eyes.

He makes this sharp noise, like he just sucked in a quick breath and then his mouth starts moving. "What if at the dance tonight we take the stage and you sing him a song? Wouldn't that be some romantic-type shit?"

"Yeah, it would, I guess." I shrug, but that's not going to fly. "But they'll run us off stage, and we'll get detention. And I'd get grounded again."

"You're always grounded, what's the difference?" He grins.

He's not wrong. But no.

"Not the point," I huff. "It won't work. We'd have to get our gear set up and hooked up, all while fighting off the band that's playing, plus the teachers."

"Oooh, teacher-student fight." Ian's eyes glaze over.

But something in it actually sounds doable. Maybe it doesn't have to be at the school. Maybe there's something in that little Ian nugget.

"No fights," I say instead, as the tiny thread of an idea forms in my head.

"It'd be cool though." Ian grins.

"Sure." I nod.

There has to be something we can do, something I can do. I know it doesn't mean he'll take me back, but I've got to try.

SKYLAR

FRIDAY, OCTOBER 18

"Did the school call?" Siri asks Mom while I put down my phone and straighten the bottle-green dress under my arms.

"Yes," Mom groans. "Not sure what they think I'm going to do about it."

I grin at her in the mirror. She's sitting on my bed watching me, a warm smile painted on her face. I twist, examining how the dress sits on my hips and clings to my thighs until it loosens just above my knee and splits open along my calf. The bottom sashays around my ankles above matching green sandals.

"I'm so proud of you, Skylar." Mom plops her hand on her lap. "It's not been easy, but you keep pushing on."

Thanks, I mouth as a thought of Jacob slips in. It's his eyes. Just his eyes.

"You do know they might not let you in tonight, right?" Mom asks.

I nod. I've thought about it a lot. It's a big if. But if they don't, I'm just going to turn around and we'll go somewhere else all dressed up. We decided in Sociology against changing if that happened. I'm just hoping someone has a little heart and doesn't make us do that.

"Okay," she sighs, looking at her watch before getting up. "Your ri—"

A car honks outside, brakes squealing up the driveway.

"Speaking of the devil," Mom laughs.

I take in a deep breath and follow her downstairs where Dad's waiting. He turns down the TV and comes over, dropping his palms on my shoulders.

"Your Mom probably beat me to it, but I want you to know I'm super proud of you, Sky." He smiles. "The dress looks good too."

He smirks, which makes me laugh. I never thought in a million years I'd have a dad, not a real one, not one who cares. I thought I'd end up aging out of foster care first. But here I am.

Thanks, I mouth.

A knock comes at the door and Mom lets Seth and Imani inside. Woah. Seth's looking dapper in his black suit and Imani's killing it in a white sequin gown that reaches the floor. I'm happy to see them, but there's still this little spot in the back of my brain that was hoping it'd be Jacob standing there with a little handkerchief sticking out of a suit pocket.

"Hiya!" Imani screams, and Seth jumps. Nothing's changed. "Oh my God, you look so pretty! And you did great on the blush."

She stumbles forward, heels clacking against the hardwood floor. She wraps me up in a hug, practically pushing Dad away, and I squeeze her back. Yeah, I did my own makeup. Okay, well Mom helped a little. It's not much. Some pinkish blush over my nose and cheeks and some eyeliner basically.

"Let me get some pictures before y'all take off." Mom prances into the kitchen.

Seth huffs, which gets me giggling.

"You'll live." Imani throws a hand his way, then motions in a big circle around the two of us. "We don't want to forget all *this* hotness though."

* * *

We've been in the school lot staring down the entrance to the gymnasium for the last ten minutes. We didn't bother going to the football game. None of us gives a shit about football.

So many cute and stylish and even tacky gowns have passed by, escorted inside by a plethora of suits. I'm surprised at some of the colors these guys chose. There was literally one guy in an all orange suit. *All orange!*

"Okay, so if they don't let you in," Imani says what we've all been thinking, "we're not going in either. Right, Seth?"

"I don't want to be here anyway," Seth huffs.

It helps, something about it makes me laugh as I type, "You sure? You don't have to, you know."

"Uh, yeah! We do." Imani bobs her head. "But they're going to let you in."

I shrug.

"Ready?" Imani asks.

I nod and let myself out the back. The only way we're going to figure this out is by walking up to that door. We just have to get past the teachers and Mr. Walters standing sentry.

"Hold up," Imani says, her heels clapping the pavement haphazardly. "I can't walk in these things."

"Why'd you wear them then?" Seth groans.

"They're pretty," she bites.

I laugh in my gut as they come up next to me at the edge of the road and a shiver runs down my arms. It's sort of cold, and my shoulders are exposed. When it's safe, we cross. The bottom of my dress flaps in the wind, exposing my left leg from the knee down. They better let us in, I shaved for this.

Imani nearly trips stepping up on the sidewalk on the other side but catches herself. I pull out my phone now that we're across and keep walking.

"Pretty or not, I'd never wear those shoes," Siri tells her.

"Aw, you like my shoes?" Imani gloats. "Thanks!"

I shake my head, smiling like I'm ready for this. But I feel weak, and my stomach is starting to hurt. I'd be more ready if I was walking up hand in hand with Jacob, but I'm starting to see that that's my fault.

"Here we go." Imani grabs my hand, and I look over to see her making Seth hold her hand too.

We start up the concrete stairs, but before we get to the top Mr. Walters steps in front of the door. I stop at the ledge. My eyes lock on him, and on cue his mouth opens.

"You can't come in dressed like that, Skylar." He remembers my name? "I think you know that."

I want to say something, to be able to move my lips and let the words pour out. To tell him it's a stupid rule and to just let me in. But I can't. I raise my phone and start typing, but Imani beats me to the punch.

"You can't be serious." Imani slings her hands out. "This isn't school. It's a dance."

"And the school dress code still applies," Mr. Walters says

back.

"But what about all the girls you let in before us with the way-too-short dresses? That's not in the dress code?" Siri complains.

Just in the time we were sitting in the car, there were at least three that walked right by them in dresses that barely reached halfway down their thighs. I know that's against dress code.

"Yeah, what about them?" Imani echoes.

I look to the other teacher for backup. She just frowns at me. I'm not sure if it's pity or annoyance.

"I don't recall that, but this," Mr. Walters lifts his hand like he's scanning me, "is not acceptable dress for boys at school."

"If you want to come in, you'll have to change into something…" the other teacher pauses to think of the right word. "Different."

"A suit or pair of slacks and a dress shirt would do fine," Jacob's dad picks up, not satisfied with her answer.

I clench my fist. My chest is trembling. I was ready for this, I swear I was ready for this. But I'm not.

I let go of Imani's hand and spin around, darting down the stairs and up the sidewalk. At the edge of the gymnasium there's a sprawling tree. I aim for it. The clicking of Imani's shoes and their shouts grow distant, but I don't stop. I just want to get away. I slump against the sturdy trunk and bury my face in my hands.

The world spins around me, and the noises swirl together. It's all my fault. I'm too different. I can't talk. I'm a faggot. And people either use me or mock me because I'm different, or I push them away when they get close. And then I go and screw

up an entire school's dress code and have the dad of the only
boy I think has ever cared about me not let me in the dance.

You're just a defect. That's all you'll ever be.

JACOB

FRIDAY, OCTOBER 18

"You know," Ian shifts uncomfortably in the driver's seat, "if you weren't stupid, you'd be walking him in right now."

"Really?" I shake my head, watching Skylar, Imani, and Seth walk up the stairs.

He looks great in that dress. It's regal how it starts just below his shoulders. And yeah, I'm jealous I'm not the one walking with him up those stairs. I should be. But I effed up.

"You ready?" Ian grumbles. "Let's get this over with. Actually, can we just like go in, grab some punch, and leave? Please!"

I roll my eyes. If he doesn't stop complaining I'm going to punch him, I swear. I might be the *only* reason he's here, but the *only* reason I'm here is because the boy I messed things up with is here, so we're staying. I'm going to talk to him tonight. I have to.

"What's going on?" Ian tilts his head.

I squint to see who just stepped in front of them at the entrance. I groan. Of course. My dad.

"Is he…" I start but stop when Imani's hands start flying. "He is!"

"What did you expect?" Ian moans. "They did just pass that thing, you know."

"Yeah, but this…and *my* dad." I throw my hand toward the windshield just as Skylar spins around and darts down the stairs. "What the hell?"

He takes off down the sidewalk with Imani and Seth in pursuit. They seriously didn't let him in.

"That ass-" Ian leans forward but stops.

"Just say it." My eyes lock on Dad, but I'm quick to trail after Skylar before he disappears. I dip my head and squeeze my fists. What do I do now?

I know what to do. The pieces start coming together in my head. Thoughts churning and moving. I prepared for this after school. It's a long shot, and it'll probably fall apart before we can manage it, but it's something. It might just work.

"Ian." I face him, a look that hopefully screams *I have a plan* and not *I'm stark raving mad* on my face.

"I know, that's so messed up." His mouth starts moving. "We can go talk to him."

I'm not sure if he's talking about Skylar or my dad, but that he'd think of either is sort of nice. But that's not part of my plan.

"No, can you call the pastor of the church—" I nod to the building about a block down the road with a massive parking lot bordering the school lot. It's where Skylar goes, and where I called this afternoon and talked to the pastor.

"Like I have his number." Ian looks at me crazily.

"-and tell them we do want to use their parking lot?" I finish my sentence, and he's looking at me even crazier now. "I've got it!"

Which gets me an even crazier look.

"I'll have Eric bring our gear. Remember how bad you wanted to take over the stage?"

His face morphs from amusement to intrigue, and I type a quick text to Imani while he's processing it.

JACOB: Don't let Sky leave. Ive a plan...

"Yeah," Ian says. "You explicitly said that wouldn't work."

"We're not going to take over the stage." I smile at him. "We're going to make our own. Right over there."

SKYLAR

FRIDAY, OCTOBER 18

Why am I still here? I promised we'd leave if this happened, but I don't want to let them win. Even if they have already.

"Let's go," I have Siri tell them. "There's no point."

"No!" Imani yelps.

My eyes jump, the tears freezing a moment in shock. The confusion on my face must be evident, because Imani's mouth does this trembling thing and she starts talking again.

"We haven't had anything to drink." She nods a little too hard, elbowing Seth when he looks at her the way I am. "Right?"

"Uh, yeah, right." Seth's face goes resolute.

I can't go in, I remind them. So I don't see how that's going to work.

"Seth can go," Imani says. His brow crinkles but he nods anyway.

"Yeah, I can go get some punch." He nods and starts off, walking away backward. "That's all I came for anyway."

What the hell is happening?

Imani plops down on the ground beside me and sighs. I try to warn her not to get her dress dirty, but she waves me off.

"Hold up," she says and starts texting someone. "Gotta make sure Seth gets me a snack while he's at it."

I laugh. The tears are gone, but I still feel like shit.

"Talk to me," she says in a lowered voice and puts an arm around me.

Ah. So that's what this was. Get Seth away so I'll open up. I roll my eyes. I think it's working. I turn to face her and concentrate on talking slowly.

It's stupid. I can't go to Homecoming because I like dresses, I tell her, smacking my lips together in a big grimace. *Like, what's so dangerous about a guy in a dress? I'm not the dude walking into school with a gun shooting it up. It's a fucking dress. A damn nice one too.*

"Yeah, it's a damn nice one for sure," Imani laughs. "Going to be honest, I only caught *most* of that. But you're right."

I wipe a tear away as a tiny laugh finds its way up my throat as a puff of air. *Slower, Sky.*

I look up through the tree branches, past the reds and oranges and yellows of dying leaves. The sky fades from shades of blue to warm orange and the sun has disappeared behind the trees.

And Jacob.

I messed up with Jacob. I drop my face toward the ground and inhale a deep breath. *I messed it all up.* It's become so clear that it was all my fault. All of it.

"You didn't mess it *all* up." Imani shrugs. "It wasn't *all* you. The dress code wasn't just you. And the Jacob stuff wasn't all you either. You were both worried, just about different things. And maybe it isn't too late, you know…to fix it."

Her words stick in my head. I've thought about it so much, but I always come to the conclusion it's too late, that it's over.

You really think? I ask.

"Yeah." She looks me right in the eye. "Jacob might not have known exactly what he wanted a few weeks ago, and you, my friend, are a ball of anxiety. And if I'm being honest, you've not given him a chance to prove himself."

But should I? Maybe he did just want a fucktoy. But honestly, for as much as I convinced myself that was the case before, it sounds absurd now.

"I mean, I can't say exactly what he wants, but I *can* tell you how bad he feels not being able to say what you needed to hear." She smiles.

I bore my eyes into her.

You've been talking to him, haven't you?

She shrugs, and her smile lifts. "Maybe."

You bitch, I grin and stick my tongue between my teeth. But I'm not mad. I thought I would be, but I'm not.

"What can I say?" She squeezes me.

Out of nowhere this noise, a screeching, rings in the air. At first it's disjointed and unpleasant. But then it settles into a rhythm, a beat.

Music? Outside?

Imani's phone dings and my eyes jump toward her. She grins.

What are you up to? I ask.

She shrugs as Seth comes down the sidewalk. That's when I notice a stream of people pouring out of the gym in their dresses and tuxes. Where are *they* going?

"Drinks, anyone?" Seth raises three small cups, two gripped precariously between his fingers.

Imani takes one and I get up and grab the other.

"We have something to show you." Imani smiles and urges me to follow.

I go along and as we walk, the music amplifies. When we round the corner I swear my eyes are playing tricks on me. I snap to Imani.

It's Jacob and The Nevermore! And so many people.

What are they doing? I ask. Like what the hell?

"They're waiting on you," Imani says like it's obvious. "Well, *he's* waiting on you. And half the school."

My lips swing upward, and I have to catch my breath. *Waiting on me?*

"He's been waiting on you for like two weeks, but we won't talk about that," Imani laughs, before pinning her arm around mine. "So what are *we* waiting on?"

I use my free hand to motion for her to lead the way. Is this really happening?

Someone's singing now. I'm guessing it's Eric, because I know that's not Jacob's voice.

At the street crossing it becomes clearer. Jacob's standing to Eric's left, strumming his guitar. And when I see him searching the crowd, my heart jumps. Is he looking for me?

"Where the hell are y'all going?" my least favorite voice screams from behind. I turn to find Blake and Bexley at the gym entrance, crowns on their heads. "Seriously?"

"Watch your language," Mr. Walters scolds him, but all of their faces are drawn in confusion.

Bexley looks pissed in her silver sequined dress. "But this

isn't fair."

I look at Imani and skew my lips. *Fair?* And shrug.

"Oh, how the tables turn." Imani grins as Bexley stomps back into the gym and Blake chases after her. "Let's go."

My heart does another leap when Imani tugs me across the street. The music is blaring, and that's when I notice we're in my church's parking lot, not the school lot anymore. There are so many people out here, dancing to the beat, bodies moving in one way or another, some more thrusting than dancing. There's none of the glitter and streamers or fancy table decorations or tables at all, like I'm sure there are inside. But they came anyway.

"Why are all these people out here?" I make Siri ask.

"For you." Imani grins. But she's already told me that.

"Jacob had us text everyone and have them text everyone they knew to come outside." Seth looks around Imani. "This is basically your dance."

My mouth drops open. They all ditched the real dance to come out here? No way.

Then my eyes lock on Jacob. He's staring back at me. I give him a coy smile, which he probably wasn't expecting. His face lights up, and I swear his chest puffs. After everything I put him through, he's still doing this...for me. He really did like me all along, it's so clear now. Nobody would go this far just to use another person. He likes me for me.

I step closer, dragging Imani with me. I want to be up front. I want to be closer to him now that I've let my guard down, and all the anger has lost its meaning now that this wall has fallen.

I want so bad to talk to him, to run up and wrap my arms

around him, but he's in the middle of a song. I hold back when we get to the front and try to let my feet move with the music. Imani and Seth join me, hips popping, heads swaying, and arms, in Seth's case, flying everywhere.

Then the beat stops and the guitars go silent. Eric scoots up closer to the mic while everyone waits for the next song to begin.

"I'd like to thank everyone for coming over here tonight instead of the 'real' dance," Eric laughs, putting up air quotes. "As you all know, because of the *stupid* new dress code, this guy my friend is absolutely crazy about isn't being let into the dance tonight. So here's a big screw you to the new dress code."

The dance floor, or parking lot, I guess, erupts in a disjointed echo of *screw you*s. And as weird as it is, it does something inside me.

"Hold up!" someone yells. I twist around to find Mr. Walters pushing through the crowd, swinging his hands in the air and stopping feet away from me. "This has to stop right now. The dance is inside. This isn't approved by the school. Everyone back inside."

Mr. Walters starts waving his hands toward the gym, but no one moves.

"No." Jacob steps up to the mic. "This is our dance, and you can't stop it."

My eyes go wide. That's his dad he's talking to.

"Excuse me, Jacob." Mr. Walters turns to face his son, disbelief beaming from his eyes. "I said the dance is inside. This is a school dance, there are rules, and—" Mr. Walters starts, but a person I wasn't expecting to see tonight stops him.

"Excuse me." Pastor Dane puts his hand up and smiles. What? What is my pastor doing here? When Jacob's dad finally stops, he continues. "I'm afraid you don't have authority here, Mr. Walters."

"I'm sorry, what?" Mr. Walters' face screams indignation.

"This is the church's property, and we've approved of this *inclusive* dance for the students," Pastor Dane explains calmly.

"You can't do that." Mr. Walters shuffles.

"Actually, we can," my pastor affirms, and then says something I definitely wasn't expecting. "We would like to ask that you leave the property though, for the safety and comfort of the students."

"I'm sorry, what?" Mr. Walters' mouth drops and his head tilts. "I'm trying to do what's best for them."

"That's not the way I see it," Pastor Dane counters.

"You approve of this? Of boys wearing skirts? You do know that's what this is all about, right?" Mr. Walters attempts to *reason* with my pastor.

I can't believe this is happening. Like, what the hell? My eyes jump to Jacob, and he looks as awestruck as me and everyone else in the parking lot.

"I do," Pastor Dane says, nodding. Then he takes a breath and considers his next words. "And we believe in the love of Christ here, not the judgement of the pharisees."

Mr. Walters stumbles back like he's just been punched in the chest. "How dare you!"

"I'm going to ask one more time for you to leave before I call the authorities." My eyes go wide as the words flow out of my pastor's mouth.

All eyes flock to Mr. Walters. He doesn't speak, he doesn't

come back with some rant or Bible verse. No, his shoulders slump and he shakes his head in disgust. But he turns around and starts walking away and disappears into the crowd.

I turn and find Pastor Dane watching, making certain he leaves. Then he looks at me and smiles. I nod, thanking him for standing up for me, for all of us. He nods back before he walks away.

"Well then, so, where were we," Eric laughs into the microphone.

"Screw you," someone yells, and the crowd erupts into laughter.

"Ah, yes." Eric laughs, and although Jacob's laughing too, I can see the reservation in his eyes. He's getting grounded tonight for sure.

"All right, so with *all* of that done, I'm handing over the next song to my friend, who you all know, to sing for that same someone we're all over here for." Eric points at me and grins.

I look away, embarrassed, but not enough to stay that way. When I look back up, Jacob's at the microphone, his tux coat hanging open over black slacks and dress shoes, unlike Eric's jeans and t-shirt.

"Skylar." Jacob's voice echoes across the crowd, eyes firmly on me as he points, his guitar swaying under his neck. He shoots a puff of air through his lips, and then looks at the crowd. "Okay, one second. I wasn't expecting that. So bear with me. Woah. Okay, so, I'm so getting grounded tonight."

Everyone bursts into laughter. Like, it shouldn't be funny, it sucks, but it is still. I shake my head at him and he grins and does the same.

"But that's not stopping us, and that's not stopping me," he starts up again. He locks on me again. "Skylar. I'm sorry. I need to apologize to you. I didn't have the answer you needed two weeks ago. And it shouldn't have been that hard."

The crowd quiets down, whispers murmuring around the lot, all eyes on us. I don't know what to do. This is all so awkward, but at the same time the sincerity in his voice, the way he's opening up about what happened in front of everyone, reaches deep inside my chest.

"So, I want to ask your forgiveness," he says, and signs *Please forgive me* at the same time.

Forgive you? Of course!

I nod furiously, and *aws* jump around the crowd. Jacob's face lights up, and for a moment it looks like he doesn't know what to say next, like he didn't expect to get this far. He laughs nervously and picks up his guitar.

"I don't want there to be any doubt between us, Sky," he starts back up. Then he signs and says the most beautiful thing I've heard from his lips. "I love you."

My eyes go wide as the hoots and cheers erupt. Did he really just say that? My eyes flinch away for the briefest moment to find Imani, who's smiling furiously at me. He did. He really did!

"I do! I know that now, and I need you to know that." He smiles and then points at me. "Now, would you be my baby?"

Before I can mouth anything or rush the stage or smother him in hugs, he starts strumming his guitar. Ian comes in from behind with the drums, and Eric follows, and a familiar tune sings in my ears. Are they going to play... Oh my! They're going to sing Myylo!

I want to scream yes! To belt it out for everyone to hear. I want everyone to know that yes, I want to be his baby. Jacob's baby! I know he can see it in my eyes as I nod as hard as I can, tears rolling down my face.

On beat, Jacob's lips part and he begins to sing. And he's singing to me. It's perfect. It's seriously perfect. How is this actually happening? He hits the second stanza, and the words don't matter. It's the way he looks at me, the way he did all of this, for me. Do I even deserve this?

There's a break in the song, and Jacob throws his guitar over his back. Maybe I don't deserve it, but I'm not letting this chance pass me by.

"Skylar, come on up here." He smiles, and the crowd screams for me to go.

Eric takes over as I walk up, foot by foot, closing the distance between us. His sweet pale grin pulls me closer, and all the doubt in my mind vanishes. He's the one. Maybe I'll always doubt what people think of me, but somehow, right now, I don't. I know he means it, that he cares, and I believe he always will.

"Hey," Jacob whispers when I'm finally there, signing it at the same time.

Hey, I sign. And then follow it up with, *Did you mean it?*

Jacob nods, the smile never leaving his lips.

I point at myself and make a circle over my chest with a closed fist, *I'm sorry.* I can't say it enough. I was stubborn and scared. And that's okay to a point, but he didn't deserve that. I keep signing, my hands moving quick, but slow enough for him to catch. I watch his eyes to see if he understands with the music still playing around us.

I was scared. I thought you were just using me. I put you in an impossible place.

"It's okay, Sky," Jacob says, signing what he can. "I was scared too. You're the first guy who's ever meant anything to me. And it took you not talking to me to see how much you really meant to me. I hate it when you don't talk to me."

You know I can't talk, I sign, and roll my eyes. Even now, under all the music and the magic in the air, it stings.

"Okay, maybe you've never *spoken* to me audibly, with your mouth," he looks at me calmly, eyes begging me to understand something, "but your hands and your eyes and your lips, they've said so much. I'm not looking for your voice. I'm aiming for your heart."

My chest flutters and my heart melts inside his words.

You have it, I tell him.

His lips curve upward in this content way that calms and excites me, and at the same time he moves in, closing the gap between us. Notes explode, voices cheer, and I swear lights flash as his hand caresses my cheek and his lips press against mine. I push into him, hoping it'll last forever, losing myself in his arms and lips.

Night fades away, and the music becomes a dull drum to the beat of his heart against my chest. His hands grip my back, pulling me closer as if there were room to spare. I kiss him back, wanting, needing this moment to never end. And it lasts an eternity before Jacob pulls away, leaving my lips empty of his touch, but my heart full.

When I open my eyes he's looking down at me with those brilliant greens, smiling like nothing else matters. I grin back and bite at my lip. He giggles and I have to look away, he's too beautiful.

What? My eyes spring open when they find Seth and Imani kissing. I mean I always suspected, but really? Jacob notices too, right before they finally let each other breathe, and see us looking.

"What?" Seth skews his mouth like he just got caught with his hand in a cookie jar.

"Took him long enough." Imani shrugs and pulls him back into a kiss while the music beats around us.

I give them a thumbs-up and turn back to Jacob. I don't think this day could get any better.

"So, you want to be my boyfriend?" Jacob laughs and proves me wrong.

I giggle. How can those words seem so completely third grade but so perfect at the same time?

Yes! I nod softly, looking into those beautiful green eyes. Yes.

NC NEWS

North Carolina Supreme Court Overturns Local School Board's Gender-Based Dress Code Policy

BY ENEIDA WALLACE AND MILTON ALLEN
UPDATED APRIL 21, 2020 10:27 AM

In a surprise 4-3 split decision, the North Carolina Supreme Court has overturned a lower court decision upholding a local school board's strict gender-based dress code, as challenged by student Skylar Gray. According to the court the previous decision had not properly taken into account the free speech of students and past state and federal precedent. The decision effectively invalidates the board's new dress code and stipulates that school dress codes in the state must be gender neutral.

ACKNOWLEDGMENTS

There was a point when I genuinely didn't think this story was going to be written. But a number of people around me had other plans and helped get this story going and then kept pushing me along until it was finished. So, here's a big thank you to anyone who had a hand in the completion of this story.

I'd also like to highlight a few who dealt with my questions, doubts, and initial ideas and story, along with the capstone pieces of the book. I'll start with a big thanks to Katie Messick and Grace Fongemy, who once again got my brain moving and provided me with the initial confidence to put this story together and helped form some of the key elements early on. A big thanks goes out to Keean Sexton for always being so ready to help and giving wonderful input on my outlines, ideas, and even promo stuff. I have to thank Kai for giving me the idea for one of my favorite scenes in the book (the first date).

You might be surprised to learn that there was a bit of research involved in writing this story. Thanks to Sandra

Farley for her information about mutism (nonverbalism), David Kummer for his help understanding more about foster care and adoption, and Amanda Jane for all the information about Wicca to help do justice to Imani's character. Thank you to Kalob Dàniel for being my fashion guru for the two main characters. I am unfortunately in no way blessed with the ability to even properly match clothes, so that was important.

As always, thanks to everyone at Editions - Coffee and Bookstore for dealing with me and allowing me to write in the shop basically all day every Saturday and more. You all are like family even though most of you do try to give me a heart attack every time I come in the store. Come to think of it, maybe that's why you're like family.

I had a wonderful group of beta readers once again. Thanks to Iris Vayle, Rachel Witte, Dominica Scudieri, Ronnie Benion, and Benjamin Wesley for reading the version of the story no one else ever will and giving me their feedback to make it a better one. I have to give a huge shoutout to Jordan Webb (@mygaybookcase on Instagram) for his part as a beta reader. Jordan went above and beyond and provided me with so much feedback that was absolutely critical to improving this story and is largely responsible for it being the way it is now. Thank you!

Of course, I have to thank my amazing editor, Christie Stratos. You are an amazing person, writer, editor, and advisor. I truly depend on you all along this process and you always come through and tell me what I need to hear.

Now a huge shoutout to Lucía Limón, the brilliant mind and hand behind all the artwork for this book. Lucía is the amazing artist who designed the character art and all the cover designs, and when I say I love the designs it's an understatement. I don't know how you do it, but you are amazing, and honestly I can't wait to see the incredible things you go on to design.

I cannot leave without thanking Laura L. Zimmerman. Laura is one of my favorite people in the world, a fellow author, my "work wife", and dear friend. I've bounced so many ideas and doubts off her I can't even begin to put them here. If it's in this book, there's a good chance she's heard about it or helped. You've also been a shoulder for me to lean on in some darker times and have made them easier to get through.

I consider everyone on this list a great friend. You are the backbone of what I do and what I love. Thank you.

ABOUT THE AUTHOR

Jordon grew up in a small southern town in the foothills of the Appalachian Mountains just south of Boone, North Carolina. Jordon is an alumni of the University of North Carolina at Charlotte with a B.S. in Political Science he'll never use, and works at the nation's largest privately owned shoe retailer as a full-stack web developer to pay off all that student debt. While not writing, Jordon spends most his time entertaining his cats, Genji & Mercy, watching Schitt's Creek and Parks and Recreation re-runs, and acting like he's any good at Overwatch. He lives in Kannapolis, NC.

VISIT JORDON ONLINE AT

www.JordonGreene.com

If you enjoyed this story please consider reviewing it online and recommending it to family and friends.

Lightning Source UK Ltd.
Milton Keynes UK
UKHW010627010522
402233UK00012B/358/J